Additional Praise:

"This unforgettable novel…slowly smoldering towards, then erupting into infernos of violence as well as passion…traces a century and a half of the Knight family as its members, both honorable and corrupt, carve out kingdoms and fight for fiefdoms. *Wyman and the Florida Knights* evolves into a Southern East of Eden, a tale that could occur only in America, perhaps only in Florida, and certainly only by the gifted Larry Baker."

—Ron Cooper, author of author of *All My Sins Remembered* and *Purple Jesus*

"In *Wyman and the Florida Knights*, Larry Baker delivers yet another sumptuous read. The Knight dynasty may begin with a Bible-thumper, but a century later they tend to find their Grail in the bedroom, and often in illicit hookups. Along the way, every affair suffers its agonies, and the high feelings can turn bloody."

—John Domini, author of *The Color Inside a Melon* and the memoir *The Archeology*

"The old snake charmer is back and once again Larry Baker's mythical Florida is weaving and casting its spell. A place where blood is poison and people say the damnest things. If I lived there, I wouldn't trust anybody. Baker's *Wyman and the Florida Knights* is not for the faint-hearted."

—Mike Lankford, author of *Becoming Leonardo* and *Life in Double Time*

WYMAN
AND THE
FLORIDA
KNIGHTS

A NOVEL BY
LARRY BAKER

ICE CUBE PRESS, LLC
NORTH LIBERTY, IOWA, USA

Wyman and the Florida Knights
Copyright ©2021 Larry Baker
First Edition
Isbn 9781948509299

Ice Cube Press, LLC (Est. 1991)
1180 Hauer Drive
North Liberty, Iowa 52317 USA
www.icecubepress.com | steve@icecubepress.com

The paper used in this publication meets the minimum requirements
of the American National Standard for Information Sciences—
Permanence of Paper for Printed Library Materials, ANSI Z39.48-1992.

Manufactured in USA using recycled paper.

Cover photo from Steve Vaughn: stevevaughn.com

Larry Baker contact: icwriter@gmail.com

Disclaimer: This is a work of fiction. Any resemblance to any actual
person, living or dead, is purely coincidental and unintentional.

SWOGGE

Book One:
The Past, as Prologue

1866:
THE FIRST KNIGHTS

Thomas Knight went to Florida in 1866 with God, a gun, and a thousand dollars in gold. His ancestors had sailed west to the New World. He took a train to the Old South. From Pittsburgh to Jacksonville, then by private carriage to St. Augustine, where a community of freed blacks were expecting him, and then by flat-bottomed barge on the St. Johns River until it met the Ocklawaha River and then deeper into central Florida. Knight had been to Europe as well as the American West. He had read William Bartram, Henry David Thoreau, Jefferson's *Notes on Virginia*. He could cite scripture in his sleep and argue with Darwin in his mind, but nothing had prepared him for Florida.

The God he carried came in two editions. One was a ten-pound, leather-bound, Old and New Testament King James Version that had been in the Knight family for a hundred years, complete with pages of art depicting the wrath of God and the love of Jesus. This edition was called The Big Word by Knight's heathen brother Hiram, to distinguish it from the pocket edition of the New Testament that Thomas Knight was always pointing at his brother right before he asked God to show mercy toward that brother. In Hiram's world, that pocket Bible was The Little Word. In Hiram's world, Thomas Knight was a pain in the ass.

The Big Word had been wrapped in butcher paper and sealed in wax, then crated in cherrywood, to be opened again only when the altar was built and consecrated in Knight's New Christ Church of the South. That altar would then be the site of his anticipated marriage to a woman he had not yet met, but whom he was sure waited for him in Florida, all part of a divine plan in which God had provided a role for him and his progeny. With a wife and children, Knight could then open The Big Word and add names to the family tree that had begun branching on the inside of the front cover with Jacob Knight in 1778.

Thomas Knight always found comfort in the word of God, big or little. He was never without it. Even as he slept, The Little Word was always within reach. But his mind was prone to signs and premonitions. Omens, as it were. He had always sensed a message in the unfilled lines of the family tree in The Big Word. It had occurred to him as he was about to seal it up for the trip to Florida. He looked at the entry for him and his brothers, and then counted lines. Assuming a new generation of Knights every twenty years, The Big Word would run out of lines in 2016. He told Hiram about this revelation, but his brother merely shrugged and suggested that he paste some new pages inside the cover. It was not a satisfactory response.

As for Knight's gun, it was useless in Florida. It was a long-bore single-shot buffalo rifle that had served him well in the American West. Safely distant from a target, time to load and aim, the barrel resting on a tripod, that gun was deadly. But there were no vistas in Florida, and no animal in Florida was as dumb as a buffalo. Knight had showed the gun to his guide as they began the barge trip up the Ocklawaha, and the guide had grunted and spit before saying, "Perhaps you could use the butt as a club."

Pythagoras Jones was Knight's guide, and he had the unique distinction of being the blackest Egyptian in America. His life since arriving in Jacksonville in 1848 had been a constant series of explaining himself to any white man who questioned his lineage. His British accent, his papers, and his usefulness as a guide had all helped keep him free, but he had still acquired a slave's habit of dissembling around white folks. Think them fools behind their backs, and never let them know how smart you were to their faces.

Before and during the recent War, Pythagoras had worked on the Underground Railroad to the North. He had been successful because he had been cautious. Unlike some others, who packed up entire families and seldom asked them questions, Pythagoras had aided only young, healthy men whom he trusted to keep quiet. Unlike some others, Pythagoras had, as he eventually told only himself, a zero percent return rate. It was a calculated phrase, and a bit too mercantile for his friends, who funneled black souls to the North as a mission, not a problem in commerce.

After the War, Pythagoras wrote to Thomas Knight to thank him for his help in Pennsylvania, a gesture he repeated with a dozen other benefactors throughout the Free States. To his surprise, Knight was the only one who wrote back. Infrequent correspondence began, discussions of philosophy and politics, and then Pythagoras was mystified to read one day that Thomas Knight and his gold were coming to Florida, that he had "been called" to Florida, that he wanted Pythagoras to help him finding "a virgin forest bourned by still waters, to be Christ's new city." Pythagoras decided that Knight had lost his mind, and he wrote back discouraging him from coming, but the letter never caught up with Knight. He had waxed The Big Word and was already descending from Pittsburgh.

Pythagoras had had his fill of religious zealots, so he retreated from Jacksonville to St. Augustine, home to a hundred former slaves who now lived by fishing and hunting. He was astonished to discover that they had been waiting for him *and* Thomas Knight. Evidently, Knight was more methodical than Pythagoras had given him credit for, so the black Egyptian resigned himself to waiting for the white man and his gold. And, as he realized, he knew the perfect spot for Christ's new city, if Knight brought enough gold.

When Knight told his brother Hiram that he was going to Florida to found a new church, Hiram looked at him and wondered if he ever slumped in a chair. Ram-rod posture was a Thomas trademark, even when seated. They were in Hiram's office at Keystone Telegraph, where Hiram had been reading about a new way to process steel that had been perfected by Henry Bessemer. Hiram's boss was Andrew Carnegie.

"I'm going to Florida, Hiram. Going to found the church I always dreamed about, the church I was promised."

On a good day, Hiram liked his brother. Thomas was usually harmless, and always good fodder for a story when Hiram and the other Knight brothers smoked cigars after an ample dinner. Thomas did not smoke, nor drink, nor curse, and, as far as Hiram could determine, he did not pass gas either. Unlike his other brothers, however, Hiram did not underestimate Thomas's capacity for fulfilling the most unrealistic of dreams. Thomas had hated slavery and became an abolitionist. He thought he could end slavery on his own, and it was only the fortuitous kick of a horse to his head the day before he was to meet John Brown on his way to Harper's Ferry that had kept him from achieving the same glorious martyrdom as his hero. He had still been in a coma when Brown shed his mortal coils, but Knight toiled again as soon as he regained consciousness, convinced that God was saving him for another mission. Borrowing from his father, he spirited a thousand copies of *Uncle Tom's Cabin* to his contacts in the Deep South, hoping to foment social and intellectual discontent, but he was crestfallen when the mislabeled crates with Stowe's poisonous book were discovered and publicly burned in Atlanta.

Hiram had been appointed his brother's keeper by the elder Knight brothers. Thomas was the youngest, Hiram born only a year before him. Their mother had died giving birth to Thomas, causing an estrangement between him and his siblings, but since Hiram had no memory of his mother, he was not part of that grudge.

All the Knight men, except Thomas, who found God, had gone into business. The Civil War had been very profitable for them, supplying blankets and muskets to the Grand Army of the Republic, but only Hiram and Thomas had served in uniform. Hiram was discharged after Gettysburg, having lost his left arm. Thomas served as a chaplain all the way through Appomattox, comforting the dying and eulogizing the dead. Hundreds of northern mothers had letters from him describing their sons' last, blissful, pain-free moments as they were about to meet Jesus. Hiram had always respected Thomas for his service, but he still wished his brother wasn't so damn judgmental about what he perceived as faint Christians, whom, Hiram eventually came to understand, were everybody but Thomas.

The moment before Thomas had told him about going to Florida, Hiram was preparing a note for his boss about Bessemer's process. Carnegie was already a rich man, and Hiram was one of the men whose own wealth had been enhanced by their association with the Scotsman. Lately, however, Hiram had noticed some incipient depression in his boss, some dissatisfaction with his own wealth. Then, hearing his brother's plans for Florida, he had a moment of insight that puzzled him: His boss had more in common with his brother than he did.

"I'm going to Florida, Hiram, and I don't think I'm coming back."

Hiram felt his missing arm begin to itch as he cocked his head to one side and studied his brother. Was he serious? About not coming back?

"Thomas, you are . . ." but he hesitated. He had given up reasoning with his brother, but Hiram still felt an obligation toward him. "You are prone to dramatic gestures. I would not be so sure that Florida is to be your final home. Your health has not been conducive to travel for many years, and Florida is such a primitive state. As well, your . . ." and Hiram tried to be delicate, ". . . your avid support for the preservation of the Union will not make you a welcome guest."

"The Union be damned!" Thomas hissed, his hands clasped as in prayer. "That Union was willing to abide the sin of human bondage for too many years in order to preserve itself. I served not the Union, nor the faint men who compromised to lash it together. I served God."

Hiram recoiled, stung again by his brother's judgment. Hiram had wept for days after Lincoln died, but Thomas had insisted that the assassin's bullet was merely delayed justice for Lincoln's procrastination in the face of absolute evil.

The rebuke in his office moved Hiram, decisively and irrevocably, back to the side of his elder brothers. Thomas Knight was, indeed, a bit too Old Testament for comfort.

"How can I help you?"

"I will need supplies and money."

"I will talk to the family."

The two men looked at each other briefly, and then Hiram stood up, extended his sole hand to his brother, and said, "You will keep us apprised of your progress, of course."

Thomas stood and took his brother's hand, and for a moment Hiram thought he saw some softness in his eyes, but that moment passed as soon as Thomas released his hand and spoke, "God's will be done."

Three months after Thomas left Pittsburgh with his Bibles, his gun, and fifty gold twenty-dollar coins, Hiram received his first letter from Florida:

> All is well here. I have seen the Beast in the Jungle, but God's Word protected me. Much good work is still to be done, and my strength often ebbs, but I see daily progress, and retain much faith that the breath of God will

carry me forward. My love and prayers are with you and the family. May God bless you and give you comfort.

Nine months after that letter, the only letter that Thomas sent, Hiram received another note from Florida:

It is my sad duty to inform you of your brother's death. Reverend Knight departed in the night and never returned. For that eventuality, he left me instructions to contact you. In particular, he requested that you be the executor of his estate. I have maintained very accurate records, so this disposition should proceed smoothly. There is much property, and the Church itself has substantial value. Your brother was much loved here, and his parishioners will miss him dearly. Their grief has led them to rename their community in his honor. They hope this will meet with your approval. Please advise of your intentions. Best wishes, Pythagoras Jones.

When they first met, Pythagoras took one look at Thomas Knight and told himself: *Dead of a heat stroke in about a week.* Knight was wearing a black suit, had bushy mutton-chop whiskers on his face, and the soaring black hat on his head made him tower even higher above the short black men teeming around him. Knight's procession had been biblical. Astride a mule, trailed by a multitude of recently freed helots, he had seen Pythagoras at the end of the open road and raised his hand in greeting. The multitude turned its collective face toward the immigrant Egyptian as well.

"Mr. Jones, I presume," Knight had said, and Pythagoras nodded. Knight waited for a response, but, getting none, proceeded. "Your state is not what I expected."

"Surprised me too. More like Africa than the rest of America," Pythagoras said, pleased to see that Knight had the same reaction that all white men had when they first heard his British accent.

It was Knight's turn for a mute nod.

"The Bible dates time from the Garden," Pythagoras continued, motioning to the men around Knight to pick up his bags. "This place predates that by a thousand millennia."

Knight's expectations about Pythagoras Jones were being confirmed. Their prior correspondence had revealed an educated man capable of abstract thought, but Knight had not expected Jones to be so conversant in Biblical imagery.

"Yes, of course, surely the Garden was itself a forest before Adam and Eve tilled its soil and tended its flocks," Knight said.

"Tis no forest, Mr. Knight. Florida is a jungle, and there's no Natural Law in a jungle like there is in a forest. This here, where you're standing, is just the opening of that jungle."

"But I assumed that this was my destination. I assumed I would meet you on that land which I had requested in my last letter to you. Indeed, this seems to be the spot."

Pythagoras wanted to say, but kept to himself: *You brought yourself to this spot, no assistance of mine. Truth be known, I came here to avoid you.* Instead, he said, "This is Lincolnville, a new community in St. Augustine. Your land is deeper down the river."

Unknown to Jones, Knight took his words as a sign of divine intervention. Lincolnville was tainted by its namesake. God would surely offer Thomas Knight an unspoiled genesis.

The next morning, barge loaded, bright skies, Knight began his journey down the St. Johns River to where it merged with the Ocklawaha. By midafternoon he was almost in the dark. The river had narrowed, and the tangled foliage on each bank seemed to reach for the other side. In that dim world, Knight heard sounds that had to have been formed and exhaled from a nightmare. Screams and caws of unseen birds, the splash and snorting of primeval water beasts, and the constant admonition of Pythagoras to not touch an overhanging branch lest it turn into a snake. At times, something thumped the underside of the barge, and Knight imagined a freshwater Leviathan rising to tumble him and his guide into the water. But he was not afraid. This journey had a purpose. No, not afraid, Thomas Knight was absolutely thrilled. All he needed was one final sign.

God did not disappoint him.

As the barge floated around one more bend, the river widened and the foliage parted to let the sun pour through. The light was dazzling, and Knight could see that the river was absolutely purely clear right down to its smooth bottom. The world below him was full of life, schools of fish shimmering in silvery communal masses, and then he saw a beast like no other, almost like a cow in the water, larger than Knight himself, but obviously gentle, already touched by the hand of God and made subservient to Man, floating just under the surface, gliding by Knight's barge to be replaced by two more smaller versions of the same. Knight put his hand in the water and reached for the beast, but as soon as his hand touched the water, he heard a growl from the shore. He turned to face that sound and confronted the head of an ebony panther, just the head, protruding out of the dense foliage. The panther growled louder, then snarled, baring his fangs, its dark shoulders emerging from the green thicket.

Knight's buffalo gun was loaded and lying in front of him, and he looked at it first. But then he reached in his pocket and pulled out The Little Word, holding it with both hands, and stood up. He raised The Little Word and pointed it straight toward the panther.

The panther studied the projecting Word and withdrew, wherein Knight turned to his guide and nodded, "This is the spot."

Pythagoras Jones thought to himself: *It might take more than a week, and it might not be the heat, but this is a dead man.*

Hiram Knight went to Florida to retrieve his brother's remains. That was his assumption, his self-imposed obligation. His older brothers had been skeptical. Why not simply send a paid agent, or have "that Jones man handle the arrangements." They expressed concern for Hiram's health, his pallid face being proof that he was not fit for travel to some godforsaken wilderness. But none volunteered to go in his stead.

Hiram took his own son with him. The boy was a robust copy of his father, blessed with two strong arms, and was destined to be the tallest Knight until the twentieth century, well over six feet. Hiram had planned a European trip with his son before the boy went to

Harvard, but Florida would do. The boy had been Thomas's favorite nephew because he never fidgeted in his uncle's presence. It was a slim reed on which to hang affection, but the boy had never feigned his own affection. Thus, the two Knights went south to gather up their kin and return home. There was only one problem. There was nothing to gather.

"I was led to believe that my brother was dead, so I assumed that his body had been found to confirm that," Hiram had said when informed by Pythagoras Jones that there was no body to recover. He would have been angry, but he was exhausted from his two-week journey, and his own body had been sapped by the Florida heat and humidity. It had been raining for two days by the time he and his son finally met Jones, and the itching in his absent arm was becoming intolerable. Hiram Knight hated Florida.

"I wrote that he had departed in the night and never returned. It is safe to assume that he is dead," the black Egyptian said. They were sitting on the shaded porch of Jones's hut.

"I wrote you back," Knight protested. "I informed you of my plans to come here. You could have been clearer. You could have responded. There was time."

"I could have, that is true. I assumed you would still want to see your brother's work. He told me all about your prior support. And, of course, you are the rightful owners of his land, and that is no small treasure."

"This land is swamp and jungle and worthless," Hiram spat back, slapping at a mosquito as he contemplated returning to Pennsylvania as soon as he felt better.

Pythagoras spoke to Hiram without looking at him, "Your brother had a vision, and he imposed it on the land around him. If that is not your vision, I'll be glad to reimburse you for his investment and take the land as my own. Perhaps even with a profit to you. I certainly understand your hesitation. This is not Pennsylvania."

The son spoke, "How long has my uncle been missing?"

Pythagoras considered the boy. Unlike his father, the boy had adjusted his wardrobe to the environment. His loose shirt and pants were not unlike those of Jones, and his wide-brimmed hat had kept his face from reddening as his father's had done. A month earlier, the boy had written to Louis Agassiz at Harvard about his plans to study Natural History. Sitting across from the boy, Pythagoras gazed at a youth on the cusp of adulthood. He had his uncle's hands and eyes, but he furrowed his brow much like his father.

"The Reverend went away about six months past," Jones said calmly. "He had done it many times, going into the woods but always returning. I waited three months before I wrote your father."

"And his congregation?" the boy asked.

"Beg pardon?"

"His congregation, what did they do while he was gone? Did they cease their attendance at his church? What held them together in his absence?"

Pythagoras looked from son to father and then back to son. Hiram Knight was surprised by his son's question. Pythagoras was suspicious. He had been wrong. His inquisitor was not a boy.

"The Reverend was missed, of course, but these people had potatoes to plant and hungry children to feed. Life must go on, young .

. . " and Pythagoras tried to retrieve the name of the evolving youth across from him.

"Stephen Jay," supplied the youth. "Stephen Jay Knight."

Pythagoras nodded, and Hiram Knight smiled. His son would accomplish all that he would not, that was Hiram's belief. Stephen had always been exceptionally bright, and the trip from Pennsylvania had cemented a bond between them that Hiram had only contemplated in silence. More than once in their southern descent, he had relied on his son's arm for support, on his mind to anticipate a problem with transportation or supplies, and on his wit for entertainment.

Hiram had never praised Stephen to his face, nor to his siblings or uncles. But his aspirations for his son had never wavered, and his son's promise was eventually the talk of the elder Knight brothers, whose own children paled in comparison to the potential of Stephen Knight. In Hiram's world, even Andrew Carnegie had remarked that Stephen was marked for great things, a blessing much valued by his father.

"I was not asking about their lives, Mr. Jones. I was asking about their souls."

Pythagoras knew to tread softly. Stephen might have had his uncle's hands and eyes, and his father's brow, but he was deeper than either of the older men. "I was ordained by your uncle. In his absence, I conducted services. I merely read from his large Bible." He noticed how Hiram Knight seemed to wince at the mention of that book. "We would sit quietly for a few moments," measuring Stephen as he spoke, "much like your northern Friends' meetings."

"That was as my uncle prescribed? You were copying his service?"

Pythagoras looked at Stephen Knight and knew this was the first test of their future relationship. He then looked at Hiram. That man had the look of his brother, the look of a man soon to die. The son had a look unlike them. Stephen Knight had pale blue eyes, and Pythagoras sensed that the young Northerner would outlast even himself.

"No, the silence was my refinement," Jones said. "Your uncle was more prone to telling us about the glory of God. He seemed to know much about it. My own knowledge was too inadequate, I did not attempt to share it. The silence was to let God speak for himself."

"You're an educated man? Am I correct, Mr. Jones?" Stephen asked, and Pythagoras knew that was not his real question.

"As much as books and travel can educate a man, I suppose I am educated," he said.

"But you do not believe in the glory of God, do you? Your education has not led you to that truth yet? Ordained or not, God's glory is not within your vision. Am I correct?"

Hiram watched his son. He had seen him do this to others, and he had always blamed his brother for his own son's confrontational streak. His elder brothers had been right. He should not have let Stephen spend so much time with his uncle.

Pythagoras looked around, avoiding eye contact with Stephen, before he finally spoke, "I see glory everywhere, young Stephen, but I've never seen God. That's the difference between me and your uncle, and, I'm guessing, between me and you."

Stephen Knight tilted his head and smiled broadly for the first time. "No, Mr. Jones, that is what you and I hold in common."

Hiram Knight felt excluded from that moment, but he was too weak to impose himself. He noticed, however, that the ever-present itching in his missing arm had been replaced with a numbness that seemed to be growing into his chest.

"Would you take me to his church?" Stephen asked Pythagoras.

"And you, sir?" Jones asked Hiram Knight.

"I will rest here. Evidently, I am not as fit as I had assumed. You two go. I have never had the interest in my brother's world as my son has had. I will rest," he said, his breathing noticeably more ragged. "We can talk about a disposition of the property when you return."

Jones studied the young man in the boat with him. Stephen Knight had the same trait as his uncle, a tendency to stare, but Jones sensed a fundamental difference. The Reverend Knight had always stared as if looking for something lost. His nephew stared as if studying something found. The Reverend's eyes were distant and unfocused. His nephew's eyes seemed to catalog everything around him.

Young Knight did not need Jones's warnings about hands in the water or reaching for branches, and he obviously knew how to maneuver a boat in tricky currents. "How much farther?" he asked, the simplest question he had asked in the past hour. Jones had already answered a hundred queries about water sources, vegetation, and animal life within and along the Ocklawaha River. Knight seemed most impressed with the pristine transparency of the water beneath him. Natural springs and a lake further inland, Jones had explained, although there were times that stormy weather and fallen rotting trees would temporarily darken the water.

"Another half hour," Jones had replied to the time question. Neither man spoke again until their boat turned the bend and Stephen saw his uncle's church for the first time. He stood up, and Jones took note of how that act was done without upsetting the balance of their craft.

Thomas Knight had cleared three acres from the jungle out of which the panther had first emerged months earlier. Jones had told Stephen the panther story and the young man had nodded, a gesture that conveyed affection, and said, "My uncle was prone to Biblical excesses, a source of some concern in our family."

Jones had winced. The ease and natural grace of the young man's body seemed inconsistent with his speech. Knight registered his guide's expression and spoke again, arching his eyebrows, "My uncle was as crazy as a loon."

Jones felt emboldened enough to say, "Religion will do that to a man. Even a good man."

Thomas Knight's New World Church of Christ had no walls, and it was five feet off the ground. It was his design. Twelve columns of pine trees, whose bark had been trimmed off, lathered in pitch, dried, and then painted white. A pine floor elevated and supported by dozens of pitch-sealed logs buried in the ground underneath, a precaution suggested by Jones to anticipate a history of periodic intrusions by a rising river. A roof with a six-foot overhang beyond the supporting columns, to keep the frequent rain off the worshippers. But, no walls.

Most intriguing to Stephen Knight, his uncle's church was perfectly round. Jones had anticipated his question as they walked toward the steps. "The Reverend had his plans drawn before I met him. Showed them to me, asked if I could supervise the work, provided funds for tools, and took his first trip inland without me. Of course, he was back in a few hours."

"But why this design?"

"Said he wanted to be able to see the outdoors as he spoke."

Knight turned to face Jones directly as they stood at the foot of the steps. "You know what I mean," he said, "and you waste too much of my time being evasive."

"I was merely . . ." Jones attempted.

Knight walked up the steps, leaving Jones below. The Egyptian looked up at him, searching for some connection to the young man above him and the frail man they had left behind. Father and son seemed incompatible. Uncle and nephew were closer, but the nephew had a weight the uncle lacked. Jones felt that weight on him at that moment, and he was compelled to contrition, an unnatural condition for him.

"The Reverend told me that he wanted no walls because he was afraid of a beast that would approach him without warning. Walls would merely hide the beast, which is why we also cleared away a goodly space between church and woods, so that the beast would have no place to hide," Jones said, taking his first step up.

Knight had taken off his wide-brimmed hat and motioned with it for Jones to follow him, "And why the circular nature of this church?"

On the final step, Jones confessed, "That, Mr. Knight, I do not know. I asked your uncle. He ignored the question. Any significance I attempted in my own mind was never confirmed by him."

"And the parishioners? They were not puzzled as well? But they flocked here on the Sabbath, took the long trip up this river as we did, just to hear my uncle?"

"These are good people," Jones said. "But they are not . . . thoughtful. I mean that they . . ."

"I understand your meaning," Knight interrupted, but not unkindly.

"These are good people who worshipped God before your uncle arrived. But he seemed to inspire them in a collective fashion . . . "

"Which you resisted," Knight interrupted again, but less kindly.

Jones looked down, but not because he was intimidated. He merely wanted to choose his words carefully. When he looked up again, he made a point of seeking Stephen Knight's blue eyes before he spoke. "I have resisted stronger men than your uncle, and his God."

Neither man spoke for a moment, long enough for them to notice that the woods around them had become silent. Rain was coming.

Stephen extended his hand to Pythagoras, and the Egyptian accepted the gesture. Knight then sealed the pact. "So, you are the man I need to teach me about this land. Come and walk with me around the edges of my uncle's church. I have a lot of questions."

The rain came, so thick that it sounded like stones on the roof, and the surrounding woods were blurred even at so short a distance. The two men talked for hours. Short questions from Knight, longer and longer answers from Jones. Where was the source of the

Ocklawaha River? Were there land trails to the church? Who lived in the surrounding land? How many different kinds of animal wild life had Jones seen? Did Jones know anything about plant medicine? Indian life? As they talked, Jones kept asking himself if there were a hidden purpose to all these questions, but there was no pattern. Stephen Knight simply wanted to know everything there was to know about Florida. Only one question made him suspicious, "How much do you think it would cost to buy all the land between here and Jacksonville?"

A day later, Stephen Knight broke his father's heart. "I will take you home, but I am coming back here as soon as I can. I would also like an advance on my estate. There is enormous opportunity here. I see a new community in this land. Not Knightville, as the Negroes have named it. But, Arcadia."

Hiram cursed his brother Thomas one last time, and looked around for Pythagoras Jones, but the Egyptian was nowhere to be seen. His younger brother and his ordained assistant had stolen his son. "But, Stephen, your future? And, Harvard?" he protested.

Stephen Knight was joyously adamant, "Florida will be my Harvard."

As he lay dying, Hiram Knight searched for his missing brother. It was a journey back to their childhood, a journey interrupted only by short stretches of coherence. A time when Hiram still had both arms and Thomas had not seen God. Hiram had taken it upon himself to protect his younger brother against the wrath of their father and older brothers. They would go by themselves to the Pittsburgh

Fourth of July parades, waving tiny flags as scarred and limping veterans of the recent Mexican War marched by with their battalion banners held aloft. But in Hiram's fevered mind those parades became labyrinths of dark blue tunnels with grotesque cripples leaping out at the boys. Headless men, men with gaping wounds, men that Hiram had known at Gettysburg, and Thomas would become lost so Hiram had to shove himself through the wall of dying blue men to find his brother. Thomas was always in the distance, calling for Hiram to help him, but then running away when Hiram got closer. And then the boys were older, on a warm Spring day, sitting on a bench outside an apothecary near their massive white wooden home. The smell of horse manure was distinct in Hiram's nostrils. Thomas was whittling soft pine as Hiram told him all about how steel was processed. And always the Great War, the War their brothers avoided. In these final dreams, Hiram and Thomas served together, and Andrew Carnegie was President of the United States. They fought side by side, never harmed even when musket balls screamed around them, slow enough to be seen, fast enough to kill. The worst of Hiram's dreams was one in which he was in the Florida swamp looking for Thomas, but he himself became lost. Time blurred, and Hiram was at Gettysburg again, with thousands of blue and gray men trapped with him in the muck of Florida. His arm ripped off again, not by a surgeon, not with whiskey as an anesthetic, but ripped off by a single cannonball that seemed to be on fire as it headed toward him, and then the searing pain. It was the worst of his fevers, him screaming for Thomas to save him, and his brother appearing with The Little Word in one hand and the other hand grasping green slime and twigs, but it was the slime and twigs that Thomas used on the bloody stump of Hiram's shoulder, shoving more and more into the shredded wound, until the slime and twigs became an arm. And the pain stopped.

Stephen had promised to take his father home, but the trip north took longer than the trip south. Hiram's fever began the day his son returned from visiting Thomas Knight's church in the woods. Father and son had arrived on the backs of mules, but it was obvious to Stephen that their return trip would require some means for his father to rest as they traced their original route. They had assumed that a wagon fit to carry a coffin would be waiting for them, but Pythagoras Jones had only a two-wheel cart. A day of construction, however, had converted the cart to a wagon, and Hiram Knight was padded on to its pine-needle bed for his journey home. Netting was found to protect him from sun and mosquitoes, two seemingly mute black men were recruited as drivers, and Stephen alternated between riding behind the wagon and sitting with his father.

Getting to Jacksonville was the most grueling part, and by then Hiram had lapsed into a coma. A day before that curtain, he had his last few hours of clarity. He had no premonition of his impending death, assuming that the further north he traveled, the better he would feel. Temporarily alert and energized, he probed his son's intentions. Surely, Stephen was not serious about returning to Florida. His future was too bright to have it thus wasted. Stephen seemed dead set on the move, but he also, in his father's mind, offered the possibility that the move was only temporary, and that Harvard had merely been postponed, not forsaken.

"Stephen, America is about to blossom," Hiram told his son. "We have grown from ocean to ocean, preserved the Union north and south, and men like Mr. Carnegie will lead a new revolution. When we get back to Pittsburgh, I want you to meet with him again, to listen to him talk about his plans. You can return here, but please don't come back without granting me this request."

Stephen nodded, and then shrugged, holding on to the side of the wagon as it traversed a shallow rocky stream, "I'll certainly do that, Father, but I also want to talk to him about Florida." And then he smiled that beguiling smile that had prompted a tremor in the hearts of a select circle of young Pennsylvanian women, a smile that stirred his father in a different way, a smile that drew him and his son into a conspiracy of truth that Hiram Knight knew he would miss when his son left home. The smile lingered as Stephen said, "Of course, my cousins will be the barons of that revolution."

Hiram laughed out loud for the last time in his life, wishing he had the strength to pull his son to his bosom. He and Stephen had often passed private judgment on the Knight family, feeling a bond in their own exclusion. "Your cousins are competent dullards, as are their fathers. Men with gold on their minds and metal in their hearts. They will get richer, and remain barren."

"And you, Father?" Stephen teased. "Can you speak verse about yourself?"

Hiram Knight was having trouble breathing. He was pooled in his own sweat, and his lower back ached. He sensed that he was lighter than when he began his journey to Florida. He also sensed a yellow smell about himself. Gazing at his son before speaking, he thought he saw less of himself and more of his dead wife in their only child. How could such a beautiful woman have loved him, he had asked himself a thousand times. Finally, in a low voice, he said, "I am as competent and as dull as my brothers." Seeing his son about to protest, he added, "Dull, but not a dullard. It is my only vanity, to be honest about myself. My final pleasure in life will not be your inheritance, although I admit that I will have enjoyed its accumulation. Stephen, I am merely a hand-up for you. And that has been my great pleasure. And, why I fear your plans."

Stephen told his father to look around. They had come to a dirt road with towering oaks on each side, their branches reaching across the narrow lane and intertwining with each other to form an arching dome that allowed only star-like dots of sunlight to penetrate. Hiram had felt the temperature drop as soon as they entered the shade, and the yellow smell around him turned to green.

The dying man looked at the branches and formed an analogy for his son to consider. "I never felt like my brothers and I came from the same branch of the family tree. Or perhaps their branch split when I was born, and your uncle was himself a branch off of mine. Am I making any sense?"

Stephen consoled him. "You don't have to make sense. You have to rest. You have a long journey ahead of you. Enjoy this road for a while."

Hiram then surprised his son, "I wish I was you, Stephen. I wish I was you and had your future. Florida or whatever it is to be." He was getting hazy again. He had more to say to his son before they got home, but he was too tired. "I just wish I was you."

Looking at his son's blue eyes and the sparkling green sky over his shoulders, Hiram took a deep breath. Stephen then reached over and loosened his father's shirt as he closed his eyes, whispering to him, "But, you are."

As his father rested, Stephen looked around at his future home. *Surely, this is how the world was at the beginning.*

In the beginning, all the Knights had been Republicans. They endorsed a Union of the States, but not for labor. Abolition of slavery, but not equality of the races. They were Christians and Capitalists. Prosperity was a virtue. Poverty was a vice. When Stephen Knight went to Florida with his father looking for his Uncle Thomas, he brought all the family history with him, fully aware that Thomas had exiled himself from that history. Failing to find his uncle, Stephen took his own dying father back North. That trip back allowed him time to imagine his own future: a future Knight manifestly destined to resurrect a fallen South rather than exploit a virgin West. He would honor his father's desire to see him graduate from Harvard before he returned to Florida with a vision of that future, a vision to be seeded and nurtured by a fifty-thousand-dollar loan from his Pennsylvania uncles, a loan paid back with interest within five years. He also returned to Florida with a bride whose own family invested another fifty thousand in his vision. Stephen understood wealth. Men were wealthy because they made money, inherited money, or married money. The latter two sources were themselves makers of more money.

Knight wanted to buy Florida. He did not consider himself a New World Adam. He was a surveyor with a Harvard education in

Natural History. He saw no contradiction between preserving Nature and profiting off of it. That was his vision. Before he returned to Florida, he had sought out Frederick Law Olmsted and engaged him in a lengthy debate, over three nights of dinner and wine, about how to "tame" a wilderness. Knight left unsatisfied. He could not convey to Olmsted his own vision, and Olmsted's vision, he decided, did not account for his own concept of *dynamic stasis*. Olmsted seemed to want to assert order on Nature first, and then freeze that order, as if Nature was to be a museum of itself. Knight wanted to preserve the natural beauty of Florida that he had first experienced, to let it grow as if it were an organism, but that primeval beauty had to be mastered and made subservient to Stephen Knight's other ambition: the creation of a Knight dynasty of enlightened heirs and stewards of his vision. It was a grand vision, for sure, he would admit to his pale and nervous bride as he described their future.

But only to himself would he admit that he had no idea what he actually meant. Perhaps he only *sensed* a vision rather than actually saw it? His initial encounter with Florida had been indelible, as if he had never had those physical senses of sight, sound, and smell until he paddled up a river into a jungle looking for his missing uncle's church. He was too much of a Knight to not sense the economic value of fertile land. Timber was obvious, and all the industries that would be spurred by that. But, also, tracts for cattle, tightly bred and slaughtered for Southern omnivores. And why should America have to import oranges and limes? Profit was the easy vision. Supply and demand were a gospel understood by all the other Knights. Hence, their investments. As he made his case to his elders, Stephen knew that he was only telling them what they wanted to hear. He knew that his other vision would not be so hospitably received. But he had a brilliant young man's faith in himself. He would figure it out later. The important thing was first to stake his claim to the land.

It took him a year, and more loans from his family, but he finally owned fifty thousand acres of central Florida. He then spent another year exploring most of it, surveying and measuring and mapping. He spent the next year platting and building his own town, naming it Arcadia, finally providing his wife the palatial home he had promised her, a home designed to replicate her family home back in Pennsylvania. In his fourth year, he established his lumber business and started selecting land for his citrus groves. At the end of his fifth year, he took his wife back to Pittsburgh to see her relatives, letting her have the pleasure of giving her parents a bank draft to repay their investment while he did the same to his uncles. He did not tell her or anyone else that part of the repayment had come from his selling off ten thousand of the original fifty thousand acres he had purchased. He had promised a return on their money within five years. Like any Knight, he knew that to get credit in the future he must pay off debt from the past on or before the due date. Credit begets credit. Money begets money. His uncles urged him to turn his Florida enterprises over to capable managers and return to Pittsburgh to assume control of the larger Knight industries there, favoring him over their own sons. He thanked them, and declined. His wife returned with him, but ceased to be his soul mate. She was mother to their three sons, mistress of their house and servants, but she hated Florida.

In another five years, Stephen Knight had repurchased the ten thousand acres he had been forced to sell, and then added another hundred thousand acres. But his vision, his *dynamic stasis*, eluded him over time. His vision had to be compromised. He could not preserve and exploit at the same time. He therefore separated the goals. He restricted his development to fifty thousand acres and simply set aside the remaining hundred thousand. He was still a young man. He had time to clarify that elusive vision that he had only sensed but never really seen. Besides, thirty thousand acres easily made him rich.

He died a day short of fifty, after making his last journal entry.

Much to do today. Tobacco barn to be cleaned. Sun-curing is behind schedule. Early crops have been bountiful after disappointing start. Proper Turkish blend seems to have been resolved after recent trip to Virginia. A scent of unsweetened dark chocolate. Very pleasant. Hope to have comparable success with cattle. Heat and humidity have been deterrents (to man as well as beast). Infestation of undetermined origin. Samples sent to Harvard. My speculation is that some version of a South American or a Texas breed might prosper here. Survival in Texas augurs well for survival anywhere. Soon to go South to look at the vast inland ocean of water that sustains the lower part of the state. Untapped potential for irrigation, but would need pumps for northern transfer. If time and sunlight permit, I will go to my uncle's church and make some sketches about future reconstruction. Thomas might prefer the concept of resurrection to reconstruction. It would be a lively conversation with him. In a perfect world, my father would himself partake, the three of us parsing theology. I might suggest to

Thomas that resurrection requires a prior existence. But since he him-
self did not finish the construction of his church, it was not born, but
stillborn. He would swell with indignation, but subside. Father would
remind me that the construction of any church was not consistent
with my own character, as I lacked faith in any God conjured by man.
I wish he were here, but hale again. I believe he would finally see
what I see in this land, proof of something greater than my uncle's
Jehovah or Jesus. Perhaps then he would understand that while I do
not believe in God, I do believe in worship.

He had stopped to rest. Up since before dawn, after a day in his jungle, he checked the sun and determined that he had another hour
or more of light. Enough time to go to church. He had his shotgun
slung over his shoulder, his sketch pad in his satchel, and walked
without thinking. He had the route memorized in his leg muscles.
The ground was lush with grass still wet from an afternoon shower.
Seeing the pillars of the unwalled church ahead, he had paused and
turned slowly around, the wide brim of his hat shielding his eyes,
surveying his land. He closed his eyes and inhaled deeply, taking a
single blind step.

Had he missed the hiss of a warning? The pain came first, and
then again, and then he was on his knees, facing the church, and then
a third penetration. He had dropped his sketch pad as he struggled
to get the shotgun off his shoulders. But where to aim? He tried to
turn while still on his knees, but all he saw was the grass parted as
if by a comb. Three narrow lines going three different directions.

This cannot happen to me.

Three punctures, two in his calves, one in his thigh. *How could I not remember to wear my high-top leather boots?* Years earlier, he had suffered a comparable wound, but only one, and he was with others who tended to him immediately and got him bathed in fresh water within minutes. At this moment, he was alone and an hour from the company of another human.

The end began as time stopped. Numbness in his legs, and then he was light-headed. He touched his face, feeling nothing. He looked at his hands, covered in sweat. How long was it taking? *I need to record this later in my journal.* He retched. He looked at the church, but it had blurred.

This cannot happen to me. I have too much to do.

His breathing was labored as he tried to walk toward the church. It seemed to keep receding in the distance. He lay down in the grass, looking up at the darkening sky. He closed his eyes and spoke to his father. *I'm sorry. I wanted you to be proud of me.* He thought of his wife and children. *I have no one to pray to, no one to ask for their protection.* His sight gone, he smelled and listened to the world around him. Had there always been that many birds, so many different trill and whistle and chirp variations? Far above him he could hear the swooping flap of an eagle's wings. The hum of branches swaying. But then the breathing, low and almost guttural. His own? Breathing outside of himself. How to distinguish between a low growl and a heavy purr? The ground under him softly vibrated as padded feet circled him. He could not open his eyes.

This cannot happen to me.

All that was left for him was the distant smell of Turkish tobacco.

JIT KNIGHT

Percy Knight had given up trying to lose his nickname *Jit*. It was always better than the alternatives that plagued his childhood. *Percy* was itself a curse, even though he eventually found a famous poet with that name. But Knightville's Percy Knight had no language talent. As a child he was taunted by other poor children, and even a few times by his rich cousin Norton Knight, the eventual Lord of Knightville. Norton had relented, some form of *noblesse oblige* surfacing against his will, and Percy was granted teenage knighthood by his cousin once he reached high school in 1960 and was discovered to have unnatural speed and quickness for a white boy. A sportswriter dubbed him the *Lightning Bug* of the Knightville Panthers. After one game, another sports Mencken called him a *Jitter Bug* for his east-west moves as well as his north-south speed. Norton began to call him *Buggs,* but that failed to adhere. But in some cosmic joke, since Percy was also inherently insecure and unable to hide his social awkwardness, Norton tossed off *Jitter* as his cousin's nickname while introducing him at a pep rally, and it was met with universal acceptance. Percy became Jitter Knight, and then the helmet of a visiting St. Augustine Yellow Jacket met his knee, and Jitter Knight was no longer swift or quick. It was the last game of his junior year. The devolution from *Jitter* to *Jit* followed, and Percy Knight went from knight to vassal in the kingdom of his cousin. His jersey was given to a promising sophomore. Jit never got his diploma.

He was granted only one dispensation from what seemed a future of small-town obscurity. He and Norton loved the same girl, Sandy Chippen, but she loved only Jit. Norton became the Lord of Knightville, as expected, but Jit became the sheriff.

Jit did not aspire to be the sheriff. He simply outlasted everyone else. Lacking a future, he began as a volunteer when he dropped out of Knightville High. He still had his football strength, but he never attempted to chase anybody. As a volunteer, he was not allowed to carry a gun, but he had a uniform. He was called most often on a Saturday night when the men from the Knight Paper Mill spent their weekly check at the Knight Tavern. Jit worked at the Knight Lumberyard, but he knew most of the mill workers from high school, those who did not escape after graduation. Knowing them, he knew their fathers and families too. They knew Jit well enough to know that he was always gracious at first, but resistance to a request from him usually meant a slap to the face and an arm pretzel-twisted. Jit might even apologize, but he was consistent. The full-timers would joke, *Jit might not shoot you, but you sure don't wanna fuck with him.*

Jit had another innate skill lacking in the full-timers. He could talk to black people. It was his most mysterious power. Knightville was a little bit black and a whole lot of white town, and each side knew its role. It was the Sixties. Civil Rights was a movement, but only in other places, like Lincolnville up in St. Augustine. Norton Knight's father had raised eyebrows when he started hiring black men for a few of the Knight businesses, but his motives were clearly economic, not social. Blacks worked cheap, and poor whites thus knew that they were expendable. Norton's family had always been on top. Jit's family had always been one rung above the bottom. He did not live on the black side of town, and he had no black friends. The decrepit black high school would eventually be closed and its students forced into Knightville High a few years after Jit had dropped out. But Jit understood how the winds were blowing. Separate but equal had always been one but not the other. Still, operating one school instead of two was going to save the taxpayers some money. Social justice was a smokescreen. More importantly, the Knightville High football coach knew that he was soon going to be competing against other *integrated* teams. And, as Jesus and Bear Bryant understood, *Black boys sure can run and the big 'uns are mean to the bone.* Jit had no illusions about himself. He was white trash. But for some reason, he never understood the necessity of having two water fountains side by side at the Knight Drug Store. One pipe eventually led to both spouts. So, when his first Saturday night brawl at the tavern had to be settled, and the fighting settled down to a piss fight between Billy Tatum, his old blocking fullback, and Johnny Clifton, a one-eyed colored boy, Jit yanked them apart and asked, "You want to tell me what the hell is the problem here," as the grinning full-timers stepped aside. Jit listened to each man and then put the cuffs on Billy, whose reaction was only a little less astonished than everybody else.

The old sheriff who Jit followed around had finally hired him as a deputy when he was twenty, but only after Jit had agreed to get his GED. With a GED and a job, he proposed to Sandy and, to his wonderment, she accepted. He asked his cousin Norton to be his best man but was rebuffed. Jit was genuinely surprised. The old sheriff had to explain to him, "Jit, for as smart as you are, and you *are* smarter than people think, you might be the dumbest white boy in town. How could you not know that your cousin was sweet on Sandy all these years? Seriously, she never told you?"

"They were sweet on each other?"

"Dammit, Jit, did I say *they*?"

"But Sandy and Norton are . . . they are not . . ."

"If you're trying to tell me that your cousin and Sandy are not running in the same circles and that Norton's daddy would disown him if he actually brought her home one night . . . hell, yes, I know that. But I know she loves you . . . Christ go figure . . . and that you are perfect for her. Explaining Norton is beyond me. I caught him outside her house one night a few years ago, like a damn window peeper except it was a full moon and he was across the damn street. I was going to haul him back to his father, but he made me promise to keep it secret. And he told me the entire story. How he had known her since grade school, just like you, but, dammit, love is too damn complicated for me. I thank the Lord that me and my wife never had to deal with it."

Jit's head spun and he swayed with the realization that he had inadvertently insulted his cousin. He went to apologize, but Norton seemed unconcerned. "No, no, Jit. Things are fine, no hard feelings. The sheriff has perhaps exaggerated our encounter and my conversation with him. No, I wish you and Sandy the best of luck, but it is still probably better for me to absent your wedding."

Almost fifty years later, Jit helped his cousin die.

If Knightville was confused by the daily routines of Norton Knight, it could charitably be described as being amused by Jit Knight. Norton was a specter in their lives. Jit was an endearing spectacle. Young people heard stories about his youth and his short-lived football career, and they had a hard time reconciling those stories with the corpulent, slow-moving, slow talking, seemingly confused enforcer of the everyday social order within which their lives ebbed and flowed without most of them having to lock their doors when they left their houses. But, old and young, every four years they voted to keep him in office. For the past twenty years, he had run unopposed.

Before becoming Jit's favorite deputy, Abraham Jones had known him when he was a child, going to Jit's house with his mother to clean and cook, with Abe doing some yard work too. Abe's friends had joked about Jit being his real daddy, but, when Abe was big enough, he stopped those jokes with a few lightning punches to the guts of his tormentors. He also pointed out the obvious problem with that theory. Abe was coal black, just like his real mother and father. Truth was, Abe wished that Jit had been his father. Jit never raised his voice, never hit him, and never forgot his birthday.

When Abe was sixteen, Jit had been called to break up that fight between him and two other teens. After he grabbed the collar of one of Abe's tormentors and slapped the other, Jit had pointed a finger at Abe and demanded an explanation. Each of the three boys was taller and stronger than Jit, but each knew that the sheriff was not to be sassed back. Abe had sulked and looked down at the ground as he told Jit that the other boys had said that Jit was his father. Jit had turned to the other two and gave them a look that said, *That true?* Silence was affirmation. Jit let out one of his trademark exasperated sighs. "Abe, I'd be proud to be your daddy . . ." turning back to the other two, ". . . but saying that sorta shit about me and Abe is a damn slur on his mama, and I ought to whip both of you, but I'm going to let you boys off easy. You apologize to Abe here and I won't drag your black asses over to his house where you can apologize directly to her. And I won't then take you home to tell your own parents about your lack of respect. Deal? If we understand each other, I want you to shake my hand."

Four years later, after getting an AA in Law Enforcement at Seminole Community College and going through police academy training, Abe went to work for Jit as a deputy sheriff. Classroom training had been the first hoop, but Abe soon learned his first lesson from Jit about the real work he had to do in Knightville. In the interview, Jit had asked him about his long-term plans, the usual *How do you see yourself in ten years?* question. Abe was quick to say, "Being your best deputy." *Twenty years?* "Being your replacement."

Jit was pleased, "So you don't see yourself in Tallahassee or Jacksonville or . . . Orlando?" Jit never said the word *Orlando* without a noticeable phlegm in his voice.

"No, sir. This is my home."

"That's good to know, so let me tell you something that will only make sense the longer you're here."

"Jit, I was born and raised here."

"But you ain't been the law here."

"No, sir, that's true, but I've watched you for as long as I could walk and talk."

Jit smiled. "Abraham Lincoln Jones, I'm not sure how it works in other places, but here's the sum total of my knowledge about how things work in your hometown, my hometown, this town. There are going to be a few times when you'll have to ignore the law in order to enforce the law. Those times aren't in the books you read. But those are times that matter. Every small town is different, different people. Knightville is different, and you're gonna see that difference, but only in a uniform."

"Sheriff, I got lots of time."

In his first ten years, Abe worked the day shift with Jit, but was available for all the night calls that the sheriff made. On Sundays, Abe's mother fixed them dinner. The other deputies accepted that he was Jit's favorite. They had a history together. But, in reality, Abe was also his best deputy. He was also the only deputy who had seen Jit break the law on a few occasions, more lessons. If an enterprising academic ever wanted to research law enforcement in Knightville, Abe would have been a better source than Jit himself. He could have pointed out that Jit had integrated his department long before it was a national goal. Four black deputies, four white. Of course, female deputies were a bridge too far for Jit until Abe kept harping on the discrepancy. For Jit, women in uniform made no sense, but Abe poked him every time a rare opening occurred in the department. "Sheriff, dinosaurs are extinct. You got to adapt." The next opening was filled by a black woman from Tampa. Abe congratulated the sheriff, and so did the editor of the *Knightville Times*. Only later did Abe learn that Jit's daughter Sandra had been poking her father about hiring more women long before he had mentioned it.

Abe could have also told the PhD researcher that Jit kept the black deputies mostly in the black areas of the county. He could have told the researcher that Jit would investigate crimes before they happened. People talked to Jit, especially black people. Eventually his black deputies were his scouts. That was his method. Something suspicious, Jit made a visit. Abe's favorite investigation, never to be admitted publicly, was when Jit heard about a meth lab in east Knightville. He took Abe with him, and since the house was owned by a black landlord named Jake, he took the landlord too. Turned out that all the tenants were white, all of them recently moved to town, all of them meaner than snakes, but all of them were asleep when Jit and Abe and the landlord showed up at midnight and walked into the house, flipped on the lights, and started yelling at the three spooked-out white men. Abe had a shotgun. The landlord had an unloaded shotgun, and Jit became Charles Laughton with a badge and a nightstick. Before they entered the dark house, Jit had also reminded Abe that if he actually fired that shotgun the entire place would explode.

The three blinking perps were herded to the front yard, where Abe stood over them with his shotgun as they lay on the ground, their noses in the dirt. From that position, Abe could see Jit and the landlord in a heated discussion inside the sheriff's car. Fifteen minutes later, the two men emerged and Jit informed the three meth dealers that their immediate future had been decided. First, they would leave Knightville and never return. They would not pack any belongings. They would surrender any cash they had to the landlord. When one objected, Jit pointed out that he had an outstanding warrant for parole violations, and so his future incarceration at the Starks prison would be a little bit longer. The other two men were eager for the deal. Abe remembered thinking, *This ain't right. These guys are prime future offenders. And we are robbing them?* Jit asked the objector if they had a deal, emphasizing the *never return* clause. "Take the fucking deal, Sid," the other two men pleaded. Sid relented.

An hour later, back in the office, putting the shotguns back in their locked storage cases, Abe was shaking his head and asking Jit what just happened. His education was beginning.

"Those guys weren't local, and they'll go be somebody else's problem now."

"But that ain't how it's supposed to work, Jit. And you took their money. I sorta think that's a crime, isn't it? Aren't you . . . and me . . . blurring some lines that ought to be clear?"

"Probably."

"And?"

"And I told Jake that he was going to use that money to get some pro cleaners in there and fix up that house, make it safe and clean, and then he was going to rent it to the Taylor family down on Juniper Street, you know the ones, with that retarded child of theirs and old man Taylor working two jobs and still drowning, and Jake was going to rent that fixed up house for half what he would charge anybody else, and still make a damn profit, and if he did that then I would ignore his other properties down by the river, for a while, but he had better start fixing those up too, and I would not start busting his duplex on Rochester Avenue where Twyla and her daughter are whoring themselves out, with Jake getting free pussy on the side. Seemed like a win-win for everybody involved."

Abe would have told the PhD researcher that he did not know whether to laugh or quit. That choice was settled after he asked Jit, "But those three men, if they get busted somewhere else, have some information about the sheriff in Knightville that might be used in a trade-off for some other charges. You're running a big risk, Jit."

"Their word against ours. Jake ain't talking. I ain't talking. You?"

Norton was not sure where to put his cousin Jit on the scale of acceptable professions. Jit was the Sheriff, but, even though he did not arrest a lot of people, the county still seemed relatively crime-free.

Norton had once asked Jit what he did to justify his salary. It was not meant as a criticism. Jit understood that and was not offended. In Jit's mind, his cousin was prone to questions that had simple answers and deep answers. Trouble was, sometimes only Norton knew what he was really asking.

The two men had been at the hardware store. Jit was buying paint for his office. Norton was . . . and *that* was the question for a lot of people in Knightville. *What* was he actually doing? Jit was carrying out a gallon bucket of paint and Norton was standing on the porch. But what was he doing? Norton owned the world of Knightville, but other men seemed to be running it. Jit's daughter Sandra had once told Jit that she and him and everybody else in town were simply part of something called *The Knight Borg*, little cogs sharing one brain and operating as one mindless unit, owned by Norton. But then she had laughed, "Sorry, been watching too many *Star Trek* reruns. But I'll get back to you when I figure it out. Uncle Norton sure does need a day job, that's for sure."

Jit had no idea what his daughter was talking about. He did not watch television. But he knew she was whip-smart, probably the smartest girl in town, even smarter than her mother, whose own wit and insights had always puzzled him. Sandra would come up with a better explanation soon enough. But on that day when she laughed about that something called *The Knight Borg*, she also almost immediately added, "You won't tell Uncle Norton I said that, will you?" Jit looked at his daughter and had to admit that, even though she was editor of the paper and a certified adult, she was still just another member of the town audience for his cousin. Norton was a mystery, and that mystery led to myths and wonders, and fear. Norton Knight did not smile, and he was prone to leaving a conversation before it was over. Nobody had ever seen him lose his temper, but everybody assumed it was there.

Jit did not fear his cousin. Norton had all the advantages in their world, but Jit had married the girl Norton wanted. Jit could also remember times when they were young boys, not yet Knight men, and they played together in the woods, hunting snakes and rabbits, sometimes working summer jobs in the citrus fields, but high school changed all that, high school and Sandy Chippen. No, Jit Knight did not fear his cousin. He felt sorry for him. That sorrow began when

Norton came back from Europe and married the second prettiest girl in Knightville, Sandy's sister.

Norton asking Jit to justify his salary was a riddle compounded by Norton's almost immediate clarification of the question. "I mean, your job, not your salary." Keeping the peace and protecting property might be self-evident to most people. Jit had to justify himself every four years to the voters, but nobody asked him why the job itself needed to be justified. He knew his cousin wanted a serious answer, but he also knew that he was not as deep as his cousin, did not go to college, did not read books. Another reason that he felt sorry for his cousin? Norton was the loneliest mind in town. Jit would never use those words . . . *loneliest mind in town* . . . because it would have required him to be his cousin's intellectual equal, to reduce the right words to express complicated thought into a metaphor. All Jit could say was, "A lot of bad people in the world, Norton. Somebody has to keep them away from you."

The two men had been standing on the hardware store porch for only a few minutes, Jit with the gallon of paint getting heavier and heavier. He knew that his answer did not satisfy his cousin, but it did almost make him laugh, if a grim smile qualified as a laugh. "Right, all the bad people . . ." waving his hand around, ". . . out there. But the worst people? They're not out *there*." And then he walked off.

If Norton had been talking to anybody else, their conversation might have been reconstructed and misquoted in subsequent conversations, more fodder for the Knight family lore of Knightville. More head scratching and pursed lips, more looks over shoulders to see who might be listening, more concern about Norton Knight's mental health. But Jit kept Norton to himself. He would always feel sorry for him, seeing how his cousin's misery began with a bad marriage, and, even though that wife was a demon to him, her drunken fatal "fall" down the stairs seemed to have destroyed him, their baby son not a comfort then and a personal burden to come as an adult. Jit would always protect Norton from the rest of Knightville. He felt he owed his cousin that much, for many reasons.

Only Abe Jones knew how Jit had managed to keep crime down in the county. He simply did not arrest a lot of people. He chose to negotiate justice on a case-by-case basis, especially if the offense was not committed in public, and almost nobody got arrested for a misdemeanor first offense or petty crime. Jit's only zero-tolerance rule was for any man who hit a woman or child. *Those bastards go to jail.* Black folks knew how the system worked in other places, black parents especially, how an early false step ruined many futures. They knew how Jit would haul one of their wayward children home and hand them over to an overworked mother or father, suggesting that his own time was better spent chasing all the big-time bank robbers and murderers that were rampaging over the county. Non-existent bank robbers and murderers. Second offenses, however, started a sliding scale of penal authority. First-time walking-drunks were packed in a squad car and taken home. First-time driving-drunks were sometimes put in jail overnight, and given back their car keys a week after they were released. The worst thing you could do to Jit Knight, poor whites and poor blacks knew, was to be ungrateful. Contrition always eased forgiveness. Resistance and sass accelerated that sliding scale of justice. But there were enough of those ungrateful folks who provided a role model for how *not* to act around the sheriff.

Sometimes he would enlist one of the two black preachers in town to go with him as he drove around the black neighborhoods. State and Church was a formidable combination. And he always carried voter registration cards with him. Abe Jones had once pointed out to Jit that he treated whites and blacks differently. Paternalistic to one, deferential to the other. It was Jones's second year in the department. Jit told him that he wasn't paying attention. "It ain't color, Abe, it's money. And that deferential thing is bullshit. Poor people got enough rocks on their backs. You come see me in a few years. You tell me how to do my job then." Jones paid more attention. He figured out that as many whites went to jail as blacks, and in central Florida that was an atypical balance. Still, Jit *was* different around whites and blacks. Jones kidded Jit about always taking his hat off around white people but never around blacks. Jit admitted, "That might be true, but all those white folks still know that I know how many of them work for my cousin. 'Course, Norton and I never talk shop, but people assume we do. Hell, Norton doesn't talk to anybody. Small towns, Abe, a lot of stuff goes unsaid, right or wrong. Then again, the wrong stuff ends up as gossip anyway."

Forty-plus years of being a sheriff provided Jit Knight with too many examples of human failure. The few murders in that time had been grisly, but crimes of passion in general are seldom an art form. The worst had been a minor stabbing that had refused to stop bleeding. If Elihu Johnson had been sober, he might have called an ambulance after his wife had shoved a butcher knife in his chest, but he chose to continue his own abuse of her, both fists rendering her pulpy, a brick rendering her unrecognizable. Jit had hauled him into jail for the second time the week before, his patience long gone, but Johnson's wife had pleaded for his release and the county attorney, over Jit's objections, had agreed. A week later both husband and wife were found sprawled in their backyard, blood pools and swatches of hair and flesh leading from the kitchen to the above-ground swimming pool. The pool water was pristine, the floatable toy flamingo motionless. Jit would always remember one detail. The wife's body was contorted on the patio, but Elihu's body was propped up against the pool. Jit noted the single bloody handprint on the metal railing around the pool. He wondered if the dying man had simply grasped the rail for support before he sank to the ground, or was he actually trying to get in the pool. It made no sense, Jit told himself. *You got a knife in your chest. You just killed your wife. And you want to take a dip?* But he thought some more. *Maybe he was trying to get some water to wash his hands off? Maybe wash some blood off his face?* But Elihu Johnson was not known for his cleanliness.

Jit had stood in the yard surveying the damage as his deputy started to help the coroner load corpses into their body bags. This was a time before Abe Jones had been hired, and the deputy that day was competent but indistinguishable from any other deputy. He and Jit would never have the conversations that eventually developed between Jit and Abe, the boy he had helped raise. The day the Johnsons killed each other, Jit had simply stood there and thought about human misery and meanness. The bloody handprint had been a small detail, but Jit was more interested in Elihu's final position. His back propped up against the pool siding, Elihu would have had an unobstructed view of his wife's body a few feet away. That was the mystery for Jit. *The sonuvabitch was alive for some time, drunk and dying, and he couldn't avoid seeing his wife. Maybe he tried to look away, up at the sky? But she was right there in front of him. Maybe she wasn't dead yet? Maybe they had one last chance to curse each other? Did they think this was just going to be another time they battered each other, and life would go on? Or, did he really know it was the end for him? Who was he cursing then?*

Jit wondered those things, and he might have discussed them with Abe if he were there, but that particular day Jit kept his thoughts to himself. Everybody in town was used to Jit and his cousin Norton keeping their own company, so to speak. In Norton's case, everybody assumed it was because Norton simply thought that they were not worth talking to. He was damn smart, everyone agreed, and he just thought his words would be wasted on them. Jit? He was quiet, most people assumed, because he didn't have much to say to anybody about anything. Norton was a mile deep, Jit not so much. He was a good sheriff, but, seriously, that wasn't rocket science.

It was true. Jit kept to himself, but Sandra Knight never understood it when other people commented on her father's silence. "You never saw him at home. My lord, I had to go to my room too many times because he was always talking to me or the women who cooked for us."

The childless and combative dead Johnsons had been unmourned by their neighbors. Relatives were contacted, but were uninterested in claiming the bodies. They weren't churchgoers, but the Baptist minister was willing to preside and invoke God's divine mystery, for ten dollars. The funeral home was not as charitable. Two bodies in one pine box, a pauper's plot shared with two other pine boxes, which had been buried earlier and deeper. A preacher, Jit, and a gravedigger with a John Deere backhoe laid the Johnsons to rest on a sunny day in June. As the Baptist entertained the gravedigger, Jit was honing his law enforcement philosophy that he would explain to Abe Jones in the future. He blamed himself for the Johnsons' death. In the clarity of hindsight, their bloody final scene had been predictable. Jit could have prevented it if he had simply ignored the law. The most notable variation on that insight was the earlier time he simply ignored a murder because he was glad to see the victim dead.

NORTON KNIGHT

His corner study had always been his favorite room, lined with a thousand books and with two large windows that offered views of the northern and western vistas of Knight land. But even the study had long since ceased to offer a space for thinking. He could still read there, and he conducted the business of the Knight empire there, receiving the managers who worked for him, listening to their reports of past problems and decisions, their suggestions for the future, and he had usually agreed with them. He understood, he told himself, that his money was working for him, not these men, who were merely extensions of that money.

It made sense to him, but when he had tried to explain it to whom he thought was the smartest manager he had, that man had simply nodded and acted as if he understood and agreed. But Knight respected that man, regardless of his lower vision. Ten years earlier he had come to Knight, asking for his protection. He had knowledge that other men were embezzling money from their positions in the Knight empire, hundreds of thousands of dollars in the past few years. They had asked him to join them, assuring him that Knight himself was oblivious. They had intimated that if he did not join them, it would not bode well for him personally. Those men had reputations. The man was afraid, but he chose to confide in Knight, who assured him that he was safe, that he would be rewarded as well as protected. Knight did not tell the man that those other men were probably right. He had been oblivious. He had been disconnected from his own money. Perhaps it was time to at least start *thinking* about his money again. A month later, the embezzlers were gone.

Knight had assured his loyal manager, "The county attorney will deal with them, as will the sheriff."

The loyal man was still concerned about himself, about having to testify in public. Knight re-assured him, "The county attorney will not need you."

But outside the courtroom?

"The sheriff will protect you. I assure you."

The loyal man apologized for dragging Knight into the public spotlight. Everyone knew how much Knight disdained public attention. Knight was not concerned. "The public will never know."

The loyal man was confused. "But the trial, the news, the talk."

Knight was indifferent. "The trial and sentencing are settled."

"But, the . . . news?"

"I own the news."

The loyal man had stopped talking then, just as he would years later when Knight told him that he was merely an extension of money. Knight resigned himself to settling for loyalty, itself a valuable commodity, over intelligence.

Norton had been raised an Episcopalian, Sunday services a foregone conclusion, his body in attendance, his mind anywhere else. His side of the family had endowed the small church for over a century. Small in size, small in congregation, but his father had assured him that quality, not quantity, mattered. Norton had announced to his shocked friends in high school that he was an atheist. His parents assumed it was a phase that all teenagers went through, and they shrugged off his adolescent rebellion as simply a necessary step toward maturing into an adult. But Norton had a secret that compounded his teen alienation, a secret more surprising than going from believer to nonbeliever, a secret he kept from everyone except his cousin Jit. Norton did not lose his faith. He never had it. Even as a child, going through the rote of Christian indoctrination, Norton never believed any of it. He feigned piety until he was sixteen. He dared not admit it to his parents, who dressed him up for Sunday display, who hosted the Episcopalian minister for dinner the first Sunday of every month, who disdained Methodists and Baptists, who slept in separate bedrooms. He eventually discovered the term *dissembling* and came to understand himself. He posed as a believer and thought he would be discovered by his parents, but they remained oblivious as long as he went through the outward motions of reverence. As he got older, it was a small crack in his respect for them. Eventually, he lost respect for anybody who believed in God, and that was his real secret. He announced his atheism but did not mock those who held to their own faith. That was another form of dissembling. And then he quit dissembling after his wife died. No pretenses. He ended the Knight endowment for the Episcopal Church. The dwindling congregation did not step up and increase their own financial support. Instead, some melted into the previously scorned Methodist and Baptist flocks, others transitioned to be among the sturdy runt Episcopalians: they became Presbyterians. Norton bought the small Episcopal church building and converted it to a hardware store.

Norton did not believe in God, but, having read his ancestor Stephen's journals, he understood the distinction between Faith and Worship. Much of the primeval jungle had been lost since Stephen arrived in Florida. Timber had been cleared. Houses encroached. But the heart of that jungle was still accessible if you were willing to park your car and walk a mile into the shrinking green darkness. That green heart was part of the land that future lawyers would want. For decades, Norton had established his own development barriers, and all of them kept that pristine heart untouched. He had always come to this spot by himself. He knew the best trails, knew how to watch for snakes, and he had usually brought a gun with him. He sometimes tried to come at night, toting an electric lantern, but even he was intimidated by the sounds he heard. He was trespassing on his own land.

The jungle had entwined itself around and through the remnants of the first Knight claim, and his destination was seemingly hidden by a century and a half of leafy growth. If a stranger had been dropped into the same exact spot, that stranger would not have seen what Norton Knight was seeing at the end of his excursion, the skeleton of Thomas Knight's unfinished church, the circular floor intact but piled with moss and fronds, perhaps a dozen of the original columns still standing. But any understanding of its first purpose would have required fluency in a foreign language that had never been recorded, a language of symbols, not words. The first time Norton had seen it, he and Jit were together, having skipped school and then trekking through acres of of unsullied land. It had taken them three hours, another three to get out of the jungle before dark. Norton had told Jit that they were searching for the El Dorado of the Knight family, the infamous lost chapel. He had to explain to his cousin the myth of El Dorado. Thinking back to that moment, Norton understood that Jit was the first person to give him that look others would often give him for the rest of his life, a look of patience and confusion, a look that said, *Okay, if you say so. As long as you know what you're talking about.* With Jit, the look had been all that, but also tinged with sibling admiration. Jit would never fail to tell people for the rest of his life that Norton was the smartest man in Knightville. The boys had made their excursion the week before Jit's knee was shattered in a football game. Back then, Norton had assured him that he had a great future ahead of him: college scholarships, a free ride, and then perhaps a shot at the pros. Jit had a chance to get away. Norton would not be so lucky. "I'll go to college, no doubt, but we both know that I will end up back here to replace my father." Jit had given him that *look* for the second time.

The two boys had walked around the decomposing church and had the last extended conversation of their lives. Norton confessed to liking a girl he had just met, but he did not tell Jit the girl's name. He knew his parents would not approve. Jit had met someone he liked as well, but he had not even spoken to her, much less presumed to ask her for a date, so he kept her name to himself around his cousin. Sandy Chippen was too beautiful for him, so why even let Norton laugh at his pretensions. So, they walked and talked and made a game of looking for Thomas Knight's body. He had disappeared a hundred years earlier, and everyone assumed he was near his church when something happened to him. Perhaps the black panther got him, the panther more legendary than Thomas himself?

Norton's greatest strength was his ability to not give a damn about the rest of the world. Or, so he told himself. A few people might have described the same trait as a weakness, as being more *oblivious* than *indifferent* to the opinions of others. After all, how could he not see the irony . . . more, the perverse oddness . . . of him marrying the older sister of the woman his cousin had married. Only Jit, and the sheriff before Jit, understood the deeper knot. Norton was in love with his new wife's sister, but Jit won her heart first. *First* was a key distinction for Norton. Perhaps if Jit had not been there at the beginning, perhaps Sandy Chippen would have given her heart to Norton? Simply a matter of chronology? Two other people, besides Jit and the elder sheriff, knew the secret. Sandy, of course, who had spurned Norton with a gentleness and sweetness that made him love her even more. The fourth was her sister.

Ashley was the older of the Chippen girls. A senior to Sandy's junior class status, as Norton was to Jit. Ashley had been her sister's confidante. She had urged Sandy to consider the future. Norton would be a step-up for the Chippen family. Norton was handsome and would be rich. Jit was Jit. A lateral, not vertical, marriage was all he could offer. Sandy admired her sister, especially her intelligence and her ambition. She knew that her older sister would go away and succeed in the world beyond Knightville. But Sandy loved Jit. His world was enough for her. Ashley confessed to not understanding her sister. Love? Ashley had heard her own parents say over and over: *You're older. You've got to set an example for your sister. She's not as smart as you are. She's much too trusting.*

Norton had gone away from Knightville after high school, but he knew it was only temporary. He would be allowed to go to college and to travel, but he was expected, required, to return and assume the role for which he had been groomed. That is, if grooming meant that he was the only heir to *the* Knight name and land. Educated and older, he waited for his widowed father to die. He did not have to wait long.

The funeral was the social event of the year in Knightville. Norton was by himself in the receiving line, standing next to the open casket, shaking hands, accepting condolences, hearing short stories about how his father had touched other people's lives. He suspected insincerity. Then Jit and Sandy appeared, and Norton almost wept as they both embraced him. The truth was, Norton had loved his father and mother, as aloof as they could sometimes be, as stern as they often were, but he was their only child. They had always been a presence in his life. At his father's funeral, until Jit and Sandy arrived, Norton had been grieving by himself. After embracing, the three of them kept talking, with Norton even laughing at times, and the waiting line got longer. Sandy finally pulled Jit away, hugged Norton one more time as Jit shook his hand, and the logjam was broken. The required communal homage was allowed to start again.

"Remember me?"

Norton did not remember her, but she did look very familiar. The line had dwindled down to a few dozen. He was tired. The church service and burial were still to come.

"I'm sorry. I think I should, but it's been a long day."

"Ashley. We graduated together. Ashley Chippen."

If people in town began talking about him and Ashley, Norton was not listening. He was not in love, he insisted to himself, but Ashley thought his resistance could be overcome. He was certainly drawn to her, a more upscale version of her sister. In a typical hierarchy, the Chippens would not be on the lowest rung. In sociological terms, they were comfortably lower middle class. But in Knightville, there was only one scale: Norton's side of the Knight family, and everyone else. Three generations earlier, the Knight family tree had split into Norton's line and Jit's line. Jit eventually became part of the "everyone else."

The trouble with Norton's status was that he had no social peers, and thus no suitable marriage pool. When he met Sandy, he simply assumed that his parents would love her as much as he did, would embrace her into their family. How could they not? The wonder of her was self-evident. He was eighteen. He was mistaken.

Ashley, however, would have been acceptable to his parents. Norton finally understood the distinction. Ashley had a seriousness absent in her sister, a superficial sophistication in her wardrobe and demeanor. That was Norton's epiphany about his dead parents. For them, a person's *surface* was just as important as their substance. If all the world saw was the surface of someone, that surface had to rise to some standards of taste and decorum. Norton split hairs as he rationalized his growing attraction for Ashley. Superficiality was not the same as shallowness. Ashley was clearly more mature than her sister, more educated, more sure of herself. In all the important realms of *surface*, she was Norton's equal.

And she was always Sandy's sister.

When Norton told Jit that he had become re-acquainted with Ashley, his old classmate, Jit was the only person in town who was happy for his cousin. Jit did not support him in public and then mock him in private, as most others did. The two had grown up together, only a year apart, and the eventual explicit gap between their statuses was not even implicit when they were boys. They were more brothers than cousins. Jit knew about Norton's teenage affection for Sandy. He also knew about the rancor between Sandy and Ashley, but if Norton was happy with Sandy's sister, then Jit was happy with him. As boys, they had sometimes talked about their plans for the future, how their lives would fall into place, and Jit could remember that his cousin's description of his future perfect wife was actually a lot like the Ashley he described. Jit's own version of the future was much less precise. He could not imagine someone like Sandy.

Sandy was uncharacteristically uncharitable toward Norton when Jit told her about him and her sister. She was also concerned. *Norton is not a good match for her, Jit. She's not good for him either.* Jit was confused. If he were asked to describe Sandy, he would often talk about her ability to clearly judge other people, finding hidden weakness or finding hidden strength. He would always laugh when someone, and someone always did, ask *What the hell did she see in you?*

She would not elaborate about her sister, consistent with *If you can't say anything good about somebody, don't,* nor would she agree to talk directly to Norton.

I would just hate to see him hurt, Jit. He's a good man, down deep.

Was it obvious to everyone, the artifice of their marriage? Even to themselves? Most people around them were polite. After all, he *was* Norton Knight. But almost everyone agreed: If Ashley had not been the sister of Sandy Chippen, the wife of Norton's cousin, she would have been perfect for him. But the sister/cousin connection could not be finessed in a small town. To the non-Knight world, Norton had pretensions; Ashley had *airs.* Norton had money; Ashley knew how to spend it. There were rumors that Norton had been sweet on Sandy first. Ashley never hid her envy of her sister, even long before Norton entered the picture. Still, everyone agreed, Ashley seemed to have made the better bargain. Jit was not a "catch" in anybody's mind.

Were they happy? They were cordial to each other in public, with Ashley making a point of holding on to Norton's arm as they walked downtown. After Sonny was born, she seldom appeared without her husband. Norton himself seemed to be a doting father whenever the three were together. After she died, however, Sonny was an orphan. Raised by hired nannies and sent to boarding schools when he was seven, returning full-time to Knightville only when he was old enough for high school.

Jit knew the truth about how unhappy Norton had been. At least, more than anyone else. He had wanted his cousin to be happy, but after Sandy disappeared Jit lost focus on his cousin. But then Ashley died, and Jit performed his first act of absolution for his cousin. He went to Norton's house and certified his innocence.

Ashley drank. She was known for her drinking, even in high school. The sheriff before Jit had taken her home to her parents more than once. But he also made the worst of well-meaning mistakes. He called Sandy to go with him to get her sister, and he would tell Jit years later about that night. How as soon as Ashley saw Sandy, she went directly at her face, and the two teenagers were in the dirt within seconds. Pulled apart, as soon as the sheriff turned his back, they were at each other again. He was not surprised by Ashley. Sandy was the revelation. Smaller, seemingly more fragile, she was walloping her sister with a vengeance, which only fueled Ashley even more. It was a lesson that the Sheriff imparted to Jit more than once.

Families, Jit, have their own boatload of cargo that none of us ever see. Piss and bad feelings, kept in the family, and you're gonna end up dealing with it more than you want. You and me, we've been lucky. Parents did us more good than harm. And, hell, sometimes you can't even blame the parents. Something in the blood, I guess. All in all, you're never going to be bored in this job.

Jit had seen it play out for himself year after year. Sometimes he would take a kid home and see what the problem was as soon as the parents opened their mouths. Other times, he understood the parents, knew the parents, felt the heartbreak in their voices as they tried to talk to their child in front of him. Cause and effect were sometimes a mystery to him. But he was paid to deal with the effect. He knew Sandy's parents well. He had seen how they favored her among all their children. Had it been that obvious to Ashley too? Jit was not sure, but Norton was reminded often.

Ashley was older but, as she and Sandy became teenagers, she slowly understood the real difference between her and her sister. Sandy was loved by everyone. Ashley was respected. Ashley was the firstborn child, but Sandy was her parents' favorite. The light-bulb moment? For their parents' twentieth anniversary, Ashley had bought them a pricey set of coffee cups, each embossed with a bright red *20*. Her parents had always made a ritual out of their morning coffee. Sandy had stitched a quilt for them, alternating squares of their favorite colors, with the center square embroidered with the date of their wedding. Sandy was not a very good seamstress, and her parents were not known for their sentimentality, but Ashley recalled every detail of that moment, to tell Norton years later.

It was like I had disappeared. They opened that box and you would have thought they won the lottery. They even wrapped that quilt around themselves as they sat on the couch. And I knew it then. I was in a goddam fairy tale. I was the wicked sister. I was the one looking in the mirror asking who was the fairest. But how could I hate her? She was too precious, remember? I was the smart one. She was the sweet one. I was pretty. She was beautiful. They had turned me into a simpering cliché.

Norton took Ashley to Paris for their honeymoon. It had been her wish. He told her to pick any spot in the world, but for some reason he did not expect her to pick the most obvious. Love, courtship, marriage, a honeymoon consummation of flesh and soul? Was not Paris the symbolic embodiment of the process? Except that he and

Ashley had consummated the fleshly union long before the legal union. That was her idea too. If he had assumed that his sexual experience was more notched than hers, he was disabused of that notion a week after his father was buried.

As a teenager, himself a virgin, Norton had desired Sandy Chippen with all the illusions of adolescent romance. She would *give* herself to him, an exchange of their mutual innocence. Their bodies, as Norton wrote, without embarrassment, in his journal, merely *vessels of our souls*. The mechanics of sex could be negotiated later. A decade later, emotions were negotiated between him and Ashley. And, like all negotiations, mutual agreement required compromises. Norton knew he was doing that as the weeks passed, compromising, but he never got the sense that Ashley was settling for less than she wanted.

Even after Reconstruction failed, and Florida turned Democratic, the Knights had remained Republicans. They all knew it made no difference in their lives who lived in the governor's mansion, or who went to Washington. Their wealth insulated them from any cracker Bolsheviks because neither party let those radicals in the game. As long as the Democrats did not tell them how to run their businesses, or steal too much in taxes, the Knights were happy. During the Great Depression, they even made the New Deal work in their favor, subletting land to the CCC and taking money for roads and a new post office. If you had asked Norton's grandfather or father why *they* were Republicans, they might have offered an olio of political clichés, but Norton knew the truth, told to him by his father the first time they surveyed the northern extremity of Knight land, debating how to extract more wealth from that land.

"Democrats are stupid fucks, son. They have neither class nor culture nor the ability to retract their heads out of their asses. How can you respect any man like that?"

Norton had been dumbfounded. His father's excessive profanity was well known within the family, a daily barrage that would eventually turn Norton himself into a man known for seldom ever using profanity. Norton had listened to his father and realized that his father was actually talking about himself. His wealth had brought him neither class nor culture. Norton also realized that his father actually believed that he had earned his wealth, not that it had been handed to him by the merest cosmic chance of having the right parents. Norton dwelled on the word *respect*. He did not respect his father, he finally understood, but he also saw how nobody else in town did either. His father avoided books and music; Norton absorbed them. His father cheated on his mother: Norton swore that he would sooner not get married than prove to eventually be unfaithful. His father seldom left Knightville; Norton left home as soon as he graduated from high school. He went to college, to travel, to find somebody he could love forever, although he knew that he had already found that person back in Knightville.

Norton had told himself that when he came back from his travels that he would be a different kind of Knight. Instead, he married Ashley. He joined the respectable civic groups. He donated to local schools and charities. He made weekly appearances at all of the Knight businesses. He would walk downtown and speak to anyone who spoke to him. He avoided any discussions of politics, knowing that he was out of step with the town. He did not proselytize for his Republican friends, nor against his Democratic friends. Down deep, he knew that Republicans were more respectable than the Democrats. They always had been. Did he aspire to office? "Never," he would say. His real reason was kept to himself. Politicians prided themselves on representing the people, of working *for* the people. The most honest thing that Norton ever acknowledged, but only to himself, was that he would never work *for* anybody, especially the *people*.

He had lived long enough to see Florida go from blue to red. Race and religion replaced capitalism as a rationale for Republican success. Norton might have been privately appalled by Republicans, but he still had no respect for Democrats. *Tax and spend* was still a true cliché for them. *Cut taxes, spend anyway, and hate your neighbor* was how he saw the new Republicans. During the 2010 election cycle, he started quoting Yeats to himself: *The best lack all conviction, while the worst are full of passionate intensity.* But then he saw the same lines uttered by a Democratic columnist, exhorting other Democrats against the mob Tea Party. Knight wanted to throttle the columnist and his implication that the Democrats were the "best" but lacked conviction. *The Democrats are stupid fucks*, he had muttered to the columnist who was a thousand miles away in New York City. That began his own political exile. He could no longer use his education to set himself apart from *the people*. His insights were not original. Even poetry he loved could be marshaled in the service of those for whom he had no respect.

His accountant had once asked him if he had ever voted for a Democrat. Norton had been adamant, *When Hell freezes over.* But he had been wrong. He realized it as soon as he hung up the phone. Jit, he had always voted for Jit.

SONNY AND ANGEL

Until he met Angel Darling in 2006, Stephen "Sonny" Knight was of a mind about himself that had crystallized after years of introspection: *I am not a bad man, but I lack some essential and elusive quality that would make me a good one.* It was a comfortable and almost accurate appraisal, as well as an effective pickup line if delivered without looking directly at the woman across from him, spoken softly as if to himself. It was the word *elusive* that set him off from other men. A touch of poetry. Women, he came to understand, would line up to offer themselves as that elusive quality which would make Sonny Knight a good man. His first wife believed it the most. Angel had no such illusions. But, then again, she wasn't much interested in good men. As for his first wife, he admitted later, his money was more seductive than his charm.

Sonny's vision of himself would also satisfy Norton Knight, the man who had insisted that humility was the most necessary quality in a man, that braggarts were fools, and braggarts with money were idiots. Norton had also told Sonny that there were three basic types of men: those who made money, those who pissed it away, and those who were smart enough to simply hold on to what they had. Sonny was happy being the third. Fortunately, Norton had always provided him a lot to hold on to.

Sonny had never measured the value of his life in money. He was born rich. He was not impressed by, did not envy, the wealth of other men. Nor did he question the disparity of wealth between him and others around him. Him having money was as natural as other men having none. Norton Knight had made him work from an early age, that was true. Norton felt that he had an obligation to teach Sonny the value of work for its own sake. It was a lesson wasted. Sonny knew that work was irrelevant to his material well-being, but he also knew that his father was not a man to ignore.

So, Sonny worked because he thought it was his father's desire, but not at any Knight business. That was sometimes awkward, because the Knights owned most of the businesses in the county. Norton had himself been born with the Knight money and all its advantages, especially since he was an only child, but the family had been scandalized by his youthful insistence of "going his own way" as soon as he graduated from Florida State. Norton had gone North, another scandal. He eventually returned home, quickly becoming a Knight again; in fact, becoming more of a Knight than his own father. He married one of the fertile Chippen girls despite the obvious class disparity, and proceeded to expand the Knight family and fortune, with Sonny as his only heir.

Sonny had begun with a paper route for the *Knightville Times*, even though he disliked having to get up at dawn to deliver the morning edition before he went to high school. However, it was that first job which began Sonny's lifetime of self-appraisal. As much as he disliked delivering the paper, Sonny actually enjoyed going around to collect his subscribers' payments. It was always on the last Sunday afternoon of the month, and everyone knew he was coming. Although he was only a teenager, Sonny sensed that people liked him. He often lingered at an open door, talking small talk with a *Times* customer, sometimes picking up a conversation that had begun the previous month, "The gift of gab" is what his father called it, but Sonny was never sure his father really appreciated that gift.

Sonny would have kept that job, but Norton Knight bought the *Times* and Sonny had to find new employment. He went to work at Mott's Drugstore in downtown Knightville as a weekend clerk in the small hardware section. Soon enough, a lot of his old *Times* customers were lingering in Mott's, and Sonny was gabbing again. Old Man Mott said that Sonny was a "born retailer," and Sonny knew that his boss meant that as a good thing, unlike his father's tone when "the gift of gab" was mentioned. Sonny's only flaw, as he would have to admit in therapy after his first divorce, was a little bit of a temper when things didn't go his way. A drawer of nails and screws not close as tightly as Sonny wanted? Take a hammer and pound it. Weekly inventory figures do not balance? Wad up the tally sheets and throw them against the wall, cursing the other clerks for mis-shelving items. Inventory still not balanced? Fudge the numbers and let somebody else do the inventory next week. Overall, Sonny considered himself a happy person, a likable person. If his first wife had finally taken to singing "When Sonny gets Blue" every time he lost his temper, just to provoke him, then it was understandable that he slapped her. After all, he had warned her that he was tired of hearing that song.

Sonny's self-appraisal began early in his life and crystallized when he got to high school and fell in love. His first love, his only true love he was sure, was the first person, male or female, to offer an alternative explanation for the basic laws of his universe. When he told her about how he liked his earlier jobs, and how everyone seemed to like him, she had pursed her lips and given him that look he had seen her apply to bad food in the school cafeteria. "Sonny Knight, you are a dim smart boy. Do you think for one fraction of a micro-second that anybody in this town . . . this town named after your gene pool *and* mine too . . . that anybody in this town has ever dealt with you without having to consider that you are a goddam Knight? Not only a Knight, but eventually you'll be THE Knight! Not like me or my daddy. We'll always be the cracker Knights."

"Do you really think I'm smart?" was all he wanted to know.

Sonny was indeed a smart boy, and he had the grades to prove it. He was book smart, could talk and write smart. Standardized tests, if he concentrated, were a snap. Looking down at his classmates, the smartness gap was a canyon. Knight or not, Sonny would have been valedictorian if it had not been for the one girl who was smarter than him. How could he not fall in love with her?

Norton once told him, "You are one lucky bastard. The Knight money, your mother's looks, and only god knows where you got those muscles, the complete package. Do yourself a favor. Don't screw it up, or you'll be like Jit's side of the family."

Sonny went to Knightville High and was blazing his retail path to the top of the prep food chain even in his sophomore year. Then he saw the girl, his first love, at the aging Knightville pool. Sandra Knight came from the same gene pool, but Sonny did not care. Soon enough, a different kind of pool gave him hope. The high school had a swim team but no pool, so everybody was bussed back to town after school to use that leaking public pool built during the Depression by the Knight family, built by them just so they could turn down a project initiated by Roosevelt's WPA. Sonny was the best boy swimmer, but Sandra was as fast as him, and she looked like a movie star in a bathing suit. He didn't know she was smart. All he knew was that sometimes he could not get out of the pool because he was sure that his wholesale erection would give away the fact that he had been staring at her as she walked around the edge of the water. He asked her for a date, and she turned him down, saying that her father would not let her go out with boys until she was a junior. *And besides, your daddy and my daddy are cousins, you know that, so we're related too. Our kids would be Mongoloids.* He told her he would wait, and she laughed. It was another sweet hook in his heart. First, her legs, then her laugh. Sonny was in love. He was also oblivious to the well-known fact that Sandra Knight did not laugh. Her response to him was more of a throat-clearing than a laugh.

When Sandra casually mentioned that she wished that their school had its own pool, so she wouldn't have to deal with the un-predictable chlorine levels or have to spend so much time on the bus when she could be doing something else, Sonny went to his father and made the case that the high school needed its own pool. Norton called his accountant to make sure the tax breaks would be needed in that year of unexpectedly high income for the Knight enterprises. The money was escrowed and fourteen months later the new pool opened with much fanfare and a ribbon cutting that was even filmed by the Orlando television stations. But Sonny's true love was not there. She had quit the team. He didn't know it then, but he would never see her bare legs again, even though on their only "date" he did manage to put his hand between them.

Sandra became editor of the school newspaper, and Sonny started taking journalism classes. That was his downfall. Of course, he eventually realized that it was not his fault, that the journalism teacher himself had a crush on the girl. It was the only explanation for why Sonny earned A's all year long while she was given A+'s. Tiny percentages of points, but in the big picture they were enough to make her valedictorian and Sonny merely the salutatorian. When the selections were announced at the end of their senior year, Sonny was gracious. After all, by the time he was eighteen, Sonny's view of himself was almost complete: I am a Southern Gentleman.

That image of himself had hardened even more after he saw *Gone with the Wind* on a big theater screen in Orlando. Sonny thought he knew the story since he had grown up with other people who talked about it, but he had never seen the movie. He walked out of that theater and intuited something about himself that would make perfect sense to the love of his life when he told her. He was sure of that.

Sonny had realized that he was not only Ashley Wilkes . . . he was also Rhett Butler. Honor and Gentility wed to Pragmatic Cynicism. And damn good looking to boot. It was not ego. Sonny knew he was good looking, but he always feigned humility. That was part of the Code. He had explained all this to Sandra, and she nodded, smiling, saying, "Funny, I see you more as a Tom Buchanan type." Sonny's blank expression told the girl that she ought to explain the reference, but all she did was suggest that he go read *The Great Gatsby*. Sonny went home and asked Norton if he had ever heard of a character named Tom Buchanan. Norton looked at him but did not speak. He motioned with his head for Sonny to follow him into his private study, an act that intrigued Sonny because his father had always made it clear that the locked study was off limits to everyone. Sonny had seen the inside a few times, but he was never allowed to linger, and was never left alone. That night, nervous because he was sure that the girl comparing him to a fictional character would provide a clue as to her true feelings about him, Sonny waited as his father stared at the hundreds of books surrounding them. It was odd, Sonny saw the book first, and he was sure his father knew exactly where it was, but he had to wait as Norton looked around the room, sometimes touching a book but not pulling it off the shelf. When he finally did retrieve *Gatsby*, Norton turned to the last page and read it silently to himself. Then he closed it and handed it to Sonny, asking, "This girl, the one you love, is her voice full of money?" Then, seeing his son squint at him like he was a stranger, Norton sighed and said, "Second best book in American literature. Enjoy."

Minutes later, alone again in his study, Norton reached for a decanter of bourbon and poured himself a drink, thinking, *He wasn't even interested enough to ask what the best one is. That's the sad part.* And he downed the bourbon.

Sonny had gone to his room and read *Gatsby* in two hours. Then he read it again. If Sandra had been there, he would have asked her to marry him, related or not. Telling him to read the thin book had been a signal. She loved him. Sonny thought Tom Buchanan was noble and admirable, a strong man that a woman would want, as Daisy did. That was her message to him, surely.

Because his father would not let him take the book out of their house, Sonny went to Knightville's only bookstore and bought his own paperback copy of *Gatsby* to carry with him to school. He did not talk to the girl about it, but he made sure she saw that he had a copy. She would understand.

First, there had been Rhett and Ashley, and then Tom Buchanan, each adding a variation to Sonny's evolving Code. Women need a strong man. They can act independent all they want, but every woman secretly wants to be carried up that wide, dark staircase to awake with a smile on her face the next morning. That knowledge was used by Sonny on his only date with Sandra. Weeks of earlier cajoling had worn down her resistance until she agreed to that first date. Her initial insistence on some sort of confusing Platonic relationship . . . after all, their fathers were cousins, their mothers were sisters, making her and Sonny cousins themselves . . . had weathered Sonny's long-term siege on her virtue. She had finally allowed him certain privileges, perhaps out of her own adolescent curiosity, and he had initially acquiesced to her limits, but Sonny decided that it was time for her to let herself be carried away. In the back seat of his father's Buick, he put his hand under her Christmas Formal gown and advanced like Pickett's men at Gettysburg. With the same results. Sandra slapped him as hard as she could, and Sonny's temper spoke, "Who the hell do you think you are? Some sorta Scarlett O'Hara? Well, let me tell you something that you better never forget. You are no fucking Scarlett O'Hara!"

"And you, Sonny Knight, are no fucking me!" she had shot back just as she slapped him again. She scooted out of the front seat of the Buick and started walking the two miles back to her house, with Sonny driving alongside her, at first seeming to apologize through the open window, but then pointing his middle finger at her as he sped off. Eighty miles an hour, an empty flask tossed in the back seat, Sonny saw a bony dog crossing the asphalt road ahead of him. He loved dogs. But at that moment, those bones were everything in the universe that stood in Sonny's way . . . past, present, and future. The Buick accelerated, and Sonny looked for the girl in his rearview mirror just as that bony dog became a bloody lump on the side of the road. Until the end of his life, if asked about the worst thing he had ever done, Sonny knew the answer, but he never confessed.

For the rest of the school year, he never spoke to Sandra, and he made himself some promises. The first was that he would never allow another woman to ever slap him again. He kept that promise until he met Angel, the woman who taught him a lot about the connection between pain and pleasure. The second promise he made to himself was that he would eventually marry the girl he truly loved, that first girl who ever slapped him. Her being a cousin was not a problem in Sonny's mind. In its own way, the blood connection made her even more desirable. But that promise was adolescent and premature. It took twenty years but he finally met Angel, the woman who would be his second wife. Sonny did truly, deeply, and madly love her. She slapped him, and she loved him slapping her. But only in bed. Pushing forty, Sonny Knight was fascinated by his good luck. Angel had forced him to look at his past and ask a basic question: *What's the connection between me then and me now?*

"You're fucking me."

"Stranger things have happened, Sonny Honey."

"No, no, I mean you're fucking with me, right?"

"So, first I'm fucking you, and now it's a joint effort?"

Sonny was falling in love and would never understand that she was smarter than he was. Drugs and alcohol might have explained his confusion at that moment, but she had been doped up hours before she had offered him his first line of cocaine. She was now making a carnal and linguistic distinction, but he missed it.

"No, no, I mean . . . I mean your name. You're just fucking me around with that name, right? That's just your club name, right?"

Sonny felt her hand rubbing his groin as she straddled him, then she settled her own exposed groin snugly on top of his lap, took her hands and put one on each side of his face and leaned down to kiss him ever so slowly and wetly as the warm center of her body took control of his future.

"I get off in two hours. If you're still here, and you have another hundred, I'll show you my driver's license. If my name is not Angel Darling, you can fuck me . . . any way you want. Deal?"

"I'll give you two hundred, regardless. Forget the name thing."

Sonny had firm standards when it came to sex. He had never, would never, pay for it. At least, not directly. He knew the rules. A man always paid for it in some way, somehow. His first wife had made him pay dearly. But only desperate men paid direct, men who had no other chance, no other appeal to women, ugly and old and loser men. Sonny was none of those things, but this Angel . . . whose perfect breasts were real and whose downy blond pubic hair matched the mane of her head . . . this Angel turned Sonny Knight into everything he feared about his future. He could not offer her his soul, since he was sure he had none, but he began desperately offering the only thing he valued . . . the coin of the Knight realm.

"Five hundred for the night."

"Sonny, honey." She whispered in his ear, "You can't afford me. But stick around. My offer still stands. Two hours."

Sonny had been to the club dozens of times. Atlanta was only a seven-hour drive from Knightville, and he loved to drive his new Lincoln on long trips anyway. The first club he had gone to, as soon as he turned twenty-one, eventually bored him. Too small, no real privacy, and the women were always the same. But then he found the Pony Tail, his home away from home. Three stages, like a three-ring circus, walls of mirrors, each stage with its own lighting system, and dozens of young women every night. Through a curtain in the back was the private lounge. Watching the dancers was free, visiting the private lounge was a fifty-dollar minimum, everything else behind the curtain was negotiable.

Two hours later, the Pony Tail began to close. The crowd had dwindled to a few men who had negotiated escorts back to their hotels or homes. Sonny was still in limbo, waiting for his license exam, when the stage lights dimmed and the ceiling lights came on. Sonny blinked as the Pony Tail became a pony stable. The most jarring adjustment was his sense of smell. In the dark, the Pony Tail was dopamine and norepinephrine, compounded by estrogen and testosterone, the air soaked in perfume and pulsating with waves of music from overhead speakers. With the lights on, the Pony Tail was cigarette smoke, spilt beer, rancid sweat, and clanging metal chairs being stacked. Two large black women were sweeping floors and wiping tables. Within a few seconds Sonny could taste the smell of the room. He felt light-headed, then nauseous, and wanted to find a place to puke. But her voice saved him.

"Hey, Sonny Boy, you wanna buy a girl breakfast at the Waffle House?"

Sonny opened his eyes and the Pony Tail was dark again, just him and her and the perfumed music. She was wearing tight red sweatpants and an oversized sweatshirt with a Georgia Bulldog logo. Her blond hair was piled on top of her head, and her face only had traces of her working-girl makeup. Sonny was helpless. How could she be even more beautiful than she had been two hours earlier?

"The Waffle House? I have a room at the Hilton. It has twenty-four-hour room service."

She rolled her eyes and exhaled a laugh. "I had higher hopes for you, Sonny. But I'm going to give you one last chance."

She had her driver's license out of her purse in a flash and held it a few inches away from his face.

Sonny stared at the plastic card and remembered her offer: If her name was not Angel Darling, he could fuck her. He stared at the card. The photo was her for sure. The name on the card was Elizabeth Susan Monroe. He blinked and looked again. He then tried to not look directly at her. But a quick glance at her face gave her away.

She had the look of a woman about to receive bad news. Years later, he could still never explain to her or himself why he quickly said, "Dammit to hell, I guess I'm out of luck, Angel. It would have been fun, but a deal is a deal. But I'd still like to buy you that breakfast at the Waffle House."

She put her right hand on the side of his face. He could see that she might laugh or she might cry, but all she did was softly stroke his face and gently pull him toward her.

"Sonny, you're either smarter than you look, or luckier than you have been anytime in your rich-boy life."

"So, we're good for the Waffle House?"

"Maybe next time. For now, I've been told that the Hilton has great room service."

Sonny was of the mind that if you admitted that you had a problem, then it wasn't really a problem. Admit it, confront it, solve it, and sometimes solving it meant simply adjusting to it. It was a version of Nixon's mistake he would tell friends: The cover-up was worse than the crime.

His first wife insisted that he was a pervert. He insisted that wanting sex more than once a week did not make him a pervert. Thus, he blamed her for his affairs. He did not deny them. She eventually demanded a divorce. His attorney told her attorney that a divorce was not possible. Her attorney said, "We'll see you in court." A week later, her attorney received sworn affidavits from three men who attested to their sexual encounters with her. Each affidavit included nude photos of the wife, photos taken by Sonny, photos whose crudeness did not rise to the aesthetic level of *Hustler*. The wife was livid. Across the conference room table in her attorney's office, she screamed, "You took those. You made me do those. I did those to please you even though I was sickened. And you wonder why I think you're a pervert?"

He described the scene to Angel as they began a future lifetime of soul-baring, their own bare bodies next to each other at the Hilton. Sonny realized something about that moment from the past, and he gave credit to Angel.

"You know, the thing is, I sat there looking at her and it was like the sound had gone off in a movie. Her lips were moving, the lawyers were pointing pens at each other, some sort of secretary was at the end of the table taking notes, and there was . . . nothing. Like I was somewhere else, like I was watching this from somewhere else. And for a second I forgot her name. This woman was pointing at me and moving her lips, but if you had put a goddam gun to my head at that exact second, I couldn't have told you her name. And the thing is, she was right. I had done a shitty thing. I was willing to lie about her, just to hurt her. I just don't understand now who I was then."

"So why the fuck did you marry her, Sonny?"

Sonny closed his eyes, as if he needed to be blind to answer a simple question.

"I don't know."

"You're not instilling a lot of confidence in me about our future perfect life together."

"We have a future?"

"Fuck, Sonny, I'm happy with right now. The future is nothing but gravy. But a girl can dream, right? How about you? You happy right now?"

He opened his eyes and rolled over to face her, his hand squeezing her bare ass. "You're very strange, you know that?"

"Sonny, I seem to recall something about pots not judging kettles. And if you think I'm strange now, you might not be able to handle tomorrow. But you still didn't answer my question. Why the fuck did you marry her? Why did you fall in love to begin with?"

"Oh, hell, I don't think I ever loved her. I might have told her that, but sitting in that office that day I realized I didn't even know her. I certainly had no reason to contest the damn divorce. I just didn't want her to get any of my money. Well, my father's money, which is all I had. I just wanted her to go away."

"Your daddy's rich, and your mama's good looking? Jesus fuck me, I'm fucking a song lyric. When do I get to meet the folks?"

Sonny sat up on the edge of the bed, his back to her. She put her thumb on the middle of his spine and began to massage his flesh, slowly going lower.

"You won't like my father," he said, still looking away from her.

"Hell, I don't even like my own father. Does this mean that we both have daddy issues?"

"He won't like you."

"Neither did mine."

"He liked my first wife. He approved of her. He made that clear."

She sat up and wrapped her legs around him, pressing her breasts against his back as she put her arms around his chest, nuzzling her face into his neck. "Sonny, you might have bigger daddy issues than me. Just don't tell me that he fucked you."

"My first wife was Knight material. You would be my father's nightmare. You would confirm every disappointment he ever felt about me."

"So, you're telling me that I'm the woman of your dreams."

Sonny was not a stranger to women who liked sex. Good looks, charm, and being a Knight had opened a lot of doors. Angel was different. She was the first woman who had ever seemed as . . . *fascinated?* . . . about sex as he was. For the first few days after they met, he would go to the Pony Tail and just watch her work. He had been married once, had even been in a few relationships he thought were semi-serious. Even if he did not love the woman he was with at the time, he was still territorial. Any perceived interest in another man from her, or interest from a man about the woman he was with, triggered pangs of jealousy. Sometimes, a physical confrontation.

For those first few nights, he would pay his money to be a spectator in the VIP Room. Angel glowed in the dim light, her blond hair luminous, her body covered in powder that sparkled. Stag men were not allowed in the VIP Room, so Sonny had to pay another dancer to escort him, a dancer picked out by Angel. More than once a night, Sonny and Angel would find themselves only a few feet away from each other on one of the overstuffed couches. Angel would always find a way to turn her partner's head in one direction, nuzzle his neck, but make eye contact with Sonny. All his life, Sonny had been told that strippers and whores hated the men who paid them, that they feigned pleasure for a price. Angel was different.

"I love my job, Sonny, fucking love it. I love being looked at. And you want to know a secret? Last night, you looking at me hump that guy, I loved that too."

"But there's more to it, Angel. You know that. Don't kid a kidder. You let them put their hands all over you, pay you and then paw you like they owned you. I've seen it."

"You mean, like you do?"

They had known each other two days. Sonny did not understand her yet. All he knew was that he did not want her to think he was like any other man. He told her that, his wish to be different from the other men who touched her.

"Sonny, all men are the same, even you. Rich or poor, you would kill your mother for what I have between my legs."

It was an early lesson for Sonny, why Angel was different.

"Look, you've got no control over that, you or any other guy. I've fucked stupid men and smart men, rich and poor, cops and doctors, too many damn doctors, and there is always that moment you're all the same. The mama-killing moment. I don't hold that against you, Sonny, you being a walking dick."

"Me too?"

"Uh, duh, honey. But you still might be different. Get yourself out from under that dark cloud you walk around with, you and me might be a role-model couple, the next King and Queen of . . . Knightcity, Knighttown, or is it Knightburg?"

"I'm the Knight*ville* joke, Angel. And my father is never going to die, just like that Queen in England."

Angel sighed. "Everybody dies. You and me, your daddy, your ex, everybody."

That was when she told him about her life before being a stripper, her two years as an ER nurse at Emory University Hospital.

"I was going to be a teacher, but one term of student-teaching convinced me that I wasn't cut out to be a teacher or a mother. I hated kids."

Sonny was skeptical. "And you went back to school and became a . . . nurse?"

"Go figure, right? Turned out I liked sick people, especially sick kids. Probably why I like you, eh?"

He ignored that comment. "But you ended up in the ER."

Angel had looked at Sonny and calculated the way he looked at her, the tone of his voice, the serious confusion. He wanted a serious answer from her.

"A slow shift in Pediatrics one night, a bus wreck out on I-75, the ER was understaffed anyway, and I guess any warm body in a white uniform would work for them. I volunteered. Twelve hours later I was still there, covered in blood, crying over a baby born dead out of a dead woman, and somebody yelled, not even sure he was yelling at me, yelled *I need a hand over here*. I was the closest hand."

"I wish I had been there."

"Sonny, somehow I don't see you being the Dr. Kildare type." She was edging away from being serious.

"No, no, I mean I would have liked to have seen you then."

"Sonny, honey, I sorta think if you had seen me then, you and I wouldn't be here now. As I recall, the first time you saw me, I was naked. Bloody scrubs are not a good first impression."

Sonny winced, started to speak, but then stared away silently before he finally said, "That's not what I meant."

Angel felt something she had not felt in a long time . . . remorse. She had hurt his feelings, and even though she wasn't sure how, she wished she could start the conversation over. She took his right hand and wrapped both of hers around it. Reflecting later, she could put it into words, but not at that moment. She was known for taking big leaps in her life, but she always checked first to see if there was a net. Sometimes that net was simply an exit plan. Her own Plan B. The way that Sonny was staring off into space, Angel started to feel like she was about to forget about a net. Years later, when they formally got married, she told him that she had broken one of her cardinal rules that first week of knowing him. The rule? *I had sworn off damaged goods I told myself. You, Sonny, were a fucking wreck.*

"I'm sorry, Sonny. Tell me what you mean."

"I would have liked to have seen you a long time ago. I mean, not know you or anything like that, just to have seen you in that ER, to watch you do that. Does that make sense?"

"I was a different person then, Sonny."

"No, you weren't. Look, I coasted through schools all my life. Skimmed every book put in front of me. I should have been my class valedictorian, but I was lazy. I'm not a truly smart person, Angel, but I believe one thing for sure. Nobody is one person in the past and a different person later. I've always been me. I don't know what I mean, except I wish I had seen you back then."

Poof went the net.

They agreed on one thing. They were either an odd couple, or the perfect couple. Sonny was an open book for her. He spoke less, especially when they were around other couples, but he did not hide anything or evade any question. Before she ever got to Knightville, she thought she knew the entire town as Sonny knew it. Once she actually got there, she was able to see what he got wrong, but at least he had shared all his past as he remembered it.

She was different. It took years before he pulled the details out of her. Sometimes he would act like he was appalled, "Too much, too much, Angel. You did not do *that*." And then he would ask for more details. But there were limits. Her childhood.

"You had a dead mother and a father who did not love you. You poor baby. I'll trade you."

"And what the hell does that mean?"

"It means one of us is going to have to be dying of some sort of terminal disease before I rehash those days. Deathbed confessions, Sonny, I'm a great believer."

"You'll tell me one of these days," he had insisted.

"Right, when one of us is dying. And when I'm dying, I'll have a list of people I'm going to make sure die before I do."

Was it supposed to have been this way all along? Sex? Weren't first times always awkward? And how could sex with her be more intimate than with anyone else in his past? Weren't the mechanics the same? But the first time with Angel that made her different than anyone else was not the actual first time they had sex. The important first *moment* that was indescribable, but indelible, came after they climaxed at the same moment together for the first time. Him still inside her, her legs still around him, she put her hand between her legs and touched him and then herself. He felt her massaging him, and then, their faces only inches apart, she rubbed her damp fingers across his lips and then raised her head and kissed him again. The smell and the taste and the touch became blurred. With his eyes closed, the smell had a color, the taste was a weight settling over him, the touch of flesh was a sound. Every sense registered as another sense. Hours later, he had tried to describe it to her, but he knew he was not finding the right words. She put her hand over his mouth and shushed him. *Sonny, don't overthink all this. It'll all come back again. Trust me.*

Sex was the easy part. Sonny had finally met a pornographer's dream. Within the first week, they had their first threesome. It was Angel's idea. She picked out another dancer at the Pony Tail, introduced her to Sonny, and set the rules. Angel always set the rules. That first time, she never took off all her clothes, never touched Sonny, never let him touch her. He sat in the corner watching her and the other woman touch each other, and then Angel changed places with him as he joined the other aroused woman. She made it clear: they could only do what she directed. The first time that Sonny tried to improvise, she reminded him, "The party's over unless you do it my way. *Capiche?*" The other woman added, "trust me, Sonny, she means it." The two women, Sonny realized, had done this before.

But he was, he admitted later, at the mama-killing moment, even if it meant somebody else's mama. Their second threesome, Angel told Sonny to set his own rules. She would do whatever he wanted. But even *that*, she reminded him, was her rule.

Angel had another rule that she told Sonny once only, and only after he had broken it. Rough sex was their mutual private pleasure. Bruising, scratching, slapping, a hand around the throat, sometimes intensity blurred self-preservation. With sex, limits were negotiable. But Sonny had an old habit that Angel would not tolerate. After a month of living together, he made the mistake one day of hitting her in anger, not passion.

She had gone to the store without telling him. He had been asleep, she had not left a note, he woke up hungover, he yelled at her when she returned. She yelled back. He slapped her. He had done it to other women. He was Sonny Knight.

She had stepped back, looked at him, then walked into their bedroom, packed a bag, and was walking out the front door without having said a word to him when he grabbed her arm. She dropped the bag and jerked free of his grasp.

"Who do you think I am?" she had hissed at him. "Do you think you can do that to me? You get no second chances, Sonny. Nobody . . . nobody hits me. You want a punching bag, it ain't me. The world is full of women who will put up with that shit. I saw plenty of them in the ER. Fuck, I felt like hitting them myself. You want that, go for it, but the biggest favor anybody has ever done for you is what I'm doing right now."

Sonny unclenched his fist. "What the hell are you talking about?"

"I'm walking out of this house and you are still alive, Sonny Knight."

Angel did not know it, but he was having a flashback at that moment, to a time when a girl he loved had slapped him and jumped out of his car when they were teenagers. When he finally spoke, he was talking to that girl as much as to Angel.

"I'm sorry. I truly am. I'll never do it again."

"You know how many times I heard that same line from husbands or boyfriends who were waiting in the ER with some pathetic woman who was so desperate, so damn desperate, to hold on to them? Sonny, I love ya, but I'll never be desperate."

They stood there, an arm's length apart, front door open, bag on the floor, and waited to see the how the map of the future unfolded.

Sonny picked a direction.

"But I am."

"You are what?"

"I'm desperate."

Angel nodded and sighed. "I'll be back in a week. This never happened."

"I'm sorry."

"This never happened." And she walked out the door.

Like almost every male in human history, the first person with whom Sonny Knight had sex was himself. Angel asked him if he remembered the details. He had had other women ask him about who was his first actual fuck, but Angel wanted the primordial origin of Sonny's obsession with his dick.

"I mean, was it something that just happened, or did you do it intentionally? I mean, what were you thinking about? My daddy told me that I was humping pillows when I was three years old, but I don't remember that."

"Angel!"

"How old were you?"

"I was, maybe ten?" At that moment, he realized that he himself wanted to know what Angel wanted to know. How did this all begin? Sonny's wife had once called him a sexual deviant. He told her he was a sexual *depriviant*.

That wife had snapped her head back, blinked, and stammered, "A what?"

"Somebody who is deprived of enough sex. You know, a depriviant. It's a term I made up. Makes sense to me."

"Are you out of your mind, Sonny Knight? You haven't been deprived of anything, much less sex, in your entire life."

Angel loved that story. "Does she still live in your town? I'd love to meet her."

Sonny was doubly smitten. "You're the weirdest woman I have ever known. Should I worry about that?"

"Sonny, you just worry about losing me. Because as long as I'm around, you'll never be deprived of anything you want."

Sonny lost count of the times they had had sex. In private, surreptitiously in public, prone, upright, with a variety of French and Greek acts, for hours at a time, a few times measured in a few minutes. Sonny discovered stamina and resurrective abilities that he had not had since high school. He also discovered that he had limits.

Angel, on the other hand, was the first truly unlimited woman he had ever known. She was also the first woman who had ever asked him about his own life before he met her. A few perfunctory *Tell me about yourself* lines from women in his past, but Angel went deeper. And then something new happened to Sonny. He started asking her about herself. Not as feigned interest, meant to create an impression that he actually was interested. He had perfected that pose while still a teenager.

A throwaway line started everything. Angel had her hand on his crotch as he drove her around Atlanta. It wasn't a sexual moment, but Sonny struggled to find the right words. They had had sex an hour earlier, and three hours before that. They had both showered and then Angel asked him to take her for a drive. "Where to," he had asked.

"I don't care, Sonny. Anywhere. I just like to be driven around."

"No place in particular? You want to show me your old neighborhood?"

"Sonny, that's sweet. But I'm not from here. And my old neighborhood is a million miles away. It's a pretty day. I just want you to be my chauffeur."

In the front seat she had scooted as close to him as she could, and they talked. Sonny's Lincoln was a big boat on a concrete ocean, and it floated. The first question she asked him was about how he learned to drive. Sonny told her all about his driver's ed classes back in Knightville, his first car, a used green Mercury Sable that he bought for himself; his first ticket, given to him by his father's cousin; his first fender-bender, the rituals of his automotive youth.

In that conversation she had casually laid her left hand in his lap. His first response was typically male, but she seemed oblivious, and that stirring in his groin subsided. Her hand remained. Neither acknowledged it. Then Sonny realized that she was not even aware that her hand was there. She was not touching his groin so much as she was simply touching *him*. If they had been walking, she might have just as naturally put her arm around his waist to be close to him. Sonny kept his eyes straight ahead, and she asked another gateway question.

"But who taught you to drive?"

"I told you. I took driver's ed."

"Sure, but didn't your daddy show you how to drive first?"

"He paid for the driver's ed course."

She pulled her hand out of his lap and slid to the far side of the front seat, her back up against the door, tilted her head slightly and asked, "Sonny Knight, have you ever been in a car with your father?"

"Of course."

"Tell me one fucking time."

"I'm an adult, Angel. We don't spend a lot of time together in a goddam car."

"Tell me one fucking time. The last fucking time."

Sonny was tense, and exasperated. "And this matters to you why?"

"Because if I'm going to fall in love with you, I'd really like to understand what a hot mess I'm about to get involved with. And you, Sonny Boy, are a hot mess."

"Love? You got some sort of preflight checklist before you fall in love? How's that worked out for you in the past? Or, are you still a love virgin?"

She was not fazed.

"Sonny, have you ever been in love? Not fucking lust, I mean fucking love. And don't give me that *I was married* bullshit. Don't be making fun of me about falling in love. You tell me right now. Do you even know what it's like to be in love?"

He stared straight ahead, and she could feel the Lincoln slowing down.

"Yes," he finally whispered, without looking at her.

"Now we're making progress."

"Why is this so important to you?"

"Sonny, don't let this go to your head, but I really . . . I really want you to be the one."

He glanced at her, then back at the road. "The one?"

"The *one* that everybody wants. I want you to be my one. I want me to be your one. It's not a difficult concept."

"So why ask me about me loving somebody else?"

She scooted back across the seat to be near him. "Because anybody your age who has never been in love . . . never will be. And here's something clear to me. You've loved somebody in the past, but you're here in this car with me now. So that tells me that that girl you loved . . . she didn't love you. If you were her one, you and me would never have met."

"You are weird. Have I told you that?"

"More than once. And you are a lucky sonuvabitch, Sonny. Have I told you that?"

"More than once."

"You got a clue why you're lucky?"

"Because I met you?"

"Is that a question?"

"Because I met you."

"Absolutely. You know something else, Sonny. I'm gonna really like meeting all those people in your hometown. Your father, your ex, your lost love. I mean, I assume she's still there."

"I'm not sure that's a good idea."

"Sonny, when you figure out I'm the one for you, you'll see that it's a great idea."

"My ex is long gone."

"And the one that got away?"

"Lord, she'll be there forever. She runs the newspaper that my father owns. Her father is the sheriff. They're cousins. My mother was the sister of the sheriff's wife."

Angel squinted and started processing. "You were in love with the daughter of your father's cousin? You were in love with your mother's niece? Doesn't that make you cousins?"

"It's a small town."

"Hell, you're making me feel better about my childhood."

An hour later, they were on I-75 headed south. Angel was asleep, stretched across the front seat, her head resting on his right thigh. Sonny listened to her breathing, more than a purr, but less than snoring, and he started pulling up memories of his father and cars.

He would tell Angel when she woke up. The farthest he could go back was to the time his father took him to the cemetery to see his mother's grave. Was he nine, or ten? Sonny had no memories of his mother. She died when he was barely past a year old. There was only one picture of her and him together, given to him by Sandra Knight when they were in high school. She had gotten it from her father, and such a roundabout circuit made no sense to Sonny.

Sandra had explained, "My mother took the picture and my father had it with all her other things. He gave it to me to give to you."

Sonny had been in Sandra's house many times, always self-conscious that she lived in a place with pictures of her mother in every room, while he lived in a place where his mother never seemed to have existed.

"Daddy wanted me to give it to you. Said it was a peace offering for having to give you that ticket last week."

"I wasn't going that fast," Sonny had said.

"Sonny, you want to think about that? I've been in a car with you and your lead foot. And, besides, Daddy said he had stopped you a few times earlier and warned you about the crap you do behind the wheel."

Sonny had kept the picture in his wallet, but he never told his father he had it. But the day he got the picture was the day he went back to the cemetery to see his mother's grave for only the second time. Decades later, driving with Angel's sleeping head in his lap, Sonny remembered those two trips. The first time, his father had simply asked if he would like to visit his mother. For a split second, Sonny thought he meant that she was alive and had come back to

Knightville. Sonny was more curious than excited. All he knew at that age was that she had died in an accident, a fall down the long stairs at home, stairs he scaled dozens of times a day. Only when he got back from that first trip did he make the literal connection with those stairs and his mother. He snuck into his father's study and stared again at the only picture of his mother in the house. He froze that image of her face in his mind and then sat at the foot of those stairs. He knew all the stories about how his father had found her at the foot of those stairs. He looked back up and studied the steps and how they curved toward the top. She had fallen and tumbled down and landed right where he was sitting that day. She had been there once, dying if not already dead, but now she was in the ground miles away. The second time he went to her grave, he had the photo with him. He had stood there and looked at the ground and then the picture, back and forth, thinking how young she looked. She would have been in her late twenties, perhaps only a decade older than he was at that moment? He noticed how much his mother looked like Sandra's mother. Not as pretty, but still pretty. He could even see some of his mother's face in Sandra's face, but Sandra was nowhere near as pretty as his mother or even her own mother. The fact was, Sandra always looked the prettiest when she talked about her mother. That mother had simply disappeared one day, when Sandra was still a baby, but Sandra could talk about her as if she had never gone. She knew a thousand details of her mother's life. Her house had dozens of pictures of the two of them together. But then she had vanished.

Sonny had been genuinely puzzled, "But you never really knew her. You were about the same age as me when my mother died. I don't know a thing about her."

"Sonny, you weren't raised by my daddy. I heard mother stories almost every day I was at home, sometimes the same story a dozen times. You know what? I bet my daddy could tell you a lot about your mother. He knew her too. Of course, you might not want to let your father know you talked to Daddy. There's some sort of weird blood there I can't figure out."

It was only long after he and his father had become estranged that Sonny realized he had questions about that first trip to the cemetery. *Why? Why not before? Why not after? Why?* His father simply announced they were going. He did not talk to him as they drove there. If he said anything while they were there, Sonny did not remember. But the day was memorable. Milder than usual for August. Just enough wind to move the leaves in the trees, but not so much that you heard them rustle. Sonny had followed his father through the rows of swollen green mounds, past mossy marble tombstones, and then his father suddenly stopped. He did not speak for a few minutes, but then he waved his hand over the grave in front of them, as if slowly fanning air, and said something that Sonny did not understand then, nor remember later, except that it was obvious that he was not talking to Sonny.

Why? Why not before? Why not after? Why?

Driving with Angel, Sonny wished he could at least remember the date. Was that significant? What did he say? His mother was not born in August, nor did she die in August. And why never talk about her? Why was no one allowed to talk about her in that house, not even the hired help that came and went over time?

Angel let out a deep sleeping sigh. Sonny drove with his left hand and began to stroke her hair with his right. *Is she the one?* Sonny wanted her to wake up, but he did not want to wake her. He wondered if she would like to go see his mother's grave with him. He laughed to himself, *Of course she would.* He realized that as soon as he asked himself the question. They would go to Knightville as a couple. He would introduce her to his world. That would be the last test for her. Then he would know for sure. At his mother's grave he would tell her about the most indelible fact of that first visit, a fact only remembered thirty-plus years later because Angel had helped him go back to that moment and relive it. That day in the cemetery was the first time that Norton Knight had ever worn a white suit. Never before, and never without afterward. He had turned into the ghost of the town he owned.

Sonny knew everybody who was anybody in Knightville, but Angel pointed out that very few of those people knew the real him. He was born there, went to school there, was married there for a short time, but that marriage was not a topic for discussion after his divorce and his new ex blazed out of town. Everyone to whom he introduced Angel when they came back together was somebody he had known ever since his childhood. Perhaps a few, like Sandra Knight, had gone away to college, but they came back. Sonny had moved away after his divorce, and even though he owned a duplex near downtown, he did not really live there. He would be gone for months at a time, once even for two years when he served in the

Coast Guard and was stationed in Miami, but it did not take Angel long to discover that most of his "friends" in Knightville did not know he had ever been in the service. He had always given them a version of his life away from town, bits and pieces, and sometimes a complete lie. His most consistent version of himself was actually true. He was a sales rep for Georgia-Pacific and worked out of their Atlanta headquarters. Knight = Lumber = Paper. Sonny was a perfect fit for GP. He had the gift of gab, and he loved traveling. He had indeed worked in the Knight Mill as a teenager, but only for one week. With the story of him working for GP, his friends simply assumed that he was preparing himself to take over the Knight empire, and it was a good idea to get out of town and see how one Knight business was part of a larger industry. Angel figured out the truth soon enough.

"Sonny, honey, you need some professional help. Serious on the couch therapy."

"You're a nurse and then a stripper, and I need . . ."

"Dancer."

"Without clothes, you were a nude dancer."

"Well, that's true. But stripping is a different art form."

In the beginning of their relationship, she did that to him all the time, parse words, not for the sake of clarity so much as she liked to keep him frustrated if he ever tried to correct her. That was their early courtship, mutual deflection, not wanting the other to get behind certain defenses that had always protected them. In the long run, Angel wore down his defenses. Her? She had walls within walls, ultimately unbreachable.

"This is your problem, Sonny. People like you, the Sonny Knights of the world, the mistake you make is that you think you know the truth about yourself, and you're not happy with that truth, so you don't let anybody see it. You let them see the Sonny they knew a long time ago."

"And you know this how? You got a license to analyze people?"

"Sonny, I have fucked more psychiatrists than you have fucked strippers . . . me, I'm a dancer, different . . . and I know self-esteem issues when I see them. So, you tell me right now, no bullshit, what is it that you're hiding?"

"Other than our lifestyle?"

She raised a mock-fist toward him, rolling her eyes at the same time. "Hiding from me, Sonny. Nothing else matters."

"I'm gay?"

She pursed her lips, raised her hand, and started counting down. "Five . . . four . . . three . . . two . . ."

"I wish I was somebody else."

"Don't we all. C'mon, you gotta do better than that, Sonny. You're talking to a woman with two different names."

"I wish I wasn't Norton's son. I'm a Knight, next in line, and that's all I am to everyone in this town."

"Ah, now we're getting somewhere. Thing is, I figured that out a long time ago. Were you paying attention to what I said a few minutes ago? I was just waiting for you to admit it."

In the beginning, Elizabeth Susan Monroe did not believe in angels. Them, or anything heavenly. Her father hated God, her mother was no virgin, but they went to church every Sunday and dragged their daughter with them. Walking on water appealed to her, but not so much the chasing of moneychangers. But the adult Elizabeth studied religion and wondered why it had not made a more favorable impression on her as a child. She had been one of the billions of people whose home, from earliest memory, made religion part of the oxygen of the soul. It was always there, invisible, an assumed necessity for existence. Her parents were deviant sinners, but they could quote red letter scripture at the drop of ice into a glass or the slapping of a child.

She once told a minister *You would have thought it would have just stuck, you know, stuck to me because I had never known a life without it. Sort of a natural thing. You know? Does that make sense?* The minister was married and sleeping with her, but he was not a bad man. Elizabeth had been replaced by Angel, and Angel did not judge him. He was just a man. And he was sincere in his concern for her soul. But she also knew that when he talked to her about faith and God and the soul, he was also talking to himself. She wished she could have helped him. He had come to the club every Wednesday night, late, and he was generous. He had offered to pay her for sex, and she had asked him, as she straddled his lap: *This is not sex? Twenty dollars for two songs and me naked on top of you. This is not sex?*

Sonny Knight was different from most men. He understood her when she told him her minister story. *He didn't get it, Sonny, like most of you guys. I tried to explain to him, Jesus Christ, I said to him, everything is sex. Even God. More than fucking. Sex is walking and talking and touching and looking and smelling and tasting. Sex is the air in the room. But he only heard me mention Jesus and then he stopped listening. So, I accepted his offer, took the hundred bucks, and sucked his soul right out of him.*

Sonny looked up at her face, the taste of her still on his lips, his hands cupping her bottom and softly squeezing it as he whispered her words back to her, *Everything is sex. Even God.*

Sonny, Honey, time to come to Jesus, just as you are.

She had known a few other men like Sonny, who understood her, but each lacked one or more other essential qualities. Innate humility was an asset, even if hidden by thespian arrogance. Lack of humor was always a bed-breaker. Generosity of spirit and pocketbook. Capable of jealousy but not to the point of being possessive. Everything in a man that would appeal to any woman, she wanted all that. And she wanted him to worship her. Sonny was not perfect, a bit unmotivated at times, but he had been wounded a long time ago and so she forgave his insecurities and public braggadocio. He was going to be a late-bloomer, that was obvious, and she had always been a patient woman. Most importantly, Sonny adored her. She knew it from the first night. He would resist it, insist that he could walk away anytime, but she saw through that. He adored her.

The pole, working the pole, never bothered her. Her freshman year of college, she had stripped at a private party. She was stoned, but that was never an excuse for her later. She was not paid to do it. She was merely encouraged. Her drunk date encouraged her. Her own best female stoned friend had encouraged her. A dozen other drunks had encouraged her. Lost in the memory of that night was a key question for her . . . how did it start? Was there some conversation about the pros and cons of exhibitionism, some movie about strippers in an earlier conversation? What prompts a nineteen-year-old girl to take off her clothes in front of strangers? She would never have an answer. But she would never forget the act itself, the center of a cramped apartment living room, the heat of the bodies around her, the eyes on her. She had never suffered esteem problems about her body. She knew she was blessed. Every man who had ever seen her naked had himself felt blessed. The "pole" in the room was merely a straight-backed chair. It took fifteen minutes to shed all her clothes. Even then she knew the difference between gynecology and mythology. Her hand always stayed near the center of her body, concealing and highlighting at the same time. Was there music? There had to be music. She did not remember. She did not remember handing every article of clothing to her girlfriend as she shed them. But she did remember a lesson she had learned in private, all the times she had sex with men before she was nineteen. The first time should always be slow.

There had been crude remarks, whistling, female voices too, and she recognized her date's voice, even as she swayed with her eyes closed. With her eyes open, she could see couples touching each other, oblivious to others and perhaps to themselves. She straddled the chair, her back to her audience, looking back over her shoulder, moving her hips as if God himself was inside of her. And she was very happy.

I thought I had died and gone to heaven.

Show over, she sat and leaned her head against the back of the chair, her long hair drenched with sweat and hanging limply on her shoulders. She looked up and saw her girlfriend clutching all her clothes, her own eyes glassy. Did they actually applaud, or did she only imagine it? She stood and walked around the chair one more time and then her girlfriend took her hand and led her to a bedroom to get dressed again. Another self-evident truth? Putting clothes on is a lot less attractive than taking them off. Best to be done in private. With the bedroom door shut, she reached for her clothes, but her friend held them tight to herself, whispering without looking up, breathing deeply, her voice lower and lower. *Liz, you are absolutely beautiful. I thought I had died and gone to heaven. Watching you. You were like . . . like . . . some sort of angel.* They had only known each other for a few weeks.

Elizabeth Susan Monroe looked at her friend. Her new friend, and something else new for her. A decision. The desire was not new. A desire often sublimated in the past, a desire frustrated. She sat on the edge of the bed.

I want you to look at me.

Liz, please, we . . . we should . . .

Does that door have a lock?

Sonny was not interested in numbers, and Angel appreciated that. He never asked her how many, but he never resisted the details of any single time. Early in their relationship, she had to make a decision: truth or fiction? She had a tendency, even before she met Sonny, to exaggerate her history. She had admitted that to a therapist she was sleeping with, who had kept asking *Are you telling me the truth?* She responded. *Does anybody tell the truth about their sex life?* She had just started her career as a nurse and was still organizing her checklist of qualities she wanted in a man. The therapist worked in the same hospital, had been counseling the parents of a dying child in her ward, was handsome, and seemed to be a gentleman with potential. In hindsight, she understood that her early choices in men were often based on faulty premises. Sex was an easy premise. Easy come, easy go. The other stuff, not so easy. With the therapist, she had made the mistake of telling the truth about her childhood. He then claimed to be not so much interested in her past as he was intrigued by her willingness to boast about her adult sex life with her partner of the moment.

Knowing you as I do, it seems to me that you might be trying to intimidate your partners, letting them know that you are capable of anything, that you are bolder and more decadent than they are. But, at the same time, in my opinion, you might be channeling low self-esteem into stories that make you look like a slut, to prove to yourself that you are not worth any serious consideration.

She told Sonny the story, quoting the therapist with more pompous prose than he might have actually said, affecting a tone of academic condescension. Sonny was laughing so hard that he began crying.

"So, I said to him, you're calling me a slut? I'm a slut and you're a fucking saint? Jesus, Sonny, the real lightbulb going off in my head was that I might be a slut, he might be right, but I sure as hell didn't want to be stupid. And fucking him was a stupid thing to do. No, wait, I'm wrong. Fucking him was fun. Having a conversation with him was stupid."

"And you actually bit his dick?" Sonny was holding his stomach laughing.

"Well, that might be an exaggeration."

Sex was not a moral issue for Angel, unless it was with a married man. She understood the distinction, but she also made sure the married man understood it too. *Deciding to do this is the only moral question, okay? You go through that door with your eyes wide open and everything that happens after that has got nothing to do with morality. We fuck upside down on a park swing is as moral as immaculate conception. Comprehende?*

In time, she met others like her. And then she met Sonny, and she introduced him to the others. Her bringing another woman to bed with them had been easy. With another man had been difficult for him. Repetition had been an anodyne. And then an aphrodisiac. By the time she met Sonny, she was pushing forty. She could look in a mirror and remember the past. She wished she had taken pictures of herself when she was younger. But memory was all she had. When she moved with Sonny to Knightville, she amended her confidence about the iron curtain between sex and morality. She was not who she used to be, but she still wanted to keep a lot of the old her. Was it a moral judgment about herself? She tried to explain it to Sonny, afraid that he might misunderstand. But, of course, he adored her.

"Sonny, I want to be Angel Darling here, but I don't want us to live like we have in the past. We have the place in Atlanta, friends in Atlanta, and we can always go to Atlanta. And the people in Orlando too. But can we just be an old married couple here? An old boring married couple. Hell, who knows, maybe your daddy will invite us to a boring dinner."

Sonny looked at her and smiled. She loved his smile, but only the smile that he had when he wasn't trying to smile.

"You want to be Angel here, but not Elizabeth, right?"

"She's history, Sonny. She died in the Emergency Room at Emory and came back as Angel at the Pony Tail in Atlanta. You know that story."

"I seem to recall a driver's license. You still got a license, right? Angel, we can be whatever you want to be as long as you stay the same. But if you want to co-own the house or have a checking account here, the law is not going to understand at all. Unless Angel Darling has a Social Security number or birth certificate, the paperwork is going to be tricky."

"Sonny, you do realize that you have not used my other name . . . ever . . . since we met, until today. I don't need to have my name on some damn piece of property. I trust you. I'll keep my bank account in Atlanta. I just want to separate me here and now from me anywhere else, as long as you are the same all the time."

They had been walking in downtown Knightville, stopping at the hardware store and then the café, on the way for her to meet Sandra Knight for the first time.

"This means a lot to you?"

"A lot."

"And you tell me how messed up I am?"

"You *are* totally fucked up, Sonny. Welcome to my world."

"Okay, we'll make all this work. But, c'mon, eventually I'll have to tell my father all about you and me. Until then, make damn sure that my Uncle Jit doesn't stop you for speeding around, like you tend to do. Him asking for your driver's license might be a bit awkward."

"Sonny, forget about your father. Eventually, this is going to be our town."

Years earlier, the first time Angel saw Knightville, she told Sonny that she thought she was in a time warp. But she also told him that it was not the town he had described to her. He had been dismissive: Mayberry without the charm, and the Uncle Jit he described was certainly not Andy Taylor. A town of colorless, not colorful, characters. Angel said she would decide about the "local color" after she had been there awhile.

"So, you weren't even little Opie?"

Sonny was not amused. "No, I was always Norton's son."

Angel kept quiet for the rest of the hour as he drove her around the town itself and then out to the lumber mill and citrus groves. Angel had been impressed, but also confused. She knew Sonny was rich, through his father, but nothing about the groves or mill seemed to scream *wealth*. Sonny had turned toward her as he drove, nodded, and then turned back to look ahead as he spoke.

"It's the land. We own all the land. Not a soul in this town, and for most of the county, own the land they live on. My family never sells land. You own a house, you pay land rent to us. You own a business, you pay land rent to us. Not a lot, but it all adds up every month."

"Is that even legal?"

"Consenting adults, Angel, every damn soul in this town is a consenting adult."

"So, what did you do here, Sonny, growing up, working here? Did you have to pay rent to your daddy too?"

Like a moth to a candle flame, he found her irresistible when she asked questions like that.

"He pays me a hundred thousand a year."

"And how do you earn it?"

"I stay away from him."

"Sonny Knight! Don't be a dick-head whiner. And when do I get to meet the old sperm donor? Or, are you embarrassed to show me off as the future Mrs. Knight?"

"You and I are not getting married, I thought."

"Sonny, that's up to you, but I still want a ring. Me not being your wife is your loss. And, trust me, you can tell your daddy that we aren't producing any future little Knights. You're the end of the line, honey."

She told him to take her around the town one more time. That second circuit, she had more questions. Something about Knight-ville was eluding her. If she had never seen it, Sonny's caricature of it as a boring Mayberry might have eventually been accepted and stored away and forgotten. He painted the town in two shades, like an old black-and-white photo. But she was seeing it more as an old fading color photo of a town not anything like the black-and-white Mayberry. Something reminded her of a different mythical town. And, besides, she had never liked that Andy Griffith show.

It wasn't architecture so much as it was ambience. Buildings had a story. Knightville was built for the heat in a time when central air was not common. Canopied storefronts, some with wooden, not concrete, porches and sidewalks; shotgun cracker homes with wide porches. And no parking meters downtown? At least the streets were paved.

"Show me your house, Sonny."

"I thought I did. Two blocks back, the duplex with the flamingos on the porch. I own both sides.

"No, no, I mean the house you grew up in. And then take me to the McDonald's. I'm starving."

"Angel, there's no McDonald's in town."

"Whatever, any burger place is fine. Wendy's, whatever."

"Nope. I'll take you to the café next to the newspaper office. Good food there, but certainly not up to the level of a Big Mac." He reached over and patted her knee.

Knightville came into better focus for her. There were no franchises anywhere. There were no new buildings anywhere. The town had been built over time and then at some arbitrary moment, it froze. But Angel still wanted to pin down the feeling she had as Sonny drove her around that first time. Amid faded colors, old homes, ripples of heat rising off the ground, sections for white people, others for black people, no outsiders, a town square with a gazebo, the only signs of modernity were satellite dishes on the roofs or attached to a side window. It wasn't fair, she told herself, to make comparisons. She was herself. Sonny was himself. There were no others like them. As she was driven around Sonny's hometown, she wanted Knightville to be unique too, because she felt almost sentimental about it, as if she could imagine herself growing up there instead of Sonny. He was spoiled. But something about his town could only be explained by comparison. She had read hundreds of books before she was twenty, few after that, and her favorite was read over and over, starting when she was in high school, and she loved the town in that book because she loved the teller of that story, and she loved the teller's father. Even before she saw the father on screen, she had loved him in her imagination. In the worst years of her life, she would return to that story. Escaping her memories, she watched that movie many more times. That girl, that father, that town of dark shadows and neighborhood spooks, not a town of sunshine and light. She imagined that book town as real even if only fictional, but if she could be that girl, and have that girl's father, she would live in that town forever. Sonny would probably never understand. Nobody else had either, but she would try to explain it to him eventually, and hope that he would surprise her.

"There it is."

"*That's* where you grew up? Stop this car right now, Sonny Knight. I want to get a good look."

"We are *not* going in."

"How long has it . . ."

He ignored her and stopped the car, keeping the engine running. He did not anticipate her actually getting out. But there she was, out in a flash and leaning against the front of his car, her arms crossed. He had no choice. He got out and stood beside her, hip to hip, afraid she would start walking toward it. But she just stared.

Angel had been surprised because as they had been driving the houses had gotten smaller and seedier and more darkly populated. And then the road dead-ended at Sonny's first home.

"I expected a white picket fence," was her first comment. Instead, the entire half-acre lot was surrounded by a waist-high stone wall. The house itself? Angel did not have the design vocabulary, but she knew it was not Southern for sure. Sonny read her mind.

"Gothic Revival." And then he started pointing. "Arched windows, arches everywhere. Steep pitched roof. That trim is called vergeboard. The tower is usually associated with churches in this style. The spire too. The overall size is a bit out of character."

Angel was looking at him, not the house, as he talked.

"Sonny, this place is so not what I expected, and it is so not *you*."

"The original Knight, Stephen, my namesake, designed and built it for his wife a million years ago. Popular design back in Pennsylvania."

She kept staring at him. He almost laughed.

"Yep, I hate the place, but I learned all about it from my father back when we were living together when I was home from boarding school." Pointing again. "I had a room up there."

Angel looked back at the house, and neither spoke again for a few minutes. Soon enough, she closed her eyes and inhaled the sweetness of blooming magnolia trees, their scent inconsistent with the house they surrounded.

"Didn't you tell me that your father always wears a white suit?"

Thirty minutes later, they walked into the Gator Café downtown.

"Lord Almighty, it's Sonny Knight. How long has it been?"

The waitress was old and tanned like leather. But Angel noted how she seemed genuinely pleased to see Sonny, another point for her to consider about him. As much as he would talk about being a loner in Knightville, it was obvious that this woman had some sort of residual affection for him.

"Too long, Penny. But here I am, like a prodigal son. And here's a good friend of mine, Angel Darling."

Angel was prepared for the usual response in that situation. A man would introduce her to friends or family and they could not conceal their first gut reaction, always some variation of *She isn't his type, so it must be something else.* Or so she would tell herself later, when she was no longer seeing that man. How could they know it before she did? But Penny surprised her. She was a waitress from Central Casting.

"Pleased to meet you, honey. You're a whole lot prettier than the last woman Sonny dragged in here."

"Penny!" Sonny was embarrassed.

"Just kidding, Miss Angel, Sonny ain't been here in years. I've missed him and his tips. But I'm telling the truth about you being pretty. Sonny always had pretty girls with him, but you're the prettiest."

Sonny was no longer embarrassed. Angel could tell that he was actually happy.

"Penny, I appreciate that, but the girl version of me left the station years ago."

"I hear that, and I'll match that and raise you another twenty. Sit down, I'll get coffee and take your order. And you, Sonny, from you I expect a big tip."

Angel was beginning to like Knightville even more.

Late lunch consumed, two cups of coffee each, she looked out the window and saw an overhanging sign for the *Knightville Times* next door.

"Didn't you tell me that the great lost love of your life worked on the newspaper here?"

Sonny had a forkful of pie in his mouth and almost choked.

"Forget it. We are headed back to Orlando as soon as we leave here."

"No, Sonny, the tour is not over yet. I'll let you off the hook about meeting your teen heart-throb, but you still owe me two other places to see."

"And they are?"

"You're going to take me to the cemetery to meet your mama."

Sonny pushed back from the table, looking at Angel. He knew he was in love, but he wasn't going to gush about it.

"And the other?"

"That, I'll leave up to you. But here's the deal. We're staying in town until after it's dark, and then you're going to find a public place, somewhere from your past, maybe the old high school football field. Hell, I don't know, but you'll figure it out. You find the spot, and then we're going to fuck. Me, I'd prefer your father's front porch, but I'm guessing that might be too much too soon for you."

They got married in Atlanta and moved back to Knightville after a few years. He kept his job as a sales rep for GP, but only to service his established clients. Traveling appealed less and less to him the longer he knew Angel, but keeping his job also allowed them to get out of town whenever they wanted, a necessary convenience for their lifestyle.

Moving back had been her idea. Sonny had been willing to settle near Atlanta, forsaking Knightville, but after their first trip back, only weeks after meeting each other, she had made it clear that she wanted to live there eventually. That made no sense to Sonny, but he agreed anyway. She had one more condition. In Knightville, she was Angel Darling. That other woman, whose name was on the marriage license, did not exist anymore. Sonny surprised her. He loved the idea. Of course, as she knew, he loved secrets. She thought she was prepared for anything he might reveal to her about his life or his past, but sometimes he took her breath away.

She had insisted that she wanted to move to Knightville, but she refused to live in the duplex he had maintained all the prior years.

"I want a real house, Sonny. Not as grand as your father's, but I ain't sharing a wall with strangers."

He agreed, but he told her it would take some time to find the right place. When he finally showed it to her, she was disappointed. It was small and run-down, and abandoned. But he had explained.

"We're going to renovate this place. You help me do it. Make it what you want. This used to be a bad neighborhood, but it's better now than when I was growing up. All this place needs is some money and taste. Keep the basics, add on to it. You decide. Make it what you want. And then we move in."

He had money. She had imagination. He only had one caveat.

"Keep as much of the original exterior as possible, repair it, polish it up, but you can do a lot to the inside, build out on the back, add some rooms, whatever."

Six months later, she had the house she wanted, and Sonny was happy too. The surprise came when they talked about Sonny's wish to not be his father's son. It was the first day in the renovated house. They had been sitting on rocking chairs on the screened-in side porch, an overhead fan quietly whirring above them, like an old couple who had lived there a lifetime.

"Sonny, are you happy now?"

"Very much."

"You know, I'm still surprised you wanted this place, but now I'm glad you did."

"I used to walk past here on the way to school here. Knew the old people who lived here."

"They're gone, right?"

"They were my grandparents."

Angel stopped rocking. It was slowly dawning on her.

"This was the house your mother grew up in?"

"The one."

"Sonny, you are absolutely, surprise, surprise, . . . a sentimental sap. And obviously more of a mess than I thought."

And I love that too.

SANDRA KNIGHT

She was born Emily Marie Knight, five pounds seven ounces, and cut out of her mother after twenty hours of medieval labor on the hottest, most humid day of 1972. Emily Marie combined the first names of her maternal and paternal grandmothers. Her mother was named Sandra Chippen, "Sandy" to everyone who ever knew her. Sandy had chosen Emily's names, and her husband had simply nodded. He loved his mother. He liked his mother-in-law. He liked most people. He adored his wife, and if Sandy had wanted their daughter to be named Johnny Cash Knight, he would have thought it was perfect.

Emily had never heard herself called anything other than Sandra. When she went to the first grade, her teachers already knew her as "Sandra, the sheriff's daughter." She never heard what they said behind her back, "Sandra, such a poor child, orphaned so young." Of course, she was not really an orphan. She was raised by her father and a line of interchangeable black women who cooked and cleaned for the sheriff, some of them with less than sterling reputations, but in Knightville any child without a mother was an orphan, especially if her father was Jit Knight.

It was Jit who named her Sandra, not by edict or law. Sandy Knight had disappeared a year after her daughter was born. After that, Jit started calling his daughter Sandra, out of the blue and without explanation. It was the only name she could ever recall hearing.

As she got older, she noted how often her father corrected anybody who called her Emily. "Her name is Sandra now. She's my Sandra." Only Norton Knight was exempt from this rule. Even if Knightville understood and finally accepted the girl's new name, nobody could figure out why it was Sandra and not Sandy. Jit himself had never called his wife Sandra. But, as Knightville had always known, Jit Knight had never been quite right in the head.

As she got older, referred to as Sandra by the adults, it was natural that her childhood friends inclined to call her Sandy, but she assumed her father's role. She corrected those friends, "I am Sandra, not Sandy." Thus, an implicit character evolved. Sandy was a lighthearted name, a casual name, a happy name. Sandra Knight was a serious young girl and then a serious young woman. Sandra was the adult version of any and all girls named Sandy, and Sandra Knight meant to be taken seriously.

Jit had always been proud of her. She excelled at everything she did in school, blue ribbons and gold stars and then valedictorian. She had failed at only one thing, and that was the only thing that actually made her laugh later, a story that got funnier the more it slipped into the past. Her friends had convinced her that she ought to try out for one of the cheerleader spots at the end of her junior year in high school. All she had to do was get on stage in front of her classmates and do a routine of peppy exhortations with three other aspirants, all the usual go-fight-wins and go-teams that were the basics of adolescent cheerdom, with a pom-pom in each hand. After all, Sandy Chippen had been a cheerleader. Her daughter should be a natural. Sandra practiced for days with the other girls.

Their entrance on stage was flawless, arms and legs in sync, poms up, poms out, pep band blaring the fight song, a Radio City Music Hall chorus line of Florida Rockettes. Sandra and the other girls had their elbows locked together and, just as they did one more kick, Sandra kicked with the wrong leg, hitting the girl next to her, knocking her off balance. Sandra fell, instinctively holding tighter to the girls around her, dragging them all down to land on their bottoms, an explosion of shrieks and pom-poms, and hysterical laughter from their classmates. The other three girls were back up in a flash, trying to recapture rhythm and dignity, but Sandra just kept sitting on the stage. Jit had been in the audience, his heart broken for his daughter. The other girls high kicked their way off the stage as the teenage audience rose and gave them a standing ovation. Sandra was still butt-down on stage, rubbing her knees, her eyes watering. He could recount the story years later but never recall, perhaps chose to consciously forget, that he had told his daughter *Your mother would be so proud of you* right before she went on stage. He had wanted to rush the stage to help her, but he knew that would only embarrass her even more. He assumed she would be up quickly, perhaps do a mock bow and win back the audience. But she had just sat there. Then, as the cheerleading coach came out and headed for her, Sandra Knight became a legend for future classes, waving the coach away and yelling to the world at the top of her lungs *I broke my goddam ankle, you morons!*

Every time she would tell that story in the years to come it got funnier and funnier, with details added or invented, and a listener might have thought it was the best experience of her high school life. Jit would sometimes ask her about it, when he thought she was sad or distracted about something else, knowing that she would retell the story and make herself smile. Eventually, she wrote a three-thousand-word essay using the humiliation as an initiation story. The *Atlantic* paid her fifteen hundred dollars. That same year, she was the commencement speaker at the graduation of a KHS class that had not been born when she broke her ankle. She read that story. Jit was in the audience then too.

Except for the four years she spent at Florida State, Sandra lived with her father until she was thirty. If anybody asked why, she would shrug. *Why not? It's not like I have money to blow on an apartment. Daddy needs me, and our house is only a block away from the office.* How much her father needed her was open to question. Even as a small child, Sandra was aware of how a string of black women were in and out of their house, cooking and cleaning, doing the necessary chores of domestic life. Her father was not a talkative man, except when the subject was his missing wife, so she was seldom a conversational partner for him. So, the real reason? Her high school journalism teacher, Jerome Guinta, would become her adult friend, eventually her adult lover, and it was he who forced her to admit, even if only to him, that it was she who needed her father, not the other way around.

Sandra had loved Guinta when she was a teenager, seduced him when she was a college sophomore, and carried on a long-distance affair with him for a few years until he broke it off, saying that everything had become too "complicated."

Sandra had been angry at first. "Excuse me, but you being married didn't complicate all this from the very beginning?" She was right, of course, but reality sometimes has unintended consequences. Guinta told her that he would rather be her friend, to have her respect, than to have sex with her. Bluntness had always been part of his appeal to her. He insisted that a few years of clandestine trysts was, in the end, wrong. She looked at him as if he had just told her that he was gay. But then she did something that few people had ever seen her do. She laughed out loud.

"I wish I had said that to you. All this time I always had the feeling that we were sleeping together because it was what we were . . . *supposed* to do, not what we really wanted to do. I mean, I know that I started it, but now I'm not sure why. Does that make sense?"

Guinta nodded. "You do know, I hope, that I have always thought I was lucky to know you."

"I'm not dead, Jerry."

He opened his arms and she stepped into his embrace. "Nope, we're both too young to retire and rot, too old to kid ourselves."

"Jesus, Jerry," she muttered into his shoulder, "too old? I'm not even thirty. I'm just a kid, right?"

"And you still live at home."

Breaking up with Jerry Guinta was not a heart-scarring event for her. They had cared for each other before, and that did not change. In fact, he would remain her only real friend. His eventual divorce did not reopen a door for them to resume their relationship. But he would remain the only man in Knightville who had ever seen her naked. She would miss that. Her Tallahassee days had taken care of her virginity, but none of those Seminoles had ever made her feel beautiful, none of them made her want to have sex with them, to remember them afterward. Jerry was different. She had loved him when he was her teacher, but that, she rationalized, was probably just a teenage crush.

When she graduated from high school, in addition to the Valedictorian scholarships she received, her father gave her a thousand dollars. It was a treasure back then, and Sandra cried in front of him for the only time in her life. She had always assumed that they were poor, but she did not recognize until much later in her own life the one trait that she had intuitively inherited from her father. Neither had any use for money beyond the basic necessities of life. Their friends had a different interpretation: *Jit Knight and his daughter were the cheapest people in Knightville.* Jit had the advantage of wearing his sheriff's uniform even when he was not on duty. His sartorial choices were thus simplified. Sandra merely had no sense of style. Fashion was an alien concept to her. She was always neat and clean, but her limited wardrobe was worn to obsolescence, replaced only when the material showed its first hint of being threadbare, to be replaced by a new version of the old clothing. Knightville agreed, in the grapevine of its community conversation, that Sandra had surely suffered from the absence of her mother as she grew up. Sandy Chippen was the embodiment of grace and style on a shoestring budget. She never looked the same two days in a row, an effect sometimes achieved by the mere addition of a scarf or a bandanna, some article of clothing in a combination never seen before, or so it seemed. More astute observers might have insisted that it was not Sandy's wardrobe so much as it was her personality that brightened up her appearance. Those same observers chose to ignore the Sandy

Chippen who terrorized her husband and her friends in the months before her daughter was born, and for months afterward, a woman suffering from a harrowing pregnancy and postpartum depression, a woman afflicted but undiagnosed. No, all that Knightville remembered, and all that Sandra was told about her mother, was that Sandy was a gift to her husband and to everyone around her. Journalism classes, however, taught her to ask questions. Eventually, she asked enough questions about her mother and the angelic Sandy became more complicated.

When she came back to Knightville, her BA in Journalism on a wall in the house in which she had grown up, she got a call from Guinta asking her to come to the *Knightville Times* office. He was the part-time editor there, while he taught full-time at the high school. She thought he was going to offer her a reporter's job, but the owner of the paper had a different offer. The owner was her Uncle Norton, Sonny Knight's father, her father's cousin, her dead mother's brother-in-law, and the only man in her childhood who had ever scared her.

"I can't do that. I . . . I . . . I am flattered, but, but . . ." she had stammered. She then looked at Jerry, whose expression gave him away. Unlike her, he was not surprised by the offer.

Knight had been persuasive. "If you don't accept, I'm going to close down the paper."

"Uncle Norton, I'm totally confused here. This makes no sense."

He pointed to Jerry and then pointed back to her. "Jerry has agreed to help you get your feet on the ground for the first few months. This is not the *New York Times*. We only have three full-time employees. Our peak subscription was twenty years ago. We haven't made a profit in the past ten years. In a few years, we'll be in the twenty-first century, and everything I study now tells me that print journalism is just like me, doomed to extinction."

Jerry tried to interrupt. "That's not true, sir. People are always going to need . . ."

Knight raised his hand and Jerry stopped. Sandra was fluctuating between panic and awe. In her twenty-three years of life, her uncle had never spoken to her as much as he had in the previous two minutes. But his offer still made no sense.

"Uncle Norton, are you expecting me to turn this around, to make a profit? I have no idea what you expect me to do, or even why you expect *me* to do it. Jerry is the person who should be doing this for you, not me."

Knight looked at his cousin's daughter but did not speak. Jerry and Sandra waited, slipping glances toward each other. Knight stood up and looked around the messy office. He saw the ancient water cooler in the corner and walked over to take a small paper cup out of a tube and pour himself a drink. He turned to his small audience and erased the rest of Knightville as he became something they had never imagined . . . human.

"Emily, everything in this office is older than you. Maybe not this cup, but certainly this cooler. I remember being the person who had the first drink from it a long time ago."

Emily? Her uncle had always used her real name in the past. But it was still jarring to hear it.

"You asked about a profit. Lord knows how much I don't care about a profit. Everything else I touch makes a profit for me. I'm awash in black ink. No, I do not expect a profit from you. In fact, I want you to spend any money you need to update this place. You're a smart young woman. Make a profit if that is important to you. Or not. You figure it out."

"But, why *me*?"

Knight smiled at her, and Sandra saw her father's own rare smile.

"I knew your mother a long time ago. As you know, I married her sister."

Sandra was preparing herself to be disappointed. She was expecting another story about how wonderful her mother was. Implicit in all those stories over the years, Sandra intuited, was an implicit criticism of herself. Sandra would never be Sandy.

"I have watched you grow up. You are very much her daughter."

"Oh, god, Uncle Norton, I am nothing like my mother."

"That is not for you to judge."

Sandra wanted to tell her uncle to stop it, to stop playing the role that everyone else in town seemed to have abdicated to him. She wanted to tell him to stop acting like he was some sort of god. For a few brief moments earlier, she thought he might be different from the talk about him, that he might actually be a good man, like her father.

"I don't want this job," she snapped.

Knight immediately disarmed her.

"I'm sorry."

The three of them sat in awkward silence. They could hear the phone ring in the front reception area. Six rings. It was after five o'clock. The *Knightville Times* was closed until the next day.

Guinta broke the silence.

"Sandra, Norton and I have talked a lot about this. We think you have enormous potential."

"Both of you are insane. This is no way to run a newspaper."

Guinta persisted.

"You were managing editor of the *Florida Flambeau* at FSU when you were a junior. You also wrote about half the stories they published, but then you had to go and piss off Bobby Bowden, so they made you focus on management. For chrissakes, Sandra, the *Flambeau* had over a hundred people on staff and a circulation of twenty thousand. And you don't think you can run this country store operation?"

"Jerry, have you ever known me to suffer from lack of self-confidence?"

"In most things, nope. You've burned a lot of bridges in this town, broken a few hearts, and you still have a reputation for not suffering any fools or classmates when they crossed you. But, yes, I'm surprised that you're hesitating."

Sandra stored away the comment about *in most things* for a later conversation.

Knight had sat down and leaned back in his chair, watching Sandra's and Jerry's body language, sensing a history between them. With a distinct inhalation, he directed their attention back to him.

"I should explain myself better. I am sorry for this confusion. I need to tell you a story about your mother."

Sandra glared at him, surprising herself, but that spontaneous ire met his eyes. She was immediately ten again, in the presence of her Uncle Norton, the man who owned the universe of her life. If her renowned self-confidence was, indeed, a fact, then it must have developed after she had stopped seeing him around town as she became a teenager.

"The great regret of my life was not helping your mother when I could have. Jerry and I agree about your *potential*. It was the same with your mother. I had planned to help her when you became older. I always had the means to do it anytime, but she resisted. She always told me that there would always be time to go to school again, to find a job that made her happy and fulfilled her. I told her that I would pay for anything, that she did not need to worry about you . . . or your father. I even offered to help Jit directly, but he was too proud. Your mother insisted that she and Jit could get by on their own, but she thanked me, she thanked me and . . ."

Sandra looked at Knight and wondered. *Does my father know all this?*

" . . . then she was gone."

Knight paused and looked at Jerry, but Jerry was looking down at the floor. Sandra tilted her head and looked at Knight again.

"I don't want your pity, Uncle Norton."

"Pity is the last thing I'm offering you. I'm offering you a future, not your only possible future, but a good one, and you would be doing me a great service by accepting."

Sandra turned to Jerry again. His head was tilted down, but he was looking over the rims of his glasses, and then with a slight nod toward Knight he gave her an unmistakable sign. *You need to do this.*

"One more thing," Knight said. "Take this job now and if you are still here when you turn forty, the paper is yours to keep."

"You're offering me a lifetime job?"

"No, I am offering you the newspaper. To own. And I was serious when I said that I would close it down if you did not take the job."

"Jesus Christ, I thought offering me the editor job was insane, but this . . ."

"Here's a story I've never told anybody else. My grandfather started the *Times* a hundred years ago, but my father sold it. He always told me that it was the biggest mistake of his life. That the paper should have stayed in the family. When he passed and I came into my own wealth, I eventually bought it back. I understood something my father did not. A town without a newspaper is a town without a heart or a brain or a soul. And that soul has to have the Knight name attached to it."

Sandra looked at Knight. *Has he always been like this? How does this man exist in this town and nobody knows him?*

"I want the *Times* to stay in the family. I want my Will to specify that you, if you want it, will assume ownership after my death. You are the only member of my family I trust with this paper."

"Uncle Norton, you have a son. Surely . . ."

His reaction startled Jerry and Sandra both. Knight laughed like Sandra had told the funniest joke in the world.

"Sonny? My son Sonny? My god, you of all people know how worthless he is. He can have everything else to sell off or run into the ground, but not this paper."

"That's not fair," she protested, but she found herself having to stifle her own laugh. "Sonny is not . . ."

"You, of all people, know that he is."

Sandra stood up and raised both her hands as if telling a crowd to back away.

"I accept."

An hour later, she and Jerry were alone in the *Times* office discussing the other staff, who did not know that they were about to have a new boss who was twenty years younger than they were. Jerry had prepared a list of problems and issues that needed immediate attention. Ad revenue was down; print costs were up; circulation was stagnant. Not an auspicious future, even if Norton Knight continued to be a blank check for it. Jerry was optimistic. Sandra was second-guessing herself.

"Did I do something really really dumb?"

"Do you have any better offers?"

"Jerry, I wasn't even looking. I just assumed that I would take a break from school for a few months and then start some serious looking."

"Sandra, I haven't been teaching for a hundred years, but long enough to know that you were the best student I ever had, the best student that school had had in decades. When Norton asked me if I thought you could handle this job, I told him 'in a heartbeat.' Like he said, it's not the *New York Times*, but it could be one of the best in Florida."

"Did you know that I had a mail subscription to the *Knightville Times* even while I was in college? I always got the paper a day late, but I always kept track of news here. Obits first, and then any news about Daddy. The more I learned at FSU, the more I'd imagine things I would change about the *Times* if I were calling the shots."

"Well, there you go. Norton and I are right about you."

"That was a game, Jerry."

"No, Sandra, that was you. And you do really think that I didn't know that all those years? I was on Norton's part-time payroll even when I was your teacher."

She rolled her eyes. "Pa-leeeze." But the fact that Jerry seemed to have been thinking about her even after she graduated and went away, even before she seduced him, was very pleasing to her. "So, let me buy your dinner. I'm free, white, and twenty-three. And since I'm going to be a newspaper mogul soon, I'll have money to burn, right?"

Jerry stood up and raised his hands, mimicking Sandra from an hour earlier.

"I accept."

"Good, and after I get you drunk, you can explain that comment about me being confident 'in most things.' You can tell me where I'm a pushover."

"Not a pushover, Sandra, just sometimes you are your own worst enemy," he said, still standing over her.

"Such as?"

"Such as when you go out of your way to be unattractive."

"Oh, Jerry, you know that I can be naturally unlikable around some people."

"I'm not talking about your personality." He leaned back against the desk, sliding his hands into his pockets. "You make yourself unattractive. A better way to say it? You do not let yourself be attractive."

She started to shake her head, as if to dismiss him, but then it hit her, what he was saying. "And?"

"I'm saying that you are an attractive woman who does not let herself be attractive. I'm saying that you look in a mirror and do not see yourself."

Sandra wondered if journalists in New York worked harder than she did. She would never complain out loud, except to Jerry, but even he was not as sympathetic as she expected. He had kept his job at the high school, but he had to get certified in another field when he was notified that the newspaper program was being scrapped. Declining interest in the field, declining interest from the students, declining enrollments in general. He had tried to salvage just an online version of the paper, so his few students could at least practice research and writing and web layout, but that was a lost cause too. When his own students preferred producing a DVD of the yearbook, instead of the traditional print version, Jerry became a remedial writing teacher, a field with a future.

"So, don't whine to me about working so hard. I'll trade places with you," he snapped at her, and she never complained again.

It took her a few years, but she finally figured out the future of the *Knightville Times*. She knew that Norton Knight would subsidize the paper even if it was losing money. Some mysterious wonders in the tax code, his accountant had assured her, exotic deductions for business losses, depreciation, and general "stumblefuckedness." Sandra liked the accountant but thought he was an odd match for her uncle. She made that comment to Jerry, which led to him pointing out the obvious. "Sandra, nobody is a match for Norton, even though your father comes close in his own Knightly way."

But Sandra knew that her uncle would judge her by how well she managed his property. She also had her own standards. She did not have to make a profit, but constant losses would reflect on her personally. Down deep, only three people's opinions of her mattered: Norton's, her father's, and her own. And she was her own worst critic.

A decade after taking over the paper, she understood the trends. More and more people, even in Podunk Knightville, knew the national news a day before the paper could print it. Technology took care of that. Television and computers, twenty-four-hour cable news programs, Facebook and whatever. She stopped subscribing to the AP. She scoured the websites of other Florida papers to keep track of important state news, citing and then printing stories from the *Tallahassee Democrat* for state politics. For news from around the world, the country, and the state, the people in Knightville had better sources than the *Knightville Times*. But if they wanted to know about their neighbors' lives and deaths, their high school's wins and losses, and who was running for the county board, Sandra had a monopoly.

She still had to make compromises. She cut the Tuesday edition instead of Monday's because Sunday generated enough news for a Monday edition, while Monday itself was the deadest day of the week. A one-seventh reduction in printing costs added up over time. Early press deadlines for every day, except Friday night, to allow complete coverage, with photos and postgame interviews, of the high school football game. Any Saturday-night college game outcomes did not get reported in Sunday's paper. Exceptions could be made to that policy if FSU or UF played at night. Fewer comic strips, but she always kept her father's favorites: *Beetle Bailey* and *Pickles* and *Garfield*. She subscribed to *Doonesbury* and *The Far Side* for herself. Fewer syndicated columnists, and nobody too extreme. George Will, yes; Cal Thomas, no. When Jerry told her that the high school was going out of the newspaper business, Sandra saw an opportunity. The *Knightville Times* added a new page devoted entirely to student reporting, supervised and edited by Jerry. The students were unpaid but given a byline and had a postage-stamp-sized headshot of themselves above their names. Once a week, she would have a student do an op-ed, with no subject being off the table. Resumes were being built. Jerry himself was the reporter for most education issues, school board meetings and bond issues, but he never wanted a byline. If an interview was required, he would prep Sandra and she would do it.

Sandra reserved local politics for herself, as well as local gossip, often pleased with a delicious overlap. But those fields had their own limitations in a small town. Reveal too much gossip and you lose your local sources for other news. The Friday and Sunday long editorials were Sandra's exclusive domain. Those editorials were the only exceptions to her basic philosophy about the paper, a philosophy she published the first day of her tenure as the paper's new editor: *This paper is the daily record of life in Knightville. You might compare it to a diary, but I prefer to see it as our daily journal. It is who we are. I want this to be about you and your neighbors. I want you to see yourselves. I want this to be a community paper. Years from now, I want your children's children to be able to pick any day in their grandparents' past and see what was happening around them at that moment in history. For you now, I want you to appreciate your own town, the good and bad, the happy and sad. It is my firm belief that a town without a daily newspaper does not truly exist. I want to be more than your town journalist. I want to be your biographer.* The editorials were meant to reflect her, not the town, but she knew she had to publicly soften a lot of her private liberalism.

Jerry called her an hour after that issue was published. "Can I speak to Sandra Hearst Pulitzer?"

"Funny man, Jerry."

"Sandra, from the bottom of my heart, you better be careful or a lot of people in this town are going to start seeing you as the next crazy Knight. I understand what you're feeling, but c'mon, there's a whole lot of this town, any town, that just does not . . ."

"Jerry, let me feel good about myself, okay? Unlike you, I grew up in this town. I do love it. I want to do it justice."

"I just don't want you to be hurt, Sandra, or disappointed too much."

It took a few years, but Sandra perfected her two-P approach: photos and profiles. Every page was at least a third visual, almost all local people or places. The front page was always half visual, a technique that Sandra adopted from big city tabloids. Lots of headlines with page numbers in small print, full stories inside. In time, high-res cell phone cameras became a budget blessing. She took photos, and she solicited photo donations from subscribers and gave them a credit. In time, she had more to choose from than she could ever use, and she had an "eye" for choosing the pictures that were as much art as . . . reality? She wanted her subscribers to think as they opened the paper: *Well, that's interesting.* And to subconsciously think: *I wonder what will be in tomorrow's paper.* She knew that her competition was not another paper, but television and the internet.

Sandra had one other goal. If she did a profile twice a week, in a year she would have profiled at least a hundred people in Knightville. It required interviews, hours of talk, hours to interview people who might know the subject, other research, but she would joke with Jerry, "Everybody's life is worth two thousand words. And a picture." She never met the annual goal of a hundred, but she tried.

Who she interviewed was based on simple criteria. First, anybody who might be in the local news in any way got shoved to the head of the line. Somebody opening a new business in town, *Let's talk.* Somebody running for county board, *Let's talk.* Older people interviewed before younger, anybody more likely to die. If the county was thirty percent black, a third of the profiles in any given year were about black residents.

Jerry was intrigued. "How do you know that somebody is going to die soon? You got sources with hospices, doctors, funeral homes?"

"Jesus, Jerry, do you remember teaching me anything in high school? About cultivating sources. Ring a bell?"

"Oh, I remember that, but I sure as hell didn't teach you how to write as well as you do. You do know, I assume, that you're too damn good of a writer to grow old and die in this town. You put a collection of those profiles together and send them to The *New Yorker* or some other national magazine. Blow this burg."

Sandra had looked at Jerry and shrugged. He had always been her biggest booster. But he was right. Her profiles were Knightville treasures. She chose people that everyone already knew. She chose people who were obscure to their own families. In fifteen years, unlike what Jerry had predicted about her becoming just another Knight eccentric, Sandra almost redeemed her family in the public eye. She had to start discouraging people from suggesting other people to profile. She had other nuts and bolts to put in the pages of the *Knightville Times*. She belonged to all the service clubs, served on the Knight Bank Board of Trustees. She published local government meeting agendas, advertised commission openings, school lunch menus, births and deaths, the communal glue.

Even Norton Knight was impressed. Circulation at the paper stabilized and ad revenue went up. He called to congratulate her.

"I look forward to it every morning. I am very proud of you, and I am very happy that I listened to Jerry years ago."

Sometimes, Sandra wanted to kick herself for caring so much about what her uncle thought of her, and she was not going to admit it to him for sure. "Uncle Norton, you know that one of these days you are going to let me interview you, don't you? You know you can trust me, right?"

Norton was silent.

"Uncle Norton?

"That is not going to happen. Ever. Nor, do I suspect, will your father submit to one of those interviews."

"Yes, I figured that, but the offer is always there. You just have to trust me."

"Emily, as far as I am concerned, I would prefer to not exist at all in the *Times*. I do not want to see my name in print ever. Can I *trust* you to do that?"

Sandra felt the old chill come back to her, the chill from knowing Norton as a child.

"Yessir."

Sandra had to grow up before she began to understand her father's guilt. It took a long time, but she finally convinced him that he was not to blame for her mother's unhappiness. Everybody knew about that famous year. Sandy Chippen seemed to have lost her mind. She was unpleasant to everybody, and for most of the residents of Knightville Jit Knight had been a saintly embodiment of Patience and Devotion.

"Daddy, you told me yourself that she didn't tell you for three months that she was pregnant. She knew she was pregnant long before she told you. And let me tell you now, something was happening to her beyond her control too. Hormones are a bitch sometimes, excuse my language, but those mood swings and anger and depression weren't your fault. And as I recall you saying, a few months after I was born things settled down and you were happy again, right?"

Sandra had been convincing even though she was not really sure herself. She had gone to college with a metaphorical list of things to learn about. The list changed with time, but her absent mother was always at the top. Science courses, married friends, and daytime television talkshows had been her textbooks. Psychological issues of the 1970s had become physiological issues of the twenty-first century.

Jit had always considered his daughter a marvel. Even as a child, she was old for her age. As a young woman, she seemed to know a little about everything, no matter how obscure or esoteric, and a lot about a few things, like politics and history. When she still lived at home with him, they would watch the evening news together. Or so she would tell her friends. The truth was that they were in the same room, but only she was watching the news. Jit had a newspaper in his lap. He would look up often enough, especially when she started talking to the screen. A commercial would come on and he would then ask her why she was so agitated, and she would retell the news but with her own commentary. Sandra was opinionated at an early age. By the time she was a senior in high school, she was subscribing to *Time* and *Newsweek*. Jit understood those choices, but he loved to tease her about her subscription to *People* magazine. She assured him that it was still "news."

Sandra knew that her father trusted her judgment. But she only understood that after she came home from college and moved back in with him. When she had left four years earlier, he had let his newspaper subscription lapse. Without her in the house, the outside world for Jit seemed to disappear. Back home, she had steered an early conversation back to her mother's lost year. She wanted him to trust her on that one issue in particular, convinced that if he could get past his guilt about that one year, he could then finally open up his life again. *Open up his life again . . .* she wasn't quite sure what she meant by that, but it was a phrase she used with Jerry and he seemed to understand. "Your father is not exactly the sunniest guy in town, that's for sure. Then again, compared to his cousin, your dad is *Cinco de Mayo.*"

To bring her father along, she made him retell the story though she had heard it many times.

Jit always told Sandra as much as he could about her mother. How he had never heard Sandy raise her voice, how she had never seemed to get mad at him. Frustrated, of course. Impatient, often. But there was never darkness between them. That darkness began with noticeable silence months before she told him that she was pregnant. She stopped talking to him. Some perfunctory yeses and nos, but never a smile, seldom a complete sentence. That lasted a few days, during which time she cleaned and recleaned an already immaculate house. Was she already pregnant then, Sandra asked him, but Jit could not be sure. He remembered that he was overworked the first few years after he was elected sheriff. He initially had no control over his own schedule. Felons and hormone-crazy teenagers did not work nine to five. He was on call for late-night crimes and misdemeanors. His future was uncertain. His salary barely paid the bills, and he had started to drink too much. Jit would tell Sandra that her mother had every right to be upset with him. Everybody in town had surely been telling her that she had made a mistake by marrying him.

Sandra had always interrupted him at this recurring point in his story.

"You really think that was the cause? You really think that she didn't love you? Dammit, Daddy, do you really think that *she* thought she had made a mistake?"

He would shrug and shake his head, never looking her in the eye. "I don't know."

Sandra wanted to raise her own voice, but she also did not want to be her mother at those moments. She did not want to embody anything about that time when Sandy Chippen was hair-trigger angry, so Sandra would calmly remind her father, "Don't you think that I have heard versions of that time from other people? Daddy, you weren't the only one she jumped on. Everybody had their own run-ins with her. They were as confused as you. And nobody ever thought she didn't love you. Nobody, never, ever. And you yourself never stopped telling me how happy she was within a year after I was born, how the two of you were happy again. You have to stop blaming yourself. Can you do that? If not for yourself, do it for me, okay?"

"If she was happy again, why did she go away?"

That was the question that Sandra could never answer. In her own mind, she had created a future in which Sandy Chippen came back, and her daughter could finally meet her. Sandra had grown up in a house full of pictures and stories about her mother. It was never going to be enough. Sometimes, Sandra was angry at her mother. *How could you do that to him. To me?* Other times, she simply wanted to see what Sandy looked like, an actual human being, one half of Sandra herself. Sandra had a secret that was inexplicable even to herself, repressed because to admit it out loud would be to admit her own desperation. Sandra had escaped Knightville, but she came back and accepted a job that would lead to her never leaving again because, down deep, she dreamed that her mother was coming back and Sandra wanted to be there.

ORIGINAL SINS

Jit had never told his daughter, or anyone else, the complete story. Everything he told her was true, but it was not everything.

A month before Sandy finally told him that she was pregnant, he had gotten a call from a woman he had known for years. She wanted to meet, to share some news about his wife. It was an hour after Sandy had melted down over an unpaid bill. She had yelled at Jit that he should ask his cousin for a loan, or simply a handout. She had been trembling. *Tell Norton he owes it to you. Tell him it's for me. He owns everything, he might as well own us too. Jesus, Jit, I'm tired of worrying about tomorrow.*

An hour later, Jit finally understood what was happening. Sandy *was* unhappy with him. This woman knew too much. They sat across from each other and drank too much. At least, he drank too much. Sandy had evidently told this woman things about her personal life with Jit that nobody else knew. The woman knew too much, and she was crystal clear as Jit became angrier.

She wants out, Jit. It won't happen soon, but it's in the cards. I mean, I love her too, we all do, but she's not happy and I'm afraid she is going to make you unhappy too. You and I go back a long time. I care about you too.

Jit had another drink and looked at the woman. He knew she was right. Sandy should have married somebody else. He looked at the woman. She said it again.

I care about you too.

Four hours later, Jit went home and sat in the kitchen until the sun came up.

A year after Sandy disappeared, Jit stood over the dead body of the woman who had told him the truth about how Sandy felt about him. Norton was standing next to him, both men looking down. It was an accident, Norton had said, giving Jit all the details. Jit looked around, not saying a word, then back down at the body. He knew his cousin was lying. Guilt oozed from every evasive glance. He knew the history between him and his wife. But he also knew that the woman was dead and he would never have to see her again and remember the night they had drinks. He would never forget it, but he would not have to be reminded of it. He looked at Norton and spoke eye to eye.

"Yep, that makes sense to me. I'll take care of the paperwork, let the coroner know what I think. Sorry about your loss."

He was lying.

Ashley had made Norton her co-conspirator. She assumed that he was merely protecting himself as much as her, that as soon as they had done what they did, he could not reveal her without revealing himself. She had never explicitly threatened him. Perhaps she wanted to believe that he might have actually done it out of concern for her, genuine affection? Perhaps their marriage was not really a sham? They did not talk about it. She never asked him, as more time passed, *why* he had done it. Cause and effect. As long as she was safe, the effect, why he did it, the cause, was irrelevant.

"I killed her, Norton. She wouldn't get out of the way."

"Take me to her."

"Go to hell," she screamed.

Norton slapped her to stop her from screaming. Then he put his hand around her throat. "Take me to her. And do exactly as I tell you."

The story unfolded as they drove. Ashley did not intend for it to happen. Of course not, nobody ever does. Norton did not intend to do what he did. That would be insane. Norton was not an insane man. But in a sane world, Sandy Chippen would still be alive. Norton drove slowly, knowing the exact spot Ashley described to him, the curve of the dirt road, the enormous fallen tree on the north side, the deep woods beyond. She told her story over and over, asking Norton to forgive her, and then a moment later she would splatter tears and snot all over herself as she insisted that it was Sandy's fault, that Sandy had not gotten out of the way, that all Sandy had to do was step aside. Norton ignored her. He wanted to find Sandy before anyone else did, before he called Jit and told him, before she belonged to anyone else again. Norton was not an insane man. He was merely a man leaving his life behind him.

He saw her body from a distance, just the feet first in the wet and high grass. He told Ashley to stay in the car. He wanted to be alone with Sandy. If only for a few minutes, he wanted her to himself.

He knelt beside her. She seemed smaller than the last time he had seen her. He picked her up, knowing where to take her, the exact spot of Knight land that had always been there waiting for her. It took half an hour, carrying her to the spot, digging by the dim light and shadows cast by a lantern he had brought, stopping when he thought he heard some noise in the woods. A hot night, no wind, but something was out there. He was not as strong as he had thought. He could only go down three or four feet into the earth. But, in the end, it was just the two of them. After he talked to her, he put his pocketwatch in the breast pocket of her blue jacket. It had been given to him by his father. She had seen it many times when they were in school together, and she had thought it was lovely. Norton remembered the word, an odd word for a watch . . . *lovely* . . . but the first time he showed it to her she had taken it and held it to her cheek and then up to her ear, listening to it tick, and she said it was *lovely, like a heartbeat.* The comparison made no sense, but from her it was beauty. In the dark of the night years later, how could he not give it to her? Then he covered her up, a few yards away from the skeleton of Thomas Knight's church.

He was aware of the contradiction, but he ignored it. The contradiction of losing Sandy but saving Ashley. Putting his drunk and sleeping wife in the back seat, he had driven back to his house in some sort of poetic stupor, choosing his interpretation of himself at that moment by choosing to remember words from a poem in his study. Chill, stupor, then the letting go. Except that he refused to let go.

He pulled the groggy Ashley out of the car and carried her upstairs to bed. He looked down at her and saw her future too. He leaned down and slapped her sleeping face, rousing her, and described that future to her. She thought she was dreaming.

"You did what? Are you crazy?"

"No one is to know. Do you understand?"

"Norton, you are crazy."

He slapped her again.

"This is your life from now on. You are still my wife. You are the mother of my son. But you and I are dead. You will stay here, but never touch me again. You will sleep in this house. Alone, in the bedroom downstairs. No one will ever know she is dead. No one will ever know you killed her. You are now just the dead weight of my life, and I will carry you forever. Do you understand?"

"For chrissakes, Norton, do *you* understand?"

He raised his hand to slap her again, and she pushed herself back up against the headboard of the bed. His hand hung in midair as he slowly put his other hand around her throat and spoke in a whisper.

"Do you understand?"

Ashley nodded, feeling his grip loosen around her throat. Only then did she notice the traces of blood on the palm of his still raised hand. The blood on his shirt, the dirt and grass stains on his trousers, and then the smell of all that . . . the blood and dirt and fecund vegetation. She was afraid he might read her mind at that moment.

If only you knew everything. If only . . .

But she forced herself to imagine being somewhere else, anywhere else, at that moment.

I told her that she wasn't as smart as she thought she was. And neither are you, Norton, neither are you.

For a year, they performed in public. The First Couple of Knightville. Like everyone else, hearing that Sandy Chippen had seemed to vanish, they appeared confused and concerned. Norton was solicitous toward his cousin Jit, lost at sea. He advertised a reward for information leading to her return, but Jit asked him to withdraw the offer. *We'll get hundreds of tips leading nowhere, Norton. We just have to give her time. She'll come back.* Norton offered to pay for all the domestic help that Jit would need as he became a single father, but Jit told him that "help" was not a problem. He had his pick of townspeople who would help him for free. Norton understood. Unlike most of white Knightville, he did not care that all the "help" coming to Jit's house was black.

Norton stepped further and further away from Jit. If Knightville noticed anything different about Norton, it was that he seemed to be more connected to his own infant son, the two of them often seen in town without Ashley at their side. A nanny had been hired. Norton had a plausible explanation. *Ashley is still much grieved and distracted by her sister's disappearance. I have the means to make her life easier. So, why not?*

In private, they lived in slow motion, doing their best to not be alone with the other. He spent the day in his study. She might venture out by herself in the afternoon, but she soon tired of the good intentions of the good people of Knightville. Their sorrow about the missing angelic Sandy. Their offers of help. Their constant praise of her husband. *He is such a good man, Ashley. Taking care of you as he does. He is much different than he was, so much more friendly, so much nicer.* She had considered a visit to Jit, but, as she approached his office one day, she realized that the last person he might want to see would be her. She turned away and had a rare moment of objective insight about herself. *Never speaking to him again will be the most decent thing I have done in my life.*

The moment passed, with no comparable moments in her future. She went home to have another drink and watch the nanny entertain her son. She studied his face, noting the Knight blood. She watched as the nanny made him laugh. Sonny seemed to be a happy baby. He seldom cried, and his eyes seemed alert to the world around him, the still small world of the Knight house, but she could imagine his first awkward steps, and then his world would open up. Ashley compared him to Jit's daughter, the daughter that Sandy Chippen would never see again. *I wish I had had a girl.*

Most of all, Ashley resented her husband loving Sonny, a resentment that bred a conclusion that made sense only to her. *He doesn't see me and him in Sonny. He sees him and Sandy, precious perfect her. Sonny is all he has left of her, the child they would never have. I was just merely the goddam surrogate. He keeps looking for his and her face in Sonny, not mine.*

It was all too much. A year of letting Sandy's ghost live the house, a year of performing mime in a marriage. A year of being afraid her husband would somehow turn on her. Perhaps exile her? Take full custody of Sonny and send her back to the crumbling home where she and her sister had grown up? She had no friends in Knightville. She had nothing except two things that were uniquely hers. Only she knew what she had done to her sister. But, more importantly, only she knew what Norton had done to her sister.

Sonny was asleep, the nanny was gone for the night, and Ashley was drunk. She finally wanted Norton to confront an inconvenient truth about his future. She ascended the stairs, drink in hand, calling his name softly and slowly.

"Norton . . . Noor-ton . . . Noooor-ton."

Halfway up the stairs, she heard his study door open.

"Norton, darling, we need to talk."

He stood at the top of the stairs, a book in his hand.

"You're drunk."

"Darling, that may be, or not, but I still need to settle something with you."

"Go to your room, Ashley."

"Go to hell, Norton."

He stared down at her. She kept one hand on the railing, the drink steady in the other, and began walking up toward him.

"We have nothing to say to each other, Ashley. Go to bed."

"No, we have a lot, my darling husband, my darling accomplice husband."

She kept walking. Norton stepped back as soon as she reached the top to stand face-to-face with him. His withdrawal was a misread sign to her. *I should have done this sooner. He's a coward. He actually is afraid of me. After all this time, why couldn't I have figured that out sooner?*

"You think that you can control me because I'm afraid to go to jail, or some shit like that? You control the world, right? But do you ever think that I might simply say that you and I both did it. Was there any other plausible reason for you to hide the body? You control the world, right? But how's this? You could have turned me in that night, but you went crazy, Norton. I married a crazy man. If

I had known you were going to be that crazy, I would have gone and found that goddam quilt she made for my parents and you could have buried her in that. But I want to be out of this asylum now. I want to be free of you and Sandy and everybody in this town. You let me go, and I won't tell anyone about you and Sandy. I won't even tell Jit. You ever think what he would do if he knew about you taking Sandy away from him?"

He took another step back, another misread sign to her.

His response surprised her, "I'll let you go, but you can't have Sonny."

"Oh, Norton, you and Sandy were made for each other, both of you oblivious to the truth right in front of you. I told her that she wasn't as smart as she thought she was. And neither are you, Norton, neither are you. Do you really think that Sonny is *your* son?"

"Get out! Get out tonight!"

"All that time she was such a bitch to everybody, even to Jit. It was so easy."

"Ashley, stop this. You've lost your mind."

"Isn't that wonderful. I've lost *my* mind. Really? That's what she was saying as she jumped out of the car. Saying I had lost my mind when I told her about Jit and me."

Norton took a step toward her, a sign she ignored.

"Take it to your grave, Norton. You look in Sonny's face, all you're seeing is Jit and me, not me and you, not even you and Sandy. And she's dead, Norton, she's dead."

He took one more step. Ashley did not move. Neither spoke.

Norton walked slowly down the stairs, never taking his eyes off the crumpled body on the floor below. He sat on the lowest step and waited. A half hour later, he touched her cold throat. He called the nanny and asked her to come back to the house, and then he called the sheriff.

"Jit, I've got a problem. Ashley has had an accident."

"Norton, call an ambulance and I'll be there as soon as I get somebody to come over and watch Sandra."

"No hurry. She's dead."

Jit waited, feeling his own heart race. Norton did not speak again, but he did not hang up the phone either. Jit broke the silence.

"Are you sure?"

Norton finally answered, "Absolutely."

An hour later, Jit listened to his cousin's story. Ashley had come home drunk, as she often did, they had argued about their marriage, as they had often done. She had been standing at the top of the stairs. She had misjudged where her feet were, stepping back and slipping off the first step.

Standing next to Norton at the foot of the stairs, Jit studied the body. Her position was consistent with a fall. It was obviously a tragic accident, right? It was not a mystery. Any injury to her body was explainable. The broken neck, the bruises, a tragic accident. The coroner would agree. That Norton was not distraught was itself consistent with his character. Everything was consistent with the deceased's personal history and the laws of physics. All Jit had to do was write it up that way. He was the Law, and the Law determined the Truth.

He sat down on the first step while Norton remained standing over his dead wife.

Staring at Ashley, Jit said, "Sorry, Norton, sorry for your loss." He then looked up to see his cousin's eyes locked on him.

"So, it's over, right? Or, do you need any more details?"

The two men kept looking at each other. Jit blinked first.

"Lord, Norton, how many years since I have been in this house? Ten?"

Norton's face softened. "A long time, Jit. A long time."

Each man had a question about the other, but it would never be asked or answered completely.

How much does he know?

"Mr. Knight, I'm sorry to interrupt . . ."

The nanny had waited as long as she could, out of deference to her employer's grief, but a baby had a more basic need than solace and privacy. "I'm sorry, but Sonny is awake and hungry, and there is no formula in the refrigerator. I'm sorry, but I thought she told me that she had been to the store . . ." She stopped, suddenly aware of the bad form, the implicit guilting of a child's dead mother. "I'm sorry, I'm sorry, I didn't mean it that way." It had been a traumatic night for her. The late call, seeing the body as soon as she entered the house, Norton's calm resolve. It was a bad dream. Still, a child was hungry.

Jit waited for Norton to respond, but his cousin simply stared witheringly at the nanny. The nanny was a tiny young woman. Her job had been a godsend to her and her family.

"Mr. Knight, I'm sorry, I just need to get some formula. Your son is hungry."

Jit offered a lifeline to the nanny. "I'll call the woman at my house. She can have one of her own sons bring over some of my daughter's formula to you. Fifteen minutes too long?"

He then looked back at Norton. "We'll get him through the night. You can stock up tomorrow."

Norton looked at Jit and saw the answer to one of his questions.

He doesn't know. He really doesn't know.

PETER WYMAN

He had no illusions about his status in the world. Talent had gotten him into the Yale School of Art, helped by both his parents being Yale graduates. Talent had gotten him the teaching position at the Savannah College of Art and Design. Talent had gotten him his first wife, a fellow Eli artist. His talent for sleeping with students had gotten him his first divorce. His parents were never judgmental about the split. For lack of a better word, their own relationship had been very *elastic*. Wyman and his brothers and sisters had all grown up knowing about their parents, but they also saw that their parents were happy with each other. Since he had told his Eli artist fiancé all about his parents' open relationship, he assumed *she* would not be judgmental about him. He was wrong.

He had no illusions about why he slept with his students. In his fine arts world, morality was easily checked at the door of the class-room. He discovered early that young girls away from home, newly surrounded by eligible young men and passably attractive older male teachers . . . those young girls pursued as much as they were pursued, especially young female artists-to-be. Or so he told him-self. If he was rationalizing abhorrent behavior, violating implicit and often explicit norms, but everybody was a consenting adult, wasn't that merely *carpe diem*? His second "wife" seemed to agree. They were faculty members, both divorced, both with a reputation, but she was the first person, male or female, who made Wyman laugh a dozen times a day. He made her laugh too, surprising even himself. She was acerbic, astute, and she cried at movies. They had met at a faculty party, where spouses were eyeing other spouses. He had been discreetly cajoling a sculptor's wife when he felt a jab in his back. Without turning around, he barely heard, "She's a screamer. Be careful." He quickly bade the sculptor's wife good-bye and turned to look for the woman who had poked him. Scanning the room, he saw her in the corner, drink in one hand, cigarette in the other.

For the rest of her life, she told him that she would never forget the look on his face when he figured out that she had been the one who had warned him about screaming women. "It wasn't love, Pete, that look on your face. It was more like . . . *you?* In fact, you almost looked disappointed, but as soon as I tipped my glass toward you, you smiled. A genuinely happy smile. Did you know that the joke in the department was that Peter Wyman never smiled? A bit too full of yourself, sir. You can thank me later."

His joke was actually the truth. "I was thinking that I would have to stop seeing the two women I was dating at that time. Two was juggling, but three would kill me."

She had not hesitated. "Pete, you weren't dating women. Girls are not women."

Six months later, Peter Wyman asked Sarah Levy to marry him. She turned him down.

"I'm not a fan of marriage, Pete. Bad track record in my family. But if you're willing to live with me, do your own laundry, and not complain if I snore, then maybe we can be a serious couple, our own version of husband and wife."

They still went through all the pre-nup adult negotiations. No lies about their pasts, but with boundaries for their future. Each agreed to allow the other their own private space. The rule? Sarah spoke for both of them. "As long as I don't know, and nobody else knows, you're a free man. And by knowing I don't just mean that I walk in on you and some bimbo in bed. It also means I don't ever see any guilt in your face. Same from you to me. Don't humiliate me, Pete, that's all I want. But I'll tell you this. If you ever fall in love with anybody else, I will kill you."

Six months of seeing each other every day, sleeping with each other almost every night, of looking for each other after every class, Wyman was sure he had found the woman that his parents must have raised too. But he was wrong. Six months after they moved in together, they both realized that each had stopped having sex with anybody else. Wyman was not his father. Sarah was not his mother. He wished he could go back and talk to his parents again, to ask them how they thought they actually loved each other. How could they separate love and sex? Real love, that is. All he knew for sure was that Sarah made him happy. And calm, as if he had been holding his breath all his life and then she let him exhale.

He would always remember, could never forget, the exact day he met Alice. He made a joke to his class about it being his mother's birthday, and that his own birthday would be the next day. He expected presents. An annual line. Nobody ever took him seriously. It was also the first day of the semester, and he scanned the small group in front of him. She was staring at him. A woman in her thirties, a yellowing white blouse, black skirt, straight hair down below her shoulders. First day of the semester was always a short class. Goals and expectations in a printed syllabus, first assignments, and then his customary *go and sin no more* dismissal. Each of the students had to have submitted a sample of their work to get admitted, and Wyman's first thought was an effort to recall those works and guess which one belonged to the woman who had stared at him. Nothing came to him.

As the class filtered out, she remained in her seat. Even though she was the only student left in the room, she raised her hand, as if to ask a question. Wyman stood motionless and then extended his own hand and turned it palm up, gesturing, *Yes?*

"Mr. Wyman, I won't be in class tomorrow."

"As I said a few minutes ago, I don't keep attendance. Keep up with the work, we'll be fine. And I'm sorry, but who are you?"

"Alicia Bulova, but everybody calls me Allie."

"Well, you can call me Peter. Allie is fine, but is it okay to call you Alice? Just between us. I'll look for you in a few days."

Where did that come from? Some sort of reflexive flirtation? Am I too obvious?

She looked at him, part smirk, part suspicion.

"I've never seen myself as an Alice. Too old-fashioned, too ... affected? But if it makes me your favorite student, knock yourself out. But, you know, I knew a man who called me the Queen of Hearts, and I don't think he was complimenting me."

And now she is flirting with me?

"I'll hate to miss your class, but tomorrow at this time is bad for me. Won't happen again. As for calling me Alice, sure, I'd like that. You can have that name all to yourself. I'll be your Alice."

An hour later, they stopped talking. Wyman went home to Sarah and told her about the odd student he had met that day. Sarah almost laughed as she reminded him, "I will kill you."

He protested, "She's not *that* attractive. In fact, she looks a little run down."

Sarah rolled her eyes. "Pete, you haven't been this excited about the first day of class in years. Run down or not, she's got your attention even though she's obviously too old for you."

When Wyman went to the department office the next day, an envelope was in his faculty mailbox. Inside were a movie gift certificate, a tin of Earl Grey tea, and a note: *Happy Birthday, Peter. I'm looking forward to our class. Alice*

After class, he went back to his office and found the sample drawings she had submitted. He self-consciously tried to separate the sketches in front of him from the woman he had met. How to evaluate them? Something was wrong. In his most objective appraisal, her work was very good, but not outstanding. Not the best of the submissions, but certainly good enough to get into the class. He needed a second opinion. He took every student submission home with him, a dozen different artists, mixed them together, and showed them one by one to Sarah.

"Do I get a prize if I pick the one that you think is the best too?" She then quickly chose the best submissions, all done by one student, who was not Alicia Bulova.

"Yep, he was my choice too."

"Pete, you sound disappointed. Am I missing something?"

"No, no. Just wondering. He seems like a sharp kid. Just thought I might have overlooked something the first time I went through these."

"My type?" She was teasing him.

"Let me get back to you in a few weeks on that. In the meantime, you want to go to a movie tonight?"

The next time he saw Alice Bulova, she was naked.

Wyman was never involved in choosing the models for his figure drawing class. He would arrive the first day, and the model was simply whoever the department hired. He did not even request male or female. He just wanted a nude body the first day, knowing that his students would not be expecting such immersion so soon. Whenever the nude sketching began, it was always going to be awkward for many of his students that first time. The moment that the model dropped their robe, he would watch his students. With a female model, he focused on the young men in his class. With a male model, he had started his career looking at the reactions of the female students, but over time he realized that their reaction was less revealing than how the male students reacted. Wyman only had about fifteen seconds before any initial reaction was erased and true concentration began. If pressed by his colleagues to explain why he began his drawing class so abruptly, Wyman would shrug off the question: *My class, my rules. No hidden agenda.*

The model was late. Wyman had made the usual first-day introductions, had the students talk a little about themselves, but that took only a few minutes. He hated small talk. Over time, he had lost the advantage of surprise. His students this morning knew all the stories about Wyman. They knew he had a nude model in the first class, but there was still a bit of edginess as they waited. They also knew that the school models were never picked for their looks. A body was a body. Impatient, Wyman went ahead and announced their assignment.

"When the model is ready, I want you to put down your pencils and concentrate on the form. I'll tell the model how to pose. I want you to concentrate on that body as a form with light and shade and curves and even angles. Do *not* look at the model's face. That's a different class. After the model is gone, I'll ask you to describe what you saw. What about that form stood out to you? I want you to tell me what you would emphasize, if anything at all."

His back was to the door, so his first vision was how his class responded to the person entering the room unannounced. They had collectively turned their eyes away from him as Alice Bulova walked in. She had their complete attention.

"I'm sorry I'm late, Mr. Wyman."

He knew the voice. He was confused for that first few seconds as he turned slowly around. She was not on the class roll. Why was she here? And then he saw her standing there in a white robe.

"Tell me what you want me to do."

Was the silence noticeable? He wondered later how long it had taken him to respond, if his students were even aware. For that first moment, she had looked directly at him, eye to eye, but then she looked around the classroom as if evaluating the paint on the walls. She obviously knew a few of the other students, and she did a waist-high wave to them. Then she spotted the small stage in the center of the room, walked over and stepped up, turned back to Wyman and made eye contact with him again.

"I'm all yours."

Wyman cleared his throat and spoke to the class, "Remember what I told you." And then to her, "Alicia Bulova, right?"

"Yessir."

"Well, Miss Bulova, whenever you're ready, you can put your robe on that stool. I'll ask you to assume a few poses. Standing today and then . . ."

She took off her robe before he could finish.

Seriously, Peter? Miss Bulova? You were able to say that with a straight face?

Thirty minutes later, she was robed and gone. Wyman polled the class about their impressions of the model's form. As usual, there was no consensus about the small details. As the discussion continued, he became confused. Had they all been looking at the same body he had seen? One student remarked about the cellulite on the model's stomach, obvious stretch marks, possibly from pregnancy? Another noticed the weakness of the chin, how the flesh seemed to sag. Another, how her legs must have been recently shaved since there were razor nicks above the ankles. Another, the pubic hair must have been shaved in the past, since it looked so coarse today. Another, the hips were disproportionate to her upper torso, too wide, the buttocks flat and starting to sag. Another, the fingernails needed manicuring. Another, she plucked her eyebrows.

"Enough!" Wyman almost raised his voice, pointing to the student who had commented on the model's eyebrows. "I specifically told you to not look at her face. Pay goddam attention to what I tell you."

The class froze. None of rumors they had heard about Peter Wyman included anger. He looked around the room, every eye on him. He shook his head and took back control of his class. "I'm sorry. Too much coffee this morning. Let's call it a day."

He knew he would talk to Sarah about the experience. He trusted her. But he would not be completely honest. He wanted to process the most important detail by himself. As he had listened to his students describe the model, he realized that he could not remember any of the details they did. He must have looked. He did not remember. He told them to not consider the model's face, but that was all he remembered. He told them not to look at her face, but that was all he did. For that half hour, as she moved at his command, he followed her. Sometimes, across from each other, she would be looking everywhere else but at him. She never made eye contact with any student. But, the moments. The moments she would slowly turn her face toward him, looking past him, and then directly at him. A moment, and then she would turn away.

Tell me what you want me to do.

From the classroom to his office was usually a two-minute walk, assuming he used the elevator. From the top floor, full of sunlit classrooms, to the ground floor, opposite end of the building, to an office with one small window. He hated his office and was seldom there, preferring to stay in the classroom and do his paperwork there, to meet his students there, to think there. The classroom smelled of paint and sunlight. His office was musk. He left the classroom that day and walked to the end of the hallway, descended a flight of stairs to the next floor, walked to the other end, descended that stairway, and then walked back the other direction to the stairway at the other end, and then finally descended to the ground floor. The hallway on the ground floor had always reminded him of the hallway at a second-rate hotel, dark, with windows only at each end, each office door recessed in even more darkness. It was a department joke, their "creativity housed in hallways of seedy assignations."

I'm all yours.

He walked absentmindedly, running his hand along the cool wall, looking straight ahead. A few doors from his own office, he saw her. She had stepped out of the recess and waved at him. He stopped. Neither moved. He started walking again, slower. He kept looking at her face. She started walking toward him. They met in the middle of the hallway.

"Seriously, Peter? Miss Bulova? You were able to say that with a straight face? And you didn't seem pleased to see me today."

"Well, you could have told me that you were going to be the model. I wasn't displeased, just surprised."

"Ah, the fine line between shock and anger. I have to work on my body language interpretive skills. But, for the record, the *Miss Bulova* was priceless."

Wyman knew to tread carefully. He had known young women in his past who had worked too hard to be witty or pseudo-sophisticated. They would be perfect future academics. Besides, he had only known Alice Bulova for less than a week. He told himself to be careful. He also told himself that as much as he might be intrigued by her, he was not really attracted to her. He had seen her naked, but not one aspect of her body, below the neck, was memorable. He just wished that she was the most talented artist in his class. That would have justified paying more attention to her. Minutes later, she was sitting on the edge of his desk, in a cramped and unkempt office, daring him to ignore her.

"I wish you had told me about being the model."

"Sorry. I had applied for the spot before I met you in your other class. Didn't get the word until later. Didn't connect the dots. Just needed some extra money. Does it really bother you, me being your model? If you prefer, I can ask to be assigned to somebody else."

"I thought you were on a scholarship."

"Enough to go to school. Not enough to eat. I sorta like to eat. You and Sarah want to feed me? I'll keep my clothes on for you."

"You know my wife?"

"Everybody knows her, Peter. Relax."

"But you've never met her."

She rolled her eyes. "Did you hear me? Relax. But she might like to meet me. I'm still looking for more work. I do house-cleaning and yardwork. And if this office is any indicator of how you keep your house, the two of you are going to need me."

"I don't think that's a good idea."

She slid off the desk. Wyman realized that nothing she was wearing seemed to fit her. Her plaid shirt was too big, as if sized for a large man. Her skirt was too long and it even had a noticeably frayed hem. Details that should have been obvious at their first meeting, but only noted now. Details that he would share with Sarah later, in a conversation in which she informed him about Alice's actual age.

"Ask her anyway. Remember, I like to eat."

Sarah was holding a wineglass when he finished telling her about his day. Peering over the top of her glasses, she looked at him as if he were a new suitor describing a pet project in his life, something that he assumed would be as interesting to his audience as it was to him. It was a "look" she had bestowed on him on other occasions: genuine interest, but distance, as if he himself was her own project, the thing that interested her. Wyman had always seemed too ironic to most people, too reserved to share his own private thoughts with anybody else. That façade had cracked within weeks of knowing her.

With his description of his new student, Sarah realized that Wyman seemed to want her to find Alice Bulova as interesting as he did, to be as drawn to Alice as much as he was, as if he were arranging a courtship between the two women. She dipped her finger into her wine and began rubbing the rim of the glass until it squeaked. Wyman noticed and stopped talking.

"Pete, didn't you tell me that she was an older woman? In her thirties, you thought."

"Yes, you'll agree when you meet her. In her thirties, and with a lot of baggage I'm discovering. But, she . . ."

"She's nineteen, Pete. Nineteen. She could be our daughter."

"How do you . . ."

"Sometimes it's a simple thing, like looking at her actual application. You ever think of that?"

"And you did?"

"Pete, you know what I find most adorable about you? For as smug a bastard as you are, as much as you think you know all the proverbial ropes, you are incredibly . . ."

"Stupid? Transparent?"

Sarah smiled. "No, Pete. Neither of those, for sure."

"So?"

"So, you are incredibly innocent. You are the most innocent sinner I have ever known. Innocent or not, Pete. Just be careful. And never forget, I will kill you."

"Would you like to know what she asked?"

"Pete, not really, but you seem dying to tell me."

"She wanted to know if we would hire her to do housework for us."

He expected one response, but got another.

"Tell her minimum wage only. Four or five hours a week. Pete, I might love this girl now. You know how I hate housework and neither one of us knows how to mow a lawn without losing a toe."

"You're not serious."

"Tell her to call me and us girls will work out the details."

"You're not serious."

Sarah smiled at him, almost a smirk. He had seen the same smile on Alice's face.

"I want to meet her, Pete."

Calls were made, arrangements agreed on, and a week later Wyman and Sarah went to a movie while Alice came over and cleaned their house. Both were impressed with the results, especially Wyman. Alice did not seem to care about her own appearance, but the cleaned house was immaculate and orderly, down to magazines being stacked in chronological order. They came home and paid her. An hour later, she left. Thirty seconds after she left, Sarah slapped Wyman on the back of his head, almost affectionately.

"You lied to me."

"Excuse me?"

"Pete, you do see the problem, don't you? We just spent an hour talking to a girl young enough to be our daughter, who has nothing in common with us, but we stood at the door for an hour, gossiping and laughing like we've known each other all our lives."

"I told you that she was very bright."

"Bright is not the word I'd use, Pete. Something harder to pin down, but it's there."

Wyman knew that Sarah was processing and would find the word she wanted. "But you agree, right? She is very impressive, especially for a teenager."

"Nineteen going on forty, and that's the puzzle. She's awfully damn . . . *familiar*. That's what I want to figure out. Not like I know her from somewhere else or some other time. I mean familiar like . . . she crowds in, she doesn't recognize some sort of boundary. I mean, I felt like I had known her for years. Some sort of intimacy that should have taken years, but here we were, old friends."

"I tried to warn you about that. I didn't lie to you."

"Darling, the slap was for something else. You either lied to me or you're lying to yourself."

Wyman waited, not sure what he was guilty of, but sure he was guilty of something.

"Pete, all the time before this, you kept saying that she was interesting, but not all that attractive. And just remember, you named her. She's *your* Alice. Old store rules apply now. If you break the plate, you pay for it."

"Sarah? I have no idea . . ."

"Pete, get back to me as soon as you figure out who the plate is."

He was not a young man when he met Alice. Even if she had been in her thirties, as he had assumed, he would have still been much older. Knowing that she was only nineteen, he immediately tagged her as having father issues, and he was not going to become a cliché . . . again.

Before he met Sarah, he knew that his young lovers had many reasons to get involved with him, and none of those reasons were related to animal magnetism. He was an average-looking older man who swam in an ocean of budding and curious, and sometimes damaged, young women. It was never love, it was never permanent, but it had been addictive. He prided himself, rationalized, by never being aggressive, never offering anything in exchange, never forcing. He never had to, he thought, because all he had to do was pay attention to the signals. He simply accepted what was offered.

Sarah had listened to that self-serving self-analysis before they formalized their relationship and moved in together. She had her own history with younger men, but she did not need to have met and fallen in love with Wyman to change her behavior. She had already grown up.

A week after moving in together, they had been walking around their neighborhood after dark, familiar terrain for both, and Sarah had asked him a simple question.

"Pete, do you think there should be more streetlights around here?"

He had paused and looked around.

"Looks like standard distancing. What, two hundred feet apart? Almost bright enough to cast shadows. Am I missing something?"

"Would you walk down this street alone at night?"

"Sure."

"I'm not sure I would. It's very dark, lights or not. Too many dark spots between the lights. Tree branches obstructing. The alley up ahead, no way to see what is a few feet from the opening. If I were a very young girl, I would walk with mace in my hands, or I would stay inside."

Wyman glanced around again and then gave Sarah a puzzled look.

"Pete, it's a different world for girls than boys. A different reality. You're a boy. Navigation is different for you. You think you're in control. Those girls in your past? Most of them just wanted to be as free as boys for once. Lucky for them, you're actually a well-lit street."

"Sarah, I don't know if you just insulted me or not."

"I'm just suggesting that sometimes there are dark streets for boys too, but most of you guys still assume you're safe and in control."

"I want you to pose for me."

"Of course, you would. I assume you mean out of class. I also assume I get the same twenty dollars an hour, right?"

"No, I'm not paying you."

"Peter, me dropping that robe is going to cost you."

"No, I want to paint your portrait."

She tilted her head and for a split-second Wyman thought she might actually be embarrassed. But only for that split-second.

"Can it be our secret?"

"Why?"

"If you promise to never let anyone else ever see it, I will pose for you. I don't want anybody else to see me. You either understand that, or you don't."

"Alice, I've seen you naked. Dozens of others have seen you naked. You're not exactly a mystery."

"That's sad, you saying that."

"How so?"

"You think you've *seen* me because you've seen me naked? Jesus, Peter, I thought you were different than anybody else. You want to paint me but you can't even see me. You can kiss my ass, which you *have* seen."

Her anger was sincere. So was his. He wanted to tell her to grow up and stop being so melodramatic. Anybody else would have accepted his offer right away. But Alice Bulova had conditions? *He* had to prove something to *her* before she would do it? Who the hell did she think she was?

They were standing next to the fountain in Lafayette Park, having gone through the Cathedral of St. John the Baptist an hour earlier. He had seen everything worth seeing in Savannah long before he met her, but for weeks he had been revisiting places with her that he had already seen. He was her tour guide. He was always in control, he assured himself, but behind that self-delusion was also self-indulgence. It was a singular pleasure, taking her back to the places of his past, as if she had always been there. He had a list of such places, far and away from Savannah, that he wanted her to see with him. He had told her about his wish to show her places in his past. Doing so, he had asked her if she wanted to do the same for him. He tried to make it a game. *If you could show me the important places in your past, where would we go?* She always said *Let me get you a list.* But she never did.

"Forget it. I just wanted to paint your portrait. Your face. Something I think I see, but you think I can't see anything. So, let's drop it. Go get somebody else to paint you. I'm sure you have lots of other offers."

"More than you'll ever know, Peter. But . . ."

A hundred feet away, the cathedral offered saints on the walls. Next to them, water overflowed the three tiers of the fountain. Hundred-year-old oak trees offered mossy shade.

"Yes," he interrupted.

"Yes?"

"Yes, it will be our secret."

In all those weeks, he had never touched her. She never gave him any overt sign that she wanted him to touch her. He assumed she recognized his own boundary signals. Knowing her true age, he knew those boundaries had to be widened. But he saw her every day. She still came to his house once a week and cleaned, sitting down with Sarah for coffee, them laughing with each other as he came through the kitchen door, as if he had been their main topic of junior high girl talk.

In the hours the studio was not used by the school, she posed for her portrait. She insisted that the door be locked. Wyman insisted that the window shades remain open. They had no set schedule, no minimum time per session. They were governed only by how long they could be alone.

For the first few weeks, she obeyed his professional rule that his model not see the work until it was finished. But one day she simply ignored his protests and walked over to look.

"I knew it, Peter. You think I wouldn't figure it out."

The canvas was still blank. For weeks he had been miming his work, letting her see the motions of art without producing art. He had taken photos over and over. He had sat at different angles away from her, different distances. All the while, they talked.

"Alice, this is how I work."

"You're lucky you have a faculty job. Anybody paying you privately would have fired you last week."

"Besides, this is not for anybody else, right? It's for me."

"Only you?"

"Actually, yes, only me. And you don't have to do this if you don't want to."

"Oh, Peter." She was slowly shaking her head back and forth, looking directly at him. "I'm going to sit here forever, as long as it takes, and you are finishing this portrait. So, whatever is blocking you now, get over it."

"Truth is, I'm still looking for you to stop acting. Your face is still acting, hiding something."

"Is this where you quote Eliot?"

Wyman blinked. "Alice, what the hell . . ."

"*To prepare a face to meet the faces that you meet.* My favorite poem of all time. You got a favorite? I know, *April is the cruelest month* gets a lot of press, but Prufrock is his best. So maybe that's why I like you, Peter? Are you Peter Prufrock? You're not too skinny. You're not balding, much, but I'm guessing that you have Prufrock potential. So, fuck off, Peter Prufrock."

And she walked out of the classroom.

Two days later, she did not show up for what was supposed to be their next session. No message, just absence. Wyman told himself to ignore the obvious self-produced drama. She would be back. But she was gone for the next session too.

"She's quoting Eliot to you and you don't see the problem?"

He told Sarah about Alice calling him Peter Prufrock. He had to invent a different setting, a different context for someone to quote poetry to him, especially someone like Alice. He said that he had been doing a word-association exercise in class. *Anybody know any imagistic poems that you would like to illustrate?* More than one student had chosen Eliot, but only Alice had compared him to Prufrock.

"Let me guess. She told you that after class, right?"

Wyman had to improvise a lie, and if Sarah accepted the lie then he would have to be prepared to make the lie consistent with a reality she was creating.

"How did you know?"

"Pete, she might be nineteen, but she's an old nineteen. She knows how anything she says around you in front of anybody else, even me, can be either misinterpreted or, more dangerously, be seen for what it truly is. Quoting poetry to anybody is a *private* matter. Some sort of special relationship between the two of you. Remember what I said about *familiarity*."

He was relieved. He was sure that Sarah still did not know about the portrait sessions. She was perceptive, but she was still perceiving only one version of his life.

"But you have to admit, in or out of class, quoting Eliot was impressive."

Sarah looked at him like she was looking at a child who still believed in Santa Claus.

"Pete, it would be impressive if she did it out of thin air, totally spontaneous."

He wanted to defend Alice against Sarah's skepticism.

"Nobody knew I was going to ask that question. Nobody could come prepared. It was all spontaneous."

Wyman surprised himself by how convincing he was. Sarah was still unimpressed.

"Here's my guess, Pete, my womanly guess. That poem was prepped long before you asked that question in class. She was just waiting for the right moment to use it. You served up the softball. She was going to Prufrock you sooner or later, not because she believed it, but because she knows how insecure you are. And I'm betting she has some other tasty allusion waiting for you."

"But, even if she was as premeditated as you think she was, just picking that poem was . . . was . . ."

"Brilliant, Pete, absolutely brilliant. Like I said, she's an old nineteen. And I find her fascinating too. Just do me a favor, okay?"

"Favor?"

"Yeah, if she ever quotes Emily Dickinson to you, don't fall in love with her. And, trust me, she's got Dickinson loaded and ready to go."

He looked at her and was about to respond when she stopped him.

"Pete, trust me."

"How can you be so sure about her? And so cynical."

"Because, Pete, my spindly legged, bald-spot, coffee-spoon-measuring love, she has already quoted Dickinson to me."

He had been asleep in bed with Sarah when the phone downstairs rang. She nudged him. It was his turn. He almost stumbled down the stairs getting to the kitchen, picked up the phone in the dark, and heard her voice.

"Peter, are you okay? I was thinking about you and I had a bad feeling. I just want to make sure you are okay."

"Alice?"

"I know it's late, but I just had a feeling. I'm sorry for calling so late. Go back to bed. I was just thinking about you."

Wyman could see the wall clock in the dark. Two in the morning. He could hear other young voices in the background of Alice's voice, laughing and telling her to hurry.

"Alice, are *you* okay?"

"Oh, I'm fine. Just taking a road trip with some friends. Go back to bed. Like I said, sorry to call so late. But I had a feeling."

Wyman chose a path, lowering his voice as if he were not alone. "Thank you for calling. Come see me at my studio when you get back. I'll buy you a cup of coffee and you can tell me about your trip. And I'd like to work on your portrait again."

How long was there silence? He kept the phone close to his ear, but she was gone. He was about to hang up when she finally whispered, "I'd like that very much. Good night, Peter."

There in the dark of that kitchen, Sarah asleep upstairs, he finally saw Alice's face.

How important are first times?

They were looking at her portrait. How do parents look on their first child, the moment the child comes into the world, ruddy and screaming but soon wiped down and beaming pink? A wonder and a marvel, and totally unique, their own souls embodied in a new creation. Wyman tried to say something like that, that the face on the canvas was more than just her. It was them. She just shook her head.

"Peter, when did you get so romantic and stupid at the same time?" Pointing at the canvas, "That's not us. That's me. Perhaps a bit gauzy around the edges. Thinner, thank you, and you have certainly done wonders with my chin. Still, all in all, it's me. It's me exactly as I wish I was."

"It's who you are."

They had been standing side by side in his studio, but not touching. The sun would set in an hour. She moved closer to him, her shoulder leaning into his. He could smell her hair. She put her arm around his waist.

"You've never kissed me," she said without turning toward him, her eyes still fixated on her own face. "Six months, you've even seen me naked, we've been alone plenty of times, but you never even tried to kiss me?"

He would never figure it out. Why was every moment with her a *scene*? Why did he willfully choose to ignore the obvious truth? She was acting. Performing brilliantly. He had begun as merely a supporting player. Knowing his *role* had protected him. Sarah had warned him, and he had not disagreed with her. But he continued, and he was becoming Alice's costar. He told himself that he could step off the stage at any time. He had told himself, over and over and over, that he was the writer of his own script.

She stepped around in front of him, her portrait visible behind her. She saw his eyes shifting from the face in the portrait and back to the face closer to him. They were the same. He put his hands on her waist and closed his eyes as she leaned forward and kissed him. Then she put her lips next to his ear and whispered, "This is the first time. Yes, it is important." And they kissed again. Longer and deeper but still slowly. An hour later, they were on the couch in his office, him inside of her, her looking directly into his eyes, and they both climaxed. He was almost fifty and for the first time in his life he could not see the future. *What have I done?* Everything he had imagined about his future . . . Sarah, his career, his art . . . every assumption disappeared. His new future was a mystery to him. Tomorrow was a mystery. Another hour later they were still intertwined. She would not let him leave her.

Another essential part of Wyman's self-perception was his absolute belief that he was a realist. He knew he was a very good painter before he met Alice, but not the best. He knew that his subsequent fame was a matter of chance as well as merit. He might not have met Alice. He might have resisted her after he did meet her. Either would have changed his future. Meeting her was not his choice. Falling in love with her? *To* fall in love; *to not* fall in love. Were those choices for anybody, even a realist? Did he consciously know he was in love with her before he painted her? Or did the painting itself reveal to him his own emotions, emotions the realist Peter Wyman insisted that he could control? All those things . . . meeting Alice, painting her portrait, falling in love with her, all of them might have made him a better painter, but they did not make him famous. His fame was pure chance.

Robert Hughes made him famous. A giant in the art world, Hughes was in Savannah a year later than he had been scheduled. The original date had to be postponed. If he had come when he was scheduled, he would have seen Wyman's work and perhaps been impressed, perhaps not. But the Alice portrait did not exist then. For Wyman, Alice did not exist. A Hughes illness had intervened.

Hughes was apologetic. The Savannah Art School quickly offered a new date, but that date had conflicted with other dates on Hughes's calendar. More chance. Hughes was gracious, juggling his other dates, insisting that "Death nor Doom" would prevent him from honoring the new engagement in Savannah. A public reading, some media interviews, private visits with faculty and students, Hughes would be the highlight of the year.

Wyman had been a fan of Hughes ever since he read *Heaven and Hell in Western Art*. But he also knew that Hughes had a reputation for being a critic whose personality sometimes did not distinguish between honesty and contempt. He did not plan to show Hughes any of his own work. Why take the chance? Nobody except Alice had seen the *Alice* portrait, not even Sarah. It was supposed to be a secret. It was supposed to be hidden, not on display for the most famous art critic in the world. Alice made sure that Hughes saw it.

His students had been waiting for him and Hughes to arrive. They had seen the portrait in the room before he did. They knew the model. They were amateurs, but they understood that the portrait was more than a face. It was a story. Hughes mistook it for art. He entered the studio and immediately walked over to stand in front of the portrait. Wyman introduced him to the class, but Hughes did not acknowledge them. The students did not know where to look. At their own, clearly shaken, teacher as he spoke, or at the wavy-haired man who was ignoring all of them, but who was clearly a *presence*.

Hughes turned back to Wyman, with a one-word question. "Yours?"

The adolescent nightmare of showing up late for a test and also being completely naked. Wyman looked at his students' faces, then back to Hughes. Two different audiences, both of them seeing him naked.

"Yes . . . but . . ."

"Interesting," was all Hughes said before he turned to the classroom and became a gracious storyteller for the next hour. As Hughes spoke, Wyman sat in the back of the studio, quite sure that Alice would walk in and introduce herself. For that hour, however, she existed only on canvas.

With the students gone, Hughes went back to the portrait and stared for too long. It was probably less than a minute. His only comment to Wyman about the portrait was both cryptic and sad. Pressed to explain, he merely shrugged.

"You should have lived three hundred years ago."

Wyman was still distracted, wondering how the portrait had serendipitously appeared just in time for Hughes to see it. Only Alice knew it existed. The answer should have been obvious.

It was not intentional, but Hughes made Wyman famous and subsequently rich. A week after Hughes's visit, Wyman got a call from the Art Institute of Chicago. Would he be interested in letting his *Alice* portrait be part of an upcoming exhibition of *Contemporary American Portraitists*? His name had been mentioned by Hughes.

The Chicago caller had laughed. "Bob wasn't sure, but he thought I should call you."

"Not sure?"

"In so many words, he told me that he thought your work represented everything he hated in art. And then he said it was absolutely breathtaking and brilliant for all the wrong reasons. But he also paid you a compliment, and if you hired a good publicist you would make it the headline to your press release."

"I'm sorry, but none of this conversation makes sense."

"Peter, Bob Hughes said that he hated your work, but that he could be wrong. You might be a singular talent. He admitted that he *could be wrong*. That's your foot in the door. You made Robert Hughes second-guess himself. All I know for sure is that I really want to see what you have done."

Sarah had always known that he was painting Alice's portrait. Alice had told her and sworn her to secrecy, so she said nothing to Wyman until she actually saw it for the first time. It was unveiled at the annual "Faculty Exposition" of work, the week after Robert Hughes came to visit. What was supposed to have been a secret was already a rumor that had spread. Why hide it any longer? Alice by herself was already a rumor . . . *Have you met a girl named Alicia Bulova yet?* . . . but the portrait spawned a newer rumor . . . *Seriously? He's old enough to be her father.*

Wyman would try to describe the moment years later, to his final model, a dying rich man.

"You know how sometimes you'll be at a funeral visitation, or maybe in a hospital room with other people visiting a gravely ill person, and suddenly the husband or wife, or father or mother, just somebody more important to the dead or dying person than you, that person arrives and you intuitively fall silent and step aside to let that person have their own private access, and you and everyone else just step back into a shadow to let the newcomer have some privacy, but you still watch that person, look for their reaction, to see how they grieve the loss that is right there in front of them? That was how it was. Sarah and I walked into the gallery and the crowd was gathered around the portrait, somebody saw us and whispered to the others, and like a sea they parted and we had an unobstructed view from across the room. But none of them would look us right in the eye. They all seemed to be looking somewhere else as we walked up to stand in front of the painting."

As soon as they entered the gallery, Wyman looked for Alice, relieved to not see her. Calmer, holding on to Sarah, he waited for her opinion, the only opinion that mattered at that moment. He could hear her breathing next to him. No deep breaths, no muffled gasp, her exhalations almost a hum.

"Are you sleeping with her?"

Both kept looking at the portrait.

"No."

"Are you in love with her?"

"No."

"One is a lie for sure, Pete. And only one of those lies really matters."

"Sarah, do you think I don't love you?"

"Ah, there's the rub. You do love me. As flawed as you are, I love you too. That's my problem, not yours. But the biggest pain I have ever felt in my life is this exact moment."

"Sarah, you are the only . . ."

"Shut up, Pete. You have no idea what I'm talking about. You have no idea what I mean. Love me as much as you do, me love you like I do, all that misses the point. If you had never met her, you would have never painted something like this. Do you even realize how beautiful this is? How utterly breathtaking? And it was her, not me, who inspired you?"

"Sarah . . ."

"I wish I could thank her. I've always thought you possessed some talent that was rare. And the appealing thing was that you didn't even know it. You didn't even understand yourself. But I always had this adolescent dream that one day you would stand on a stage, being recognized for your talent, and you would look into the camera and tell the world that you would have never been there unless you met me."

"Sarah . . ."

"Here's the deal, Pete, my most important order for you. Whatever happens to you in the future, don't ever blame her."

"Do you love me?"

They had been sitting across from each other in a booth in a Charleston bar, their first trip together out of town. A Paul Simon song overhead, competing with the clash of dishes and a hundred conversations around them.

"Yes, absolutely. I love you, and I probably have for a long time."

They had never used the word in all the time before then. Sarah had warned him. Love was more damning than sex. He looked at her face as he confessed. Was it a smile, or a smirk, or simple disbelief?

But she did not say that she loved him. Not then, not when he told the truth. She did not say that she loved him. After that, hundreds of times. If ten years of knowing her was a series of scenes, public and private, shouldn't *that* scene have been better scripted, with her admitting her own love for him? She looked at him, then away, but it was another month before she said she loved him.

The next day they took the boat to Fort Sumter. Choppy waters in the bay, neither had worn enough warm clothing, so they held tight to each other. A dozen other tourists must have thought them odd. The May-December couple. Inside the fort, the wind blocked by what was left of the rubbled walls, they followed the guide, Wyman's arm around Alice's shoulder. That had been new to him, the experience of public touching. Not even with Sarah had he been affectionate in public. Another moment? The guide was explaining how Abner Doubleday had served as Major Anderson's subordinate during the shelling of the fort. "Most of you probably know him for inventing the game of baseball."

As the small crowd nodded, she raised her hand. "That's not really true. It's a myth."

It was another example of something he had found fascinating about her from the very beginning. She knew things. Something about almost any subject. For as long as he knew her, he would send her books. If he raised a subject in a conversation, no matter how casually, she would come back later having read something about that subject. Correcting the Sumter guide was typical. He had seen her in conversations with older adults, conversing as if she was their peer. What did Sarah say . . . *familiarity*? But, more, he was fascinated by how others reacted to her. *Who was this young woman? Why is she with him?* And often the implicit undercurrent . . . *I want to know her.*

Her portrait made him famous. His fame made him rich. Even Sarah acknowledged that. *Tell her thanks for the new car.* He left academics and became a painting mercenary. Art galleries offered him exhibitions, as long as *Alice* was the headline draw. More exhibitions, more interviews, more guest lectures, more portrait requests, more travel. Eventually, Alice traveled with him after Sarah stopped going with him.

Pete, unless you get invited to Rome, you're on your own. I've been everywhere I ever wanted to go, and I've heard you speak about painting so much that I can quote you in my sleep. And your punch lines? Only funny the first hundred times. So, go, young man, and I'll keep a light on for you.

Did she ever know? After all, she seemed to accept his version of reality. Wyman eventually knew the answer. She had warned him. And then he wasn't allowed to deceive even himself any more. He told Sarah that he would end it. When he said it, he believed it. He was lying more to himself than to her.

"Pete, remember Danny Pryor, the young man who we both agreed was the best painter in that class with her? Remember? Did it even register with you when he dropped the class? Did you wonder why?"

He had not even unpacked his bag yet, as she stood in the bedroom door looking at him.

"She was fucking him, even before she fucked you, Pete. She made herself irresistible. Shocking, right? But here's the cosmic joke. I knew it all along. She told me about Danny. She made it sound so innocent, so like a teen romance, but she swore me to secrecy because she thought you would be disappointed in her. Your opinion of her mattered so much, right? But she thought I would be interested. You know, girl-to-girl talk, and I fell for it. Even suspicious me, I fell for it. But you want to know real girl to girl talk, Pete? That boy's mother called me yesterday to tell me that he had committed suicide. Why me? Well, because I was the one who answered the phone. She was calling you, but she got me, and she told me what she wanted to tell you, how her son had never recovered from your opinion of him. Your opinion of him, as told to him by Alice. He stopped painting. Yeah, you mattered that much to him. You want more? She had never heard about that damn portrait. She had no clue about the connection between you and her son's so-called girlfriend. But then she saw it in a magazine on her son's desk and she figured it out, the triangle. And she wanted to tell you to go to hell, but she got me instead. "

"But I never . . ." he had stammered.

"There's something wrong with me, Pete, some emotional dead end that I didn't think possible, some place where I go but have to turn around and start over again. I should tell you to pick that bag up and walk back out the door, but all I can think of is something she told me about you years ago, and I never forgot. I had asked her how she put up with your incredibly dumb humor. Dammit, Pete, I loved being around you. From the very beginning, you were the most fun man I had ever known. But she looked at me like I was talking about somebody else. You never ever made her laugh, Pete. Whoever else you were around her, you were not the man I knew. And that has probably saved your life at this moment. Whoever she loves, if that is actually how she feels, he's not the same man I love. I'm not sure I would even like the man she is involved with."

The unavoidable question: *Mr. Wyman, how well do you know Miss Bulova?*

He looked at his credit card statement and saw a thousand dollars' worth of charges made at a Jacksonville Target store. He had opened the account in secret and given the card to Alice after she left Savannah, in case she needed anything and was in a bind. His commissions were almost criminal. A few dollars here and there were insignificant. He called her. She insisted, *Peter, I have no idea what you're talking about.* But then she called back. *Peter, I'm sorry. I just checked my purse. Everything is gone, my license, that card, everything. I'm sorry, but all you have to do is call the insurance company and they will take off the charges.* The insurance company told him that a police report would have to be filed. To confirm a theft. He told her to file the report. Explain that he had loaned the card to her. It was stolen. Necessary paperwork for him to have the charges taken off his account. No harm, no foul.

The Jacksonville police called him: "Mr. Wyman, how well do you know Miss Bulova?" They had investigated. The card was used at a specific time and at specific locations. Those charges had been made by her. Cameras followed her out of the store, showing her with the packages. The credit card charges were one issue. Her bigger problem was that she had filed a false police report. She was going to be arrested. He improvised a lie. *I wish she had simply asked me. I would have let her make those charges. I know that she has been under a lot of stress lately. She was probably embarrassed. It was me who made her file that report. Is there anything we can do here?* The detective on the other end of the line hesitated. *If she or you will make full restitution to the credit company in 48 hours, that would help.* Wyman exhaled. *That won't be a problem. I'll see to it.* That was a truth. The detective wanted more. *I'll need for you to sign a statement, attesting to everything you told me here. Vouching for her. Make it part of the record, in case something like this happens again. She only gets one free pass, as long as you vouch for her. And I'll need for you to do that in person in my office.*

A month later he got a phone call from a collection agency. A credit card in his name had a five-thousand dollar unpaid and long overdue balance. He insisted that he did not have any such card. The name on the card was not even his. But the application had his Social Security number. Proving nothing, those numbers were stolen all the time. Where had the bills gone to begin with?

Mr. Wyman, how well do you know Miss Bulova?

All the bills had gone to Alice's address in Jacksonville. Some were paid in the beginning, but later ones were ignored. He had the collection agency send him copies of all the monthly invoices. A lot of ATM cash advances, but in cities other than Jacksonville. Plane tickets charged. And then the obvious harsher truth dawned on him. All this had happened months *before* he lied to the police to keep her out of jail. She had been movingly contrite when confronted about that problem, but she had done worse earlier and . . . what? . . . simply assumed that since his name was not on that earlier card he would never know? She had let him lie to save her, knowing that she had already done worse?

"I have a gift for your trip, Pete."

"You're kidding, right?"

He had just opened the tissue-wrapped box to discover a pair of pajamas. He looked back at Sarah. She was wearing a matching set.

"I've never worn pajamas in my life, Sarah. And, as best I recall, neither have you."

"C'mon. Humor me. Couples get matching stuff all the time. T-shirts, glasses, sweatshirts. We're both getting as old as dirt. I'm sicker than death. Humor me. Wear it for me, okay. Any aspiring arty coeds want to spend the night with you, make sure you wear these bad boys. That will scare them off."

Two days later, he opened the garage and found her behind the wheel of her car. She was wearing her pajamas. The note was in her breast pocket. He never told anyone about it.

. . . *I'm sorry, Pete, I really am. I'm not even sure you deserve this, but you're getting it anyway. The treatments are wearing me down, making me crazier and crazier, and it all seems so pointless anyway. Pump me full of meds as I get smaller and smaller? I suppose I could have waited for one of those storybook death scenes, friends and family gathered around the still breathing corpse in some hospice somewhere. That was where it was all headed. Right? And those friends and family would console you. Poor pitiful Pete, weeping as you held my hand. Or am I over-scripting? Like you always did. Would you cry? Would I be your only thought? I'm sorry, Pete. She went away but never left you. I always knew, but I was a much better actor than you . . . You have been incredibly sweet to me ever since we got the news about the cancer. Was taking care of me how you atoned? Your penance? You holding my shoulders as I puked in the toilet. How the house must have smelled of my rot. You cooking and cleaning. Was all that going to erase the past? Did you think you were going to get off that easy? . . . I am beat. I give up. You never said you were sorry, Pete. You never asked for forgiveness, but I gave it to you anyway. Hell, I would have even forgiven her. Just remember, whatever happens to you in the future, don't ever blame her. Or me. I still love you, Pete. I wish it had been enough.*

In the beginning, Wyman knew it would happen sooner or later. It always did. He would struggle with an image, something about a model escaping him, but he eventually saw it. And the rest was easy. That was his experience for the decade after his *Alice* portrait made him famous. He was in demand, and he took the work seriously, but then Sarah died and he no longer looked for the essence of any subject. The works between *Alice* and the death of Sarah were gallery and museum-worthy. His fees had risen in proportion to his fame. After Sarah, the fees remained high. After all, his rich models could always say that they had their portrait done by Peter Wyman. *The* Peter Wyman. After Sarah died, his productivity went from three or four a year to more than a dozen. He never disappointed his clients. He made them look good, their beauty frozen in oil on canvas. If not beautiful, he made them look wise or pensive, any version of themselves that he thought they wanted. He always had more requests for his services than he had time to fill, so he invented a pseudo-interview. He made them believe that he had chosen them, that they had convinced him that they were worthy of his time and talent. They believed that he saw something in them that separated them from his other besiegers, that *he* actually wanted to paint *them*. They could tell their friends, *You know, he doesn't take just anybody.* After Sarah died, he took anybody who would pay his ascending price. He did not look inside them. He did not wait and wait. In their first meeting, he would ask a direct question: *How do you see yourself?* And he would find a way to paint that. Not how he saw them, but how they saw themselves.

Decisions? Signs? Roads not taken? While he was still appearing in art magazines and his work was still being solicited by galleries, he had been contacted by an agent about writing a memoir. Wyman called it his *fifteen minutes.* The agent said that he knew a few publishers who were looking for properties. Memoirs were hot. The more famous, the better.

Wyman protested, "I'm a painter, not a writer."

"I can hire a writer to write it. All you have to do is talk."

"My life story?"

"I think that's the general rule."

"Isn't the expectation that I will tell the truth?"

The agent was losing patience. "You obviously don't read a lot of memoirs. You don't get to totally make up things, but you can shape it, give it meaning, talk about the key moments, ignore what you want, the decisions that paved your way, the people. I know enough about your life and reputation to tell you that people will want to know more."

Wyman had declined. He could not explain to the agent that he had come to the conclusion that his life had all come down to one choice, one road taken. The problem with reaching a crossroads and having to choose a direction? Free Will or Fate? Character is Fate? Only in hindsight, alone in a barn in Florida, did Wyman understand his life well enough to tell the truth. But nobody cared anymore.

Ten years after Sarah died, Wyman was interviewed by a radio talk show host in St. Augustine at one in the morning. Wyman was stoned. The host was drunk. The host had assured him that nobody was listening.

"Hell, I am the most invisible man in St. Augustine, unseen and seldom heard."

"So, I'm a bit confused about how you found me and why you'd even be interested in talking."

The host cleared his throat, and Wyman heard him slurp a drink and smack his lips. "I met you a long time ago, doing news in Chicago. Yours truly, Harry Ducharme, had a national audience then. I was headed to NPR. Everybody assumed that. I went to the Art Institute, met you in person."

Ducharme continued to talk about himself, and Wyman began to get irritated. But he was also embarrassed. He had no recollection of being interviewed at the Art Institute.

"Harry, I'm sorry, but are you sure it was me?"

"Right, right. No, no. It wasn't an interview. I was there on my own to see your exhibit. I had seen pictures of that painting before and I wanted to see the real thing. I got in the line, inched up for a half hour or so, and finally got in front, and damn, there she was. I would have stood there a long time but the guides kept the crowd moving."

Wyman was still confused. "Nobody knows who I am anymore. My fifteen minutes of fame are over. And you have no listeners. What are we doing here?"

Ducharme laughed, and Wyman could hear what sounded like a spoon being tapped on glass. "Exactly! That's the sixty-four-dollar question."

Dead air for almost thirty seconds.

"Harry, are you still there?"

"Sorry, sorry. Had to do some business. Back to us now. It was at that show. I walked away from the painting and then I saw you sitting on a bench. That painting and your picture had been in the *Tribune*, but I think I'm the only person who recognized you, so I plop down next to you and start asking questions. Just wanted you to tell me about the painting."

"Harry, I really do apologize, but I do not remember that."

"No problem, you were distracted."

"Distracted?"

"You were staring at some woman across the room."

Wyman suddenly remembered the moment, the bench, Harry beside him, the line of people inching toward his painting, and Alice watching the crowd as he watched her.

"But we're back to my original question. Why did you call me?"

"I want you to paint a woman's portrait for me. Her name is Nora. I'm not even sure she would sit for you, but I really need for you to paint her."

"Harry, I don't paint anymore."

"Pete, you're lying. Sorry to be so blunt. Unless your two hands are crippled, you are still painting. Writers write, painters paint."

"I'm not for hire."

"Then do it for free."

"Harry, this makes no sense. I said no. And why are you calling me at one in the morning to ask this question? And why on-air?"

"Because I don't exist any other time or any other place."

Wyman began to wonder if he was actually awake.

"Harry . . ."

"Do you remember what I asked you about that woman? I asked you who she was, you being so fixed on her, and you told me that it was her. It was Alice. So, I looked again but she was gone, and I was thinking that my daily four ounces was tricking me. That woman I saw and the Alice in the painting were not the same person. You remember that?

"Yes."

"Pete, I thought about that a lot, almost like I knew a secret about you, but you disappeared a few years later, and I had to call a lot of old reporter friends of mine to finally find you again. And here we are. I need you to paint Nora's picture before she's gone. I want my own *Alice*."

"She is that important to you?"

"Pete, you understand. I know you do."

"You will never sell it, right?" He regretted saying it as soon as it came out of his mouth. "I mean, you will not show it to anyone else. Can she exist just for your eyes only? If you can do that, your friend will be my last portrait."

Harry had asked Wyman what happened to the *Alice* portrait. It had been exhibited around the country, but then it had disappeared.

"I assume you have it somewhere, right?"

"No, Harry. My studio burned years ago. Everything is gone. I did a lot of other portraits for hire after that, made more than I ever had up to then. And then I stopped painting for anybody but myself. I look forward to meeting your friend. Perhaps I'll see what you see. And I look forward to meeting you too."

Harry never called back.

Eventually, Savannah was too full of ghosts, so Wyman sold his world, all except his art work, which he put in a private studio. He set the thermostat and told the landlord he would be back soon. He paid a year's inflated rent in advance. And then he went looking for a place to . . .? Not to die. Just to disappear? He left no forwarding address because he had none. *Just put the mail on the table*, he told the landlord. He tossed his cell phone and let the contract lapse. He had a debit card and money in the bank. He had everything he needed for a road trip, except a destination. He headed south on I-95. Six hours later he saw a sign that advertised St. Augustine as *The Oldest City in America*, and that seemed like the right place to stop. *Why not start again from the very beginning?*

He exited at State Road 16, headed east, and was almost in St. Augustine when he saw Harry's Curb Mart. The name began ringing bells for him. Across the front of the store, from one corner of the building to the other, was a sign made of yellowing plastic letters. *Through these doors walk the finest people in the world: Our customers.*

Wyman walked through the sliding glass doors and headed for the blond cashier. She was obviously a smoker, a hazy odor of tobacco on her clothes, and her teeth showed a lifetime of coffee and cigarettes. She was hardly young, but she had full lips and a firmly round figure, and, when she smiled at him, it was sincere, and that smile made her teeth seem whiter. He looked at her name tag, fascinated by how it seemed to rise as she took a deep breath. Polly Jackson. He had never known anybody named Polly in his entire life.

"I'm looking for a man named Harry. He was on the radio here a few years ago. Wanted me to paint a picture for him, but I lost contact. You got any idea who I am looking for?"

Polly took a drag on her cigarette and looked around the store before answering him with a soft tremble in her voice.

"Harry Ducharme was his name, but he's dead. Harry's dead."

Wyman was not prepared for the finality of that. A few minutes earlier, he had actually thought that the connection between Harry somebody and St. Augustine might mean that St. Augustine was the predestined spot for him after all these years.

"You know him? A friend?" she asked.

"No, no, just a call from a long time ago. He wanted me to paint a portrait of a woman."

"Do you mean Nora?"

Wyman was hearing bits and pieces of a conversation from his past.

"Yes, yes, that sounds right."

"Nora is dead too."

He thought he had left all his ghosts back in Savannah, but here he was again, reminded that he was still bumping into them. He stood at the counter, but he was out of questions. St. Augustine was no longer a destination. He was lost again.

Polly tilted her head and looked at him.

"You okay?"

Wyman shook his head. "Truth is, I'm looking for a place to settle down. For some reason, I thought this might be it. I'm a painter. Any room for a painter here?"

"Oh, lord, this town is full of painters, lots of galleries downtown. Big tourist draw."

"I'm not looking to sell anything. Just a place to paint. And I guess, to not even be seen."

"Mister, that makes no sense at all. And, excuse me, you wearing your pajamas during the day is not going to go unnoticed around here. But there is one place you might go look for, town north of Orlando, if it still exists. I heard stories about it for years and then it seems to have disappeared. Hasn't been in the news for decades. Ex-boyfriend of mine came from there and told me it was full of crazies. Which I thought was funny, since he turned out to be an asshole meth dealer."

"It doesn't exist?"

"Mister, all I know is what I heard. A town full of crazies, and for Florida that's saying a lot. You want to disappear, you go to Knightville."

BOOK TWO:
DOORS CLOSE,
AND OPEN

2016:
NORTON GETS AN OFFER

Norton had never trusted lawyers, even those he hired. Were they born to be lawyers? Something genetic? In the entire Knight lineage, he was told by his own father, there had never been a lawyer. All other professions were permitted, even preachers. Market profiteering was admirable. Teaching was noble. Law enforcement was necessary, but lawyers?

"That's a lot of money, Mr. Knight, but, if you want more, I suppose we can go back to our clients and see how far they're willing to go."

The tall lawyer, who looked like a television lawyer, leaned back in his chair and waited. The other lawyer, overweight and balding, whose presence for an hour had been merely physical and not verbal, leaned forward. Norton expected him to finally speak, but all he did was slowly rock back and forth in his chair. Norton waited. The lawyers waited.

Norton had been feeling ill for weeks. His urine was dark. His back ached him into insomnia almost every night. He had an appointment with his doctor after meeting with these lawyers. He did not like doctors, but not as much as he disliked lawyers. The doctor he had been seeing for forty years had died a year ago. Norton was handed down to the new doctor who had bought the clinic, a doctor not much older than his son Sonny. As he sat across from the Orlando lawyers, Norton had a thought: *I should have bought the clinic myself.*

"Norton, nobody lives forever." The balding lawyer finally spoke.

"I'm not sure of your meaning."

"I mean that we are offering you twenty million dollars for ten thousand acres of land. I've looked at your books. We are offering you more now than you will clear in the next ten years. You're not a young man."

Norton admired his blunt self-assurance.

"So, take this deal and relax. Start a charity, a foundation, do good with the cash. Make your heirs weep at your death and thank you for their inheritance. Land prices are at an all-time high now. *This* is the time to sell."

The balding lawyer's blunt self-assurance met Norton's blunt self-assurance.

"I'm not sure which books you've been looking at. My tax records? My land appraisals? And the only argument you have is that I'll have more money to spend? Like I am some cartoon figure who bathes in gold coins? But you . . . your clients . . . want my land, my family's land? For what? To cut timber, grow limes and oranges, raise cattle? As my family has done for over a century. Or perhaps you want to grow concrete streets and shopping centers and houses for sad souls trying to escape Orlando or their jobs of pandering to pasty-skinned tourists at that Disney whorehouse? I'm not even sure why you called me. You obviously haven't read the right books about me."

The television lawyer tried to interrupt. "Like I said, we can talk to . . ."

"You can talk to God for all I care. One of my ancestors once had a direct line to him. His bones are somewhere on the land I own. Other bones too. This land . . ."

"Norton, you're bleeding. Out of your mouth. Should we call someone?"

The balding lawyer stood and was about to come around the table, but Norton waved him off. "No, thank you. And please excuse my outburst. The blood is . . . I have some gum problems, seeing my dentist later. My apologies. I should have been more forthright with you when you called. I fear I have wasted your time."

"No, no," the balding lawyer almost smiled. "Our clients will get the bill for our time. And you have our number, in case your interest . . . or circumstances . . . change."

As the two men drove back to Orlando, the television lawyer was disappointed. "Do you think he knew we were lowballing him?"

The balding lawyer was driving, and he kept his eyes straight ahead as he said, "No, he wasn't interested in the money. I've had a few like that in the past. At some point, money just stops making you happy, usually when you have too much. I should have figured that out before we called him. My mistake."

"You got a Plan B?"

"Folks back in Orlando can wait a few more months. But, as I recall, Norton has a son. Let me see what I can find out about him."

An hour after talking to his doctor, two hours after talking to the Orlando lawyers, Norton went to his ancestors' church. He did not go for solace, nor for guidance. He went to think. Knight seldom sought the advice of other men, but he often sought solitude. In the past few years, he had found it more and more difficult to stay in his own house and think. Even before the young doctor told him that he was a dying man, he had been downsizing his life. Sonny Knight had moved to the other side of town decades earlier, a few miles that might as well have been an ocean. Norton was left alone. His house was full of the same furniture that Norton himself had grown up with. The house itself was immaculate, the beneficiary of wealthy maintenance. But its interior domain had been shrinking over time. A room would be arranged as if for a real estate viewing, and then he would shut the door and never enter again. His domestic existence was confined to his upstairs bedroom and study, and the kitchen downstairs. Three rooms out of fourteen. Even his bedroom was nearing extinction since he started sleeping on the couch in his study. Only his closet and the adjoining bathroom served a purpose anymore.

Walking out of his doctor's office, Norton walked out of himself. That office was fifteen minutes walking distance back to his house, but he did not recall the act of returning to the house his great grandfather had built. He might have been thinking all that time, but those thoughts were erased when he opened his front door. The house seemed huge to him. He passed the dining room, went through the kitchen, and back into a foyer that had once hosted a reception for Governor LeRoy Collins, who shook Norton's hand, a gesture that required him to bend down to make eye contact with the boy Norton, the future Knight heir.

He wanted to go up to his study, but the first step of the stairs stopped him. He put his right foot on it, but then paused and pushed his weight down on that foot, as if testing to see if the step would support him. He looked up those stairs and suddenly felt nauseous. He went quickly back into the kitchen and retched in the sink, splattering yellowish bile across the counter, and then he settled into a chair at the breakfast table. He needed to go to his study and find his Will, but the energy for a simple ascension up the stairs was nowhere inside him.

The doctor had assured him that his diagnosis was not an immediate death sentence. Treatments were being perfected, and time could be extended. Months for sure, and years were possible. Still, the doctor had suggested: *You should make some arrangements. You know, bring your family together.* Norton had stared at the doctor, realizing that this had only been the second time that he had seen him. His old doctor would have never made that suggestion. His old doctor was as close to a friend as Norton had had. His old doctor had been the closest thing to a priest as Norton would ever know. His old doctor knew more Knight history than anybody else in town who was not a Knight. His old doctor was gone.

Arrangements?

Two hours earlier, Norton had been offered twenty million dollars for land he had inherited and that he had assumed would be his forever. But forever was suddenly closer than expected. He went back to the stairway and looked up. He needed to change clothes, from stained white to fresh white. Top of the stairs, he looked at a hallway of closed doors. *Arrangements*? Everything had to go, all the sealed rooms had to be emptied. Every chair that a Knight bottom had strained, every bed in which a Knight had slept and dreamed, even the bed in which his own father had died, it all had to go. Eventually, the books in his study, the pictures on the walls, the memorabilia of his years away from Knightville, had to go.

Refreshed, re-dressed, Norton was about to leave when the phone rang. It was his hardware store manager.

"Mister Knight, that man I told you about, the weird fellow in the pajamas who buys the paint stuff, he's due to be here in a couple of hours, called to let me know he was running late. You said you wanted me to let you know when he might be back."

"Yes, yes, I remember. Thank you. I will do my best to be there. I'm going to church now, but two hours should not be a problem."

A few minutes later, the hardware manager called his wife and told her that Norton Knight was getting even more strange.

"He said he was going to church. Everybody knows that man hasn't seen the inside of a church since his wife died."

Norton was exhausted. He knew he had been foolish to come to this spot on this muggy day. He would have to wash and change clothes again when he got back to his house. But he had come with a purpose. He found the iron pole he had staked into the ground a lifetime ago. The pole had a small tin sign at the top, lashed to it with crisscrossing wires. His back to it, he looked east and paced off ten steps, a ritual observed only by him. He faced the pole and then knelt down to the verdant ground, knowing that his white trousers would be ruined by the stain. They could be replaced. He closed his eyes and just listened to the green heart around him. He had done it many times in the past. Today was different. But he still had to talk.

"I said I was going to church. I told my hardware man, but here I am and I realize that I have never referred to this place as a church before. The old church here is not mine. But I said I was going to church."

His confession was unanswered. No absolution offered.

"I do not know how many more times I can do this."

Except for trees swaying and birds cawing, silence.

"I am not well."

Silence.

"I have to go now. There is a man I want to meet, a stranger in town. I've heard about him for months, but he has escaped me. No time to spare now. But I will come back as much as I can. I suppose I should tell Jit, shouldn't I?"

Silence.

ARTIST MEETS MODEL

Peter Wyman had arrived in 2015 without any announcement. He was simply seen one day at the Knight Hardware Store, asking for a brand of portrait oil paint that the store manager had never heard of, much less stocked. Wyman gave the manager a list of supplies and asked him to order them, giving him a hundred dollars in cash as a down payment. The manager offered to have the materials delivered, but Wyman simply stared at him as if the offer was a trick. A week later, Wyman came back with a wheelbarrow and more cash. His reputation began. An elderly man wearing silk pajamas and a giant straw hat, pushing a wheelbarrow, ignoring anybody who happened to speak to him. An invisible man for six days a week, shopping or doing other odd errands on Mondays only. The store manager had once asked why he needed all the painting supplies, but Wyman ignored him, and then flummoxed the man by saying, "I'm not a painter. I'm a photographer."

If his initial weeks began his reputation, his continued presence provoked an accumulating compilation of rumors. Fact: he always paid cash. Fact: He came out only one day a week, almost always shortly after noon. Fact: He lived in a rented barn on the outskirts of town. Fact: He seldom spoke to anyone. Fact: When he did speak, it was obvious that he was not a Southerner. Fact: He had his hair cut every other month at Stan's Barber Shop. Stan would tell people that the pajama man seldom spoke but he always seemed to be listening intently to the conversations of the other men in the two-chair shop. It was through Stan that others found out the eccentric's name, or so they thought. They did not know it was a fake name.

Norton had been told about the mysterious stranger in town by the hardware store manager, who liked to tell himself and others that he knew about everyone and everything in town. Norton had rebuked him once, telling him that gossip was a petty and salacious pastime. The manager feared for his job and was appropriately contrite, but the real lesson he had learned was to not gossip around his boss, who was also the richest man in town. Still, something about the cash-only customer drew Norton to the store on a Monday afternoon, hours after having been offered enormous wealth, followed by the certainty of death. He sat on a bench outside the entrance, under a canopy ceiling fan that was merely pushing heat down rather than away, waiting for the mysterious and eccentric man in pajamas. It had never occurred to Knight in his adult life that anybody would consider him to be as eccentric as the mysterious stranger. If that stranger's pajamas were his signature identity, Norton's daily white suit had become equal fodder for "talk" over the years.

Norton watched him approach, his face partially hidden at first by the straw hat, and then the two men locked eyes. Wyman's pace slowed but did not cease. Norton spoke first.

"You must be the new photographer in town."

Wyman pushed up the brim of his hat.

"You must be Mister Knight."

Neither spoke, but Wyman stopped with one foot on the first step up to the wooden porch where Norton sat. He cocked his head to one side and asked, "Mind if I sit?" Norton scooted over to clear room for him. Inside the store, the manager was on the phone whispering to his wife about the scene outside.

"You're not a photographer, are you?"

Wyman did not respond.

"The materials you purchase, the oils, the brushes, the wood strips for frames, you are not a photographer."

"I paint like a photographer," Wyman said, looking straight ahead.

"I would like to see your work."

Wyman turned to Norton, his expression the outward sign of a question. "You *are* Mr. Knight, right?"

Knight nodded.

"I hear that you own this town."

Knight sighed. "More like this town owns me. But I do own the barn you live in."

A week later, Knight was admitted to Wyman's barn-studio. His first thought was also a profound regret: *There is nobody with whom I would share this moment.* Not that he *could* not. He had a family. He even knew people who considered themselves to be his friend. But he *would* not tell anyone. He would keep it to himself.

He had entered a world of the most beautiful women he had ever seen. On the walls, hanging from the rafters, women motionless and serene on canvas. Knight stood in the center of the room and everywhere he turned he saw a face or form that almost froze him in place, but the next portrait in line was its own force that pulled him away from where he stood and turned him ever so slightly to confront and yield to a new seduction. Portraits framed and unframed. Some merely sitting on the dirt floor and leaning against the wall. And more and more. Women with children. Women with horses. Women in front of mirrors, admiring their reflections. Women asleep. Women in mourning and women in ecstasy. It took a few minutes, but Knight realized. *Not a man anywhere. Not a man in any of these women's lives.*

Wyman had not spoken since Knight entered his world. The two men exchanged glances, but Knight kept turning and turning to absorb the women around him. The only sound was the low fatigued hum of three overworked air conditioners and the gasoline-powered generator outside.

And then Knight saw her.

"Oh my god," he whispered to himself. "I remember her."

At the far end of the barn was the *Alice* portrait. Knight walked toward it, but slower and slower with each step. A few feet away, he had an absurd thought. *Why do I feel like I should kneel?* He turned back to find Wyman, but he was gone. Knight scanned the world of women, only to hear a voice above him.

"Would you care for a drink?"

Wyman had ascended to a converted loft.

"You lied to everyone about you. The name you gave. That's not you. Give me time and I will remember it. I saw you in Chicago, at the Art Institute. Twenty years ago, right?"

"Closer to thirty."

"You were famous." Pointing back to the *Alice* painting, "She was famous. I can remember me and a hundred other people just staring at that face."

"Thank you, Mister Knight. That was a long time ago."

"Tell me your name. I knew it a long time ago. I wanted to buy that painting but it wasn't for sale. I offered a small fortune, but I was told that the artist would not sell."

"Peter Wyman. I am Peter Wyman."

"Pleased to meet you again, Mister Wyman."

Wyman raised his right hand, tilting his drink toward Knight to acknowledge the formal introduction.

"Any of these for sale?"

Wyman shook his head. "No, but if you see one you like, please accept it as a gift from me. They're not my best. I consider them practice, even though I did them after I sold my best."

"Truth is, I'm shedding my possessions, not adding to them. But I would like your permission to come back and study all these again."

Wyman shrugged. "I'm cursed in the reverse. I can't stop accumulating. My work, my memories, I can't shed anything."

"But I would ask another favor of you." Knight hesitated. "Would you paint my portrait?"

"You cannot afford me."

"I have more money than God, at least the God who looks over this town."

"You cannot afford me."

Knight kept looking up. "I'm a dying man, Mr. Wyman. I want you to show me what I look like before I die. For once, I want to see myself."

"The price you cannot afford is how I would render you. And, please, call me Peter."

"I'm dying."

"As we all are."

"Peter, all I want . . ."

"Is what I see."

Norton looked up at Wyman and thought, *He has a high opinion of himself. Are all artists so self-absorbed? But he is all I have.*

Arrangements were made. Wyman would bring his brushes and paints and a canvas to the largest house in Knightville. He did not question Knight about why the house was empty except for the book-lined room they would use for the sitting. The rest of the mansion was empty, as if vacated before demolition, devoid of furniture, devoid of life.

"It would be easier on you if you sat on a chair," he had suggested. "Even while sitting, posing can still be a tiring experience. And it is obvious that you have less energy than you did a week ago."

"No, no, I'll be fine. Let me stand by that window. If I tire, I can rest on the window seat. I have looked out that window for fifty years. I think that's how I want to be remembered."

Wyman studied the dying man. "I only have one rule."

"Just one?" Knight tried to joke. "I thought artists were supposed to be temperamental and finicky."

Wyman ignored him. "You do not see my work until it is finished. You do not make suggestions. You do not *own* it until I am finished."

Knight nodded.

"And I don't talk to you. Don't ask me questions. It has been my experience that my subjects soon forget I'm in the room. You should not be surprised to find yourself talking to yourself. I'm not your priest, your confessor, not even your audience, but you will still hear yourself talk."

"Will you ever talk about yourself? I have questions."

"Not here. This is your space."

Knight nodded again. "Shall we begin?"

Wyman pulled a camera out of his bag. "First, I want to take some pictures."

"Photos?"

"All my portraits began as photographs. I'll take a few dozen of you. All angles, lots of up-close shots, every blemish on your face, the dark spots on your hands. I'll study those throughout the process. Refresh my memory when we're not together. Fact is, all those paintings back in my barn began with a lot of pictures. I've got plastic containers full of pictures."

"Your work? Prose and poetry? Fact and fiction?"

Wyman smiled as he raised his camera and took his first picture of Knight. "Yep. Been my experience that most people prefer to be turned into a poem. Took me a few years, but I also realized that was where all the money was for me, turning prose into poetry."

"So, you have pictures of the real Alice?"

Wyman lowered his camera, slightly tilted his head, and looked directly at Knight. "A few more of you today, and then we can start the first session tomorrow. I'll look at all these tonight and know what to look for. I'll also need some pictures of the view from that window, to see what you are seeing."

Knight had a list of confessions. Foremost of all, he knew that he should confess to Jit Knight that he had spent his life knowing the answer to the one question that had haunted his cousin: What had happened to Sandy Chippen? Jit had been deserted, left with an infant daughter, by the woman he adored. Gone without a note, gone without a word, gone without a trace. Norton knew the answer.

Before he met Wyman, he had listened to his doctor tell him that he only had a few months to live, that pancreatic cancer was terminal, that he should put his affairs in order and gather his loved ones close to his heart. The doctor's suggestion that he might have years was, Norton knew, a lie meant to give false hope. Faced with months, not years, Norton had looked into his soul and understood that the only person he still cared about was Jit, the man who had won the heart of the only woman that he had ever loved.

After a month of progressing agony as he posed in front of the silent Wyman, Knight finally forced himself on the artist and began confessing.

"What's the worst thing somebody has confessed about themselves as they posed for you? Surely they ignored your vow of silence and forced you to pass judgment on them."

"Never."

"Never?"

"I'm not your priest, Norton. I told you that."

"But you know secrets, right?"

Wyman paused. "We're through for today. You need a few days off."

Knight was afraid that Wyman would not come back. The weeks of looking out that window, of listening to himself talk about his past in front of an artist who seemed oblivious, as if his life story would be words in the air that simply disappeared like dust swept up and put away.

"I want to tell you something about me, the worst thing I ever did."

Wyman did not speak. He did not look at Knight. He just cleaned his brushes and capped his tubes of paint.

"I need to tell you . . ."

Wyman stood and walked toward Knight.

"Need? I understand need. Tell me what you need to tell me."

Knight took in a deep breath, only to be reminded how painful that could be.

"I murdered somebody a long time ago, a woman. And nobody knows. I will die both unjudged and unpunished."

Wyman walked over to stand next to Knight, looking out the window to see what his subject had been looking at all those weeks.

"Here's *my* secret, Norton. In its own way, worse than yours. You murdered a woman. Me, I created a woman, one who should have never lived. We have a few more weeks. I might break one of my rules. I might *need* to tell you that story. I can tell you because I know that you will take it to your grave."

BLACK IS BACK

Jit heard the news but, as Abe Jones expected, he did not respond.

"Black is back. Killed some dogs up near the county line. Folks up there want to know when we're going to do something about it."

Jit nodded, but he did not make eye contact with his deputy.

"He's getting predictable. About once a month, seems to me."

Jit took a deep breath, and Jones thought he was about to answer but then he just exhaled and kept looking down at his desk.

"Sheriff?"

Jit finally spoke. "The dogs pinned up, or running wild?"

"It was the Twains. You know their dogs are roamers. Pretty much left to themselves to get fed."

"Then we ought to give Black a medal. Or put him on the payroll. He's doing our jobs. Besides, are they sure it was him? Did they see him? Lots of folks blame him for shit, but they never see him."

"Sam Twain said he saw a panther, said he knew it was him because of how black his fur was. Coal black, and Sam's biggest dog was in his mouth. Hard to miss that."

"Abe, Sam Twain is a lying sack of shit, we know that. Said he actually saw Black? *Nobody* has actually seen Black. There are no black panthers in Florida."

"Sheriff, so how come we all call him Black? Even you. Sam, my mama, everybody."

"Makes for a better story, I guess. Maybe it's the heat. Maybe it's just a big damn dog with a bad attitude. But, you're right. He's always been Black to me. So, I'm guessing that Sam went for his shotgun but Black was gone, right?"

"Yessir."

"Too bad. Black could have solved *that* problem for us too."

"So, Sheriff, what should I tell him?"

"Tell him the usual. We'll contact the DNR and let them go looking for Black again. But you might also suggest to Sam that you heard a rumor that Black likes chicken best of all, especially at night, so Sam should whack some of his hens and go looking for Black some night. Take his sons with him. They can tree Black and become national heroes. Of course, Black might have other plans too."

"Sheriff . . ."

"Yep, I know. In my dreams."

"One more thing. Mama invited me to dinner tonight. That okay with you?"

"Abe, you really need to ask?"

"Just being polite, like I was taught."

Jit smiled and looked up at his deputy. "She did good by you, but ain't it time you had a wife to do dinner for you?"

"*You* telling *me* to get a wife? Sheriff, if it weren't for my mama you would have starved years ago. And, excuse me, but seems like you get some credit for my upbringing too. I spent as much time at your place as I did at home."

"Yes, that's true. And you're still just as skinny, but I suppose age will take care of that. Take a good look at me, Abe, I am your future."

"I'm gonna be an old fat white guy?"

"Well, old and fat probably." Knight touched his own cheek, "And you'll always be kin to Black, scaring all the white folks."

"Black man with a badge and a gun, I could have done worse. Lord knows, Mama thanks you every day."

Knight almost laughed. "Me and Sandra owe your mama a lot too, for sure."

"You know that you might have an opponent this year, right?"

Jit looked up at Abe Jones, shrugged, and then went back to reading his newspaper.

"You hear me, Sheriff?"

Jit had been reading the regular Friday column by the paper's editor, another plea for the state legislature to stop cozying up with the Sugar Lobby and start protecting the Everglades before it was too late.

"You read Sandra's column today, Abe?"

"She's tilting at windmills again." Jones always read the *Knightville Times* editorial every Friday before he talked to the Sheriff because his boss always asked him if he had. "I mean no disrespect, you know that. But your daughter hasn't been on the winning side of an issue in a long time."

"That might be true, but she did get Norton to start phasing out his cattle business," Jit said. "Some sort of environmental mumbo jumbo."

"Excuse me?" Jones was skeptical. "How come nobody seems to know this except you? Seems mighty hard to keep something like that a secret."

"That might be so, but I suspect that Sandra knows a lot more about her boss than the rest of us do."

"Well, I just hope she plans on endorsing you this coming Fall. I'd like to keep my own job. As for her knowing Norton's secrets, I'm guessing that she picked that up from you."

"Picked up what?"

"Collecting information to be used later."

"I suppose so. Not a bad habit for you to develop too. Now, tell me again, endorse me for what?"

"Dammit, Sheriff, you keep forgetting shit and I might have to run against you myself. This is serious business. Those damn full-mooners are coming for you and most of the county board."

Jit folded his newspaper and set it on the corner of his desk, motioning for Jones to sit down. "Speak to me."

"Bad enough the Republicans screwed my man Barack around for all that time, and now they have some sort of television clown running for President himself. Tea Party wacks on fire. Taking over a lot of low-hanging political fruit here too."

"Abe, that has nothing to do with me."

"Tell that to the guy about to run against you. This is your future opponent."

Jones handed the brochure to Jit and waited for a reaction.

"He's a Republican," was all that Jit said, as if that settled all questions. He had run as a Democrat for forty years.

223

"Sheriff, in case you haven't noticed, this town, this county, and this state have become Republican while you've been wearing the same uniform you bought a decade ago. You probably still think that Jeb Bush is governor."

"Nope, I know who the governor is . . . the insurance crook, right?"

"Sheriff, please don't tell me that you pull this dumb-ass routine with anybody else."

"Nope, just you and Sandra because I know it drives both of you crazy. Everybody else thinks I might be losing a few steps. You and Sandra think I'm losing a few marbles."

"Just don't lose the damn election. I'd miss you."

After Jones left, Jit read the brochure again. He had never worried about getting re-elected. It was not a prize position, did not pay all that much, and, he told himself: *It ain't exactly like I've been doing a bad job.*

Jit slid the brochure into his top desk drawer, wondering, *What the hell is the Constitutional Sheriffs and Peace Officers Association?* He made himself a note to call his daughter. She would know whatever he needed to know.

March 5, 2016

"You know, we have a divided country, folks. We have a terrible president who happens to be African-American. There has never been a greater division than just about what we have right now. The hatred, the animosity. I will bring people together. You watch." Trump said. (Jeremy Diamond and Eugene Scott, CNN.)

It was not that far away, not much more than an hour. Sandra had never been to the arena, but she was familiar with the UCF campus. She had done guest lectures for the journalism/communications department. The rallies were always national news. She was the editor of a newspaper. She was supposed to be a professional journalist, but she would not go even though Jerry Guinta teased her about going where "the news was newsing."

She resisted, but he persisted. "Sandra, the primary is ten days away. You do intend to endorse somebody, right?"

"Jerry, I don't need to go to a car wreck to know that I hate drunk drivers. And I don't need to go see him to know that I'll never endorse him."

"Then let's go for the entertainment value. Admit it, politics in this town would make a coma look exciting. You gotta give him credit for stirring up some interest in the process."

"Jerry, you cannot be serious. Stirring up interest in the process? Is that the same as debasing the process?"

Sandra raised a finger, shushing him before he responded. "I'll go. But I'm not giving that man a line of ink in the paper."

Sandra had grown up as a Democrat. Until she became editor of the *Knightville Times,* she just assumed that most people in town were Democrats. Her father was a Democrat, as were all the county board members. They always won. She first voted in 1996, holding her nose to vote for Bill Clinton. Asked to explain her disdain for a man and then voting for him, she would have had a quick answer, "Because the Republicans are going crazy." Clinton had lost the popular vote in Florida in 1992, and Sandra told her friends that she would have voted for Ross Perot that year if she had been eighteen. The difference between 1992 and 1996? Bob and Libby Dole seemed benign enough. Surely, they were okay? Clinton was still Clinton. Sandra would drop a name, and then have to take a half hour explaining: Pat Buchanan.

Jerry Guinta had been her first audience, and when she was finished, he simply said, "You know, you could make the same case against Reagan in 1980."

"Reagan was a tool, Jerry. An actor. He didn't believe all that bullshit. He was old-school Republican, picking up some stuff from Nixon too. Buchanan was different. He actually believed all that bullshit about immigrants and welfare and abortion and homos coming for your sons and God hating atheists like me. And it was obvious to me that the Republicans were itching for more Buchanans. The real deal. Better a philandering Democrat than any Republican was my goal that year."

Jerry and Sandra would discuss politics and seldom disagree. But she soon learned that not everyone else in town was as sympatico. That realization led her to stop talking about politics with almost everyone else in town. She knew more and more; understood, she thought, more and more, but said less and less. Any of the few newcomers to town after 2001 would read the paper and would never guess what the editor's personal politics were. The 2000 campaign had been the turning point. Sandra's public anger toward Jeb Bush and Katherine Harris had not been subtle. She wasn't too fond of Ralph Nader, Cubans in Miami, and the Supreme Court either. Circulation dropped 10 percent. She had to get an unlisted home phone number. In that time, she suspected that her father had made some personal appearances at a few houses and politely told a few people that it would be in their best interest if they never contacted his daughter ever again. She never knew that Norton Knight had also made a few private phone calls.

Jerry was her confidant, her political ally, and he had been the essential opinion that had convinced her to take Norton's offer years earlier. He would never tell her, but he had come to regret that encouragement. He wished that she had not come back to Knightville. He wanted to tell her that she was too smart for Knightville, too talented, and that she was wasting her life there. But he also knew that if she left town now, he would never find anyone else like her, and that he would be incredibly lonely.

"We will build the wall, don't worry. We will build the wall. And who's going to pay for the wall?"

"Mexico!" the crowd shouted.

"Who?"

"Mexico!" the crowd shouted.

"You better believe it."

From the parking lot to the arena, Sandra and Jerry began as ironic outsiders to the crowd around them. They shared a *Can you believe these people?* attitude that wilted the closer they got to the front gates. Sandra was soon thinking: *Who are these people?* Snake lines of red hats and American flag clothing accessories. But, energy. Buoyant and contagious energy. She and Jerry had gone to a Springsteen concert years earlier. She could imagine a lot of these same people being there too, younger and slimmer, and less well-armed, but antsy to get in and rock to the music.

Jerry would nudge her every time he saw what he called another "money shot." Up ahead of them was a man in neck-to-ankle white spandex, with black lines drawn to represent bricks. Across his chest in big letters: *Mexico Will Pay*. He kept walking back and forth in front of a CNN reporter, with camera crew, who was trying to interview a husband and wife brandishing handcuffs meant for Hillary.

"You want me to get some pictures? You know you do. How about you with that Tammy Faye Bakker look-alike over there, the one with the Dolly Parton boobs?"

"Jerry, I do not want any proof that I was anywhere near all this today."

"All I know for sure? America is a great country."

Their first mistake had been to go straight to the press table, get their credentials checked and plastic ID tags issued, and head for the enclosed press area. Even before the main event, they had become part of the "Fake News." When the main event started, and Trump began his act, Jerry had to raise his voice so she could hear, "Now I know how Custer felt."

In two hours, Mexico had paid for the Wall a dozen times, a fist fight had broken out behind the stage, Hillary had been sent to Leavenworth, a swamp had been drained, and a woman had fainted in the front row as Trump was riffing on Chris Christie and Marco Rubio. Without missing a beat, he said, "We love people who faint. Are you okay, darling? Those are the kind of people we love. She's been here seven hours. Get better. We love you." On stage behind him, the spandex wall man was holding a "Veterans for Trump" sign.

Ten thousand voters became part of the performance. In spite of herself, Sandra began writing a story, connecting Trump and P. T. Barnum and Elmer Gantry and Ron Popeil and Billy Sunday and Huey Long. She knew she would never publish it, but she had to put it into words. But then came The Pledge.

"Let's do a pledge. Who likes me in this room? I've never done this before. Can I have a pledge? A swearing? Raise your right hand. Repeat after me: I do solemnly swear that I, no matter how I feel, no matter what the conditions, if there are hurricanes or whatever, will vote on or before the 12th for Donald J. Trump for President . . . Now I know. Don't forget you all raised your hands. You swore. Bad things happen if you don't live up to what you just did."

She had looked at Jerry, wondering if he was seeing what she was seeing. The gesture was simple enough. Thousands of raised right arms pointing at Trump.

Jerry said what she was thinking. "All that's missing are the brown shirts."

Sandra nodded, but she kept writing a story in her head, but the story ended as she and Jerry were finally leaving the arena. They had weathered the middle fingers pointed at them all night long. Jerry had resisted the visceral urge to punch a woman who had spit on his shoes as she screamed, "You fake fuckers." Sandra had looked the other way when a bearded MAGA had grabbed his crotch and yelled at her, "Print this, bitch!"

Just when she thought she had finished the gauntlet, she heard her name. A voice in the crowd, a familiar voice.

"Sandra, Sandra! Over here. Over here!"

He was waving at her with one hand, giving her a thumbs-up gesture with the other. Sandra froze. It was Chuck Hubbard, the hardware store manager from Knightville. He was being pushed along by a surging crowd headed for the exit, but he kept shouting at her.

"Great to see you. Great to see you."

Then he was gone in a blur of red.

Jerry had seen him too. "Looks like you've been busted. Chuck will be telling everybody in town about seeing you."

Sandra stopped writing the story in her head. She did not want to connect Trump with her hometown. But another variation of that story became unavoidable just as she and Jerry left the arena.

Another voice called her name, an unfamiliar but pleasantly baritone voice.

"Sandra Knight, aren't you Sandra Knight?"

He was tall and handsome in the way that a handsome young man ages into a handsome older man. Lean in body, with closely trimmed gray hair, but with a squint in his eyes that could not be explained away by blaming the glare of the sun.

He walked toward her with his hand extended.

"I'm Frank Morris. I had planned on calling you soon anyway, but seeing you here today . . . well, it seemed like I ought to go ahead and introduce myself. I'd like to come by and talk to you about the race this Fall."

She was confused. He was talking as if they had a history of prior conversations, as if she already knew why he wanted to talk to her.

"I'm sorry, Mister Morris. I'm not sure what you mean."

"I'm running for sheriff this Fall."

"Okay, but I'm still confused. Sheriff where?"

"I'm running against your father."

They drove back to Knightville in almost total silence. Jerry tried to make a joke, but failed. Sandra was not in a mood for humor. "I feel like somebody told me that I had been adopted. That my entire life has been a lie."

"Sandra, you can explain that later. The only thing I know for sure is that we're going to have our first female President in a few months."

"I'm not as sure as you, Jerry. All I know is that I wish she wasn't the one."

"Sandra, you're just a sore loser because your man Bernie got shafted by the party."

"At least he believed in something other than himself."

"Right, right, no argument from me, even though, you remember, he's not really a Democrat. All in all, I'm just glad you aren't wearing your *Feel the Bern* button tonight."

Sonny Knight was not convinced that Angel was right about him, but he was flattered that she, unlike his father, actually had high hopes for him. They were coming back from Orlando, both still buzzing from the pre-rally drugs and the post-rally adrenaline.

"You ever think about that?"

Sonny was letting Angel drive his new Lincoln. She tended to speed, especially when Sonny put his hand between her legs.

"I think about this a lot," he said, pressing firmly against her.

"Sonny honey, you'll be thinking about *that* for the rest of your life, but I'm talking about the other 'P' word."

"Are you about to start a serious conversation? Maybe now is not the time?"

In the back seat, another couple was having sex, seemingly oblivious to their front-seat chauffeurs. Angel gently lifted Sonny's hand from between her legs, looked in the rearview mirror to make eye contact with the backseat lover who was being straddled by his partner. He was looking over her shoulder to see Angel's eyes focused on his, and then Angel jerked the wheel hard to the right, swerving from the outside lane to the inside, and throwing the immediately disconnected lovers up against the left passenger door.

"Goddam it, Angel!" Sonny and the crumpled lovers yelled in unison.

"Oops, sorry. Thought I saw a deer."

The woman in the back seat started laughing. "Hell, for a second there I thought Jack here was finally giving me the Big-O. Knocking me into outer space."

Jack was not amused. "You damn near broke my dick, Angel."

It was Sonny's turn to laugh. "Angel did that to you last week, as I recall."

Angel began humming, winking at Sonny. The woman in the back started moaning.

"Angel, I think you need to pull off to the side of the road," the woman said.

"Next rest stop?"

"No time."

Angel quickly checked the rearview mirror, put her foot on the brake, and went from right lane to right shoulder to right grassy slope in five seconds and slid to a stop. A minute later, she was holding the retching woman's shoulders as a night's worth of entertainment spewed out of her mouth. Jack and Sonny were gentlemen, looking in the other direction. Her stomach emptied, the woman's knees started to buckle, but Angel held her up with a bear hug, smearing her own clothing with the remnants of puke and foamy spit that had been on the woman's blouse. Sonny turned and marveled again at the woman he loved. Angel had nudged the woman back to the side of the Lincoln, letting her lean back against it, but Angel still held on to her, as if embracing, as if slow dancing, as if seducing, and she kept whispering in the woman's ear that everything would be fine, that she would not let her fall, that Angel would take care of her. Sonny had seen variations of the scene many times in the years he had known her, variations of her life as an ER nurse before she was a stripper.

Cars were speeding by, honking and blinking their lights. Angel told Sonny to get her a bottle of water from the trunk and open the bag of spare clothes she kept there. She then washed the woman's face and took off her soiled blouse and dressed her in one of her own. Then she started issuing orders.

"I'll get in the back with . . . Jesus, I forgot her name."

"Stella," Jack offered. "You know, I told you about her last week, wanted her to get in the group."

"Right, right, now I remember. Stella by Starlight."

Jack and Sonny looked at each other, processing another of Angel's obscure allusions.

"Forget it. We'll sort it all out later. Right now, you two get in the front. I'll take care of Starlight in the back, but we need to get off this highway soon or some damn Dudley Patrolman is going to stop and see if we need any help, and his help is going to get us hauled into court."

Safely back on the road, nobody spoke. Angel was sitting behind Sonny, with Stella's head resting in her lap as she held a damp cloth on her forehead. Jack was soon asleep up front, and Angel leaned forward to pat Sonny on the shoulder.

"Things settle down, I still want to talk to you about an idea of mine."

"That other P-word? You wanna give me a hint?"

"Not now, just a thought. I want you to think about how you felt tonight at that rally. I could see it. You were happy, Sonny, you were having a good time. But you kept looking around too, looking at the crowd more than you did that orange pecker up front."

"Angel, I had a great time. It was a great show, but I still don't understand where you're going with this."

"Sonny, how many times have I told you that I'm the perfect woman for you?"

"Not counting the times in bed?"

She reached up and pinched his ear.

"I'm the perfect woman for you because I know what you want even when you don't."

"Angel, it was just a shit-show rally. That man is an idiot and he's going to get slaughtered in the Fall. But you're right, I had a great time."

"He might be an idiot, but a channeling idiot savant in some ways. That crowd was him, Sonny."

"Where are you going with all this?"

"I watched you, man of my dreams. That idiot had what you wanted. He had that crowd and they loved him."

"Angel?"

"You need your own crowd, Sonny."

"Angel, that man's crowd won't help in the Fall. That crowd is just him jerking himself off. He's a bad joke and a loser. Is that what you're saying about me?"

"But it was you who wanted to go, right? You say he's an idiot now, but you made all the arrangements to get us there. I think you let it slip even if you didn't know it. You said you wanted to see the crowd too. It was you who stood next to me while everybody else was yelling *lock her up,* but you were doing a three-sixty like you were trying to memorize every damn face in that crowd. You weren't listening to him, Sonny. You were listening to the crowd."

"Angel, sometimes you scare me. Are you saying that I should get into politics? Have you forgotten who we are, how we live?"

"I'm saying that right now, this year, none of that shit makes a difference. Now keep your eye on the road and get us home."

Confessions and History

Wyman stood next to Norton after an afternoon of more sketching and only a little painting, finally trading secrets with his dying model. The two men were looking out the window at Knight's estate. Wyman had just told him most of the story about Sarah and Alice.

"I was asked to write my memoir a long time ago. I didn't do it then. It was too soon. But I'd like to write a book now. Just about Sarah. About her life before she met me."

"She does sound . . ." Knight wanted a precise word. "Unique?"

Wyman nodded, his eyes fixed on a citrus field in the far distance. "That's it. Of all the people I've ever known, and I include you and me in that bunch, as much as we think we are singular, only she was truly unique. The biggest mistake of my life was not figuring that out until it was too late."

"She is gone now?"

"Decades ago. Dead."

"I am truly sorry. I would have liked to meet her."

"She killed herself."

The two men kept looking out the window.

"Arcadia?"

Wyman had been silent for most of the morning. He was having trouble reconciling what was in front of him, a frail man dressed in white, with the image that was forming in his own eye and mind. The *essence* he wanted to paint was not in front of him even though it could only be inspired by Knight's actual presence. Something was missing. The night before, back at his barn studio and looking at the photographs he had collected of his subject, he had been frustrated. He could not tell Knight about his dilemma because he did not want him to pose as anything other than what he was. This morning, Wyman had been looking at his canvas intently while Knight talked about his family history, but, even after weeks, he did not yet see Norton on the canvas. There was an outline of a man, standing next to a red chair, looking out a window, but that man was not yet Norton Knight.

"You said he named his town Arcadia. What happened to it?"

Knight cleared his throat and turned back toward Wyman.

"Oh, we're in it. After he died, his widow renamed the town after him, and then she waited a respectable few years before packing up her three sons and moving back to her family in Pennsylvania."

"And this was the house that he built for her?"

"Minus most of the furniture, but it probably still has the original palmetto bugs and termites. In the beginning it was isolated away from the rest of the sticks and stones that housed everyone else, but the town grew and finally became our neighbors."

"You grew up here? And your own son too?"

"Yes, this was my home."

Wyman looked at the canvas. A flicker of Knight appeared and then disappeared. But he now knew it was there, somewhere, and it would come back.

"What will become of this house after you die?"

Knight was back to staring out the window. He ignored the question and picked up on his family history where he had left off a few minutes earlier.

"Of Stephen's three sons who went back north, only one returned. That was my grandfather. I often wonder how different this place would have been if it had merely been named after my family rather than ruled by it. Then again, I cannot imagine myself in Pennsylvania."

Wyman stifled a laugh. For some reason, he thought Knight was attempting irony. But he quickly realized that he had never heard Knight himself laugh about anything.

"Can I ask you a question?" Knight said, shifting the topic.

"Of course."

"I am sure you have read many books, many novels. Correct?"

"Yes, but, no, I didn't learn to paint by reading a book."

"Oh, I am sure that is true, but I wonder something. I wonder . . . my university professors, the literature professors, would often relate a book back to its author, showing how the author himself was in the story, the author's life the source for all his work, but disguised. Is that true about painters too? Are you in your paintings?"

Wyman put down his brush, but he did not answer. He looked over at Knight, expecting to meet his gaze, but his model was staring out the window. He had asked the question without looking in Wyman's direction.

Wyman stood and walked over to stand next to the seated Knight, both men looking out the window. Neither spoke for a minute, until

Wyman said, "It's a fair question. Ask me again later. I want to think about it."

Knight started to stand but it was quickly obvious that he was having trouble, so Wyman grasped his arm to help him rise.

"Can we stop for today?"

"Absolutely. I can come again tomorrow. After all, you're my only project."

Wyman helped him over to the faded couch. An afternoon nap was an inviolable ritual for Knight. Soon sitting upright on the edge of the couch, he swept his hand around the room.

"Those books on that shelf there, all I have left. All I told you about Stephen Knight, in those journals. You should touch them. Bound leather covers. He wrote that he had killed the rabbits himself, skinning them and then tanning with the bark from mimosa and quebracho trees. He kept detailed accounts. He was very proud of how soft they were when he used them as the cover for his journals. He wrote with great fascination about himself. And his land. He wrote every day. His sons and their sons, never."

"And you? Surely you wrote about your own life. I would be surprised if you didn't."

"Up until my wife died, almost every day. After that, I stopped."

"Are those journals on those shelves too?"

"No, they're gone too. A fit of pique, years ago, erasing myself. I regret it now. So, I suppose you are all I have left, Peter."

"Do I have your permission to read Stephen's journals?"

"If you wish. I have made arrangements with the state archives in Tallahassee to receive them after I die. I will tell my attorney to let you have access to them before they are boxed up and sent away, but if you are looking for any insight about me you won't find it there. God knows, I have tried to see the connection, but it is not there. Whatever was his essence, it died with him. You can do what I have done many times. You can go to the cemetery and find the Knight family plots. His is the oldest marker there. You can talk to the stone. Trust me, it will not answer."

Norton would not reveal to Wyman his greatest disappointment in his ancestor's journals. He wanted to know if Stephen Knight ever thought about his own death. In the darkest moments of his life, after his wife died, Norton thought about ending his own. He had read the journals again. Stephen Knight would contemplate the mysteries of the world around him, marvel at a jungle that seemed to pulsate with life, and record precise details of plants and animals, but he never contemplated the possibility that the world around him would continue to exist even if he did not. He had never had an ill day in his life.

"He died young, you said. Is that right?"

"His last entry. He was going to survey the remains of his uncle's church. He wanted to finish the construction. Unlike the rest of his family, he seemed to appreciate that crazy uncle. Stephen was hardly a believer, but he wrote a wonderful line. You can find it on the last page. *I do not believe in God, but I do believe in worship.*"

Wyman was standing over Norton, who had fully reclined on the couch, his eyes closed.

"And then?"

"And then they found his body the next day. Mangled and swollen, but still recognizable. Probably a panther. Others said they had seen bears around there too. They found his shotgun next to him, empty. For almost a hundred years, nobody ever went near that church again. Not until me and Jit. I was there a few weeks ago. Probably my last time."

"Go to sleep, Norton. I'll be back tomorrow."

As he was about to leave the room, Wyman saw something he had not noticed before, an oversight which puzzled him because he had always prided himself on taking note of all the small details in his own art environment, wherever it was. Had the wooden box always been in the room? Polished cherry wood, on a small table, placed on a red velvet cloth. He looked back at the sleeping Knight and then stepped over to the box, lifting the lid as softly as he could. Inside was a huge black book, wrapped in waxy paper.

"It belonged to my deranged ancient uncle. His big Bible."

Wyman did not turn around at the sound of Knight's voice. He simply froze, as if lack of motion would make him invisible.

"I'm not in it."

Wyman touched the waxy paper but did not turn around.

"Neither are you."

Knight closed his eyes and became silent again. Wyman walked back to the window for one last look. He knew then that he wanted one more photograph to finish his Norton Knight portfolio. He just needed somebody to take him into the woods. Knight was coming into focus, but different than the man Wyman thought he had been painting.

The next day, Knight was a different man, almost as if a miracle cure for death had been found. He asked if he could stand rather than sit, and he kept offering Wyman coffee that he had brewed right before their session was to start. He wanted to talk, to finish answering questions that Wyman had asked him the day before, questions that had started with a simple *What do you think of the election this year?* Wyman had seen these bursts of energy in other days, but they only lasted a few hours and then the dying Knight returned.

"Let me tell you how my wife died."

Wyman listened to Norton, but he also slowly put distance between him and his subject. As Norton finished his story, Wyman found himself looking out the window overlooking the Knight world.

"I knew all the rules, Peter. I knew what should have happened. I could have easily told the truth. A good lawyer would have gotten Ashley off. But I ignored all that. A good therapist could come up with a textbook explanation, I suppose. Doesn't matter now. I sat in the grass next to Sandy. I didn't plan anything. I didn't think about the law or consequences. To my shame, I didn't even think about Jit at that moment. I could feel the blood on her jacket. I could feel her hair. She was all I thought about."

"Norton, how is all this possible? I thought I understood you, and this town, and that I was too old to be surprised by anything anymore, but I am beginning to think that I don't understand a damn thing. All I know for sure is that I am almost through with your portrait, and all this doesn't change it at all."

"Thank you."

"Save your thanks. You haven't seen it yet. But I do have a question for you. Is it possible that Ashley was lying to you?"

"No, she killed Sandy. Intentional or not, she did that."

"No, I mean, could she have been lying about your son?"

"Science does not lie."

SAND(RA) SHIFTING

No, thank you. I'm flattered, but I'm happy here.

Sandra told Jerry later about the job offer. His response was a variation of what he had told her all the earlier times she had turned down a job offer.

"So, the *Sentinel* has a quarter-million subscribers and you have, in a good year, maybe fifteen hundred. They offered you a six-figure salary for an editor/reporter slot, and I know for a fact that you haven't bought a new pair of shoes in years. And I'm sorry, darling, but I know there are afternoons when you have to go deliver some of the papers yourself, acting like it's a personal service, when the truth is that some kid missed an entire block. Tell me again about your professional career path."

"Jerry, one word . . . Orlando."

"Okay, okay, I'll give you that one. But you also turned down Miami and Jacksonville. And, for god's sake, you turned down the *Journal* in Atlanta!"

"I wasn't ready."

"You weren't willing. Big difference. You were ready ten years ago. You won't be willing in ten more years."

"Jerry, I told them the truth. I'm happy here. I've got a comfortable life. This is my home. People like me. You like me too, right?"

She knew how he felt about her. But she truly regretted not feeling about him the way he felt about her. She could offer soothing explanations, rationalizations that evaded the deeper truth. Sandra wished she could love Jerry half as much as she knew that he, hidden behind his stoic acceptance of just being her best friend, that she could love him half as much as he loved her. She had no unmarried girlfriends. Everyone in her past had found love. Some were mistaken, of course, But they found love again. Others had left town and never looked back.

Sometimes she wanted to yell at Plato's ghost that he was wrong about everyone having an ideal half that completes them. *Liar, liar, pants on fire.* She had constructed a life of compensating equilibrium, her own unwritten philosophy: *Compensating Equilibrium.* True love was never going to happen, but she still could be happy. Being Sandra Knight did not require Sandra Knight to love someone else. Plato could kiss her Knight ass. Only once did she want to apologize to Plato. Five years earlier, Sonny Knight had moved back to Knightville, wife at his side. Sandra had no one, not even Jerry, with whom she could share the bottom of her emotional barrel. But, Sonny? *Just shoot me. Even Sonny has a one true other-half ideal love.*

"And, besides, Jerry, I'm not leaving this town until I get the final four profiles written that are still on my list."

"Four? You've always told me about two big fish that are getting away from you, and, trust me, your father and uncle are not ever going to let you interview them."

"That's not the problem. You know that. Profiles of uncooperative people are written all the time. The *New Yorker* has made it an art form. But I'm going to have to wait on Daddy and Norton to die before I write their profiles."

Jerry cocked his head and waited.

"You know something I don't?"

"Norton's dying. Daddy told me."

Jerry leaned back in the swivel chair and tried to process the news. It was true that Norton had been seen less and less lately, and he looked more pale than usual, his white suits almost matching his face and hair, but Norton Knight dying was still an alien concept. Jerry started counting backward. He had lived in Knightville for almost thirty years. He had met Norton that first year, a fresh teaching certificate in his back pocket and ambitions for a job in a bigger town. He only found out later that his being hired at the high school had to be privately approved by Knight himself. He was told by his principal that it would be in his best interest to never ask Norton about it. He was hired, that was all that was important. Over time, he and Norton achieved a relationship less than friendship and more than employee/employer. Jerry was one of the few to even achieve that. In time, it became obvious that Sandra had gotten closer to Norton than his own son or his cousin Jit. Jerry knew how unique that made her. He was still always going to be, like everyone else, an outsider to Norton.

With the news about Norton, Jerry just wanted to sit in his chair and look out the newspaper office window. He should not have been shocked. Old people die. He would die. Still, Norton Knight was not supposed to die.

"So now you know. You and me and Daddy."

"Sonny doesn't know?"

Sandra just shook her head. "You know, I've always felt sorry for him."

"Norton?"

"No, no, Sonny. Oh, hell, I suppose I've felt sorry for both of them. As much as Sonny drove me crazy when we were growing up, we all knew something was wrong between those two. Losing his mother was bad enough, but something else was happening that none of us could figure out."

"Sandra, you remember what Norton told you when you took over the paper?"

"Sure, try not to lose too much money, as I recall."

"And you've done that. No, when Norton dies, you own the paper."

"Oh, Jerry, I'm sorry. I should have told you before now, but Norton made me promise to keep it between him and me only. He signed ownership over to me about a month ago. Told me that he didn't want our agreement to get thrown in with all the other issues when his Will was probated. He didn't tell me about his health. I just found out about that. I just assumed that he was being cautious. But this paper has already been mine for a while."

"Is that the real reason you didn't accept the Orlando offer?"

Sandra looked at him and thought, *I wish you were the one I'm looking for. It would have been nice.*

"Who knows anymore, right? I *am* happy here. I do have those four profiles to write. After that, who knows how I will feel?"

"Norton and your father, who else? Whose life do I have to look forward to finally reading about? You know, I told you, you are better than you give yourself credit for."

"I want to write about Sonny eventually, but his life is still a mess. I need for him to sort things out. I'd like to figure him out and let everybody else in this town give him a second chance. With Daddy and Norton, they are who they are. No more evolution. I just need to figure out something about them that has been escaping me for years. And I'll wait until they're both gone."

"I understand waiting on Norton, but why wait on your father? Don't you think he would be pleased with anything you say about him?"

"Daddy still escapes me. If I figure it out, I might do it while he is still alive. I just never want to hurt him. Dead or alive."

Jerry had one more question.

"The fourth?"

"You, Jerry."

Sandra stood on the sidewalk in front of her office and waved at Frank Morris as he got in his car to leave. She was acutely aware that another man, in another car, had been waiting outside while Morris talked to the editor/owner of the *Knightville Times*. She did not wave to him. He was even more drably dressed than Morris had been. But his affectation was obvious. Sunglasses, a dark suit and big red tie, but the suit did not fit and the tie was spotted with food crumbs.

Odd, a man running for sheriff has his own individual security guard?

Morris had called and asked if she would be interested in a casual conversation, a chance to introduce himself. She had been expecting the call ever since she saw him at the Orlando rally. The hour before he got to her office, she had Googled the *Constitutional Sheriffs and Peace Officers Association* and was ready with a set of questions. But the basic question-and-answer was not to be found on the internet. Why was he running against Jit?

"It's my pleasure to see you again." Extending his hand.

She was forming first impressions. Morris was a charmingly insincere gentleman.

"I'm beginning to think you don't remember me." Grasping her hand.

"We met in Orlando, right?" Something *was* coming back to her.

He laughed, too hard, throwing his head back and almost clapping his own hands. "Sandra, we went to high school together. I think my feelings are hurt."

That was it, the name came back, but not the look. There was a Frank Morris in her class, but all she remembered was a name. He proceeded to fill in the gaps.

"We were in different circles."

Sandra remained expressionless. *Our class wasn't that small.*

"But I dropped out my junior year, KHS and I weren't a good mix, so I joined the Army, became an MP, put in my twenty, and here I am back home."

"And now you're running for sheriff?"

"The military put the bug in me. Public service, serving others."

Sandra's bullshit detector started clanging. She wanted space between her and the man in front of her.

"Frank, I appreciate you stopping by, but you surely don't think this paper is going to endorse you. You might be Wyatt Earp and Elliot Ness all rolled up in a bow, but, and I'm being absolutely professionally and objectively honest here, Jit being my daddy not a factor either, this county doesn't need a different sheriff. And why the hurry? Jit's going to retire after this next term anyway."

Morris's squinty eyes got squintier.

"I don't need your endorsement. I just wanted to introduce, reintroduce, myself, make a courtesy call. Tell you to feel free to call me any time you want answers to any questions. All I want from you is a fair shake. Some unbiased coverage."

"Frank, Frank, I am seriously confused here. Why Jit? Why now?"

"Sandra, you have lived here too long."

"And what the hell does that mean?"

Morris was angry, she could see that, his face almost pink, but he then did something that Sandra found unnerving. He blinked a few times, inhaled and exhaled slowly, and became serenely calm, speaking to her as if they were debating abstract philosophy in a classroom.

"I mean that we all live in our own closed groups, that, after a while we do not see ourselves as outsiders see us. We do not see how social conditions have changed because that change has been so gradual. Even if that change has been detrimental to us, we still don't see it from the inside. Me, I am on the outside looking in."

This is not the Frank Morris that was in my class.

"I'm having a press conference tomorrow. I hope you'll be there. I actually trust you to write a fair story. And you have to understand, I have nothing personal against your father. He's a good man. On the wrong side."

"Frank, Jit has never lost. You know that. People trust him."

Sandra realized that she was implicitly pleading with Morris, asking him, in so many words, to leave her father alone and let him retire on his own terms. She was not being a responsible journalist. She was being a daughter. Jit's daughter. Sandy Chippen's daughter. And then her fear for her father's future turned to resolution. If anybody voted for Morris, she vowed to herself, they would not be doing it because he fooled them.

"Like I said, Sandra, this is not personal. But you have to understand. A change is coming."

"I'll be there tomorrow."

Morris stood and extended his hand. "I appreciate that."

A few minutes later, as she was leaving her office, she called Jerry and told him about her meeting with Morris.

"And what could be more perfect. I watch them drive off and there it was right there on the bumper of his friend's car. A decal, a damn Confederate flag decal. And Frank had an NRA sticker in his back window. I read all about their group. I'm going to make mincemeat of these guys."

Jerry did not respond.

"Jerry? You there?"

"Sit down, Sandra. You are about to enter Wonderland."

"Jerry, you can't surprise me anymore this year."

"Sit down."

"You gotta hurry. I'm headed over to see Daddy and talk to him about Morris."

"Sit down."

"Jerry. . ."

"Sonny Knight has filed papers for that open district seat for the state legislature. No incumbent, no other Republican has filed, and the Democratic nominee is a joke."

Sandra unlocked her office and went back in to sit down. Everything was the same. The desks, the piles of papers, the water cooler, the bulletin boards, the two computers, the fan slowly turning overhead. All the same. Different.

MORRIS CODE

Well, I guess I'm gonna have to come over to you then.

Morris was pleased with his visit to the newspaper. He knew he was not getting an endorsement. Simple research had shown him that the *Times*, with Sandra as editor, had never made any endorsements in the sheriff race. His memory of Sandra from high school, everything that people told him about her since that time, confirmed her reputation. She never showed any favoritism to her father, even when he had a serious opponent twenty years earlier. Jit never needed it, of course. In fact, the paper seldom endorsed any candidate in any local race. So, why go? All Morris knew for sure was that as soon as he left her office, she would be headed to see her father. He was not surprised that Sandra did not remember him, but he wondered whether Jit would.

He had grown up knowing all the stories about Jit Knight, his rising athletic star, his falling star, his new career as sheriff. His own father had taken him to a game in which Jit had scored three times and rushed for almost two hundred yards. Morris, still a child, had been dazzled. He got to KHS a decade later and failed to make the junior varsity. He was never fast. He was not strong. Determination to be great was not compensation for a lack of skill or talent. But he did meet Jit.

The Morris family was the whitest of trash, and for them all Knights were the same. Norton had all the money, but even Jit was a different class above them. Jit's people worked in the mill with local Negroes, but they were royalty compared to the Morris people who worked in the citrus fields with the Mexicans and Puerto Ricans. It was the Blue Moon Bar, down the road from the sawmill, where Morris finally came face-to-face with Jit Knight. Morris, his three brothers, and two cousins were drunk, as were two Mexicans, a reverse Alamo. Morris's father had been called before the sheriff. He showed up with two pistols, and then Jit showed up with two deputies. Morris himself was the least significant actor in the ensuing drama, not even a speaking role. Both Mexicans were bleeding, but so were the two Morris cousins. Jit talked to the bartender, then to a few other patrons who had steered clear of the melee. Blame was assigned. Jit motioned for Morris's father to come talk to him. The father told Jit to go to hell. Jit asked again. Frank Morris was paralyzed with dread. Even then he knew that his father was making a mistake. Right or wrong, Jit was the law. Jit had the badge. Morris could not articulate that epiphany until years later, but at that moment he wanted to be Jit, not his own father. He made note of how the two deputies, without a word from Jit, were separating away from Jit and slowly forming a perimeter, with the bigger deputy blocking the door behind Morris's father, the other easing between the father and the rest of his family, facing them, his back to the father. Jit took off his hat and asked the father again to come talk. He got the same suggestion to go to hell. The father had one gun in his back pocket, the other stuffed inside his belt in the front. Jit was unarmed. Morris would never forget what Jit said, every single word, every single softly spoken word, uttered as if in sorrow.

Morris looked at his brothers and cousins. Did they not hear what he heard? He wanted to scream at his father to shut up and go over to the sheriff, but he was speechless.

Well, I guess I'm gonna have to come over to you then.

Jit almost seemed to limp as he walked the few steps over to stand face-to-face with the glowering father. Not a word. He looked the father in the eye and then slammed his fist into the man's stomach, buckling him over, dropping him to his knees.

And then he took away the father's guns.

Turning to the other Morris men, Jit asked if they were armed. Both deputies had their guns drawn. Frank's oldest brother handed over a twenty-two pistol. Jit explained that he would keep the guns for a while. *For your own good.* A gasping father on the floor muttered something about *More where those came from.* Jit did not respond. He just looked at the other Morris men, settling his gaze on Frank. Or, so Frank thought.

Morris might have been just like the other men in his family, but the Army saved him. He dropped out of high school, with no discernible ripple in the social pool of that world, and went to Fort Jackson, South Carolina. Asked by his senior drill sergeant if he had a goal for life after his stint in the Army, he told his Sergeant that he would like to be a cop. After basic training, he was sent to Fort Leonard Wood in Missouri. Morris had not planned a career, but he re-upped and re-upped and retired before he was forty.

The Army gave him a career, eventually a small pension, and it also gave him training that he never had from his own father. The importance of self-discipline, a respect for authority, physical self-confidence, and a fetish for weapons. Morris went to the shooting range almost every day, availing himself of guns that were out of the reach of most other free Americans. He collected guns. He sold guns. Wherever legal, he carried a concealed gun when he was in civilian clothes. Eventually, he carried a concealed gun even where it was not legal to do so.

The Army also gave him an education. His first wife had helped. She convinced him to get tested for some sort of learning disability. She said that his troubles in school were not his fault. He was too intuitively bright, she insisted. Diagnosed and accommodated, his life accelerated. MP training was the ground floor, next came an AA in Law Enforcement. Then he earned an AA in Political Science, despite hating his teachers and having to keep his mouth shut in class. He told his friends that he was finally seeing "the big picture."

His wife divorced him, with a parting shot that made no sense to him. *Frank, people always say that booze just makes a person more of who they are. I think education did the same for you. It made you more of a goddam Morris.*

He finally had a language to express the obvious truths he had learned in his life, seeds of truth planted when he was dirt poor in Florida, truths that his liberal poli-sci teachers would never learn. They had never actually worked in their lives, they had never lived with black people or brown people. They did not understand *real* life. They did not create wealth, they were parasites on working people, those who paid the taxes that paid their salaries, but who had no job security. In his last class, he had finally let loose with his honest feelings, leading his teacher to snap back. *You do realize that you are a government employee, that you want to go be a cop, with a cop union and a cop pension, and all that is paid for with tax dollars.*

Morris had a simple, irrevocably true response. *That's different.*

He knew that he could stay in the Army until he died. Tours in Iraq and Afghanistan did not bother him. But he kept wondering what it was he was supposed to be defending. America? The government? He knew history. He knew the difference between big and small government. He understood something about the Civil War that his teachers did not. It was not about slavery. It was about Freedom. Guns were about Freedom. America was about Freedom, but government was about Control. Freedom flowed up, not down. He believed in Law and Order, but even the Law could get in the way of Freedom. He wrote a long paper on the concept of Individual Autonomy being necessary for Social Freedom. It was his best work, but the teacher gave it a C-, telling him that *it lacks historical weight and relies too much on cosmic generalities.* But Morris had no respect for that teacher anyway. He passed, that was all that mattered. Outside of the classroom, people killed people with guns and all the government could do was restrict gun rights? And more of his family saw their own futures usurped by those outsiders given preferences because of . . . and Morris learned to disguise *those* thoughts. His own superiors insisted on public lip service to diversity and equality, but Morris knew what they really thought. All they needed was permission to speak freely.

With the election in 2008, Morris knew he was going to call it quits with the Army. He did not want to serve that Commander in Chief. He moved back to Knightville, and he became a cop in Orlando. The commute every day gave him time to listen to the radio.

TIME

"Peter, you do realize that I am not going to live forever."

"Your point?"

They were taking another break, sitting on the shaded front porch of his home, a different view than from the upstairs study window. A narrow street stretched from the front gate, straight for half a mile and then curving in the distance, each side of the street intermittently housing a much lesser home than Knight's. Wyman's first impression, after walking from the center of town to Knight's house weeks earlier, had been that he was passing the servant quarters en route to the master's manor. He told Norton about that impression, a lighthearted conversation opener. Norton had not been amused.

"Outsiders often make the same mistake, Peter. Thinking that Florida is just another Southern state. It is not. My ancestor Stephen understood that. So, please reserve judgments for now. And, trust me, seeing me as a Southern gentleman-farmer is a grievous misperception."

A thunderstorm had just rolled through central Florida, drenching dirt and trees and asphalt alike. A storm of blinding and thunderous intensity, lasting perhaps a half hour, and the two men had sat silently rocking on the porch, spectators to the confirmation of their own insignificance, or so Wyman observed.

"Nature is indifferent to us." He was pleased with his insight.

Norton had simply shrugged. "Stephen Crane."

Wyman did not respond.

The August sun returned to scorch the earth again. Moisture from the previous dark sky soon became oppressive humidity, and both men noted, as they drank their iced water, how ripples of heat were rising from the street in front of them. Wyman suggested that they go back upstairs, where they at least had a giant ceiling fan to cool them. Knight stood and accepted Wyman's offer to hold on to his arm as they went back inside and up the long stairway.

"My comment about my impending death, your awareness of it, was actually about the pace of your work."

"I'm making progress, Norton. I want to do it right."

"I would like to see it before I die, to see what you see. At this current pace, I have my doubts."

"Fair enough, and that's my goal too, but I can't rush this."

"And if I die before you are finished, Peter, can you even finish?"

"Norton, don't be offended, but if you dropped dead right now, I would still finish your portrait. I finally have a clear idea of who you are. Hell, without a time constraint, it might even be better." He saw Knight nod and force a smile. "And, hey, did you ever think that me taking so long is actually keeping you alive longer? I don't think you're going to die as long as I keep painting. No model has ever died on me."

Back in the upstairs study, the two men resumed the process. Knight looked out the window as Wyman feigned the act of painting. When he thought that Knight might be totally relaxed, he asked him a question that had always intrigued him.

"Why do you always wear white? Any significance to that?"

Wyman could only see the back of Knight's head as he replied.

"Why are you always in your pajamas?"

"You were a fool, Peter."

"Norton, I never murdered anybody."

"True, but you destroyed someone."

Wyman had almost finished the story of Alice, but Norton was not satisfied.

"You have talked about the two most important women in your life, but I still only understand one. I think I know Sarah. I know why you could love her, but Alice is still a mystery, and I am beginning to think you don't know anything about her either. Ten years, and you still cannot explain why you wasted your life with her."

"And you, Norton, did you know your marriage was a mistake before Ashley died, or did you figure it out later?"

"Peter, I knew it was a mistake before I married her. It doesn't matter anymore. She's dead. Sandy is dead. I'm dying. Tell me anything that matters anymore."

Wyman put down his brush.

"Hindsight, right?"

"Of course. Foresight is usually blind."

"Permission to speak honestly?"

"You're only starting now?"

"Oh, I'm not always sure I'm right, Norton. Sometimes I think I have, have had, things figured out, but then I see how wrong my assumptions were."

"About me?"

"Your family, you. You come from Yankee carpetbaggers. You weren't royalty. You're not the House of Windsor. Nobody picked out your bride for you, to keep the throne intact. You married a woman you did not love. For what? Because she was the sister of the woman you *did* love?"

"And you fell in love with a young woman who manipulated you all her life? You want to chalk it up to Chance? Fate? What? You think that Hughes seeing that portrait was Chance? She knew Hughes would be in the studio for your class. You walked in and there it was, unavoidable. Peter, there goes your theory about *chance*. Him seeing that portrait was not a matter of chance. She made it happen."

"I had told her that I was afraid for him, or anybody else, to see it."

"And her making sure he saw her portrait, that was her controlling you too. Imposing herself on your fears. She wanted him to see your work. Was that such a bad thing? In the long run, that moment also led you to this moment, here with me."

"Norton, she didn't care about him seeing my work. She wanted him to see her. And you're forgetting about that moment also leading to a lot of other moments before I met you. Don't be offended, but I'd forfeit this moment in a heartbeat if I could change some of those other moments. That is so obvious to me now."

"Hindsight, Peter. Sometimes, excuse my language, hindsight can be a bitch. But, the thing is, I am not sure you would."

Wyman frowned. "Would what?"

"You say you would do it differently, knowing what you know now, but I am not sure you would. You have all these pieces of your past, Peter, but I am not sure you have really totaled them up."

"Fair enough, so I'll do that after I finish your portrait. You want to know another story she told me?"

"Sarah?"

"Yes, about her and Alice. I had kidded her about how she and Alice seemed to get along so well. She slapped me on the arm, that slap thing she liked to do when she was happy with me, I thought, and she said something about *Pete, I'm a firm believer in the old saying that you keep your friends close, and your enemies closer.*"

"And you didn't see what she was really telling you?"

"But, Norton, if I was blind it was because, and this I believe with all my heart, Sarah *did* like Alice. She would warn me about getting too close, but she was also the person who wanted to adopt Alice. She always talked about Alice being a *lost soul*, Sarah's words."

"Peter, you're trying, you do realize, you're trying to use Sarah to absolve yourself for what happened."

"Who knows? All I do know is that Sarah was wrong about Alice. She wasn't a lost soul. A lost soul has to have a soul."

"Peter, even I could see I had made a mistake with Ashley, just not how bad, and the end wasn't really predictable. But. . ."

"But you went ahead, right?"

"Is it important to you that I was as foolish as you were?"

"I want a little less judgment, that's all. But here we are, two men who finally have the . . . there's a song . . . there's always a poem or a song about everything . . . something about distance. We finally have the distance to see ourselves clearly. And I finally can see everything that she saw. The sad thing about you, Norton, is that you never had your own Sarah."

They had been standing side by side, looking out the same window at the same land they had looked at dozens of times before. Wyman saw Norton in that land. Norton saw Wyman in the past. *You had your own Sarah, Peter, and she was wasted on you.*

To Be or Not to Be

It was the nausea more than the pain. But the pain was never far away. And then the loss of appetite, more nausea. Constipation and diarrhea competed. The color of his skin made his condition too obvious, so he spent less time doing anything where somebody else might see him. He took pain pills, but resisted morphine or Valium. He persisted. But he knew that he had to eventually make a choice: some sort of overmedicated home care . . . or suicide. Either would require him to make another decision: to tell Jit, or not.

"If you were going to kill yourself, how would you do it?"

Wyman was focusing on his canvas, knowing that Knight only had a few more weeks of coherence. He was close to finishing. He owed Knight that much.

"I have several guns." Norton went through his options. "But that seems a bit ghastly."

"Only if you plan an open casket."

"Pills are imprecise."

"Yes, and if you do that wrong you end up puking your guts out. I assume you want to go out with some sort of dignity."

"Would you help me, if I asked, at the right time?"

"Absolutely not."

"Fair enough, Peter. You've already done enough for me."

"Your portrait?"

"Oh, that for sure, but I was thinking more about your willingness to listen to my story."

Sometimes Wyman wanted to scream at Knight that he was too damn melodramatic. Too full of self-pity. But he knew that Norton would say the same of him.

"Norton, you do have a family, you know. You might be surprised by how much support you could get from them. That's more than I have. If I dropped dead downtown tomorrow at noon, nobody would claim my body. And when you die, my story dies too, since you're the only person who has heard it. But at least you have people you *could* talk to. I mean, Jesus, they must know you're dying."

Knight had been thinking about his own death more and more. *How does anybody not think about it when you can see how much sand is left in the glass?* He had told Jit, assuming he would then tell Sandra, but he had asked Jit to not tell Sonny.

"Norton, if the expression *getting your affairs in order* means anything, it's got to mean something now."

"My Will is set."

"Forget your Will, Norton. You know exactly what I am talking about. Getting your life in order."

Norton was well aware what he meant, but he could not admit, even to Wyman, the emotional paralysis gripping him. On one level, he knew that some sort of reconciliation with Sonny was necessary, but coming this late, under these circumstances, he knew that Sonny would see it for what it was . . . insincere. As if Norton wanted Sonny to absolve *him* of decades of neglect and indifference. For once in his life, Norton wanted absolute contrition from himself, atonement from himself, and absolution for the sins of his life. Sonny could not offer that. God could not offer that. Only Jit could do that. He needed to talk to Jit, beg his forgiveness, and then kill himself. Perhaps Jit would help? It might just be a gesture, but it would not be an empty gesture. Norton had lived a life of self-control, why not end it the same?

"I knew what I had done as soon as it happened."

"And Jit knew?"

"From the first moment he stood at the foot of the stairs. Something about him that I never appreciated until that moment. He had always been a better man than I was."

"Memory isn't always reliable. You might just be wanting to think that he never knew."

Norton had given Wyman the last piece of the puzzle, but all Wyman seemed to want to do was complicate things again. Norton was beginning to think that it was Wyman, not him, who was avoiding the truth. They had been debating the possibility that the accuracy of any memory of the distant past, unless you had film from every angle, was inherently inaccurate.

"It's science, Norton, figured out by smarter men than us. Something happens, you remember it later, and then you remember it again after that, but the first memory is itself an approximation of the original moment, and each subsequent remembrance is actually the recalling of the past prior memory, itself slightly altered, always imprecise, and so your most recent recollection of a distant event is actually a surface coated over another surface coated over another, and another, and the original moment will never be remembered as it actually happened. All you're doing is remembering memories. Why the hell do you think I take so many pictures of my models? I don't trust my memory."

"I killed her, Peter."

"You had been drinking, right? And her too, right? The words, what she said to you, after all these years, you are absolutely sure of what she said?"

"Absolutely."

SARAH'S DESTRUCTION

Norton shook his head as he looked at the photographs.

The two men were in Wyman's studio, Knight's barn. October in central Florida was still hot and humid, and the barn's air conditioners were groaning with compressor death rattles. The photos had been sealed in large Tupperware containers, but they had not been totally protected. Some were curled, others faded, all of them warm to the touch.

As Norton looked at the photos, Wyman asked, "You know everything about your land and property, you tell me, so you must know the history of this building."

Norton looked up and nodded, speaking as he looked back at the photos.

"She's nothing like her portrait, Peter. Wasn't that obvious from the very beginning? Surely everyone told you that."

"Nobody ever said anything."

"Not even Sarah? But, perhaps even she loved you so much that she allowed you to have your own delusions, as long as you were happy, as long as you painted so well?"

"All I know is that Alice had disappeared, just as Sarah had predicted. We were settling into that stage of life where our hurts might not be forgiven, or forgotten, but they were set aside. And then she was diagnosed with breast cancer."

Norton grimaced at the sound of the word, still holding Alice's photos in his hand.

"We thought the long-term prognosis was good. Still years to live, with treatments, perhaps remissions and then relapses, the pattern for breast cancer, but I was going to be there with her. And then she killed herself."

"Peter, dying people often think of taking their own lives early. Present company included, as you know. Sarah's decision was about herself, not you."

Norton wanted to go home, but that would mean he had to leave the barn and go to his car. A five-minute walk, and Wyman would certainly help him, but it was thirty degrees warmer outside than in the barn. The thought of that short walk was exhausting. He handed the container of Alice pictures back to Wyman and then pointed to his own nose.

"You asked about the history of this barn. Can't you smell it?"

Wyman looked around and inhaled deeply through his nose, thinking that perhaps Knight was referring to some residual horse manure odor or other farm odor that he might somehow have missed. But, nothing.

"Jit and I used to love this place. Stephen Knight had a thousand acres of tobacco planted, Samsun tobacco it was, from Turkey, and it was wonderful to smell. This is all that's left of the original tobacco barn. You don't smell it?"

Wyman shook his head.

"The curse of air-conditioning, I suppose." Norton closed his eyes and smelled the past. "Everything is cooler now, but sterile. Then again, this state would not exist for humans without air-conditioning. Perhaps in the early days, for Stephen and the few to follow him. They were tougher than us. But I'm guilty too. Comfort, I don't know. But Jit and I loved this barn. And we would go home and our fathers would accuse us of sneaking off to smoke, we smelled so much like the air we had been breathing. Our clothes probably reeked."

"There was no smell like that when I was shown the place."

"Oh, it's been over fifty years since this barn was full of tobacco." *A half century*, Norton thought to himself. *Two generations? But I can still smell it.*

"Seriously, I don't smell it."

Norton held his hand out, signaling to Wyman that he needed help to stand up.

"The first time you kissed that girl, do you remember how the room smelled?"

Wyman squinted and went searching for a memory.

"Turpentine? Dried oils? Old brushes? After all, we were in a studio."

Norton almost laughed, but only almost.

"I thought you were a hopeless romantic, Peter. Alice and Sarah both agreed about that, right?"

Wyman took both of Norton's hands and held him steady as he stood up.

"I remember how the light was dimming, how quiet it was, how her head on my shoulder felt, even the feel of her wool skirt. Especially that, because it was new and she never seemed to have new clothes any time before then, and she made me touch it, joking about new wool, making it sound exotic and sensual and decadent, but it was just an ordinary skirt that I remember now."

"I'm sorry."

"Sorry?"

"Sorry that you do not have something else to remember, some smell that you will want to experience again before you die. Me, here with you now, I realize that the last thing I want to smell before I die is what I had with Jit, right here, the Turkish tobacco from when we were young."

"Norton, stop it. You are getting too damn morbid, even for me. And you're getting to be like too many dying people I've known. Rehearsing your own death. Making the grandest of exits. But you know as well as I do . . . life . . . and death . . . never cooperate."

"True enough. But there is one condition I'm still requiring before I go meet the Knight ghosts."

"Yes?"

"I want to see my damn portrait, Peter."

"*That* I can arrange. A few more weeks. Can you hold on that long?"

Norton shrugged. "For you, sure. But you haven't made my waiting any easier with all your revelations about that girl, and now seeing these pictures."

"Excuse me?"

"Your portrait is nothing like the real her. And nothing you have said to me leads me to believe that you were seeing some inner beauty. She was pretty enough, but not a beautiful person, Peter.

Your work lied about her. So, I wonder now what your work will say about me."

"You're wrong, Norton. You and everybody else. She was as beautiful as I painted her. I painted what I saw."

"Peter, the face in the portrait . . ."

Wyman put his finger to his lips, stopping Norton, and then he pointed to the *Alice* portrait a few feet away. "Look at *that* face. Nothing else. Squint, look at each feature. Slowly, look at the whole face. Don't look at me. Look at her. Absorb her."

Norton studied the portrait. He had seen it dozens of times, in the past, and more closely now. It was still uniquely mesmerizing. Breathtaking and beautiful. He looked back at Wyman.

"Am I missing something?"

"Look at the photo again."

Norton looked down, then up. His eyes blinked as he looked back toward the *Alice* portrait, then up again at Wyman, and then back down at the photo. His head began to turn slowly side to side, and then he tilted slightly. He spoke to Wyman without looking up.

"They are the same. How is that possible? The photo looks different than it did before. It's not the same face it was before."

"That picture, all photos, are shadows, Norton, shadows of the real. Dancing on a wall. My portraits are the real reality. Not any photo. People who are not really looking, they tell me that my photos of her are different than the portrait. But they're wrong. They are judging the portrait by the photo. You now, you understand, you are judging the photo by the portrait. My painting changed everything. My painting is real, not the photo. Nobody has ever seen you, Norton. You've never seen yourself. That's what I'm doing for you. And make no mistake, if I had never met Alice, I wouldn't be able to do that. We both owe her that."

"But she was evil, according to you. Peter, everybody in this town thinks you are crazy. And now you are talking like a crazy man."

"Truth and Beauty, Norton, Truth and Beauty are not the same thing as goodness. Everybody else is wrong. Sarah was right."

"Peter? What are you talking about?"

"It hit me weeks ago, how I needed to paint you, and it doesn't matter what anybody else thinks of it. If I'm right, you'll see yourself. All I can tell you is that it won't be what you see when you look into a mirror. It's not in any of those photos of you either. But I know it's you."

Norton looked back at the photo of Alice. *You might be stark raving mad, Peter. Thinking you see something that is not there. But, me? All I see in the photo now is what you painted.*

The next day, they were back in Norton's study.

"I made the right choice. I told Sarah that I was going to end it, and I told Alice that too. I thought that was my choice."

"But?"

"Sarah made a mistake."

Norton was starting to feel nauseous, but he waited for Wyman to explain.

"A week after I said it was over, we got another call. From a doctor in Jacksonville. Alice was in the hospital. Something about a heart attack. I was listed as next of kin. Sarah was watching me as I talked to him. It made no sense. Alice was too young. I looked at Sarah as I listened to the doctor."

"She had no family?"

"That was her story."

"And you believed her?"

"Sarah believed her too."

"She never talked about her family? Peter, wasn't that a sign too?"

"They were dead, or gone, or out of her life. She was alone."

"And you believed her?"

"Goddam it, Norton, we both believed her. I was telling the doctor that I was sorry but I wasn't sure what I could do. I was just a friend, but the doctor said that she had specifically asked that I be told, that I would help her."

"And you helped."

"Worse."

"Worse?"

"Sarah told me to go to Jacksonville."

"Peter, I am not sure how to . . ."

"She told me to go to Jacksonville and bring her back to Savannah. She told me that we were both responsible for her. And I did it, brought her back for us to care for her. A month, and then she was gone. As if it never happened. Ten years of my life, gone. We had told each other over and over, *This has lasted so long, it must mean something. It must be different. We must be different.* I was wrong."

Norton put his handkerchief over his mouth and coughed, but he did not look at the cloth afterwards.

"Peter, all those photographs you have back at the barn, do you have any of Sarah?"

"Dozens, lots of them."

"But you never painted her portrait?"

"No."

"Did you ever see Alice again? After your wife died, did you see the girl again?"

Wyman did not answer at first, taking time to look around the room, noticing more and more empty shelves.

"Sometimes I wonder what would have happened if I had never met you. Except for Sarah, I've never talked about Alice with anybody else."

"But you never told Sarah all the truth, did you? I'm dying, Peter. It all dies with me. Truth or lies, everything dies with me. So, tell me, do you know the answer to the question yet?"

"The question?"

"How well did you know her? And before you answer that, I am willing to wager that you forgave her everything, right? Credit cards and everything else."

"I was enraged. I told her that we were finished. My line had always been that it would either end sadly or badly. It was up to her. We split three times. Twice sadly."

"Did you ever see her after the third time?"

"Norton, I wanted to. I wanted some sort of *The Way We Were* ending, a reunion after a lot of years, both of us older and wiser. That sort of crap. After Sarah died, I sent her a note. She wrote back, told me that she had 'moved on.' All I wanted was one final conversation with her. She was the only person who could answer the most important questions for me. Maybe if she had answered those questions, then I might have actually figured out who she really was."

"Important questions?"

"Simple stuff. Like, was it ever *real* to her? All the ways we explained ourselves to each other, that we were different than anybody else, that the rules didn't apply to us. I always thought that was true, from the first time I said I loved her. But was it really true for her? And if it was true, when did it stop being true? How did I miss *that* moment? Long before the credit cards, long before I found out she had seduced an artist friend of mine named John Murray in New York, after I had introduced them, other things I knew at the time but chose to forgive and forget, long before all the other things I found about her after we finally split. Norton, I just want to understand it all, finally."

Norton was standing, looking out the window. He motioned for Wyman to join him.

"I love this view, Peter. Sometimes it looks different. Time of the year makes a big difference. Sometimes even the wind." He pointed. "See that one tree there." Wyman nodded. "Sometimes the light catches it, a white cypress, out of place with the others. Much thinner than most cypresses. An oddity. I've watched it all my life."

"Norton, am I boring you? As for this view, how many times have you and I looked out this window together? I think I see things out there that you don't. You might be surprised."

"No, no. I was just thinking about you and your questions. Seems to me that the real answers you wanted from her were not about her, to help you understand her. Seems to me that the real question is how well do you know yourself? You needed her to help you answer that question."

"Maybe. Let me total things up again, for the hundredth time, and get back to you. Can I ask you an obvious question now?"

"Will you be disappointed in an obvious answer?"

"Do you regret what you did to your wife?'

"Yes."

"If you could go back, would you still do it?

"Yes."

SANDY RETURNS

"You got any ideas, Sheriff?"

Abe Jones had waited for what seemed like an eternity, waited as Jit stood speechless over the bones, waited as the sheriff looked at the rags in his hands, waited as Jit began talking to himself in whispers. Abe waited.

"Sheriff, the Twains are at it again."

Jit did not want to leave his air-conditioned office. Mention of the Twains was just another burr under his saddle this afternoon. He had just listened to his opponent being interviewed on the radio. His conclusion? *I am getting too old for this shit.* And then Abe showed up and compounded his funk with news that the Twains had lost another of their dogs and had gone hunting for old Black, heading out to the Knight woods and the old Knight church, swearing retribution against a black panther that nobody had ever seen. That was yesterday. Twain and his son had not been heard from since.

"And I should do what about this?"

Abe was trying to be deferential.

"Sadie Twain, the old lady, she's worried. Asked me to check on them. But you know that land better than me. I figure we could go out there. You could show me how to get around. You know, more of that education you keep promising me."

"Abe, if I haul my ass out there, they better be dead."

"From your lips to God's ears, Sheriff."

Off the main road, down a dirt path, following tread tracks in the lush grass, they saw the pickup first. Riding in the department Jeep four-wheeler, they had no trouble, but it was obvious that the Twains had gone too far in their old heap, and there it was, stuck in the muck.

"You say they were after old Black?"

"That's what Sadie said."

Jit had reconciled the existence of the Twain family existing in a human universe by simply allowing that God made mistakes. Or, perhaps he provided good examples of bad examples?

"Abe, you know the stories about this part of the woods?"

"About the first Knight folks, the old church? Sheriff, I grew up on those stories."

"Yeah, I know, probably heard a few of them from me. But people like the Twains, they invent their own stories about this land. Where the hell they get them is anybody's guess."

"So, is old Black a Knight story or a Twain story?"

"Oh, that's ours. Fact or fable, I heard it as a child, me and Norton together. No, people like the Twains have other stories. For them, there's a treasure out here somewhere, some damn pot of gold in the ground, hauled down from the North by the first Knights. Exact location one of those family secrets, passed down in some sort of midnight ritual. And people like the Twains have snuck out here for a hundred years, looking for some goddam golden snipe. I suspect they weren't after old Black. I'm guessing they were after old gold. And I bet they didn't intend to tell Sadie if they found it."

The two men had been sitting in the cab of the Jeep, motor running, air conditioner still blasting.

"Sheriff, you talking so much must mean you don't want to get out, right?"

"Hell, no. But let's get it over with. Sandra's going to be waiting for me when I get back."

The first thing they found was Sam Twain's panama hat, his trademark fashion statement. Thirty feet further, they found his right hand. Gnawed off, not severed. Thirty more feet was his handless and faceless body.

Abe began his waiting ritual as Jit processed the scene. A shotgun was in plain view, one of two barrels empty. A crime scene? But, the hand? Abe began his own processing, the logistics of an investigation. How big, actually, was the scene of the crime? Yellow barrier tape seemed like a silly artifice. The coroner was not going to be happy about trekking through the jungle to retrieve the body. And where was the son? Abe looked around again.

"Sheriff, is that what I think it is, over there, about thirty yards?"

Jit did not need to turn around.

"The one and only."

"The church?"

"The church, indeed."

Abe kept staring. It was not what he expected. But, then again, how could he know what to expect when meeting a myth? Something flashed next to the composting remains of the church. Abe blinked. He could see a dark pole, and then the top of the pole flashed again. He kept staring. The brief bright flicker flashed again. A puff of wind and it flashed again. Abe walked toward the church, soon seeing that there was a scrap of tin attached to the top of the pole. If the breeze moved it, and the overhead sun was at the right angle, the serendipity of metal and breeze and sun welded into a momentary sparkle. He forgot about the sheriff and walked toward the source of that sparkle. It was there and then it was gone, and then there again, but the closer he got it disappeared completely.

"Sheriff, you might want to come over here. We've got another body."

The Twains had been digging. Two shovels were sticking upright in a pile of dirt and grass, a gunnysack next to them. Abe and Jit stood next to the shallow excavation, each wondering at first if the bones below them were actually human. They were barely more than shards, but something human seemed to be there. Something buried with leather shoes, something wrapped in the gossamer remnants of a blue denim jacket, the metal buttons still snapped shut.

"How long you think it's been there?" Abe was still trying to process a crime scene, imagining the coroner having one more reason to be perturbed, having two difficult autopsies to perform. Jit had kneeled down on the wet ground, reaching into the hole to gently brush away more dirt from the fragile remains, seemingly afraid that if he were to apply too much pressure the *thing* that was there would disappear. He found the collar and turned it over. He felt a bulge in the jacket pocket and reached inside.

"Sheriff?"

Jit looked up, but his deputy was invisible. He was alone in his green world.

"Sheriff?"

I love it, Jit. Thank you.

I knew you wanted something like it. It's not much. Next year I'll do better

No, it's perfect. And a perfect fit. See, I can stitch your initials right here under the collar, in giant red letters. I'll keep it forever.

"Sheriff?"

"Abe, sometimes I feel like you're my son. Does that make sense?"

Abe was more concerned than confused. The sheriff was almost panting, as if gasping for breath. He was old, he was overweight and out of shape, the heat could not be good for him, the stress was obvious.

"Sheriff, I think I need to get you back to town right now."

"I need you to do something for me. Please. Will you do that?"

"Sheriff, you're the boss. But I'm not sure where you're going here."

"Not your boss, Abe. This is not a boss favor."

"Jit, you want a friend favor, right?"

"I want you to help me cover all this up for now. I want you to come with me later and find this all over again. I don't want her found like this right now, part of that," pointing to the other body in the distance, "part of that."

Abe stifled the obvious question. *Her?* Time for that later.

"And I want you to help me move Sam back closer to his truck. I'll have a story to explain him soon enough. Will you do that for me?"

Abe had often felt like he was being tested by Jit in the past, to see how much he was willing to bend the rules to maintain order more than law. That was his professional education. This was personal.

"Yessir, I'll do that for you."

Jit exhaled but did not get up. Abe reached down and offered his hand to the sheriff, an offer accepted without acknowledgment. The two men stood in the sweltering heat, making small talk, with Abe sensing that the sheriff was merely stalling, not wanting to leave. "You want me to leave you alone for awhile? I should go look for the Twain boy. Save us another trip out here."

"You won't find him, Abe."

"Sadie's going to want answers."

"He's gone. If he wasn't there with his old man, he's gone for good."

"Sadie won't be happy. She'll still want answers."

"She can get in line."

Jit was looking at Sandra but not hearing her. He kept studying her face, looking for traces of her mother. Cheekbones for sure, those were definitely not Knight cheekbones, too distinct, too perfect. The eyebrows? Jit looked over Sandra's shoulder to look at the picture of Sandy that he kept on the shelf next to his desk. Yes, the Chippen eyebrows were passed down from mother to daughter. Nose and lips? Unattributable. The eyes? Definitely the eyes, brown. Sandy had always joked about her own brown eyes. *People with brown eyes are calm but possess an underlying passion. Me, right?* Sandra's brown eyes were calm for sure, but Jit could not imagine any passion inside her. His daughter never seemed . . . *intense?* . . . about anything except politics. He had seldom seen her excited. Her rare bouts of anger were quickly stifled. And she never smiled. Her mother, everyone said, was born smiling, and, except for the one year in which she seemed to have lost her mind, she was contagiously happy. Jit had often wondered why his daughter was so different. *Did I make her this way? Why was she so blessed to look like her mother but to act like me? Would she be different now if Sandy had raised her instead of me?*

"Daddy, these people might be crazy, but they're dead serious about this election."

Jit tried to remember if Sandra had been happy as a child. Everyone considered her a serious child, a thoughtful child. Thoughtful in her consideration of others, but also thoughtful in how she always seemed to be thinking. She was not a spontaneous child. Did all that mean she was not happy? Smiling does not mean you are happy, Jit knew that. But he wished he had heard her at least laugh more as she grew up.

"And you're sure you don't remember the Morris family? And don't get me started about Sonny's plans. Sonny, and Frank Morris, and the Orange Blossom Special . . . nothing makes sense this year."

Jit had been thinking about all those things as Sandra was talking. About his daughter's past, her future, about his afternoon with Abe in the woods, and he had missed most of her conversation.

"I'm sorry, honey, tell me again."

"Daddy, I'm beginning to think that Morris is right. You're getting too old for this job."

"Is that what he said? I'm too old for the job? And who is he?"

"No, I am saying that. Morris is saying that you don't respect the Second Amendment and that he thinks the next sheriff needs to be able to stand up to the federal government and all the laws coming down the pipeline. Whatever the hell that means."

Jit stifled a cough.

"He does realize that the legislature over in Tallahassee is doing a good job all by itself ignoring the Feds, doesn't he? But I suppose he's right about me and the Second Amendment thing. Biggest damn mistake in the Constitution."

"Daddy!"

"Forget it. I'm not worried about this Morris fellow. But I am surprised that Sonny is running. I'd bet that he's never voted in his life."

"I already checked with the registrar's office. Never voted? He didn't even register until a month ago. If he had a serious opponent, he'd get crucified just on that one issue, him being a Knight or not."

"So why are you so agitated about all this? Sonny going to Tallahassee might do him a lot of good, and he's sure not going to do any harm over there."

Sandra looked around her father's office. How many times had she been there? Thousands? Growing up, it seemed like she was there every day after school. Everything seemed the same as it was the first time she had been there. She had pointed that out to her father many times, his "space" never changing. He had always reminded her that the same could be said of her own newspaper office. Even the damn watercooler had not moved.

"Tell me this, Daddy. How would any serious journalist cover Sonny's campaign? Any serious journalist who asked any serious questions. Your campaign I can ignore. In this town, nobody is going to wonder why your daughter is not writing about your campaign. I get a pass on that one. But, Sonny? I know too much about him."

"Your name is Knight too. Nobody is going to fault you for ignoring his campaign too. Not in this town."

"Daddy, I know too much about him."

"We all know Sonny. That's why he's going to win, even if he had a strong opponent."

"Daddy! I'm not talking about the voting thing, or the drinking thing, the being out of town most of his life thing. I'm talking about the . . . lifestyle thing. How am I supposed to ignore that?"

"Lifestyle?"

Sandra and Jit were at a recurring moment in their adult relationship. She had made her livelihood, lived her life, by knowing as much as possible about what happened in her small town. She also knew that her father always knew more than he let on. She knew that he knew things about people in Knightville that she would never know. How could he not know about Sonny and Angel and their out-of-town friends? But Jit would often feign ignorance, act puzzled, as if the sunrise was a constant surprise to him. Here he was, either coy or oblivious. But, if coy, he was also signaling to her that he was not going to talk about it anymore.

"Sandra, you'll do the right thing. You always have. Just figure out what you owe this town, and if you owe Sonny anything."

Jit studied his daughter's face. He had no choice. He had to tell her that her mother had come back. But he wanted to memorize the face in front of him at that moment. Intense but happy, serious and bemused? But, not a trace of pain.

He took the frayed and fading jacket out of a large manilla envelope. He did not anticipate that Sandra would recognize it immediately. Before he could find the right soft words, she knew. Admitting that knowledge was harder.

"That's Mama's jacket."

And then the look. Confusion at first, and then fear. And then the shortness of breath, a paralysis of the heart.

"Sandra, I need to tell you . . ."

"How long have you known, Daddy? Why didn't you tell me before?"

"We just found her. Out by the old church in the woods. Me and Abe."

"I saw him an hour ago. He said nothing."

"I wanted to tell you myself."

"And you waited?"

Jit had no defense. How to explain him swearing Abe and the coroner to secrecy? How to explain keeping Sandy to himself, if only for a few hours, before he had to finally let her die? He was not a poet, not a philosopher. He could not even explain it to himself.

"How do you know about this jacket? You never saw it before."

Sandra lost all self-control. How to describe anger and grief both manifested in tears?

"Daddy, Daddy, I've seen that jacket every day of my life!"

Pointing to a picture on a shelf directly across from Jit's desk.

"Every day of my life. Your favorite picture. You and her and that jacket. The same picture on a wall at home. The same picture in my office. Your favorite picture. You said over and over it was one of the happiest days in your life. How many times have I looked at that picture and wished I was in it, so we would all be happy together forever?"

They sat without speaking, but he held her hand as she wept. He let her cry into his shoulder. He heard Abe enter the outer office, saw him through the glass door of his own office. The two men made eye contact, and Abe nodded as he raised his hand to tell Jit that he would be back later. He turned to leave, but then turned back to nod again. He was more than a deputy, not quite a son, and Jit loved him at that moment. He wished his daughter had a brother.

Jit had seen it before. A parent being told about the death of a child, a spouse asked to come to the morgue to identify a body. As if denial was a magic power. Wave disbelief in the air and life could be restored. The world would be right again. Seeing it in his daughter was different.

"You're sure? I mean, you said yourself that there was almost nothing left. You could be wrong, couldn't you?"

"No, she's gone. The jacket, dental records will confirm it, other bits and pieces of evidence."

"But I don't understand. All these years, without a trace or a word, and still so close? And somebody must have done this to her. Who would do that? Who would do that?"

Jit self-consciously did not look down toward his desk drawer, in which another manila envelope was hidden.

"I suspect that we'll never know."

"You're the sheriff, Daddy. The goddam sheriff."

Jit nodded but had no response.

"Oh, Jerry, I was so cruel to him. How could I forget that his heart was broken as much as mine? He loved her first, in real life, and I loved her only because of the stories he had told me all my life. But I was angry. I wanted him to know all the answers, like he seemed to know for all my life. I wanted the answer to that, but he just sat there like he was somewhere else."

Guinta had just heard the news. Sandy Chippen Knight had finally come home, but the mystery from the past was even more of a mystery now.

"He's going to need you a lot more than you think."

"He's lost his mind, Jerry. Not wild crazy, just more silent crazy, like my entire family. How else to explain what he wanted me to do?"

"Grief, Sandra, grief. But the important thing is that you told him no, right?"

"Nobody else knows for now. I mean, Abe knows, but he will do what I want. The coroner will do an autopsy, and he will know who it is, but he owes me a few favors."

"Daddy, what are you talking about?"

"Nobody has to know."

"Daddy?"

"I mean, this doesn't have to be a story. She doesn't have to be a story in the paper. It can be our secret. You already know about the Twains. Father mangled and son disappeared. That's a story for sure. A lot of local interest. But Sandy is different. We don't have to share her with anyone."

Sandra did not believe he was serious.

"Daddy, listen to yourself. What you want is impossible. You think that if I don't put it in the paper, then it never happened? You think that you can keep this a secret forever? You and Abe and the coroner some sort of airtight conspiracy?"

"And you as well."

She looked at him like he was having a stroke. He was not making any sense.

"In case you missed it, you're running for re-election. Trust me, Frank Morris would love to hear that you were hiding a crime. And a lot of people in this town, I know, already think you're a bit daft in the head and should have been put out to pasture years ago."

"For me, please."

"No, Daddy, not even for you. I'm not going to let her disappear again. This is for me. My mother is going to be front-page news, as bright as the goddam sun. I never thought about it until now, but I'm going to write her profile. I have been collecting notes for my entire life, and you're going to help me finish it. And we're going to have a funeral service and I'm going to cry like a banshee, and you will too. But you and I are not letting her disappear again. *That's* what *we're* going to do."

Jit was looking down, but she could see his shoulder start trembling. She had never seen her father cry.

"I'm sorry. It's just too much for me. After all this time. Too much."

Sandra walked around the desk, grabbed her father's chair and pulled it away from his desk, and then knelt down in front of him, holding his hand, going from being consoled to being the consoler.

"It's going to be okay, Daddy. But I'm warning you now. You have one more pain to bear. I'm going to write that profile, and I'm going to bring her back to life. And then you and I are going to say goodbye to her."

Looking down at his daughter, seeing traces of her mother, Jit leaned forward and kissed Sandra on the top of her head, asking a different favor.

"Can you make all the arrangements?"

"Of course."

For the next half hour, she quizzed her father about other details, processing how to frame the story for the rest of Knightville, surprising herself by how calm she seemed. As she listened to Jit describe the actual discovery, the search for the Twains that led to her mother, the missing Twain body, she realized how she could honor her father's earlier wish.

"Daddy, here's what I can do. The Twains will be tomorrow's news. More print than they deserve. I'll have Jerry write the story. He'll interview you and Abe. You make sure the two of you agree on things. And I'm depending on you to keep the coroner in line. A run-of-the-mill murder mystery, with that damn panther thrown in for local color. God, how many times has that thing been talked about in this town? Thing is, you make it sound like the truth, understand? As if it *is* the truth. And I'll wait on the news about Mama. She won't be connected to the Twains at all. Next week, seven days, maybe more, I'll break the news about Mama. I'll write that story myself. I'll write it and then show it to you and Abe before I publish it. I'll quote you. I'll quote him. I will make the discovery totally unrelated to anything about the Twains. You tell Abe not to cross me. The news next week, and then the front-page profile after the funeral a few days later. You don't get to read it ahead of time. I'll read it at the service. I don't want you or anybody else trying to correct me. Her life story is all mine."

Jit nodded, his daughter a marvel to him, again.

"Daddy, I'm breaking a lot of rules here. But this will only work if you and Abe and the coroner sign on. I'm depending on you to make that happen. But I'll do all this for you. And for Mama. Do you understand how I'm breaking the rules?"

Jit looked past his daughter toward the picture of him and Sandy.

"Yes, I understand. Thank you."

An hour later, he was telling Abe about Sandra's plans and how he would have to be complicit. Abe almost laughed.

"Jit, am I the only person in this town who finds that funny? Her wondering if *you* understood about breaking rules."

"Sandra, you do realize that one of the reasons we should have gotten married is that if we were married, I couldn't testify against you."

Jerry had listened to the owner-editor of the *Knightville Times* outline a conspiracy that violated professional standards of journalism, not to mention a few state laws regarding the misuse of evidence in a criminal proceeding. A cabal that would include the local sheriff, his senior deputy, the county coroner, the owner of the local newspaper, and . . . himself?

"Count me in. I'm beginning to love this job even more."

"Jerry, I knew I could count on you."

"And that, boss, is the story of my life. I am a dependable man."

She rolled her eyes, "Your ex-wife might disagree."

Guinta ignored the comment. "Sandra, I have just two questions for you."

"And?"

"Does Norton know yet? Is he in the club too?"

"I asked Jit that. All he said was that he would tell Norton at the right time, but I'm assuming that he will not be in this particular loop."

"Well, that just proves that you and Jit don't know what the rest of this town knows about Norton. He knows *everything*. You seriously think that he will not figure this out?"

"All I know is that Daddy said he would handle Norton."

"Well, all I know is that I would pay good money to listen in on that conversation."

"You had two questions?"

"Right. Seems like a good time to ask you something I've always wanted to ask you over the years, but I never thought you would understand it until now, after me hearing you make all these plans."

"Get to the point, Jerry."

"Simple. Do you really understand that you are, and always have been, a Knight? The Chippen blood is there, for sure, but you are a Knight."

She kept looking at the picture of her mother and father, and the jacket. Jerry waited for the answer, but he was thinking something else.

You just found out your mother is dead, murdered, body discovered after decades, and you are calmly plotting an alternate reality for public consumption. You're acting like you can control all this. But you're headed toward a total meltdown. You can delay it, focus on a million tiny things, but soon enough, Sandra, you are going to become a little girl again. It's all going to crush you. But I'll still be here. Old dependable Jerry. When you really, really, need me, I'll be here. Will you even notice?

Is this how it ends, after all these years?

An hour later, Jit had not moved. The sun was taking too long to set. He just sat there flipping open and shut the rusty gold pocket watch he had found earlier that day, rubbing his thumb in circles over the engraved initials: NK.

Jit looked at his phone. To call, or go see him in person? Before they went to high school, he and Norton had seen each other almost every day. Both had been the only child in their family, and they gravitated toward each other more as brothers than as cousins.

Adolescence changed that, but Jit did not overinterpret their distancing. Norton was older. More was expected of him. Jit might be an athlete, but Norton was book smart. Jit accepted his own limitations, assuming that Norton had none. But he missed their ventures into the darkness of the Knight land. Eventually knowing that Norton had been sweet on Sandy even before he was, Jit had been almost embarrassed. Sandy deserved somebody like Norton, not like him. It would have been the natural order of things. The irony was that it was Norton who went away, not Jit, who everyone assumed was headed for football fame in college. But Jit's atomized knee meant that Jit was never leaving Knightville. Norton came back after a few years, noticeably thinner and with a streak of gray hair that some assumed was a tinted affectation. No man his age has gray hair, right? Jit was gaining weight while Norton seemed to become more handsome. And then Norton's father died, and Norton married Ashley, and the two cousins became brothers-in-law.

It was all still a mystery to Jit. Sandy loving him but not Norton. But he had eventually stopped being embarrassed by Sandy choosing him over his cousin. Norton had everything else, why should he have her too? And as long as Jit had Sandy, he was happy. Having everything but Sandy, Jit understood, made Norton unhappy. If there really was a natural order, wasn't Sandy loving Jit part of that order? But Sandy exploded for a year, and Ashley floated into his life with a different version of that natural order, offering him knowledge that confirmed his own insecurities. In the most secret part of his heart, hidden from everyone and carried for the rest of his life, Jit assumed that Sandy must have found out about him and

Ashley. He thought it the first day that she was gone. He had broken her heart. He deserved to lose her. But, to abandon her daughter? It was all a mystery.

It was still a mystery to him, the line from the night Norton had called him to tell him that Ashley was dead and this moment in his office. He rubbed his thumb around and around over the engraved initials, trying to eliminate all sorts of obvious conclusions. But the circle always came back to a conclusion that he had never considered. Norton had always known about Sandy's death.

I knew about him and Ashley. I knew it that night. Any other sheriff might have figured it out too. But, may God damn me, I was glad she was dead. She was daily proof of how I had wronged Sandy. And the great delusion of that night was me thinking that if Ashley were dead, and Sandy found out, then Sandy would come back. But he knew, he knew that night as I was protecting him, he knew what had happened to her. He knew she was not coming back. So, what do I do now?

Jit looked at the watch, and around his office, over to the picture of him and Sandy, and back to the watch.

Did Ashley know about him burying Sandy? Did she know what he did, and that is why he killed her? I thought I was protecting him, but I should have protected her.

But there was no conclusion that made sense. Norton could kill Ashley, but in no sane world would Norton hurt Sandy. But he knew she was dead. He marked her body with that watch. He had kept her to himself all this time? And that spot? Finding her bones yesterday, he had wondered how she came to be at *that* spot. That part of the mystery was solved. It was the heart of the Knight myth. It was where she belonged.

Surely, he could have told me. I would have understood why he buried her there. If he had not been the one to hurt Sandy, I would have helped him. She could have been ours together. But there has to be a reason he kept her to himself.

Jit tried to rationalize a world in which Norton could be forgiven. But the primal mystery remained. Norton was responsible for the death of one woman and the disappearance of another. That was the most generous interpretation of the facts that Jit possessed. But, still, nothing made sense. Jit was the Law. Justice must be served.

Norton had been cruel. Anybody else would agree. But he had been the cruelest to the only person in Knightville who had still cared for him, even after all these years.

I don't know what to do. I don't know what to do.

He felt his stomach growl with hunger pangs. He had not eaten since morning. His left hand was cramping, a recurring malady for months. His hearing was getting worse, the tinnitus deafening. He had been diagnosed with diabetes, but he had not told Sandra yet.

I don't know what to do.

He did not want to leave his office, ever again. He wanted time to stop, the world to freeze itself in place. But he had to admit: The world did not give a tinker's damn about him. He had survived Sandy. Sandra would survive him. But he still wanted the final pieces of a puzzle to be revealed to him. He knew that Norton was a dying man. How many months? Jit was the Law. Justice was different.

How many times had he made that distinction in the past? How was Norton to be judged?

He owes me that much. The truth. And then I'll know what to do.

He picked up the phone. "Norton, we need to talk.

HISTORICAL REVISIONISM

Abraham Jones began his career as a deputy by working the evening shift, which began at 3:00 in the afternoon and ended at 11:00 that night. From light to dark. Like deputies everywhere, he would see the difference between day people and night people. Day people were busy. Night people had too much free time on their hands. And night people drank too much. The riskiest call for law enforcement was always stepping into some sort of domestic dispute. Booze, spousal abuse, and darkness . . . Abe had seen a lot of bad combinations, even in sleepy Knightville. With enough seniority, he became eligible for a different shift, but he opted to stay on patrol from light to dark. Jit respected that.

Abe had inevitably become Jit's favorite deputy. He had an advantage that the others did not: Jit had helped his mother deliver him. Jit had cut the cord. So, Abe had grown up with Jit always there, and he had seen how Jit had grown old.

Sheriff, you sure you wanna run again? You've got a good pension. You could be some sort of Sheriff Emeritus thing. Assuming, of course, I'm your replacement.

Abe was often called even when he wasn't on duty. Personal favors for Jit. Off the books. Outsiders might have seen it as an abuse of power by the sheriff. Abe did not. Abe saw it as trust. Of all the personal favors done by Abe for Jit, the most private was how many times he acted as a chauffeur for Norton. He would get a phone call from Jit and then go pick up Norton, who always sat up front with him, who always called him "Deputy." The calls were most often after dusk, so seldom seen by the day people. Abe tried small talk, but Norton was not interested in civil discourse. He simply told Abe where he wanted to go, and where he wanted to go was usually nowhere. Sometimes he would pick up groceries and deliver them to Norton's house. Sometimes Norton simply wanted to go to the edge of the Knight dark woods, get out, and walk around as Abe waited in the car. How often? A couple of times a month, a few dozen times a year, for at least the past ten years. Those trips seemed to have stopped ever since the pajama-clad stranger had come to town. Jit had told him not to over-interpret.

He's dying soon, Abe. I think he's finally got a friend. And friends don't have to be normal, like me and you.

Abe knew that Jit was not offended when he said, *Normal like you?*

Tonight was different. Abe realized that in all the time he had been dealing with Norton at the request of the sheriff, he had never seen the two men together at the same time. Nor had anyone else in town. Norton's public sightings were more and more rare. Jit was a daily presence in the town, but seen so often that he became part of the background, eventually invisible because he was always "there" anyway. Abe would sometimes take the sheriff to Norton's house and wait while Jit went inside to see his cousin. Then Jit would return and the two of them would go see somebody else in town, but that was obviously Norton "business" and Abe was never allowed to be privy to the conversation. He would wait in the car, and Jit never explained anything afterward, except for some variation of *a favor for Norton.*

Tonight was different. He drove the sheriff to Norton's house and waited as usual. But then the abnormal occurred. An apparition of Knights. Norton in his white, which first reflected the glare of the headlights and then almost seemed to glow once they were in the dark. Jit in his khaki uniform, seeming huge beside his thin and frail cousin. Jit held his arm as they descended the steps. It had been months since Abe had seen Norton. The physical decline was jarring.

Jit opened the back door for Norton and helped him in. As Norton settled in, Abe looked in the rearview mirror and made eye contact. Tonight was different. "Nice to see you, Abe. Thank you for helping Jit."

Jit got in front with Abe and told him where to go. "Take us to where we found Sandy. Get as close as you can, and then help me with Norton to get further in. You'll need that big flashlight in the trunk, and the shotgun."

Abe was momentarily confused until Jit added, "I doubt that we'll be alone out there. I'll need you to give us some space to talk, but I want you to keep your ears open for any visitors."

"Sheriff, you sure you want to do this?" Abe looked in the rearview mirror again, but Norton was staring out the window, as if memorizing the house in which he had lived in for over seventy years.

"It's okay, Abe. It's all going to be okay."

"You know you can trust me, right? I just want you to be careful."

It took an hour, the drive to the edge of the forest, and then the walk to the church. With Jit and Norton where they wanted to be, Abe walked about fifty feet away. Jit was holding the flashlight and Abe could see the beams shoot around in the dark as Jit moved his arms, sometimes unconsciously, sometimes as if searching for something specific, sometimes directed up at the swaying cypress trees around them, sometimes pointed directly down at the ground, forming a small circle of light in which only their feet were visible. Only once was it clear that Norton was in danger, but Abe kept his distance. The two men talked, but Abe could not hear them.

"Norton, how did it happen? You owe me that. After all this time, you owe me that."

As Norton told his story, Jit wondered how much to believe. Sins of omission were still lies. Norton told him how a drunk Ashley had come home after running down Sandy, how she had described Sandy's anger toward her, their arguments from a lifetime of sibling rivalry gone off the rails, curses and slaps and then Sandy refusing to get out of the road as Ashley sped up toward her. Alcohol and physics, misjudgments, death.

He's still not telling me the truth. Jit needed the truth.

"And you killed Ashley. We both know that was a bullshit story, her slipping and falling. I knew it. You knew I knew it."

"Yes."

"Norton, this makes no sense. You killed Ashley over a year after you say she killed Sandy. A year? You know, I might have killed

304

Ashley too, made *her* disappear, if I had been there that night when she told you about Sandy. But she tells you, and you wait a year. She tells you and you do not call me?"

The two men could not see each other's faces.

"You want me to believe that Ashley killed Sandy, intentional or not, and you protected *her*. Ashley killed Sandy? That's the truth? You took Sandy back here, to this spot, Norton, to *this* spot, put your watch in her jacket, and you went home to Ashley and protected *her*?"

"Jit, I cannot explain it. I wish I could."

"You stole her from me, Norton. You took her away from me for all these years. You took her away from her daughter."

"I was wrong, Jit. I know it now."

Jit raised the flashlight and shoved it into his cousin's stomach, knocking him down.

"Too goddam late, Norton. She wasn't yours. She was never yours. But you had her all these years."

Norton did not respond. He was gasping for breath, down on his hands and knees, barely able to grasp Jit's pants leg, trying to pull himself up. Jit dropped the flashlight, its beam flush with the ground, pointing away. In the dark, he loomed over his cousin. He looked up, trying to find the moon or a star, but the sky was hidden by trees and the thick clouds of a gathering thunderstorm.

"I want the truth," he whispered to himself. "Nothing makes sense anymore."

Then he reached down and pulled his cousin up and held him close. He could feel each bone in the dying man's back. If he squeezed hard enough, he could break them all. But he put his hand on the back of his cousin's head and held him as he started to weep.

"I am sorry, Jit. Truly sorry. I don't know why I did it. After all this time, I still do not understand. You have to forgive me. You're all I have left."

Jit had a sermon for his cousin, but he kept it to himself.

That's the sad thing. After all these years, you've got nothing. You abandoned your son years ago, after he lost you and his mother at the same time. At least I had Sandra. But you threw Sonny away. You're going to die, and the only person who will care will be me, and part of me wants to kill you right now. Nothing makes sense.

"I'll take you home, Norton. You need to rest. We can talk more later."

He felt Norton hug him.

"Jit, can you do one thing for me? Can we go to the old tobacco barn tonight? Will you take me there?"

"That's it? Take you to the barn?"

"No, but it is where I want to ask the favor. Even before tonight, I've wanted to talk to you there, like we used to do, and you're the only person who can help me with something I need to do."

"You want me to help you *now*?"

"Yes."

"Why not ask me right here and now?"

"This is not our place, Jit. This is her place. The barn is our place."

Jit looked over his cousin's shoulder, scanning the darkness, trying to see his deputy. So far, the night had not gone as he planned. He understood less than he did before.

How long? Perhaps only half an hour. Abe assumed that Norton was not capable of standing up for long. After a while, he heard Jit call to him, "Where you at?" Abe answered and Jit swung the flashlight beam in the direction of his voice. "Can you come help me with Norton? We need to go one more place."

Back in the Jeep, Abe was told his new destination. "You know the old tobacco barn?"

"Sheriff, you mean where . . ." and he hesitated.

Norton spoke quietly from the back. "Out on the other side of town, where the cemetery is."

"Yes, yes, I know that place. But I thought . . ." and he hesitated again.

"I suspect he will be up. You can tell him that we would like to borrow my property."

"Mister Knight, it's almost one in the morning. Might be two before we get there."

"He'll be up."

A half hour later, the barn came into view, light seeping out of every crack in the walls, every mossy window illuminated from within. Only the roof was seamless, covered with double layers of tar paper. Abe was sent to the door as Norton and Jit trailed slowly behind. A few hard knocks and he heard an irate voice from within. "Go away or I'll call the law."

Abe tried not to laugh. "Sir, I am the law. I'm here with the sheriff and Mister Knight. They would like to come inside."

The barn door creaked open slowly, and a rush of chilled air poured out. Abe thought, *it must cost him a fortune to keep this leaky place cooled down*. He had seen the man a few times before, in his pajamas, pushing a wheelbarrow. Tonight, he was only wearing the pajama bottoms. He peered beyond Abe to see the two Knights approaching, looked back at Abe and said, "Give me a couple of minutes." And then he abruptly closed the door. By the time Norton and Jit reached the door, the man was back and wearing a complete, but different, pair of pajamas.

"Peter, this is my cousin Jit and his deputy Abraham Jones." To them, "This is Peter Wyman. He is a painter."

Wyman did not move from the door entrance. "I'm a bit confused right now."

Jit was about to speak, but Norton put his hand on his cousin's arm, almost whispering to Wyman, "I asked Jit to bring me here, to finish a conversation. Would you mind leaving us alone for a few minutes?"

Wyman kept staring at the three men, as if they were not really there.

"Can you give me another couple of minutes?" And then he shut the door again.

Five minutes later, Wyman and Abe were leaning against the Jeep. Norton and Jit were in the barn.

"I've heard a lot about your boss. Been the law around here for a long time, right?" Wyman said, watching the dark clouds get thicker. Getting no response from the deputy, he tried a joke. "Norton once called him the Lone Ranger, so I guess that makes you . . ."

"The deputy. You know, I've heard a lot about you too. But seems like nobody really knows anything about you."

"I'm doing some work for Norton."

"You're a painter?"

"I'm doing his portrait."

Abe just nodded.

"That's why I had to put you off for a little bit. I just finished his portrait. I had to find a place to hide it before they went inside. He hasn't seen it yet."

"You paint pictures of people for a living?"

"I used to. Norton is my last subject."

"You know he's dying, don't you? I suppose it's good that you finished. I'm looking forward to seeing it too. He's an odd bird. Be interesting to see how you got that."

Wyman looked back toward the barn, wondering where the two men were standing.

"Odd? I suppose. But I like him. I'm going to miss him."

"You're odd too, you know."

Wyman seemed to mock himself. "I'm an artist."

Jones shrugged. "For sure. An *arteest*. The pajamas should have been my first clue. But tell me this. Do all you artists have real names and fake names? Nobody in town has ever heard of a Peter Wyman."

In the beginning, Norton simply let Jit wander around the barn and stare in wonder at the world of Wyman. Jit would stop in front of some paintings, as if studying them, but ignore others.

"Do you smell anything?" Norton asked.

Jit turned back to him, suspicious.

"I smell paint."

Norton was obviously disappointed, but Jit redeemed himself.

"And I smell tobacco."

Hours earlier, Jit had an agenda. He wanted answers from Norton, answers that would lead to some sort of resolution, some sort of clear path to follow for the future. Standing in a barn full of portraits now, he was lost again. He had some answers, but not the truth. The future was as muddled as it was yesterday. And he was very tired.

Norton was sitting on one of the few chairs in the barn. "I think this was my favorite place to visit when we were young. You remember the time we found that rattlesnake . . . over there . . . and I was scared to death, but you took a shovel and killed it. I thought you were incredibly brave."

"Hell, I was incredibly stupid. That damn thing could have sprung at me anytime. I was just acting without thinking. You know. Just protecting my own ass."

"And mine. You remember when we thought that there was gold buried in this barn?"

"Nope, that was you, not me."

"Probably so, and I was the one who brought that shovel with us, to dig for gold, the shovel you killed that snake with."

Jit had seen this pattern before, many times in the past. Norton would start making connections between things, connections that were supposed to make a bigger point. Trouble was, Norton usually stopped before he finished, keeping the point to himself, as if understanding something that he did not want to share with anyone else, as if the other person was merely there to help Norton get on some sort of train, and then be left behind. Norton had spent his entire life leaving other people behind. Jit would not have used the word *epiphany*. But, as he stood looking at a man who had murdered one woman and secretly buried another, he did have a flash of clarity. Norton wanted more than absolution. But, what?

"Why are we here, Norton?"

"You're just now asking *that* question?"

"Don't start, Norton. Don't start philosophizing me. I'm not the man you need for that. Go ask your painter friend. I just want answers for here and now. Why are we in this damn barn, after all these years, why did you want me to bring you here tonight?"

"I want you to do me a favor. And I have to ask you in this spot."

"Christ almighty, Norton, I've been doing you favors all my life. Running your errands. Speaking for you to people you wouldn't let in your own house. Isn't it time you owe me something?"

Jit, Jit, all I hope is that you don't figure it out after I'm gone. The favor I have done for you. Lying to you.

Norton motioned for Jit to come closer and sit in the wooden chair next to him.

"I need your mercy."

Jit listened to his cousin's very specific request, but he kept looking at the women's faces that surrounded them, two old men. When Norton finished, Jit sat silently for another minute. He heard raindrops plopping on the tar paper roof, heard the wind begin to huff and puff and throw itself against hundred-and-fifty-year-old wooden walls. He looked at his cousin, who was looking at the women he himself had been looking at a few moments before. He knew that Norton was making some connection between the wind and rain and the moment they were in, all some sort of cosmic "scene." Norton was on the train again. Jit was left behind, wondering if Abe and Wyman were keeping dry in the Jeep. Still, somehow, the question of mercy versus justice kept forcing him into abstractions, and, in that world, Norton had the advantage.

"I have to think about it. I've covered up crimes. You know that. But this is different."

Norton nodded. "Fair enough."

"It's just hard to think about anything right now."

"I understand."

"It's odd. Tonight. It's not what I planned."

"Nor I."

"One thing, Norton, one thing I want you to do. All I know for sure is that I don't want you to be at Sandy's service on Friday. I'm not going to share her with you anymore. If you show up at the service, I'll never speak to you again. And I will not, for sure, do the thing you want me to do. Do you understand?"

Norton nodded again. He then tried to make eye contact with Jit, but his cousin turned away from him. Both men sat silent as the thunder began to boom outside, and then they heard a different pounding. Somebody was knocking loudly on the barn door. Jit hauled himself up and limped to the door, opening it to see Abe and Wyman trying to share a giant umbrella. Both of them were drenched.

"Jesus Christ, boss, you guys need to wrap this up. The Jeep is sinking in the mud, and Pete here is freaking out. And we need to get him in some dry clothes soon."

Wyman sheepishly shrugged his shoulders. "I told Tonto here that I'd be fine, but he's right about the Jeep." He looked past the sheriff. "Hey, Norton, you okay?" Norton waved back weakly as the sheriff spoke.

"Abe, I think I'm going to have to carry Norton. Can you keep that umbrella over us?"

"Sheriff, you're carrying nobody. You try that and I'll end up carrying both of you. I'll take care of Mister Knight. You hold the umbrella."

As soon as the barn door was shut, Wyman went to where he had hidden Norton's portrait, soon satisfied that it had remained unseen. He wanted to see Norton's face when he unveiled the portrait. A ceremony was required. A proper handover. Tonight was certainly not the night for that. Perhaps he should take it to Norton's study? Set it next to the open window. Stand back.

He looked at Norton's portrait as the storm raged outside.

I wonder if I'll ever be this good again.

NECESSARY RITUALS

Angel loved weddings. How many had she attended in her life? Forty? Fifty? Often a bridesmaid, and she never spent the night alone afterward. Weddings were always hopeful. A few times they were also a self-evident delusion to everyone except the love-struck couple at the altar. *I'll give them six months.* Weddings were also cauldrons of passion. She was not the only person who felt aroused by the explicit premise at the altar: A few more hours and those two people will be naked and contorted into a hybrid beast of fucking. That was her description. She had to explain it to Sonny. *Separate the words, Sonny. Naked, that's obvious. Contorted, you know, twisted into some shape that you never thought possible. You've done that yourself a few times, darling. Hyrbid, something new, something that is more than just the one thing. You and me, Sonny, us together are like nobody else. Beast? Good sex is animal sex. And beasts are the best animals. Fucking? Do I really have to explain fucking to you?* They had been at a wedding reception when she walked him through her carnal explication. They were slow dancing, a hundred couples around them in a giant ballroom, listening to Johnny Mathis sing "Chances Are." Just after Angel said, *Do I really have to explain fucking to you?* Sonny did something that few men knew how to do. He said the perfect thing at the perfect moment. His hands on her waist, he pulled her closer and whispered in her ear, *I love this song.* Angel melted, almost laughing, almost crying. *Sonny Knight,*

I have a dozen Mathis albums, some from when I was a kid. If he was straight, I'd fuck him in a New York minute, as long as I could hear him singing to me. They stopped dancing, standing motionless as oblivious couples swirled around them. *So do I,* he said. *Do you want to get out of here soon?* Angel had closed her eyes and imagined a future in which she would remind him of that exact moment, the totally inexplicably happiest moment of her life, thinking to herself. *Grow old with me, Sonny. I'll be a pile of sagging flesh for sure, and you'll be a limp dick cranky bag of bones. And we'll both still be trying to figure out how we got there.*

Funerals were different. Angel hated funerals. She avoided them if possible. She only went to her father's funeral to make sure he was dead. After that, she checked her emotions and grieved for few people. A nurse she had worked with, killed in a car wreck, Angel had been in the ER when she was brought in, just another crisis to handle, until she recognized the bloody face. She went to that funeral. A teacher from her high school days, an old man of forty to her sixteen, who gave her books to read out of class, who was the first man she ever desired, the only man who made her feel special by not accepting her sexual proposition. She asked Sonny to take her to that funeral visitation, and he held her hand through the eulogies. But she did not approach the open casket. As she and Sonny had walked into the funeral home, Angel knew they were looking at her, her classmates who had heard all the rumors about her and the teacher, a few of the boys she had known, their high school girlfriends who were now their wives or ex-wives. They all looked at her like she had just stepped off a movie screen. She had gone to the restroom and looked in the mirror; Elizabeth Monroe was looking back at her. For the next hour, Sonny held one hand and she held a book in the other, a tattered, rubber band-bound copy of *To Kill a Mockingbird*. But she never approached the casket.

Sandy Chippen Knight had no casket. Her ashes were in a mahogany box centered on an altar draped in white linen. Next to the altar, a posterphoto was propped on an easel: Jit and Sandy a few months before she disappeared, him in his uniform and her in a blue jacket. Angel had heard stories about Sandy, but only bits and pieces. She was not from Knightville. She was an outsider. Sonny knew more, all variations of stories that Sandra had told him. Sandy Chippen was his mother's sister, gone before his mother had died in a fall. Angel had seen a few pictures of Ashley Knight, but they had been studio shots, over-posed and overdressed. Sandy's funeral picture was different. She looked like a real person. Angel kept looking at the poster, trying to see some resemblance to Sonny's mother in Sandy's face. She had met the sheriff a few times, polite public occasions. He had always been gracious, but always seemingly distracted. The Jit Knight in the picture was not the man sitting a few rows in front of her. The man in the picture was a hundred pounds lighter, a thousand years younger? But Sandy would never get older.

Angel studied the room. It was a bigger crowd than she expected, and she noted how she and Sonny, and only a few others, were much younger than everyone else. *If she had been found twenty years from now, I'd bet that this would be a much smaller party.* The newspaper had run a front-page, but short, story a few days earlier, written by Jerry Guinta, using the photo that was now a poster. It had announced the memorial service, but the facts of the story were boilerplate journalism. Missing woman's body found, investigation ongoing, Sheriff Knight had no comment, parents and siblings were also deceased, survivors include brother-in-law Norton Knight, husband Percy, daughter Emily Marie Knight and nephew Stephen Knight. But it had promised "a full profile of Sandy Chippen will be published after the memorial service, where it will be read by her daughter." Angel had read the story and looked at Sonny. *You are so NOT a Stephen. And all this time I thought her name was Sandra.*

Angel had wondered if Sandra knew that Sonny had told her all the stories about how much he had loved her when they were teenagers. Until she and Sandra actually met, Angel had dismissed those stories. Everybody had a high school crush. Sandra probably did not remember it the same way Sonny had. Perhaps Sandra still thought Sonny was just another guy who had a crush on her. No big deal now. But, still, it could have been awkward. But there had always been the fascination. *Whoever she is, Sonny loved her, and I know he loves me now. Is there any connection between her and me, any part of her in me, since she came first?* Meeting Sandra had not answered that question. He had taken Angel to the newspaper office one day and introduced her. It *was* awkward, but only for Sonny. Angel had spent a life dealing with wives and girlfriends of men who were sleeping with her, requiring a diplomatic facade of denial, even if the other woman knew. But this was new. Out in the open, she was a proper girlfriend, soon to be wife. The past was long past. Sonny, however, stammered his way through the introduction, and Sandra had first seemed cool toward Angel. Ten minutes had changed all that. All it took was for Angel to be herself, to drop two *fucks* in one sentence and roll her eyes at Sonny's embarrassment. It also helped that she had spent the previous year reading the *Knightville Times,* including all the profiles that Sandra had published. She praised one in particular, of a deputy sheriff's mother, a black woman who had helped take care of Sandra after her mother disappeared. Sandra's expression gave her away. *You're not what I expected.* Angel had read her mind and answered out loud, "Yep, Sonny likes the brainy types." Dam breached, Sandra laughed out loud, "Well, you couldn't tell it by his first wife." Sonny had blushed.

Years later, Angel watched Sandra go to the front of the church and prepare to speak about her mother, the anticipated profile. *We could have been friends. It would have been fun. I could have made you laugh a lot. But you stopped somewhere, went back in your shell. Not sure when or why. It took time, but I figured it out. It wasn't me. You don't have any friends. In a town you grew up in, you don't have any friends. I'm an outsider, but I have more friends here than you do. You're the loneliest woman I've ever met. You're up there with a hundred people in front of you, all by yourself.* She felt Sonny squeeze her hand and stifle a sniffle at the same time.

And the bastard does not even come to the funeral? In and out of Knightville for five years, eventually Mrs. Knight, she had never met Sonny's father. She and Sonny had been downtown years ago when Norton Knight had driven by. She only knew it was him because Sonny had stopped in his tracks as the car approached but turned his face away the closer the car got. Asked what was the matter, Sonny had simply said, "*That* was my father." Angel had jerked her head back around but the car was shrinking. She had always accepted Sonny's rule about meeting his father: It was not going to happen. Norton sightings were rare enough.

Looking at Sandra, Angel thought about the Knights. *That was on my list. I figured you might know the answer, because Sonny sure as hell doesn't. But, then again, Sonny doesn't care anymore. Or, so he says.*

My mother is a picture to me. She is a story my father told me. She was born here, died here. I do not remember her holding me or feeding me or putting me to bed, but I do remember her parents. Her mother told me a story about how my mother took care of her when she broke a leg. My mother was ten. She would sing to my grandmother, about flying to the moon and playing among the stars. My grandmother always told me that my mother was going to come back to me. But I knew the truth. She was hoping more that her daughter would come back to her. Even after all her other children died, and my grandfather died, and she was, as a lot of you remember, she was feeble and could not climb the stairs anymore, moving her bed down to the parlor, reducing her world to that parlor and the kitchen, even after all that, she refused to go to the county home. I asked her why, and you have to remember that I was not even a teenager yet, I asked why she refused to leave that house, and all she could say was that Sandy would not know where to find her if she moved. But she also added an extra bit of history that a young girl like me was not prepared to hear. She kept that bed all those years, she told me, because it was the bed in which Sandy was conceived. I was, of course, mortified with embarrassment. But now, this day, I can go to my father's house, my home, and touch the same furniture my mother touched, sit on the same wooden chairs, sleep in the same bed she slept in. I know, I know, a lot of you might attribute all that to my daddy being the cheapest man in town, too cheap to buy anything new, and he always had the kindness of others to keep my mother's old home presentable. But I want to say to my daddy right here and now, Sandy's home again, she's here on this altar next to me, and, after today is over, she will go back home with you.

Angel wept, along with Sonny and everyone else. She could see Jit in front of her, his shoulders shaking and his head down. *Jesus, I'm living in that house she described. Where Sonny's mother grew up. I've known that, sure, but how much more about that house does she know that not even Sonny knows?*

Frank Morris had been one of the first mourners to arrive. Sandra was not surprised. It was an expected courtesy. He had even been gracious to Jit, the boulder in his political road. Others were in line behind him. No time for more than a handshake and condolences. Jit first, and then Sandra. As he walked away, Sandra watched him start shaking hands with a few others in line waiting to talk to her and Jit. Not a hearty political handshake, but a handshake that said, *Oh, hey, I remember you. Yes, I'm back in town. Yes, sad time here. See you around.* And then he disappeared as she turned to the next hand extended to her.

After the funeral, she would describe herself to Jerry as being a "zombie." Walking dead, not remembering anything that she actually did or said. She only remembered Morris because Jerry had taken notice of him as he worked the line in reverse.

Morris did not sit during the service. He stood against the back wall, next to a bulky companion. As Sandra began speaking, he nodded to his companion while keeping his eyes straight ahead. The other man glided past him and went into the lobby. With a quick glance to make sure no one was looking, that man pulled out a small camera and took a picture of each page of the visitor's sign-in book. A week later, each of them got a short hand-written note from Frank Morris. Not a hint of politics, just a short note saying that he was glad to see them at the funeral, sorry that he could not talk more at the time, but he hoped that the person would join him in helping Jit and Sandra through this difficult time for them. Many of the recipients wondered who Frank Morris was, especially since he seemed to know them. But, still, it was a kind note. He must therefore be a kind man.

Morris surveyed the room, processing his impression of Jit. The sheriff seemed much diminished since even the few weeks it had been since they last crossed paths. With the news of Sandy Chippen's body being found, Morris had issued a press release calling for an outside investigation. Jit had ignored him. The morning of her funeral, Morris had been interviewed by the Orlando papers, so his opinion would not be news until after the funeral. Jit and Sandra had shaken his hand not knowing that the next day he would be quoted as saying that "Simple protocols require the sheriff to hand this investigation over to outside authorities. He was married to the victim." Left unsaid, but sensed by Morris, was another police truism: Suspicious death of a spouse, always suspect the other spouse. Did he have any grounds for this suspicion? Common sense supported him, regardless of the sheriff's reputation for folksy martyrdom when it came to the case of his long-missing wife. Any other grounds? From personal experience, Morris knew that Jit Knight was capable of violent judgment. From his own marriage and professional experience, Morris knew that how couples were perceived in public was not always how they were in private. Looking at Jit mourning his wife, Morris weighed the future. *You better win, Sheriff, because, if I win, I am going to find out what happened to her.*

Sonny knew his father would not be there. Jit had told him, and then he had told him about his father's illness. Sonny knew that the sheriff had been disappointed in his response to the news. Jit's eyes were watering as he revealed the diagnosis and then the prognosis, but Sonny's face must have revealed someone who was hearing the news of a distant relative's illness, a relative he had never met. Still, Sonny was surprised that his father was not going to be at the funeral. After all, it was *Sandy's* funeral. Sonny had always known some of the rumors about his father and Sandy. Before they had gotten married, he had told Angel as much as he knew. It was not enough for her.

Do you really think your father loved your mother's sister more than her? Goddam it, Sonny, this is why adult children reconcile with their parents. To finally know the truth before it all disappears. To understand themselves. Fuck Jesus, Sonny, go ask him just for me, so I can understand you better.

Sonny had shrugged, hesitating before he responded. *This is coming from a woman whose life before she was eighteen seems to be some sort of permanent amnesia? Let me get this straight, you were born already old enough to vote?* She had dropped the subject.

Norton and Sandy might have been a sad story, if told sympathetically, but most people in Knightville let that history slide and simply put Norton in the more obvious tragedy. Not unrequited love, but more like love cut short by the death of his young wife, the young mother of his son. Just as the perpetual dark cloud over the sheriff's head had been explained by the disappearance of Sandy, Norton's eccentric behavior, his spectral appearances, his conversion to white, all were explained and justified by the death of Ashley Chippen Knight.

Until he met Angel, Sonny had resigned himself to a life without a father. He had grown up that way. Before meeting her, he had dug a moat of rationalizations. From a childhood in which he blamed himself, to an adolescence in which he blamed the world, and finally into his thirties, when he simply accepted everything as *the fucking way it is.* His mother was dead. His father was dead to him. He took the annual check from his father's accountant, thanked that man, and spent most of his adult life away from Knightville.

But then he met Angel. If someone had asked him just an hour before he walked into that club if he was ever going to go back to Knightville, he would have laughed. But she made him take her back to his home, and each time he discovered that he was actually more connected to it than he had imagined. Not to his father, but to the town. The school, the places he played, many people he had grown up with. Angel made him see a town that was always there, but never seen by Sonny. From waitresses to mill workers, everyone knew Sonny, and she soon noticed how many of them never asked him about his father. It was if they had found him abandoned in a basket, their collective orphan, and they had raised him. He might have been a hothead as a teenager, a wastrel as a young man, a bit spoiled by his father's money, but Angel pulled a curtain back for him. *Sonny, these people like you. This is where you belong. You're the Knight they want.*

On the drive to the church, he had told Angel that he was incredibly sad about how he had treated Sandra when they were in high school, that he wanted to make a long overdue apology to her, ask for her forgiveness. *Hold that one for a while, Sonny, don't overload her with any more of the past today. But it's the right thing to do.* When they arrived at the church, he went straight to Sandra and hugged her, followed by Angel. He shook hands with Jit and then Angel put her arms around the sheriff and hugged him. As he and Angel were turning to go sit down, Sandra grabbed his hand.

"Sonny, will you stand here with me and Daddy. I mean, you're part of the family too. You and Angel, both of you, please stand with us, okay."

Angel was first in line, then Sonny, then Jit, with Sandra to accept the final condolences. Within a few minutes of the procession beginning, Angel leaned over to Sonny and whispered, "I think she's already forgiven you, Sonny. Now all we gotta do is work on you forgiving yourself."

He knew most of the people who shook his hand, some he had not seen in years, and the cumulative *sorry for your loss* was like a current pulling a swimmer back to shore. It *was* his loss, not the same as Sandra's, but more than one of the mourners added some variation of, *I knew your mother too. You were just a baby. It was so sad. I'm glad you're back home.* Angel noticed as well.

Angel also noticed how one stone-faced man in the line had held Sonny's hand too long, had violated a mourner's space and leaned in to whisper in his ear. She noticed how Sonny had feigned a smile, nodded, but did not say a word. Walking back to their seats before Sandra spoke, she also noticed that man standing at the back of the room, as if looking for would-be assassins.

Driving home after the funeral, she asked Sonny, "So, who was the Dick Tracy guy who was trying to French your ear? Him and his pal in the back of the room looked like extras in *The Godfather.* Tracy or Don Corleone, I'm not sure, but he sure as hell looked out of place."

"He's Jit's opponent for sheriff. Frank Morris. I think I knew him in high school."

"And his little secret for you back there in line?"

"He told me that he looked forward to working with me after the election."

"Well, all I know is that he stuck out like a sore thumb, but not as much as the guy in the pajamas."

Jerry had been wrong about Sandra. He assumed that she would be tightly in control of herself at her mother's funeral. He had read the profile the day before, writing which would end up in some national publication eventually, if she ever submitted it. A five-thousand-word narrative of a life lived in obscurity, cut short, resurrected by memories of those who knew her, fleshed out by notes and letters that Jit had saved. A small-town life, a small town made darker by her absence. That was Sandra's achievement. She had re-created the Knightville that her mother grew up in, Knight warts and all, and she had been brave enough to include Norton and Jit and much of the Knight history from the Founding. It was a profile of the town as well as its lost child. Sandra had re-created her mother from the past and imagined how that woman would fit into the present. When he read it, he had looked at her with both fear and admiration.

"You're really going to publish this?"

"Not good?"

"Too good, Sandra. But I'm not sure this town is ready for an honest portrait of itself."

"Jerry, I love this town."

Sandy Chippen Knight, known in real life by only a few hundred people, would eventually be loved by tens of thousands of readers, perhaps hundreds of thousands. Jerry was sure of that. He just wasn't so sure that Knightville would love her daughter.

Sandra had been sitting by her father, with Jerry on the other side. He had seen her slowly rocking herself back and forth in her chair, as if either calming herself down, or, conversely, generating enough energy to propel herself forward. As she stood up, he had leaned forward and caught her eye. *You'll be fine.* He watched her walk to the altar with the profile pages in her hand. She set the pages down next to her mother's ashes, turned, began to speak, and never looked down at them again.

Jerry recognized bits and pieces of her prose, but the story she told in church was mostly different than the words she had written. Tomorrow's front-page profile would be Sandra Knight's best writing. Today, she merely talked about her mother, not the town. Fragments, sequences out of order, almost a rehearsal, but Jerry, who often mocked himself for actually believing in God . . . Jerry felt blessed.

It was not the words. The words in her written profile were more precise, more illustrative, more objective. But there was something about her voice. It was a voice that dimmed the room, focusing light only on her. Jerry had heard that voice before. For years, Sandra had told him about imaginary conversations she would have with her mother. She would re-create those conversations for him, being herself and imitating the mother of her imagination. That was the voice today, as if Sandy Chippen was talking to him, the others, and to Jit. Jerry recognized the voice. Jit surely did too.

The day before, as he had sat across from her in the newspaper office, after having read the profile, Jerry had told her, "You need to take a break after this is all over. Seriously, go away for a while. Hell, if Jit wasn't running for re-election, I'd tell you to take him. Go away, Sandra, go find a beach. I'll take care of the paper."

"That was the best week we ever had, Jerry. Thank you for reminding me."

It was not his intent, to connect his wish for her future to their past. He had thought of only her at the beach, erasing him from that past. They had gone away together, leaving the Knightville versions of themselves behind. In the office that afternoon, all he remembered was Sandra on the beach, under a giant umbrella, eyes closed, a towel over her feet. He had thought she was asleep, but she opened her eyes and he had asked *What you thinking about?* And she had looked at him with a languid smile, *Nothing. Absolutely nothing. I'm just listening to the ocean.*

"Go listen to the ocean, Sandra."

Listening to her at the funeral, Jerry told himself that he would remind her again tomorrow. He knew that she was running on fumes right now. Like everyone else in the room, Jerry felt himself being pulled into the story of Sandy Chippen, but, before he completely surrendered, he looked at the slumped shoulders of Jit Knight and made a wish.

Jit, please die soon. She's waited all this time for her mother to come back and all she got were the ashes. She'll never leave you by yourself. It's only you now, keeping her here. Jesus, Jit, please die. Don't have a damn stroke. Don't get Alzheimer's. Don't linger, Jit, making her take care of you. Let her mourn, and then let her go away. She is so much better than this town deserves.

Jerry knew that tomorrow's front-page profile would be read by every literate person in town, and read to every illiterate person. He also knew that she loved a town that would not love her back. A week from tomorrow she would publish her editorial about the Presidential election. After that, even friendship would be problematic. Sandra's town was not the town of her mother.

After reading an early draft of the editorial, he had warned her.

"You know, a lot of people are going to be pissed about this. Surely you know that even though he will lose the election, he's going to win big here."

"Tough love, Jerry, every parent knows when to use it. I love this place. I'm not letting it slide. It's my paper. This is how I feel."

"You know, you could let the Orlando paper have it as a guest opinion. Keep your hands clean here."

"Jerry, I pretty much hate Orlando."

I never really knew her. I think she would have been fun. Does that make sense? I grew up seeing other mothers and daughters. Some of you in this room are mothers of girls I went to school with. They all talked about you. I had nothing to share. If I believed most of the stories, I'd say that all of you were awful mothers. All of you obviously did not understand them. All of you were too old-fashioned. But then I would go to your houses and I would see them with you. I wanted to scream at them how lucky they were. Most of all, I wanted to see my mother and daddy together. I wanted to see them as a couple. You know my daddy. I know I'm their child. But I wanted to know how much I was her child. Here's a story I never told anybody. Sorry, Sonny, it's about you too. Some of you know that Sonny drove me crazy in high school. Teenage boys, can't live with them, can't shoot them, right? I liked you a lot, Sonny, but it took years for me to figure it out. You and me were too alike. I knew that even then, I suppose. Hell, we were cousins. We were both orphans, and the fact that our mothers were sisters made it more special. And I would think about what might have happened if Mama had lived longer, that maybe she would have had another child, a brother, and he would be my best friend, and we would have stories to tell our own kids about our mama and daddy. Sorry, Daddy, but I always felt so alone. And if I am throwing out apologies, you get one too, Sonny. I was so wrapped up in my own sad story that I never tried to understand yours. And here I go on another pity party. This is about her, not me. So, let me tell you one more thing about Sandy Chippen. When I was a little girl, my grandmother gave me a present and told me to keep it a secret. It had been her secret, and she swore me to not even tell Daddy. It was to be our girl secret. It was an old reel-to-reel tape of my mother talking to herself. She was still in high school, but it was before she met my daddy. Less than an hour, and you could tell that it was little bits and pieces recorded on different days. Sort of a diary, but I could also tell that she was trying to practice speaking. She would have trouble with certain vowels. My grandmother told me that Sandy was self-conscious about how she sounded. So, some parts are like she was reading aloud from something else, but most of it was her talking about how she saw herself in the future. The stuff of "when I grow up and leave this place." But she always said she was going to come back home and raise a family, and hopefully teach at the high school. She didn't have cosmic career plans, but she wanted to see the world before she settled down. She really wanted to go to New York City. For her, that was the most exotic place in the world. Sonny, you might remember how our class had a senior trip to New York. Everywhere we went, I'd have a conversation with my mother, describing what I was seeing. You were a jerk, to remind you, since you had already been to New York before anybody else, so you acted like the rest of us were rubes. You did that a lot back then. But that's okay. You didn't have a mother to talk to, like I did, even if only in my head. So now I have revealed my grandmother's secret. I listened to those tapes over and over, and over. I would talk to her. But I always hid them from Daddy. And that was an awful thing to do. I'm sorry, Daddy. I did worse to you, Sonny. There's another voice on one of the tapes. Your mother. She had come in the room while my mother was recording, and you can hear them yell at each other, and then laugh, call each other awful names, and laugh. Were they, what, thirteen or fourteen? But she's there, Sonny, for a few minutes, and I want you to hear it now, not here, but we'll get together. She was teasing my mother about having babies, how my mother was going to have ugly babies and she was going to have the most handsome son in the world. My mother said she was going to have the most beautiful daughter in the universe. I think your mother was more right than mine.

Peter Wyman sat in the back and had one thought. *I don't know why he's not, but I'm sure glad that Norton isn't here right now.*

Angel knew that something was bothering Sonny as they drove home. Him being quiet was not unusual. After all, they had just gone to a funeral. She assumed that he was processing everything that Sandra had revealed about their past and his own mother. As they approached the house, the old home of his mother, he slowed down, as if he were lost and looking for an address on a door or curb. Finally seeing it, he kept driving.

"Sonny, you missed the turn."

"Just want to go for a drive. Okay?" He spoke as if asking permission.

He had given her a tour of Knightville years earlier, but that was in the daytime. Night was different. More was in the dark. Angel had not given it much thought, the times they went out at night, but an hour of the entire circuit at night was what she needed to understand what Sonny said as they finally got back home.

"I hardly noticed it before," he said. "Did you? There are almost no streetlights in town. Some streets, sure, the better parts, but for most people this place rolls up the sidewalks and people are stuck at home. Nobody walks at night. And speaking of sidewalks, did you notice how many places didn't have any?"

Angel looked around. Even in their own neighborhood, the streets were illuminated only, if at all, by the light that might escape from inside the houses.

"I mean, it's Florida. It's warm most of the time, even at night. People ought to be able to walk around and feel safe. And look at downtown. After five, it's a ghost town. The town square is a dump. This place hasn't changed since my mother died. My father could have done more with his goddam money than just make more money."

"Sonny, honey, I'm not letting you go to any more funerals if you're going to start beating Norton's old dead horse."

"No, you're right. If he didn't have the decency to show up today, he can go to hell. But this isn't about him."

"I think we need to talk. Something's bugging you, but I just can't make the connection between you now and you at the funeral and you yesterday."

Waking up the next morning, with Sonny spooned behind, and inside, her, Angel wished she could stop time as they both lay there motionless. *This just seems the right way to die.* But she also saw the problem with that thought. She had never wanted to live forever more than she did at that moment. Under the covers, Sonny was still asleep behind her, snoring softly, his right arm draped over her hip. It was not the first time she had woken up in this position. After a night of consuming sex, they would sometimes go to sleep like this, still joined. This morning was different.

Ten hours earlier, they had still been awake, home from a drive around dark Knightville. In the renovated space once occupied by his mother and aunt, as well as his grandparents and an earlier generation of Chippens, in a room lit by a dozen candles, in a conversation primed by Turkish coffee and overheard by ghosts, they had finally seen a future for themselves that had always been there but that any earlier incarnation of themselves would have laughed at. They had seen their futures separately, but would wait until the next day to reveal themselves. Until then, they went to bed, shedding clothes from kitchen to bedroom.

She lay in bed thinking about the future, and the day before.

Funerals are funny things. Or was it just hers? And I might have to change my mind about funeral sex.

The morning after Sandy's funeral, Sonny told Angel that he was only going to serve one term in the legislature. His plans had changed.

"Sonny, I thought you were looking forward to it. And I thought you were a natural."

"Just been thinking, that's all. I go to Tallahassee and then what?"

"The election is next week, Sonny. We both know you're going to win."

"Jesus, Angel, I'm not even a Republican. That was your idea."

333

"Well, I figured that was the obvious pony to ride this year. But, yep, those people are nuts. You'll have to excuse my cynicism here, but I think they're all nuts, both sides."

"I don't want to be part of that."

So, why did we do this?"

"We?"

"You know, you and me, Bill and Hillary. Sarah and Ronnie. Nick and Nora." Seeing Sonny's confusion. "Nick and Nora, from old movies."

"I don't want us to be anybody else."

Sonny Knight, how do you do that? Come out of nowhere and make me love you more?

"Sonny, this got anything to do with the funeral yesterday? Thing is, your ex did a number on me, or something did, but you go ahead and drop the other shoe here, and then I want to ask you something else, an idea that surprises even me."

"The House term is two years. Then, I'm out. In two years, the Mayor's office here is up for a vote, a four-year term. I want to come back here and run for Mayor. I want to stay home. With you."

Angel took another sip of coffee. She had a thought, but inadvertently said it aloud. "My twenty-fifth high school reunion is coming up in a few years."

Sonny tilted his head, and waited. Angel was blushing.

"I mean, I was just thinking. I went to my tenth. I hated it. But somehow the thought of going back as a Mayor's wife appeals to me. Call me shallow and petty. I've been called worse. Didn't I make a joke awhile back about you and me owning this town, being the King and Queen or something like that?"

"Angel, this ain't Atlanta. And the Mayor doesn't really have a lot of power. We're in a tiny pond."

"But you're going to get some goddam street lights. Right, Mr. Mayor?"

It was Sonny's time to blush. "And a new water plant."

Angel shrieked with laughter. "Oh, Lord, Sonny, you are so right. I guess I've gotten so used to stanky-tasting tap water that I assumed it was some sort of biblical curse, here forever."

For the next thirty minutes they talked about his plans. Angel's refrain was always *yes, yes, yes* to every idea. She only had one vague reservation.

"You're not going to change this place, are you?"

"Not sure what you mean."

Angel struggled. "I mean . . . mean . . . some things can't change. Oh, forget it. I'm just remembering my first day here. How I loved it, shabby and old-fashioned. But you're right, a lot of things are overdue."

He reached for her hand. "I just want to make it better, not different."

Sonny Knight, where does that come from, you knowing how to make me feel safe, and happy?

"Angel, are you okay with all this?"

"Ecstatically okay."

And now seems like the time to tell him.

"Sonny, my turn. But I'm hungry now. Buy me breakfast at the Gator Cafe. I suspect you'll want to discuss *my* plans on a full stomach."

Oh, for a camera, Sonny, to freeze the look on your face and show it to you when we're both in wheelchairs in a fancy nursing home.

"Sonny, are you okay with all this?"

Angel was patient. She knew that her reimagined future was a more pronounced right turn to him than his had been to her. But she also realized that unless he had made his own adjustment, she would have probably never revealed her own wishes to him. Funerals, indeed, were unpredictable catalysts.

"You're serious? I mean, neither one of us is . . ."

She knew where he was going. She had already been there.

"Sonny, neither one of us is parent material, you think, right?"

The waitress Penny was standing next to the table, coffeepot in hand. "Sonny, you okay? You need another cup?"

And there it is, the sign I needed. That look on your face. You just haven't got the words yet.

Sonny looked up at Penny, not speaking, just smiling as he shook his head, then facing Angel.

"This wasn't what we planned, Angel."

"Funny how that happens, eh?"

"We're not parent material, and we're not Spring chickens. I mean, look at us."

"I like what I see, Sonny."

"It's not so simple. Neither one of us will ever see any form of thirty again."

"Sonny, I don't hear you saying no."

"And we can't live our life like we've been doing. At least, I can't. I won't do that, not sure about you. So, there is *that* problem. And I sure as hell haven't learned a lot about parenting from my own childhood."

"All I hear from you are reasons not to do it, but I still don't hear you saying no. And here's the deal, you look me in the eye and answer yes or no, no iffy bullshit, you tell me, Sonny Knight, have you ever wanted to be a father? Me, I never wanted to be a mother, but you came along and we have had a great time, and somewhere along the line, even before I realized it clearly this week, I wanted to have a family with you. I just figured you didn't, and I was willing to forget it as long as we were still happy together."

"You'd be unhappy if I said no?"

"Sonny, yes or no? What do *you* want?"

Do it, Sonny, tell me true. I already know the answer, but you have to say it. And whatever you say, it better not be "let me think about it."

"I never thought you would want to."

"Same from me about you, Sonny, but here we are at the Gator Café with Penny and her bottomless coffeepot and you about to get elected to office and this town loves you and I do too and I never gave a shit about my future until I met you and this exact moment is absolutely fucking perfect and . . ."

"Yes."

Angel wept.

Yes, yes, yes, yes, yes, of course it's yes. How could it not be yes.

Penny walked briskly over to their table. "Angel, you okay? Sonny Knight, she better be crying 'cause she's happy."

Angel started waving her hand at Penny, trying to catch her breath and stop crying at the same time, but it was hopeless. Penny swung around to Sonny. He was crying too. "It's either another death in the family or you two won the Powerball. If it's the Powerball, I expect a bigger tip today."

They stayed at the café another hour. Sonny continued to surprise her.

"You know that having a baby after forty can be rough on the mother, right?

"Sonny, why is it that all men think they think the big thoughts that no woman ever thought? Rough on the mother? But I guess we're gluttons for punishment, eh? After a few million years, we still keep making it rough on ourselves."

"That's not what I meant."

"I know. I know. Just giving you a hard time. This discussion is still weird to me."

He hesitated. "I was just wondering. Do you know anybody who has adopted their kids?" He did not look at her.

"Sonny, if I could buy our kid from a vending machine and skip the bloating nine months and less than pleasant actual childbirth, I'd do it in a heartbeat. Unfortunately, motherhood requires pregnancy."

"No, no. Our child. Do you really think it needs *our* blood to be *our* child?"

Sonny Knight, you were thinking about this long before I brought it up.

"Sonny?"

"I mean, I know that people talk about seeing themselves in their children's faces. I used to look in the mirror all the time, but all I ever saw was my father's face, not my mother's. No telling what he saw. I'm not saying this is what we do. I was just wondering how you felt."

"Sonny, having a Knight baby without the Knight blood, is that what you want?"

"I'm not sure what I want, except I want you and me to see ourselves in our children, even if they don't look like us. Make sense?"

Angel looked around the empty café. Lunch rush was over. Penny was behind the counter, filling up ketchup and mustard bottles. The Cuban cook had come out of the kitchen with a broom and dustpan, softly singing in Spanish as he started sweeping. For a brief moment, she remembered her father's face.

This is all going to work, Sonny, isn't it? I was scared to death a few hours ago, but here we are, figuring out stuff we should have figured out a long time ago.

"Sonny, I'm completely fine with buying a baby boy for you and a baby girl for me, spoiling them rotten with all the Knight money, and raising them in this town. You're going to be the father you never had. Hell, the father I never had. Me, I even get to keep my schoolgirl figure. But, trust me, we are *not* naming them Adam and Eve."

"There's the other issue too."

"Our favorite activity?"

"So to speak."

"Sonny, have you noticed that we haven't hooked up with anyone else in almost six months. You haven't been bored, have you?"

"Angel, that was never about *me*."

"Touche."

"I know we know people like us who have families, and they seem fine, but something seems wrong to me. I was thinking about this anyway. How we live our lives. I don't want to share you with anybody else anymore."

They were sitting at a table next to the large front plate-glass window. They had a clear view of downtown Knightville. Angel looked out the window and saw the overhanging sign of the newspaper office next door.

"Sonny, do you know anybody in this town who can sew?"

"Angel, if you don't want to talk about it right now, I understand, but sooner or later . . ."

"I want to get something for Sandra, a gift. I have an idea, but no talent."

Sonny was willing to drop the subject. "Sure, I actually know two good ones."

"Terrific, get me in touch with one of them."

You think I haven't thought about it, Sonny? Sure, I love it all. Even before I met you. Meeting you was probably, inevitably, going to make me figure out why I do what I do. Life is funny. Funerals too.

"About that other thing. Sonny, you keep lead in your pencil. I'll keep a supply of Botox in the cabinet. We're gonna be fine. You and me. But we're eventually gonna need to put a lock on the bed-room door. I've heard rumors that kids don't respect their parents' privacy."

Election Eve

"So, you didn't take my suggestion."

"Remind me."

"I said that you were taking chances with the editorial just with what you said about Trump and the Republicans. But there was no need to point out that you supported Sanders. The point of an editorial, I remind you, my best student, is that it expresses the objective view of some sort of journalistic abstraction, not the chip on the writer's shoulder. Editorials are not signed, but you flip this middle finger on the front page and put your name on it."

"You said all that?"

"Yes, Miss Knight, I also said that you were going to piss off everybody in town. Trumpers and Hillary people too."

"But I'll be a hero to the Bernie Bros, right?" Sandra was trying to calm down Jerry, but humor was not her strength.

"Yeah, all two of them in this town. Sandra, did you ever see a single Sanders yard sign around here, even in your own yard? For that matter, did you even see a yard sign for your father?"

"Jerry, you know he doesn't campaign. Never has."

"He never had a serious opponent before, and G.I. Joe Morris is as serious as death."

Guinta was not sure how to understand her. The earlier front-page profile of her mother had half the town scratching their heads, not sure exactly what her "point" was, since the profile had described Knightville as much as Sandy Knight. Anything profound or perceptive had been missed by that half of the town she was describing. He also resisted the temptation to ask if she thought that Norton Knight might be a little, just a little, miffed about the town being called a "fiefdom presided over by an absentee lord." But, then again, he also knew that Norton would probably not care. What *do* the dying care about? But the profile had already agitated a lot of people, who were reading this morning's paper and getting even more agitated.

The most perplexing question: Why did she wait until the day before the election to publish her editorial? It was too late to *inform* or *persuade* the voters. Old-school norms. Guinta read the paper and feared that Sandra was coming across as the town scold: *Do you know what you are about to do? What are you thinking? How stupid can you be?*

"Sandra, I'm worried about you."

"Hell, Jerry, welcome to my world. I've lost ten pounds in the last three weeks. A bag of burning dog shit on my porch last night. Subscriptions being canceled. Not sleeping much. Daddy is more distracted than ever. I wish he hadn't run. And I just have this awful feeling about this election. We just seem on the cusp of totally screwing ourselves."

"Yeah, I think you made that clear in print."

"I could be wrong, right? I mean, the past few weeks, forget the election, the past few weeks . . . I might be letting all that get in the way of my job, right?"

Was this the moment, he asked himself, *the moment she needs me?*

"Sandra, remember what I said about the beach. Figure it all out with your toes in the ocean."

She was about to respond, but she needed a deep breath first. She looked at him, through him, and then leaned her head back to stare at the ceiling. Then, looking back at Guinta, she exhaled, afraid she was about to hurt him.

"Jerry, here's the real kicker. Down deep, I don't believe what I just told you. I had a come-to-Jesus talk with myself last night. The thing most wrong with me at this moment is that I have never felt more right. The profile of my mother, the front page this morning, I've never been more honest in my life. Honest with this town, with Norton, with myself. That thing about feeling whipped and confused? All true. Me feeling like shit, worried about the damn country and this damn town. All true. But I've never been happier. I've never felt more free. I've never looked more forward to the future than I do right now. Does that make sense?"

He was ten years older than her. At that moment, it felt like a century. He looked up at the ceiling that she had been looking at. Water stains, cracked plaster, a fan with wooden blades turning in slow motion.

"Do you remember the first time we met?"

"Every detail, Jerry. You in that short-sleeve white dress shirt, totally a loser. A clip-on tie, for chrissakes. Skinny as a rail. And a crewcut. You were up there about to call roll and you had a bottled Coke on the desk and you knocked it over, busting glass all over the place. You were so trying to be an adult, and the very first day we were all laughing at you."

"Guilty as charged."

"Do you remember what I did?"

"All I remember is that *you* were the only one not laughing."

"Well, the truth might be that I was just the first one to stop laughing. And then you saw me."

"Do you remember what you told me after class?"

"Oh, god, no. All I remember is the first assignment you gave us. To go write a story about ourselves."

"Your first profile, yourself. I wish I had kept it. But, my question, do you remember what you said after class?"

"Jerry, I must have said something about looking forward to your class. You know, polishing my teenage nerd girl brown-nosing skills."

"No, you just casually said that I would look better with longer hair."

Sandra's eyes almost welled up, wide and wet at the same time.

"Jerry, oh Jerry, and you did. By the end of that first term, you had longer hair. Jesus, I do remember."

"And here we are now."

"Jerry, where we are now is not where we were five minutes ago. You were worried about me having a nervous breakdown and now we're tripping down memory lane."

"You were talking about your future, Sandra. Every future has a past. I think I'm still stuck there."

Their eyes met, and then she looked away. They both knew that a door was closing.

"Election's tomorrow," he finally said. "The future begins."

"Jerry, I have no idea where we're headed. It's as if the past few weeks have reshuffled some sort of cosmic deck for me. You want to know the oddest thing that has happened to me this morning, totally unconnected to that damn editorial?"

"Sure."

"I got a call from Sonny's wife. She wants to come by and talk to me, just her. I have no idea what she wants."

BFF's

Sandra wondered if Sonny's wife had ever lived in a small town before. You want to keep a secret, tell your dog. You tell one other person and all it takes is a little time before a lot more people *think* they know your secret. As soon as Sonny came home with Angel, gossip was fueled by history. Everybody knew that Sonny had always been a "Ladies Man." Angel, of course, was not a lady. That was obvious. A bit too flashy, a bit too bawdy. But even Sandra had to admit there was something infectiously likable about her. But nobody, especially Sandra, expected the Sonny and Angel show to last. But then Sonny renovated his mother's old home and brought Angel back as his wife. They might be gone for out-of-town trips a lot, but Sonny had always done that. He was the same old Sonny, just without the dark cloud over his head that had been his trademark for years. He had come to the newspaper office before marrying Angel and introduced her to Sandra. It had not gone well at first, but Sandra knew that was her fault. She had known as soon as they left the office what she did wrong. Jerry was the audience for her confession.

"You know I never liked Sonny's first wife, from the very beginning. She was a bitch after Norton's money. I was just pissed that Sonny seemed oblivious to the obvious. And the other women he dragged around town? My shoes were smarter than they were. And, dammit, Sonny was a lot of things in high school with me, but he was never dumb. He was damn smart, a lazy smart, but smart. And then he opens the door and walks in with her and I keep looking for her particular problem, as if I was interviewing the suspect in a murder case."

Jerry had laughed, having seen *that* Sandra Knight many times.

"I kept thinking that no woman that gorgeous could be real. Bells about gold-diggers were going off. I know, I know, my feminist credentials were tossed out, with me assuming she was like all the rest. But she was funny, Jerry. And smart. And you could tell that Sonny was bat-shit gaga in love with her. And then they were gone and I'm sure that she thought I had been a bitch to her."

Jerry had seen *that* Sandra too.

"And did she think I wouldn't do some background on her? My god, who has a name like Angel Darling? Three seconds on Google and I had two stories mentioning a dancer named Angel Darling in Atlanta and then another click and I had a dozen pictures of her on stage. Did they not think we would all know eventually?"

Jerry had asked a simple question: "Does it matter that much to you? Seriously, does it matter? Hell, Sandra, you think you're the only person in this town who Googled her? You knew all that before she walked in the office. But you didn't say a word, did you? So, why does it seem to matter to you now?"

"I don't know, Jerry. It's just all too damn confusing to me. I expected to hate her, but I like her. Sue me. But the thing is, I just don't want Sonny to get hurt again."

Jerry did not respond. He just looked out the window.

Waiting for Angel to arrive, Sandra was ready for anything. Sonny and Angel had become old furniture in the years they had settled back in Knightville. As Norton was seen less and less, Sonny was involved in more and more. When he announced that he was running for the state legislature, Sandra seemed to be the only person surprised that he was a Republican. She made sure that Jerry covered all the local political news, but Sonny's race was a no-brainer. He was going to win. The Democrat was a few steps away from senility. All his opponent needed to win was a pulse. Sonny had a pulse, an arm-candy wife, and a name. He refused to debate, but he did dozens of neighborhood coffees. Even more surprising to Sandra was how Sonny and Angel both went around together knocking on doors, handing out slick brochures, shaking hands. Sonny even bought unnecessary ad space in the paper. In fact, his ads were her single largest source of revenue for September and October. He did his own radio spots too, and everyone agreed that his bedroom voice was an audio asset. Still, Sandra had been holding her breath, wondering if anybody was going to make an issue out of the rumors about Sonny and Angel being somewhat "open" about their marriage . . . how could that not be brought up by somebody? Nobody knew for sure, and nobody in town ever claimed to know anybody else in town who were "open" in the same circles with Sonny and Angel, but then there *were* all those out-of-town trips. Still, everyone agreed: Sonny and Angel were a great looking couple.

Sandra told Jerry as he was about to leave her office, "But all that doesn't matter this year, does it?"

"Ask me that tomorrow night. As soon as the returns are in. We're either in the same old world, or the inmates are running the asylum. I'm betting on the inmates."

"Jerry, at this point, all I care about is whether Daddy wins."

Thirty minutes later, Sandra looked up and saw Angel waving at her through the glass door of her office. She waved back, and Angel smiled, walking in with a blue-ribbon-wrapped box in her hand.

"Sonny and me wanted to give you something, but first you gotta promise to keep a secret, okay? And, hey, I really liked your editorial this morning."

Sandra was a bit leery about Angel's praise. She had attacked Republicans and Sonny was a Republican. And why the gift?

"Thank you, but I'm curious about . . ."

"Ah, the old cat killer."

Angel seemed to almost wink, but Sandra furrowed her brow.

"Sorry, I was joking, Sandra. You know, about curiosity."

"Angel, can I be honest with you?"

"Shoot."

"You are very strange to me."

Angel started to speak, but she stopped the thought in her brain from escaping her mouth. *That's sad, Sandra. I've known lots of women like you in my life, but I am strange to you?*

"Join the club, darling. The who-is-Angel-really club. Eventually, you'll see that I'm just a stripper with a heart of gold. But you already knew about the stripper part, right? Anything else about me that you find strange?"

The two women locked eyes, and Sandra realized that Angel was daring her to go ahead and admit that she had found out about her and Sonny's "lifestyle." Jerry's question came back. *Does it matter?* Looking at Angel, she decided that it did not. In the big goddam picture, it did not matter.

"I'm sorry. I was being rude, as usual. This has been a rough few weeks for me, and I've already had two more people cancel their subscriptions today. I'm just trying to make sense of things. Forgiven?"

"You and me both. No apologies necessary. Hell, Sandra, I've spent most of my life assuming that I had things figured out, and then out of left field, somebody or something trips me up and I start over again. Just like this week."

"We okay?"

"Well, let me tell you about something that Sonny and I decided, our secret for now, and then you tell me if me and you are okay. And even if you're not okay with me, we still want to give you something."

Fifteen minutes later, Sandra had gone from rational astonishment to irrational joy, and Angel kept meticulous mental notes about her face. Sonny would be pleased.

"Angel, I don't know about you being strange anymore, but I'll probably never be around you anytime in the future and *not* expect you to surprise me. You and Sonny both. I suppose that's a good thing, right?"

"I was surprised at first, about Sonny, but the more I've thought about it, I think all this was inevitable for him. He just had to grow up. He needs this town, and I need him. And *that* was the surprise for me."

"I guess I do have one more question. Why are you telling me now? All this is a long way off. Why tell me now?"

"Because, as soon as Sonny and I took this leap, I felt like I was already pregnant. Those babies are coming. Might be a few years, they might not even be conceived yet. We even talked about adopting babies from Korea. Those kids are gorgeous." She pointed a finger toward her head and then her chest. "Here and here, I'm pregnant. And when a woman finds out she's pregnant, she wants to tell her best friend. Sandra, sooner or later, we're going to be best friends. Sonny is sure of that. I'm sorta warming to the idea myself. You're going to help me and Sonny raise those kids. So, get used to being called Aunt Sandy."

Sandra sighed. "Oh, Angel, I'm not even sure I'll still be here in a year. Nothing is clear to me."

"The other thing, Sandra. Sonny being Mayor. We're going to need your help with that too. You and this newspaper."

"Sonny won't need my help getting elected."

"Nope, but he will need your help with all the things he wants to do for this town. Being Aunt Sandy is for me and him. Running this paper is for everybody else. Now, please accept this gift from us and we'll talk later."

"I appreciate this, but you don't really need . . ."

"Sandra, sweetie, shut the fuck up. I promised Sonny that I'd let you open this in private. I had to find somebody to make it for us, and all she had was an old photo, but I think it turned out great. Especially the color. If the size is a bit off, we can fix that. So, here it is. We hope you like it. Now, I'm outta here. You keep fighting the good fight, okay?" Halfway out the door, she stopped and turned around for one last request. "One more thing, BFF, I want you to help me convince Sonny that he would look good in a white suit."

A few minutes later, Sandra put the gift box in her lap and opened it. Wrapping paper carefully pulled off first and set aside, white cardboard lid lifted, tissue paper parted, she saw the blue jacket.

Sandra thought about calling Jerry and asking him to come back to the office. She felt like saying, *I'm a bucket of mush, Jerry. I'm crying and I don't know why. I'm just not sure I can take any more surprises in my life.* But she did not call. She sat in her office and cried alone, but she was not unhappy.

ELECTION DAY

Norton, Norton, you can't do this to me.

"I'm supposed to take you to Mister Knight's house."

Wyman had to make a decision. He was ready to show Norton his portrait. He had planned on unveiling it tomorrow, after he finished framing it, but if Norton wanted to see him today, why worry about the frame? Wyman was about to flip a mental coin when Abe Jones made the decision for him.

"I was told to get you there before noon. Unless you need to change your *pajamas*, we should leave now."

Wyman ignored the deputy's inflection on pajamas.

"No problem. Lead on, Macduff."

The portrait was left on an easel, covered by a blue cotton cloth.

Sitting next to the deputy, Wyman tried to make small talk.

"You vote today?"

Jones just nodded.

"Any predictions?"

Jones shook his head.

"Any idea what's on Norton's mind?"

For that, Jones had an answer. "Nope. Never have."

Wyman quit trying. He had liked the deputy the night the two men waited outside the barn while Norton and his cousin talked inside. But today was different. Jones was distracted. Quiet. Wyman was merely an assignment, or so it seemed to him, so he was confused by what Jones said next.

"It's lay on, not lead on."

"Beg your pardon?"

"The line is *lay on, Macduff.*"

"I just . . ."

"No big deal. We'll be there in a few minutes. I was told to drop you off and come back and get you in an hour. You're supposed to wait on the front porch until then."

"Wait, I thought you told me that Norton wanted to see me."

"No, sir. I said I was supposed to take you to his house."

This is too much melodrama for a hot day. And I am too damn old to sit out in ninety-degree heat.

An hour had passed and Wyman was tired of waiting, but more time passed and Jones did not return. He had tried the front door soon after he was dropped off, but it was locked. At least the porch offered shade, so he stayed there until he decided to see if any other door was open. He went to the garage in the back, lifted the folding door, and walked past the tarp-covered automobile to find an open door to the house itself. That door led to an empty kitchen, which had a door leading to an empty dining room, which opened into an empty first floor, which had a stairway leading to an empty second floor. Wyman had seen all that emptiness before, but he was unprepared for the emptiness of Norton Knight's study. Everything was gone. The few pieces of furniture, all the books on the shelves, Bibles and journals, all gone.

Norton?

He went to the window out of which they had both often looked, and peered through it again. The view was different. Without Norton there beside him, Wyman did not see what he had seen before.

He heard shouting downstairs.

"Mister Wyman, are you here?"

He went to the top of the stairs and looked down to see a deputy looking up at him. It was not Abraham Jones.

"I'm supposed to take you back to the barn. The sheriff and Abe are waiting for you."

"Pete, some bad news."

Wyman had seen all the TV crime shows, the obligatory visit by the police to the next of kin, but he was a nobody. He was not Norton's kin. Still, Abe seemed genuinely sorry to be the one telling him. He and Wyman were friends again, not an assignment.

"Norton?"

"Jit and I found him an hour ago."

"I don't understand. You said he wanted me to go to his house."

"Are you able to come inside? The sheriff has a few things to tell you. Maybe ask some questions."

"But you said . . ."

"We'll understand if you'd rather not see the body. But it's going to be a few hours before we can clear out and let you have the barn again."

"But you said . . ."

"Pete, you need to decide what you want to do."

Jones put his hand on Wyman's shoulder and gently patted him. "It's going to be all right."

Wyman was led inside, to see one familiar face and one stranger. The familiar face was Jerry Guinta, talking to the stranger. Jones read his mind. "That's the coroner. Just dotting some *i*'s and crossing some *t*'s."

"Abe, please, none of this makes sense."

"It's okay, Pete. The sheriff will explain it all to you."

Norton Knight's life ended with a heart attack. He had been severely weakened by his battle with cancer. His death was inevitable. He was an old, frail man, and his passing marks the end of an era.

That was to be the story that Jerry Guinta was writing. That was the story that the Sheriff and coroner would confirm. It was to be the public and official story, told to the press by the sheriff.

Wyman was led to the sheriff, who was standing over the covered body. Jerry followed, taking notes.

"He told me that this barn was where he wanted to die. This is where I found him."

"Sheriff?"

"He called me earlier today. Said he was ready to die. I passed that off. You know how he can talk like that. You, of all people, you know how he talks. But then I had a bad feeling. So, I came out here."

Jit turned to Guinta. "Do you *understand* what I am saying?"

Wyman knew that he was on the outside looking in. The other men were operating on unspoken assumptions, creating a reality for future public consumption.

"But Abe must have told you that Norton sent for me."

"No, that was me. I sent Abe for you. I told him to take you to Norton's house."

Wyman stared at the sheriff, and then around the barn. All of them, Wyman and the others, were surrounded by his art. Beauty. Every sense but sight disappeared. The sheriff continued to talk, lips moving, but Wyman heard nothing. He looked at his own hands, putting the fingertips together, but felt nothing. He took a deep breath, and smelled nothing. Beauty, created by him, was all he had. Not Truth, not Justice, not Honor, not even Love.

He kneeled down next to the covered body, then he looked up at the sheriff as if asking permission to remove the sheet. The Sheriff nodded.

Norton, Norton, you can't do this to me. You cannot leave me alone. He touched the cool flesh of Norton's throat. *You were the only one who would understand your portrait. I need you.*

He went from kneeling to sitting, his pajama-covered bottom resting on the dirt floor of the barn. Jit and the others walked away and left him alone.

Was he aware that they were all staring at him? He was not even aware of time. From his sitting position, looking up, the barn seemed huge, the ceiling even higher, himself even smaller. After a while, Abe walked over and extended his hand down to him, helping him get off the ground.

"Pete, me and the sheriff have a question for you, about the painting."

Wyman jerked his head around to see Jit standing in front of the *Alice* portrait. Next to it was Norton's uncovered portrait.

I didn't set them side by side. He felt his knees weaken again. *Norton did it. He did see his portrait. He did, he did.*

He stood between Jit and Abe, with Abe's hand on his shoulder as Jit spoke.

"He showed me this one the night when we were here, said it was what made you famous. I told him that I wasn't an art critic, but, yes, it was very nice. But so were all the others too. I dunno, I'm not an expert. But I can see why he said you were a great painter. He put these two side by side that night, said he thought this other one was better. I agreed. It was much different than the one of that girl's face, and the others, but better, but then he told me that it was your portrait of him, and I was confused."

He didn't see the portrait that night, Sheriff. It was hidden. Wyman did not speak. *You're constructing some sort of story here. A story, some sort of story. About that night, about today. You did not find him dead. You were here when he died. You and Abe helped him. You got me out of here to make it happen.*

"He said it was his portrait, but he's not in it, Peter. I've seen that view a few times, from the window in his study. All the land, the Knight land. I had forgotten how beautiful it was, that view. Damn beautiful, and you got that right. And Norton was very pleased. But I don't see him. He said it was perfect, but I didn't understand."

"He's right there, Sheriff." Wyman and Jit both turned toward Abe as he put his finger close to the canvas. "That thing there that looks like a white tree. Look closer. Easy to miss. But that's Norton. That's a skinny white man, pretty sure. Might be lost in the woods, might be hiding. But you're right for sure, Sheriff. I've never seen trees and water look so beautiful." Wyman looked at Abe as Jit leaned forward and squinted. Abe was looking directly back at Wyman as he whispered, "Pete, it *is* perfect. Norton was right."

"Ah, so it is. My mistake," Jit said. "But, still, I thought portraits were different."

Silence for a moment, and then the sheriff added, "Well, Peter, it is, indeed, a wonderful painting, and Norton said he thought it was perfect. Not for me to understand, I guess. I'm not an expert."

Thank you, Norton.

"I don't know what to do with it, now that he's dead."

"You should give it to Sonny."

Jit and Wyman both stared at Abe. Jit spoke first.

"It's his land now. You're right, Abe. If it's okay with you, Peter, I'll take it to him. I have to go give him the news anyway. That okay with you?"

Wyman kept looking at Norton's portrait.

"Pete, you okay?" Abe tapped him lightly on the arm.

Wyman shook his head as if clearing cobwebs. "Yes, yes, sorry. Yes, please take it to his son, a gift from me to him. And, Abe, when you leave here, can you take me to the hardware store?"

Mr. Wyman, how well do you know Miss Bulova?

I promised you a list, Norton. Total things up. Make sense of it all. You asked if I really knew her. Knew myself. I knew her for almost eleven years. Made love to her in London and Paris. Rowed a boat with her in Central Park. Toured the Tate and the Louvre with her. Took her on trips to go back to places from my childhood, so that, I told her, she would become part of that past memory too. Became part of her circle of friends in Savannah, and then in Jacksonville. We were a scandalous "couple" for them, but in the end, I was really only a cliché to them. They had always known who she was when I was not around. I was the butt of a joke, the older foolish married man whose mistress offered some sort of illusion, some sort of eternal youth. Was that it? She and I both knew how we must have appeared, but surely, we were different, right? And I painted more and more, better and better. Private commissions poured in. I was asked to paint governors and senators. I raised my price, to discourage offers, but somebody always paid. We emailed every day. Talked on the phone almost every day. Sometimes I would invent a reason to leave Sarah alone to go find some privacy to call her. Sarah talked about me being two people, but all I see now is that even though I lived in two different places, I really only led one life, with Alice. And the times I checked her desk when she was asleep, reading letters from her friends asking about the other men in her life. There were even letters from those other men. Graphic letters. I didn't care. I still thought I was different than them. I can see you now, Norton, shaking your head, telling me that I was very foolish. You called her an emotional parasite. Do you remember the one thing that you said to me for which I had no response? How that I kept insisting that she was so different than anyone else because if I had to confront the fact that she was indeed not so different, that if she was merely "common," then so was I? You were right, Norton. To rationalize what I did to Sarah, I had to make Alice uncommon. To look in a mirror and not see the monster that I was, I had to paint an Alice that did not exist. So, I guess the answer to one question is sim-

ple. I did not know her at all. Or myself. It was never real, right? Here's one final story. A month before I found out about the credit cards, she and I were at a restaurant in Jacksonville called "Sliders." Near the beach. It was her thirtieth birthday. I thought we would know each other forever. I thought nobody else could be happier than I was that night. But it was all gone soon after that. I never saw her again. But every year after that, on her birthday, I went to that same restaurant, sat at the same booth. On her fortieth birthday, I took all the photos of her that I had, took them with the intent of finally burning them, and I sat and talked to her ghost. I reminded her ghost about her thirtieth birthday, about how we had been in love. I never did that again, go to that restaurant, but I still kept her pictures.

Wyman walked back to the barn with a sack of candles. Going through downtown Knightville, he had shocked people by actually acknowledging them, waving at many, speaking to a few. He made jokes about red hats, but no one was offended. He pointed to a few Hillary buttons and told the wearers that she was going to jail. No one took him seriously. He was an old man in silk pajamas, walking downtown in his bedroom slippers, someone not to be taken seriously.

Back at the barn, he waited for sunset. The heat and humidity had been oppressive all day. He arranged a large candle at each corner of a long workbench, and then he made himself a drink.

But here's the thing I cannot total up, Norton. I might have been a common man from the beginning, but until I met Alice, I was also merely a talented, but common, painter. If I had never met her, created her, I would have merely just been a talented painter forever. Perhaps Sarah and I would have gotten old and fat together, obscure academics. But there were those moments in my life that would never have happened if I had not made some sort of emotional deal with Alice. How many times was I at a showing, the anonymous artist standing near his work, listening to some patron stop and stare and linger and whisper to himself or to someone with him "... this is stunning ... this is amazing ... I have never seen anything like this before." More than once, Norton, more than once. And they were right, Norton, I was an uncommon painter. All because of Alice. And I still am. Your portrait is proof.

He turned off the air conditioners. The he went outside and shut down the electric generator. For the first time since he had moved into the barn, he was surrounded by silence. The incessant white noise of aging motors had muffled the outside world all the time he had lived there. The cool inside air had protected him and his art. Wyman stood in the center of the silent barn, listening to that outside world, feeling its heat start seeping through the cracks in the walls.

I'll go to your funeral, Norton. That should be interesting. Did you tell your cousin not to have one? If you did, he will ignore that wish. Did you write some sort of private note to Sonny that you did not tell me about? Perhaps your portrait is that note? Or am I making myself too important here? Me, the world's most uncommon painter, remember? I'm not sure about anyone else, but I will sincerely mourn you. But here's the thing. After that, I'm lost. Without you, I'm just an outsider.

No reason to stay here. No place to go. I know what the sheriff did for you, but I have nobody to do the same for me.

For the first time, Wyman heard the birds outside. The sun was setting, and the air was pulsating with life. He lit the candles and sat at the table. He wondered how long the paintings around him would survive in their new environment of heat and humidity, the real world. He brought his plastic containers of photographs to the table, holding each photo over a candle and then dropping it to the dirt floor. He hesitated when he got to Alice's photos, but not too long. They were dropped in flames. The only photos remaining were those of Sarah. He set them back in the containers and sealed them tight.

I wish I had more time. I still owe her that.

The sun was completely down, and he blew out all the candles except one. How big was the circle of light in which he existed? He tried to make a profound statement, as actor and audience both, but the last candle flickered out just as he smelled the aroma of sweet tobacco floating down from the dark rafters above him. He fumbled for the matches in his pocket. But then the door opened, and he was not alone.

Acknowledgments:

Steve Semken: Twelve years ago he took a chance on me, and I've been proud to be published by him ever since. My books never made him rich. I suspect that they did little to help him even pay his bills. He and his Ice Cube Press are the best of American independent publishing.

Nat Sobel and Sonny Mehta: My career began with them, and I will be forever grateful.

Mike Lankford: He knew me when I was showing adult movies at my Oklahoma theatre. He knows where a lot of bodies are buried. He read the first draft of this book and told me how much more work I needed to do. He is also one of the very few writers in America whose prose intimidates me with its brilliance. His only problem? He writes too slow. We need more than two books from him, and he's not getting any younger.

Steve Vaughn: Florida photographer of renown, whose work graces the cover of this book.

Dan Campion: A terrific poet; but, more importantly for this book, a surgical proofreader and copy editor.

Ginger Russell: Her friends warned her, but, lucky for me, she ignored them.

Other Works by Larry Baker

A GOOD MAN (2009)

Harry Forster Ducharme is at the end of his rope. Booze and bad decisions have taken him from the A-list of talk-radio fame down to a tiny cinder-block station, WWHD in St. Augustine, Florida. He talks mostly to himself from 10 p.m. to 2 a.m., not sure anybody is listening, reading books and poetry that he likes, not caring if anyone agrees with him, playing golden-oldies from the Sixties, and wondering how he got there.

Then, as a hurricane pounds north Florida, with WWHD broadcasting to a town without electricity, Harry gets a visitor just as the eye of the hurricane passes over. An old black man who calls himself The Prophet wants to borrow a Walt Whitman poem that Harry read the night before. He wants "A Noiseless Patient Spider" to be the core of his next sermon, in which he announces the imminent arrival of a New Child of God. Harry is a bit skeptical.

The story weaves back and forth in time, revealing the history of an orphan named Harry Ducharme. From Iowa farm to Florida beach, Harry is finally surrounded by men and women with their own burdens to carry. Captain Jack Tunnel is the morning host, more rightwing than Rush, with a cranky co-host parrot named Jimmy Buffett, but also with a gentle secret life. Nora James is the mysterious "cooking woman" who broadcasts from her home kitchen, but whom nobody has ever seen. Nora cooks on-air and discusses women's issues. Harry spends his first year in town trying to find her, only to discover that Nora's whereabouts are a communal secret, revealed only to a select few. Carlos Friedmann has the 2–6AM slot, a fourth-generation Jewish Cuban who cannot speak Spanish, but whose forte is to broadcast fake interviews with Fidel Castro. Friedmann's great desire is to kill and cook the parrot Jimmy Buffett.

Harry had arrived in St. Augustine in November of 2000. Living in America's oldest city, Harry reveals profound insights into American politics and history throughout *A Good Man*. Eventually, his role in the New Child's arrival becomes intertwined with contemporary politics, Iraq, 9/11, old-time religion, and classic literature from writers like Flannery O'Connor and Emily Dickinson, as well as the music of Harry Chapin.

A Good Man opens with the first sighting of The Prophet and ends on Election night-2008 in Florida with the revelation of the New Child. Or perhaps not. Still, Harry is there, in the parking lot of a Jacksonville football stadium, surrounded by thousands of pilgrims, as witness to and participant in one final act of death and redemption that might be a sign of the beginning, or the end.

Praise for *A GOOD MAN*

"Larry Baker's *A Good Man* updates the world of Flannery O'Connor s characters through the Bush years and into the age of Obama. Fans of O'Connor s fiction will be intrigued by Baker s imaginative reunion, in the home of the fountain of youth, of Bevel Summers with a very grown-up Harry from O'Connor s The River. Without imitating O'Connor, Baker does serious honor to her legacy." —Marshall Bruce Gentry, Editor, *Flannery O'Connor Review*, Georgia College & State University.

"In Harry Ducharme, the hero of *A Good Man*, Larry Baker has created a main character as memorable and complex as John Updike's Rabbit Angstrom or Richard Ford's Frank Bascombe. Not since Robert Stone's A Hall of Mirrors have we been this privy to the troubled soul of a disc jockey. Fans of Baker s previous novels won t be disappointed while readers new to his work will be bowled over." —John McNally, author, *Ghosts of Chicago* and *The Book of Ralph*.

THE FLAMINGO RISING (1997)

In this touching, hilarious novel of the heart and mind, of dreams and memory, of desire and first love, Abe Lee comes of age in the 1960s, living with his unforgettable family at the Flamingo Drive-In Theatre on a scrubby patch of coast between Jacksonville and St. Augustine, Florida. There, some of America's last sweet moments of innocence are unfolding.

For Abe's father, Hubert, there's nothing better than presenting larger-than-life Hollywood fantasies on his vast silver screen. Nothing, that is, except gleefully sparring with Turner West—a funeral home operator who doesn't much appreciate the noise and merriment from the drive-in next door. Within the lively orbit of this ongoing feud is Abe's mother, Edna Marie, whose calm radiance conceals deep secrets; his sister, Louise, who blossoms almost too quickly into a stunning, willful young woman; and Judge Lester, a clumsy man on the ground who turns graceful when he takes to the sky, towing the Flamingo banner behind his small plane. Then Abe falls for Turner's beautiful daughter Grace. That's when, long before the Fourth of July festivities, the fireworks really begin.

Praise for *THE FLAMINGO RISING*

"A first novel that dares mix the Icarus, Oedipus and Earhart myths, risks a Romeo and Juliet update, plunders Dante, references the Bible, rewrites movie history and inside-outs the American past. Yet Baker's book is far from pretentious. It's one of the more endearingly adept debuts to come along in a while....A novel that is as fully realized as it is inventive, humorous, and heart-aching."— *Los Angeles Times*

"What could be more all-American than a longstanding family feud between an earnest funeral director and the visionary, grandly egotistical owner of a drive-in movie theater in Florida called the Flamingo? Especially when the owner's son, who narrates the tale, is an adopted Korean boy named Abe. And the owner's daughter, Louise, also Korean, overcomes a slight limp to become a famous movie star. And the son falls for the daughter of the funeral director in one more classically star-crossed romance. And, what's more, in the pre-Civil Rights Sixties, the hired hand who helps keep a lid on the boiling tensions is a wily black man. Young Abe Lee's narration is partly a tender coming-of-age tale, partly an astute view of a family coming painfully apart. Everything goes up in smoke at the end, including Louise's crazy, beloved dog, Frank, whose imprisonment in a tower above the family quarters is a painful reminder that everyone else in this story is also boxed in, but not everyone breaks free. Highly recommended." Barbara Hoffert, *Library Journal*

THE EDUCATION OF NANCY ADAMS (2014)

Nancy Adams is a childless widow who has spent the previous four years slowly spending her dead husband's estate and drinking too much. Afraid of becoming the town's official spinster and overall spook, she finally accepts her first real full-time job ever, as a history teacher at the Florida high school from which she graduated almost twenty years earlier.

The principal who offers her the job, Russell Parsons, was her history teacher when she was a student. They had an intense, but platonic, relationship then, but he was too old for her and about to get married. He is now 47, she is 37, so age is not a factor anymore, and he is married to a woman that everyone in town hates and they assume he must be unhappy. Nancy thus sees an opportunity to start her life over with her first love. She is wrong.

Looming in the back of Nancy's mind is the intellectual ghost of Henry Adams, the Harvard historian whose *Education* was required reading for her in college. Her own education sends her back to him, requiring her to first acknowledge her debt to him before she eventually becomes his teacher.

Other key characters include: Dell Rose, the basketball coach who most people believe is sleeping with any and all living females of any age or color. Dell is charismatic, charming, absolutely politically incorrect, but eventually becomes heroic at the end. Agnes Rose is Dell's mother and also a teacher at the same school, a wonderful teacher who has a hard time reconciling her strong religious beliefs with her favorite son's behavior. Donna Parton is the school counselor, a witty woman who knows everything about everybody. Fred Stein is an over-achieving senior who becomes Nancy's favorite student. April Bourne is headed for valedictorian, super intelligent but also malicious and unprincipled.

Finally, Dana O'Connor, the eighteen-year old unwed mother who is brilliant and mysterious. Dana was headed for the valedictorian honor until she had to drop out of school to have her baby. Back now, child in tow, Dana is being allowed to make up all the courses she missed in addition to her regular class-load. Russell Parsons is letting her do this, fueling rumors about him and her, rumors that April exploits. Nancy slowly uncovers the "truth" about Dana and Russell, but it is not what people think.

Praise for *THE EDUCATION OF NANCY ADAMS*

"First of all, I finished Nancy and continued to love it. It really was very hard to put down… I'm no critic, just a reporter who's done a lot on books and publishing for NPR and an enthusiastic reader of good books. The writing was vital and under-lineable without being intrusively writerly…" Martha Woodroof, WMRA Public Radio, author of *Small Blessings*.

"There's much to love about *The Education of Nancy Adams*, especially Nancy herself, widowed, childless, unemployed, approaching 40 – and wielding a gun – when the story opens. Life seems to have passed her by, but it's actually just beginning. Under Larry Baker's masterful pen, you are immediately transported back to high school with the once student, Nancy, now suddenly among the teachers. Baker's cast of characters, weird and distinctly Southern at times, are nonetheless a microcosm of people we all know, real but by no means stereotypical. Among them you will meet yourself either as you are, imagine yourself to be or aspire to become. There is of course no Nancy without the people she's about to both teach and learn from. And others are not always what they seem. As you begin to know more of who they are, you will also begin to know more of yourself. A compelling – and often funny – read from start to finish, Larry Baker now has a permanent place on my short list of favorite novelists." Beverly Willett, essayist and columnist, *Salon* and *Huffington Post*.

The Ice Cube Press began publishing in 1991 to focus on how to live with the natural world and to better understand how people can best live together in the communities they share and inhabit. Using the literary arts to explore life and experiences in the heartland of the United States we have been recognized by a number of well-known writers including: Bill Bradley, Gary Snyder, Gene Logsdon, Wes Jackson, Patricia Hampl, Greg Brown, Jim Harrison, Annie Dillard, Ken Burns, Roz Chast, Jane Hamilton, Daniel Menaker, Kathleen Norris, Janisse Ray, Craig Lesley, Alison Deming, Harriet Lerner, Richard Lynn Stegner, Richard Rhodes, Michael Pollan, David Abram, David Orr, and Barry Lopez. We've published a number of well-known authors including: Mary Swander, Jim Heynen, Mary Pipher, Bill Holm, Connie Mutel, John T. Price, Carol Bly, Marvin Bell, Debra Marquart, Ted Kooser, Stephanie Mills, Bill McKibben, Craig Lesley, Elizabeth McCracken, Derrick Jensen, Dean Bakopoulos, Rick Bass, Linda Hogan, Pam Houston, and Paul Gruchow. Check out Ice Cube Press books on our web site, join our email list, Facebook group, or follow us on Twitter. Visit booksellers, museum shops, or any place you can find good books and support our truly honest to goodness independent publishing projects and discover why we continue striving to "hear the other side."

Ice Cube Press, LLC (Est. 1991)
North Liberty, Iowa, Midwest, USA
Resting above the Silurian and Jordan aquifers
steve@icecubepress.com
Check us out on twitter and facebook
www.icecubepress.com

To Fenna Marie
because once it wasn't
in an LB book HaHa